In the end, the suicide jump ended up not finishing by the preset forty-one-second timer that Crispy had set, but instead it killed out at the thirty-three-second mark due to catastrophic engine failure.

Every alert on Crispy's boards went to full-red status and *Opal* tumbled out of translight like a rockslide. It ragdolled through space ass-over-teakettle. Crispy was jostled like a stone in a tumbler. His body strained against the straps. His stomach was spinning, and he fought to keep down the protein bars he'd had for breakfast that day.

In the depths of the ship, the emergency engine protocols kicked to life. The Last Ditch, as it was called, was barely more than a basic life support system dribbling a thin stream of power to an impulse engine. Usually, if the Last Ditch engaged, it automatically launched an SOS beacon, too. Crispy had disengaged the auto-launch because of the situation, so no one would come looking for them. When the Last Ditch started, air and gravity returned to Earth normal. The ship fought to regain its posture and stop turning cartwheels. Eventually, many spins later, the ship's barely functioning nacelle was able to slow and right the vessel, and everyone on board took in a deep breath.

Pageant used his fingers to brush hair from his face. "Crispy, make a note: let's never do that again."

"Sounds good, Captain. Permission to throw up?"

"Sure, let's all take a minute to vomit."

Sean Patrick Little

STRANGE ANGELS

SPILLED INC. PRESS

Published by Spilled Inc. Press, Sun Prairie, Wis.
Printed and bound in the United States of America.

ISBN: 979-8-218-57638-7

Fiction - Sci-fi - space opera - sentient vessels - first contact

This one's for my mom,
the original Trekkie

STRANGE ANGELS

1

CRISPIN OKINO CROUCHED next to the open gap on the side of the hulking cargo ship *Shy Opal*. The transport vessel offered ample shade from the relentless heat of the as-yet-unnamed planet's red sun. Ten minutes prior, the ship's captain, Nathan Pageant, had removed one of the heat panels and disappeared into the exterior port-side maintenance slide, wriggling into the tight corridor like a snake. Crispy leaned against the ship and watched the vast swath of empty prairie spread out before him. It reminded him of the prairies in the Great Plains on Earth, just a sea of grass and sky with the occasional small tree disrupting the endless waves of wind-blown scrub vegetation. A guy could get to enjoy it there, if there were any sort of outposts to be had, but none of the corporations had been out there to erect one, yet. The planet was still a few years away from being ready for colonies. Bored of waiting, Crispy clanked a wrench against the bulkhead. "You seeing anything, Cap?"

There was a groan of disgust. The captain's voice sounded metallic and distant; it echoed on the metal in the repair tube. "Nothing that blowing this old bitch up and starting over with a new ship couldn't fix."

Crispy had heard that empty threat many times. Cursing the ship was the captain's favorite hobby. "Did you win at the casino and not tell me, Cap? I hear new ships are mighty pricey."

"So's repairing old pieces of hateful, derelict junk that can't fly anymore." There was a pause. "Send down the rover, would you?"

The nanobot repair droid sat waiting for assignment on the ground next to Crispy. With its large, half-circle housing and tiny appendages, Crispy always thought rovers looked like oversized mechanical ladybugs. Rovers didn't look like much, most were barely the size of Crispy's pudgy hand, but the 'bots could glide on the coils and beams too small for even Crispy to climb, and they could repair the little tears, cracks, and frayed wires that tended to make a ship get skittery. A vessel without an active rover was just waiting to die in space and become a mausoleum for its crew.

Crispy lifted the 'bot into the slide tunnel. The rover went straight to work zipping down the crawlspace toward the captain as if it had just been waiting for the chance to fix the ship. Rovers were smart, as far as 'bots go. A lot of people claimed the little robots had become sentient in the last few decades. They knew what to do and required little in the way of commands. They even did self-repair and diagnostics. They were better than pets that way.

"Rover's heading toward you." Crispy waited for further instruction.

"I don't know why you're not down here, Crispy. You're the dwarf. Shouldn't you fit in places like this?"

"I'm a pilot, not a mechanic. You're the one who loves *Opal* too much to let it go, so you're the one who gets to get greasy." Crispy leaned a shoulder against the ship. The hull was still warm from reentry, almost too hot to touch. Truth be told, he loved the ship, too. There was just something about her. The STS *Shy Opal* was outdated—long discontinued, actually—and most of her ilk hadn't flown in the Black for decades. She was a classic. When you told other spacers you flew a Lux-class Roundbelly, they usually gaped in awe at either your piloting prowess or your stupidity. Roundbellies weren't the fastest ships, and they weren't the most powerful vehicles out there, but the crew that could keep one in the air and making steady credits was close to being legendary. It took a special captain to run a Roundbelly. It took an even better pilot to fly one. Crispy liked being that sort of pilot, and he knew Pageant *lived* to be that sort of captain.

Crispy took a deep breath of air, savoring the roasted-grain scent of the grassy plains where he had set *Opal* on the turf. As much as he loved being aboard ship, there was something rejuvenating about getting planetside occasionally. The recirc air aboard the ship was always stale and flat. It had no depth, no life, no flavor. Breathing real air was a treat. Being able to open the loading ramp in *Opal's* belly to fill the hold with fresh air would stave off the flat, stale feeling in the recirc for at least two days.

A few hundred yards from *Opal*, Crispy could see a couple of animals at play, deer-like creatures. He didn't know if they were a native species to that rock, some sort of alien quadrupeds, or if they were actual Earth-species deer or antelope released on the surface of the planet by travelers in order to start the long process of making the place habitable for the human colonizers who would come eventually. Birds, or bird-like creatures, darted through the sky around the ship. They were too fast to recognize their species. Most planets in the Outer Rim were terraformed by colonial corporations from Earth in the Sol Prime galaxy, so their animals were all of Earth origin, too. A few planets, like the one where they'd had to land *Opal*, had been capable of supporting Earth-quality life before the colony terraformers got to them, so they'd had their own native animals in addition to released Earth-origin creatures. Over the decades of colonizing, a lot of the documents on who dropped what beasts on what planets were lost or purposely destroyed, so for all intents and purposes there really wasn't much difference between natural planets and T-formed planets anymore. The Rim worlds were still too new to know if that was going to be a good thing or a bad thing.

Footsteps on the grate flooring of the cargo hold broke Crispy from his daydreaming. He snapped out of his thousand-yard stare in time to see Quick Huffman's silver-blond mop and flushed face peek out at them. She was still tousled from sleep, and her long, thin arms were stretched above her head in an effort to wake herself up. "Hot out here." She arched an eyebrow at Crispy and jerked her head toward the maintenance panel. "Cap'n in the ship again?"

"He is."

"Know what's wrong?"

Crispy shook his head. "Not yet."

"We gonna fly soon?"

Crispy shrugged. Quick returned his shrug. She stepped out from the cargo hold onto the extended loading ramp and arched her back, hands on her hips. She was a thin, sinewy, iron rail of a woman, athletic and lined with ropy muscle like a Greek statue. She had a nose that had seen a punch or three in her time, but it served to give her a rugged quality, a look that said she wasn't anyone's arm decoration. She was wearing the skintight, navy blue workout togs she favored on board the ship. Usually, if she was going planetside, she wore leather and denim, maybe even a merc's tactical suit, if necessary. Aboard the ship, she was constantly stretching, lifting weights, or doing push-ups to stave off the Black Bloat, the unfortunate expansion of the waist suffered by many interstellar transport crews who got too comfortable with the lengthy, lazy periods aboard ship.

Quick leaped off the loading ramp of the hold and marched to Crispy's side. She yelled into the open access panel. "Cap'n, we ain't gonna make Fenton on time at this rate. You want I should send a message to Traxler?"

"Traxler can go snort glass." Pageant's voice was grumpy. "We'll get there when we get there, and he can kiss our feet for showing up at all."

Quick took in a deep breath of the fresh planet air. "Feels like it's coming on fall here. Smells a lot like fall, doesn't it?"

"Sort of." Crispy inhaled again. Definitely late summer, at least. There was a slightly sweet, baked quality to the air, like hayfields in September back on Earth. "I wonder if there's anything we could harvest nearby. Be nice to have some fresh food tonight."

"You want I should take the runabout and go see?" Quick cocked her head back toward the cargo hold where the little two-man hovercraft waited for a chance to be used.

"That's not a bad idea." Crispy leaned into the maintenance slide. "Cap, Quick says she might take the hovercraft and do a quick recon of the area. Maybe find us some fresh food. How much time you think it's gonna take Rover to fix *Opal?*"

"Not long," Pageant called back.

"Long enough that she *should* go, or long enough that she *shouldn't?*"

"If she goes, tell her to be back inside of half an hour. Quick scout, nothing too deep. Try to keep the ship in sight."

"On my way, Cap." Quick was already in motion. A few seconds later, the little hovercraft started up with a whir of noise and blasted out of the cargo hold, wheeling across the empty plains behind the ship. Quick was still wearing her workout gear, but she'd taken a few seconds to strap on her favorite gun belt. Her preferred weapon, a steely black Mengler-A7 blaster, was hanging at her hip.

Crispy watched until the hovercraft disappeared into the low, red sun on the horizon. The prairie winds obscured the sound of the hovercraft's engine. After that, there was only silence and the occasional sound of Pageant complaining about the ship, or the electric *zzzt* of the rover doing some sort of repair with one of its little arc-plasma multi-tools.

Crispy slid to a seat in the grass and leaned back against *Opal.* This wasn't quite the life he signed up for when he agreed to pilot for Nathan Pageant several years ago, but given he was a self-taught pilot who needed special accommodations to fly a ship, like extenders on the control pedals and a condensed panel to make it easier for his stubby arms and short fingers, he hadn't been in a position to argue. Any job was a good job at the time.

When he was a boy, Crispy wanted to fly combat ships for the Colonials. It seemed like exciting duty. He never would have passed the basic physical fitness exams, though. Some days, when he was being depressive, he really let it bother him that medical science had cured so many diseases and conditions over the centuries, but achondroplasia dwarfism was still occurring, especially in the Outer Rim where medicine was limited and good doctors, prenatal care, and gene therapy were practically nonexistent. They had been able to genetically snuff out a lot of things, but not everything. He probably could have gone in for bone-lengthening as a child and gotten a few more inches of height, but what was the point? He was still going to be a little person, no matter what. Instead of the glamour of a military pilot's life, Crispy ended up as the pilot of a clunky cargo ship that skirted a fine line between being a legitimate transport-and-delivery vessel and a black-market smuggler's ship. It could have been worse, though. At least he wasn't flying some god-awful public transport or long-hauling stellar freight for a faceless corporation. Nathan Pageant was a good boss. He treated everyone on the crew fairly, like family, and most importantly, he loved his ship.

People, especially the land-bound and those who don't pilot the same ship on a regular basis, underestimate how important it is to really love your ship. Public transports and corporate pilots don't get to fly the same ship every time. They get assigned to vessels based on current need, and needs were always changing. They might fly a newer cargo ship one day, and a long-distance fast transport the next. Crispy believed it was important for a pilot to fly the same ship as much as possible. You had to become one with the thing, learn its quirks, learn its strengths and weaknesses. You had to learn its secrets. You had to know exactly how close to an asteroid you could get, just in case you ever had to shake a pursuer. You had to know when the ship was truly maxed out on speed, or if you could coax a little more from her in a time of great need by subverting core processes and dumping that extra power to the engines. Corporate pilots never get a chance to learn that, and most of the time they did not need to know those things, anyhow. They did what they were told, stayed in the standard shipping lanes, and followed strict regulations. Private piloting was better in that respect, even if it was often far less profitable. Being an owner-operator allowed you to fall in love with your ship, and sometimes that little bit of love made all the difference.

Crispy closed his eyes. He would have liked to stretch out on the grass in the shade of the ship and take a nap. He'd been flying from Wilco to Fenton when *Opal* threw her tantrum. It was a several-day haul even at max translight. He'd been at the panel for far too long that day. He was tired, but not exhausted. Pilots had to know the difference. It's like the difference between being *hurt* and being *injured*. You can play hurt, but an injury is a time to shut down. Same for exhaustion. Even with the ship's autopilot, you still needed someone who could jump on the conn and make the human decisions in times of emergency or unexpected events such as an SOS call or a strange ping on the radar. Usually, that was Crispy's job. Pageant and Quick took their turns when Crispy needed a break, but he was the pilot, so the bulk of that chore was his. Quick took care of the guns and made sure the cargo was properly loaded and unloaded. Pageant did everything else, including making sure they all got paid and the ship's fuel cells and kitchen stayed full.

A squeal and the sound of something sparking from within the bowels of the maintenance slide shrieked into the afternoon sky. Crispy heard Pageant barking something at the Rover. After a minute, the captain's voice floated out of the tunnel. "Crisp, radio Quick and tell her that she can have an extra five minutes. Maybe ten."

"Problems, Cap?"

"Fix one issue and find another; that's how this old gal works."

Crispy hauled himself to standing and hustled around the rear of the ship. It was times like this that he envied Quick and Pageant's ability to just leap up the ramp instead of having to run to the end and walk up the full length. Stupid, stunted legs.

He ambled up the ramp and pulled down the mic on the radio next to the cargo door seal. "*Shy Opal* to hover unit. Quick, you hear me?"

There was a moment of static before Quick's voice crackled over the speaker. "What's up, Crisp?"

"Cap says you can feel free to take another fifteen minutes."

"Repairs going that well, are they?"

"More or less." At that moment, there was a squeal over the comm unit and the radio went dead.

"That's my fault!" Pageant's voice was thin and tinny. He was deep in the tube. "I think I snipped the wrong wire. Rover'll have it up in a few."

Crispy chuckled to himself. It was always an adventure on the *Opal*. He hung the mic of the radio back on its hook and turned toward the ramp.

A woman he'd never seen before was standing in the middle of the cargo hold with one of Quick's rifles pointed at him.

Yessir, always an adventure.

2

CRISPY PUT HIS hands in the air just enough to let the woman with the rifle see he was not carrying a weapon and had no intention to go scuttling off for one. He plastered a big smile on his face in an effort to be less of a threat. "Easy, there. Good afternoon. Can I help you, ma'am?"

The woman looked as if she had been dragged through three miles of cactus and rocks. She was young but looked older because of exhaustion. She wore ragged, torn clothing that looked like it used to be an orange tac-suit, but now was little more than rags and mud. The woman was even thinner than Quick, more sickly thin than athletic thin. Her hair, though matted and filthy, was what some called *hi-tech red*, an ultra-bright shade of crimson that came from gene modifications. Crispy had not seen that shade on someone in a long time. Usually, it was a mod forced onto prisoners in penal colonies to help identify them if they tried to run.

The woman began to walk toward Crispy, if you could call a limping stagger walking. She leveled the gun at his face. "You a pilot? Get to the bridge. Get it in the air."

"Can't. She's under repair. Won't be able to fly for at least thirty minutes, maybe more." Crispy backed into the cargo hold, hands still raised. The woman's eyes darted around the room. She looked crazy. Maybe panicked. Or was it just exhaustion? Crispy couldn't tell. He had been driven a little wonky from lack of sleep more than once. She definitely had that look about her.

"We need to leave. Start the ship."

"Ship's getting repaired right now. And, it's not even my ship." Crispy stomped hard on the bulkhead three times. "Hey, Cap, you might wanna see this."

7

The woman did not move the gun from Crispy, but she glanced left and right out of the sides of her eyes. "Someone else is here?"

There was a grumbling of complaints and the sound of boots on bulkhead grates. "What? What is it?" Nathan Pageant emerged from the maintenance slide, his face barely over the edge of the ramp.

The woman turned the gun on Pageant. "Move slowly. Get up here on the ramp where I can see you."

Pageant froze, a cocksure grin plastered on his mug. "A visitor. How nice."

With the gun no longer in his face, Crispy looked for any sort of weapon. There was nothing within easy grasp. Eight feet to his right, a large wrench was laying atop a shipping container. If he were average-sized, he might have been able to make a quick lateral move, grab the wrench, and throw it, but at his height, with his stumpy legs, it wouldn't happen.

Pageant moved carefully. He was not exactly a young man, but no one would consider him to be old, either. He wore well what few years he had, and despite the flecks of gray at his temples, he still could pass for someone in his early thirties with a boyish face that had seen a few miles. His waist was still narrow, although not nearly as narrow as it had been once, and his shoulders were still broad. His face was a little rough for wear, if the general definition of *rough* meant it had been hit by at least one or more barstools.

Pageant kept his voice easy and level, nonchalant. One of his best traits was his ability to be unflappable. "Afternoon, ma'am. You're on my ship. This is the STS *Shy Opal*, and I'm Captain Nathan Pageant. The tall drink of water over there is my pilot and second-in-command, Crispy Okino. I think he and I would both appreciate it if you took the gun off of us, 'specially since neither of us are inherently violent men and mean you no harm."

At that moment, Pageant's torso cleared the edge of the sloped ramp and revealed that he had his pistol drawn at his waist, barrel pointed at the woman's heart. "I'll ask again—please put the gun down. We mean you no harm."

The woman did not flinch, did not hesitate. The barrel of the gun barely moved, and she simply squeezed off a round from the rifle before Pageant could react. The shot knocked the gun out of Pageant's hand but left him unharmed. The pistol clattered to the ground, smoldering and permanently unusable.

Pageant shrugged, not taking his eyes from the woman. "Well, I guess now we *really* mean you no harm."

The woman's eyes were large, red-rimmed. She begged them, "Please. Please get this ship in the air. I don't mean you any harm, either. I just—I mean, *we* just need to leave."

"Ain't gonna happen." Pageant tilted his head at the maintenance hatch panel leaning against the ship. "We're a little broken at the moment. Should be up within the hour. Be glad to take you where you'd like to go, provided you can pay, of course. We are a private shipping vessel, after all. We transport all manner of passengers, be they animal, vegetable, or mineral."

The woman's eyes were scared. "We need to leave *now*. Please. We have to go."

"Demanding won't make it happen any faster, you know." Pageant shrugged one shoulder. "Go ahead. You're welcome to try. I'm telling you, the ship is not flight-worthy at the moment, hence why we're sitting here in the middle of nowhere, twiddling our thumbs while our semi-useless rover unit plays tiddlywinks with a tumble of wires and chips in the bloated belly of this beast."

The woman hesitated. "Do you always talk like that?"

Pageant gave her his best used-ship salesman smile. "Not usually. I'm trying it out. Do you like it?"

"No."

"Crispy, that's one no vote. Write that down. What about you? Did you like it?"

"Not especially," said Crispy. "It might grow on me, though."

"Two no votes. Well, if Quick was here, it'd probably be unanimous. I shall take the recommendation to heart and use less alliteration."

The comm panel at the edge of the opened cargo bay door lit up as the rover completed repairs on the broken connections. A scrawl of text sped across the face of the panel. Roverspeak. The little bot was sending updates.

The woman glanced at it. "What's it saying?"

Pageant squinted to read the gibberish of symbols and letters. Roverspeak was only slightly more readable than binary, but not quite as easy as standard ship common. "He says we'll be ready to get airborne in fifteen minutes. It still doesn't change the fact that I'm not someone who likes passing out rides for free. You're on my ship, you're either crew, passenger, or cargo, and we charge for passengers and cargo."

The woman raised the rifle. "I could stage a mutiny, make myself captain."

"Technically, you have to be crew to mutiny," said Crispy.

"Are you plotting on me, Pilot Okino?" Pageant raised an eyebrow.

"No more than usual, Cap."

Pageant seemed satisfied with that answer. "As long as you're consistent, I guess."

"Consistency breeds success. Isn't that what they say?"

The woman's eyes narrowed. "You both speak oddly."

"You may have a point there." Pageant took a step toward the woman. "But, so do you. You have a slight accent. It's not Earth-standard, and it doesn't sound like any colony accents I'm familiar with, so I'd have to say

9

that you're not from any civilized colony I've heard of, and I think I've heard of them all. You were probably born on a distant, barely-settled planet in the Outer Rim. You've got gen-mods. I can tell that by your hair. You might have some sort of eye-hand-muscle mod too, considering how you blew that gun out of my hand without even tipping off what you were going to do or breaking eye contact with me. And those clothes you're wearing: they're tattered, torn, and dirty, but I know a penal colony-issued jumpsuit when I see one. I was not aware of any sort of prison on this planet. I was not aware of any human settlements on this rock, yet. So, that makes you something of an anomaly." Pageant took another step toward the woman. She tensed. Her finger moved to the trigger of the rifle.

"C'mon now." Pageant inclined his head toward the weapon. "If you were really going to shoot us, you'd have done it already. If you could fly this ship, you would have put holes in both our heads without thinking. I'm betting you can't fly. I'm thinking you needed a crew. Now, if you just lower that weapon, we could have a civilized conversation about who you really are, what you really need, and how we can facilitate it. We're not savage men, ma'am. Honest. We like to help, if we can. Out here in the pan-galactic wilds, we all have to look after each other."

Out of the corner of his eye, Crispy saw a pinpoint flash of metal on the prairie. "Cap?"

"Not now, Crispy."

"But Cap—" Before Crispy could say another word, the whine of a high-velocity blaster round exploded in their ears and the woman with the gun was suddenly pitched in a hard circle, spinning her to the floor of the cargo bay. The blaster rifle skittered away. Crispy and Pageant froze for a second. Crispy, arms still raised from when the woman held the gun on him, turned his index finger and pointed out to the prairie. "Quick is coming back. She just did what she does."

"Maybe not a bad thing." Pageant dropped to a knee next to the woman. "Let's hope she didn't kill her." Pageant flipped the woman over. She was bony, emaciated. There was a spreading glossy red stain high on the woman's shoulder. It was not a killing shot, but it was definitely not good. The woman's eyes popped open, and she gasped for air, sucking wind through her teeth as the pain made her seize.

"Easy there, friend." Pageant motioned for Crispy to help him.

The woman looked scared, confused. "How? What happened?"

Crispy crouched next to the woman and grabbed one of her hands, squeezing it to comfort her. "What do we need to do?"

Pageant assessed the wound. He'd seen plenty of blaster wounds in his time. "It's not too bad, but it's not great, either. I think we need to fetch the Doc."

Crispy cringed. "Really?"

"You see any other choice? We're a little short of medical staff at the moment. If you would actually buckle down and start taking those med-training courses I signed you up for, maybe you could do this."

Crispy glared at Pageant and wiggled his stubby fingers. "Do these look like hands that can handle surgical tools? I jerk control sticks and mash conn panels. That's all I'm good for."

"Then go get the Doc, like I said."

"I hate the Doc."

"Everyone hates the Doc." Pageant smiled at the woman. "Hang on there, miss. You're not dying. We'll get you fixed up."

A second later, the whir of the hovercraft filled the bay. Quick pulled the machine to its spot and killed the engine. "Did I kill her?"

Pageant smiled sweetly at Quick. "No, but not for lack of trying."

"Pageant says I should get the Doc." Crispy released the woman's hand. Quick made a face. "I hate the Doc."

"Everyone hates the Doc. Crispy, go get him."

"Aye-aye, Cap." Crispy marched up the metal grate stairs of the cargo bay to the residence deck.

Quick's preferred weapon was a Mengler-A7 concussion blaster. At close range, it was a devastating gun. The charges it fired tended to do what the makers of the ammunition called *ripple explosions*. If you got hit with a Mengler, the initial blast tore you up like any standard bullet. Then, the electricity the gun used to shoot the bullet would shudder through your body for several moments, causing you to have seizures and tremors. At close range, if the initial shot did not kill you, the electricity would. Under fifteen feet, the pistol was always lethal, even with a shot that did not hit a vital target. At long distance, you'd probably live but you wouldn't be happy; the electrical discharges would work you like a stun gun. At that moment, the woman with the hi-tech hair was going through alternating periods of being frozen rigid with electrical discharge and going limp from the pain thereafter. There was a reason the more civilized worlds in the Inner Rim banned the gun, and there was a reason it was Quick's favorite weapon.

Quick dropped to a knee beside the woman. "I only winged her. I must not have accounted for the cross-breeze correctly."

"Lucky...for me." The woman's face contorted as another ripple of electricity discharged.

"Well, you made it through the first three or four blasts of that thing. Likely you'll make it through another three or four before it finally decides to ease off." Pageant took a pleasant tone like a man discussing the weather with a stranger.

Crispy emerged from the portal at the top of the cargo bay stairs. He carried a large, covered, clear glass jar filled with a roiling black liquid. He held it out as far as he could away from his body and kept his face twisted away from it. He also looked like he was holding his breath as he walked. "Got the Doc."

"You ever seen one of these?" Pageant put his hand on top of the glass jar. The oily black liquid inside of it began to roil faster and froth.

The woman shook her head. A cold sweat broke out on her brow, and she was dangerously pale. Another blast of the electric hit her, and she went rigid. Her toes pointed, her fingers trembled.

"This is actually an alien. I know it has a technical name, something fancy and probably with a Latin root, but most people just call it the Doc. The debate on whether or not it's an animal, or if it has some form of sentience in it, has never been settled. Technically speaking, it's a parasite. Don't worry, though. For whatever reason, this parasite actually heals humans while it does whatever it does inside you. Ships without a med officer, such as *Shy Opal* currently, tend to keep one of these on board for emergencies."

"You're kind of overselling it, Cap." Crispy squatted next to the woman's head. He leaned into her field of view. "This thing is going to fuck you up, but only for a little while."

"Ever had a tooth pulled?" Quick mimed holding a pliers and yanking out an abscessed chomper. "It's like that. You'll feel better once it's out, but until then you'll wish you'd never agreed to it."

"Hurts like a demon, but it works." Crispy pulled the front of his t-shirt over his nose. "Also, it smells."

Quick followed Crispy's lead, tucking her nose into her shirt. "Like nothing you've ever smelled before."

Pageant pinched his nose with his fingers. "There is no possible way for us to prepare you for the smell, or even describe it for you. I'm told that it smells like a combination of swamp water, vomit, and a spoiled plate of tuna."

"That, plus ass," added Crispy.

"And something that died and has been sitting in the sun for three days with a side of wet dog." Quick shuddered.

"As a side effect of having the Doc in you, that smell is going to come out of all your various…uh, *parts*." Pageant tried to give the woman a reassuring smile. "Until it's done working its magic, you're going to reek to high heaven. Your sweat, your urine, your saliva—everything is going to smell like the Doc."

The woman's teeth were clenched and grinding. "I can do without the lecture."

"We're just trying to mentally prepare—"

The woman cut off Pageant's warning. "Please, just do it." The final dose of electricity shot through the woman. Her eyes rolled back into her head. She went limp.

"Probably best she's passed out." Crispy pulled a pair of steel tongs from the cargo pocket at his thigh. No one touched the Doc unless they needed his services.

"Five credits says she still pukes, even though she's passed out." Quick pulled a cred-counter from her pocket and thumbed in the amount. "Anyone?"

"I'll take that action." Crispy pulled out his own cred-counter.

"I'm in." Pageant added his counter to the mix.

"Do it, big man." Quick took a deep breath and closed her eyes.

Pageant followed suit. "Crispy, go."

"Why do I always have to be the one to administer the Doc?" Crispy held the tongs out toward Pageant. "You do it."

"It likes you more than me."

"That's because it has only had to fix me up once. It wants another shot at me. You do it."

"You both are big babies. Just do it, already. I can't hold my breath forever." Quick gulped another breath of air. "Do it."

Crispy gritted his teeth. "Fine. Here goes." He gulped a quick breath of air and popped the lid on the glass container that held the Doc.

It's been said that one is never ready to smell the Doc the first time they're subjected to it. It has also been said that it actually gets worse every time you smell it in the future. The moment the seal of the jar was broken, the entire cargo bay, and a good portion of the well-ventilated prairie around *Opal* immediately filled with a thick, noxious rot, an eye-burning, stomach-churning scent that coated the tongue and clogged the nostrils. It was like being plunged directly into a dead animal's colon. Even though they were holding their breath and closing their eyes, the three crew members of *Shy Opal* gagged on the smell. It was impossible not to gag.

Crispy jabbed the tongs into the viscous liquid of the jar, stirred it around for a second, and pulled out the Doc. Outside the jar, Doc resembled a cross between a leech and a squid. The vile little parasite immediately squirted a foul liquid all over the floor. Whether it was a defensive liquid, like squid ink, or the little beast's urine and feces was a point of debate amongst the scientific community, as no one wanted to do the testing to figure it out. The little bastards always did it the second they were clear of the jar, though. Crispy dropped the creature onto the wound site. The second the Doc touched the blood, the woman vomited.

13

"Told you," Quick gasped through gritted teeth. "Pay up, fools." Pageant and Crispy groaned and thumbed the release on their cred-counters. Five credits disappeared from their totals, and ten credits appeared on Quick's. She flipped her middle finger at both of them. "Suckers."

The parasite, black as space, wasted no time in sinking into the woman's body. Crispy jammed the lid back onto the jar and sealed it. They waited several seconds before taking a tentative gasp of air. The smell still lingered, but it was much better than it had been. It was still enough to peel paint off a bulkhead, though. Crispy wiped tears from his stinging eyes. "I hate the Doc."

Pageant and Quick replied simultaneously. "Everyone hates the Doc."

There was a moment of lull, and then the woman's eyes suddenly snapped open. She screamed. This was not an uncommon reaction to the Doc. Everyone screamed the first time. There was something entirely unsettling about having the Doc inside you. You could feel it. You could feel it sliding between your organs, knitting the wounded tissues, and repairing the damaged muscle as it feasted on entropy and destroyed cells.

No one was quite sure what sort of magic reaction happened between the little demon slug and the human body. It was extremely difficult to study them. A while back, a group tried to find enough astrobiologists with anosmia to make it work, but the smell was too much even for people without a sense of smell. An entire research study ended up being done on that fact alone. All people knew for certain was the Doc worked miracles, despite its drawbacks.

"Let's quarantine her. We'll use the brig." Pageant grabbed the woman beneath her arms. "Quick, get her legs."

"Do I have to?" Quick was still gritting her teeth, nose tucked into her shirt.

"I'd have Crispy do it, but you take longer strides, and time is of the essence."

The strange woman bit off her scream long enough to gasp, "Get in the air. Get me out of here."

Pageant paused. "I guess we're back to that. Yes, ma'am. You're welcome for saving your life. Perhaps now you'd like to enlighten me as to why am I taking you anywhere on my ship?"

"I'll tell you everything. Please—just get us into the air."

"She stopped screaming." Quick's eyebrows arched high on her forehead. "I'm impressed. First time I got the Doc, I think I screamed for a half-hour straight. Burned out my vocal chords. Luckily, the Doc fixed them, too."

The woman tried to twist and clutch at Pageant's arm. "They will be coming for me. You have to get out of here."

"Who is this *they* you speak of? If you're an escaped prisoner, there might be a bounty on your head. To be honest, we could all use the money."

Behind Crispy's head, the comm panel beeped. The pilot figured it was just Roverspeak, but he turned to look at it, anyhow. It was a sensor alert from the proximity buoy they kicked out into space just before they dropped into the planetoid's atmosphere. Crispy frowned. "Cap?"

"I'm telling you, we need to go." The woman was remarkably lucid for someone undergoing her first experience with the Doc. "They will be in pursuit."

The comm panel beeped again. Crispy tapped it make sure it was not an error. "Cap?"

"Who are these fabled pursuers?" Pageant set the woman down and knelt next to her. "Just give me a name. Syndicates? Triads? The Mob? Maybe a state, federal, or planet-based authority? Who are you running from that you'd rather piss around and waste time arguing with us about needing to get running rather than gritting out the pain from the Doc?"

The comm panel burst into a red alert klaxon. The proximity alarms had picked up another ship. Something big was coming. Crispy's fingers danced over a flat panel and another alert popped up. It was not good news. "Cap, we got company."

Pageant glanced at the comm panel. "Well, now we know she wasn't lying. Who's coming?"

The woman, eyes wide with terror, hissed two words: "Shea Mannion."

3

THERE WAS A moment of profound silence. Pageant looked to Quick. Quick looked to Crispy. Crispy looked back to Pageant. Pageant took a deep breath. He leaned over the woman. "Who?"

"Shea Mannion." Her voice was a whisper. The woman tensed. Exhaustion, emaciation, and the stress of bearing whatever pain the Doc was currently causing in her frail body finally got the better of her. Her eyes rolled back into her head, and she lapsed into unconsciousness.

"She said his name twice like that helps me." Pageant wrinkled his nose. "She's starting to secrete the Doc's stink. We have to move her to quarantine. Quick, get her feet."

Quick reluctantly grabbed the woman's ankles. "Aw, hell. She's already got the foot funk." Quick fought back a dry heave, retch-gagging like a street cat. "This smells like the breath of someone who's been eating skunk shit, puking it up, and eating it again."

Crispy used the comm panel to send a message to the rover. A second later, the arcane lines of Roverspeak popped up on the panel. "Rover says the ship will be running in five, Cap."

"That's not a lot of time, Crisp."

Crispy did the math in his head. "Take a ship at least ten minutes, maybe fifteen, to get here from the top of atmo. Probably more if it's a big one."

Quick scowled, always the pessimist. "It'll take us at least five to get up and running again, and that's only if the rover's repairs actually work. If that little bot screwed something up, we're pooched."

"Wouldn't be us unless we were cutting something close." Pageant took a quick breath out of the side of his mouth, trying to avoid the smell of the

Doc. "Get things going, Crispy. I want engines firing the second Rover says they're good to go."

"Aye, Cap." Crispy hustled toward the stairs to the residence decks, his flip-flops slapping against the steel.

"Quick, maybe you can launch a decoy." Pageant jutted his chin toward the little storage hold where they kept the drones.

"Maybe I can." Quick had a whole cargo container of odd little gadgets and gizmos she collected from various ports, and she never turned down the chance to use one.

The *Opal's* brig was not a true brig. It was a small cargo hold just off the large main hold which Pageant converted into an all-purpose room a number of years back. Sometimes it held people. Sometimes it held weapons. Sometimes it was empty. It locked from the outside, it had basic toilet facilities and a pull-out bunk, as well as access to a dumbwaiter from the ship's galley, so it worked very well as a brig.

Pageant and Quick hauled the woman into the little room. Quick dropped the woman's ankles the second she crossed the threshold. "She's your problem now." Quick turned on her heel and hustled back to her drones.

Pageant lifted the woman onto the bunk. She felt impossibly light, a waif more skin and bone than substance. He tried to make her as comfortable as possible. The wound in her shoulder was already starting to knit, thanks to the Doc. The smell emanating from her was harsh, though. It was a thick, choking miasma of general funk, like being trapped inside of a metal tin of heated pig shit. He closed the door and locked it behind him. The pain of having the Doc inside her combined with her weakened state would hopefully keep her unconscious for quite some time. For her, it was better that way.

Quick hauled out a small drone missile, dart-like in its design. She programmed it with a copy of *Opal's* ship ID codes. "Drone's ready, Cap."

"Fire away."

Quick ran the little machine off the end of the ramp, planted it in the dirt, and fired the engines. It took five seconds to warm up and then blasted upward, a disproportionately excessive explosion sending the thing flying. The drone disappeared into the hazy sky, never to be seen again. It was somewhere far away from them, pumping out a duplicate ship transponder ID on a lower frequency. Any scanners would find the drone's ID signal first, and the real *Shy Opal's* signal second. The scanners would assume the second signal was an echo, ignore it, and the deception would be complete. It was an old trick, and one that was unworthy of newer, higher-tech ship scanners, but for some reason it always seemed to work. If nothing else, it usually bought the *Opal* a few extra minutes, and at that moment, a few extra minutes was a big deal.

CRISPY RAN TO the flight deck as fast as his legs could carry him. He was fast for a little person. Surprisingly fast, some said. He was still young, though. Age caught up to all people afflicted with dwarfism at some point and slowed them considerably. He was not looking forward to that inevitable day, and the occasional pings of pain in his knees and hips told him it wasn't too far away. He didn't like to think about it.

Crispy burst into the ship's bridge. The conn panel lights were blinking in their familiar patterns. The engine switches and geo-map were waiting for someone to start working them. He felt most at home on the bridge of the *Opal*. He dropped himself into his modified pilot's chair and strapped in, snapping all the buckles shut and making sure the straps were tight. He had a feeling he might need them.

The flight decks of Lux-class ships were built for utility, not style. The deck of *Shy Opal* was no exception. The main flight deck was little more than a pentagonal bubble atop the ship's body, barely large enough to hold four or five crew members comfortably. The top point of the pentagon was the rear, and the opposing flat edge was where the large, oval bubble window was positioned. At its widest point, the window ran floor-to-ceiling giving the widest possible viewing angles.

A trio of crew chairs were positioned behind the main controls. A basic gunner's chair for aiming and firing what few exterior weapons the Lux-class ships carried, a navigator's chair, and the obligatory captain's chair positioned ostentatiously behind the pilot's conn. As was common throughout interstellar travel, only the captain's chair was truly comfortable, and the pilot's chair was heavily retro-modded into being comfortable. The nav and guns chairs were little more than implements of extreme backside torture with fancy fabric covering them because the crew who used them did not tend to sit there for many hours a day, every day. They were chairs for people who needed them only for limited times.

The flight deck was usually dim. In space, without a star in the vicinity to cast light through the view screen, the only lights came from instrument panels, various buttons, and a dull blue overhead bulb which gave a pale, flat light. Since they were planetside at midday, the flight deck was flooded with the brilliant pink-white light from the late afternoon sun. Crispy liked it better when it was dark. It was cave-like, perhaps even womb-like. It felt safer in the dark.

There was no such thing as a quick launch when going from dead engines to flight. It took a minimum of five minutes for engines to get to the necessary heat and power levels to propel the ship vertically. Nav and weapons computers had to be brought on-line. The ship had to run through a self-check, and the pilot had to double-check that self-check. The standard preflight protocols had to be followed. The space flight controls had to be done. All in all, even with cutting some corners and ignoring a few things that *probably* would not get them in trouble later, the fastest Crispy had ever been able to launch *Opal* was just a few seconds shy of five minutes. An ideal and thorough preflight check would have taken at least twenty minutes, maybe thirty.

The rover projected more Roverspeak to the pilot's conn. The ship's engine was ready to ignite for systems check.

Crispy flipped the switches that lit the *Opal* with the preflight warning lights. He leaned toward his conn mic and opened a channel to the ship. "Preparing to fire up the dragon. Quick, is the cargo bay closed?"

Quick's voice came through the speaker a second later. "Light it, Crisp. All good down here."

Crispy started the countdown to ignition. While he waited for all the systems to get in line with each other, he leaned over and checked the ship's database for any mentions of Shea Mannion. The ship returned a standard info sheet with a picture of the man in the corner. There was nothing immediately unusual about the man. It listed his occupation as an industrialist, shipping magnate, and futurist. He was older, at least in his sixties, but he looked like he was forty, a few wrinkles at the corners of his eyes tipped off his true age. Whether his looks were enhanced with surgery, gene therapy, or if he was just naturally youthful was unknown. Crispy would have bet money it was surgical.

Mannion had a strong nose and chin, a good head of perfectly styled hair, and a stupidly expensive suit. He looked athletic, strong. He had not let money or age soften him. Crispy scanned the list of Mannion's investments and interests. It was all boilerplate standard wealthy guy stuff: insurance, real estate, ships, trading, exploration, genetics, and tech speculation. The guy's background certainly did not read as someone worthy of the woman's fear. Just another in a long, long line of rich assholes with too much money.

"Hey, Cap?" Crispy thumbed the conn mic. "I'm looking into this Mannion guy—he's rich, but that's about it. He's not the bogeyman."

Pageant's voice returned over the speaker. "I'm betting she owes him money or something. Probably an indentured servant. You know how those rich guys love their property."

"Slavery is illegal in the Rims."

Pageant knew that, but he was also realistic. "These rich guys always have loopholes. Pretty common for someone to sign themselves over to indentured servitude for a year or two to get transport from old Earth to some distant moon where their family has moved. Cargo prices can be damned expensive to get to the rims from the Sol Prime System."

"Slavery is illegal, but indentured servitude isn't. What's the difference?"

"Servitude has an exit date. Slavery doesn't. Otherwise, it's the difference between a beer and a microbrew. One is just a fancier word for the other." There was a pause. "How soon until we're off the ground, Crisp?"

Crispy checked his panels. The rover was sending a steady stream of info. "Gonna fire the engines now, Cap. Hang on." He tagged the panel for full ignite. The giant sparkers clicked a few times and the big translight engine fired. The ship whirred, shuddered, and bucked as the various machines and functions in the engine room kicked into gear. Crispy's eyebrows raised. That was a surprise. The engines almost *never* started on the first—

The engines sputtered, coughed, and died. All panels went dark.

"Horseshit." Crispy pounded a fist on the conn. He couldn't even tell Pageant and Quick what happened since the comms were part of the ship's electrical collapse. Although, if they were in the cargo bay when it plunged suddenly into blackness and silence, they could probably figure it out on their own.

The only thing in the flight deck still lit was the rover's comm panel. Since the rover was independent of the rest of the systems, it had a direct link to the panel through its own radio system so it could still relay necessary communications throughout the *Opal.* At the moment, a steady stream of Roverspeak was spitting across the bot's panel. Roughly translated, it was repeatedly questioning whether or not the engine had sexual relations with its own mother. Crispy keyed instructions to the bot on its panel. *Full reboot. Double-time.*

The rover replied in Roverspeak: *Aye-aye.*

It was a twitchy little bot, and often more of a pain than it was worth, but when the chips were down, it tended to come through. In the following sixty seconds, various lights and panels came back online as the rover went into overdrive in the bowels of the ship.

Heavy footsteps coming up the stairs from the residence decks to the flight decks told Crispy Pageant was coming. The captain was using an emergency glow-stick to light his way. "What the hell's wrong with my ship?"

"Cap, if she was a horse, someone would have shot her by now."

The corner of Pageant's lip curled. "She ain't a horse. She's been flying for more than three centuries."

"Okay, if she was a horse, she would have died of natural causes more than two-hundred-and-eighty years ago."

"Get her in the air, Crisp."

"That's what I'm doing."

The main sparkers came back online, and the Rover sent a message that the engine was ready for a retry. Crispy hit the preflight alert again. He grabbed the comm mic. "Trying it again. Hold onto something."

The engine spat and sputtered but refused to fire. Crispy swore under his breath and goosed the fuel, drenching the core. He fired again. This time, the extra fuel lit in a large explosion that challenged every inch of the engine's power containment. The ship rocked, farted, and groaned, but the translight rippled to life and began to flame.

Crispy felt the corner of his mouth curl into a half-smile. It truly took a special kind of pilot to keep a Lux-class ship in the air. "I think *Opal* is ready to see if she wants to get airborne, Cap."

"Take her up, Crisp. I want her at least a hundred klicks from here immediately." Pageant sank into his chair and threw on the shoulder restraints, clipping them to the anchor point between his legs. He checked his own panels on the arms of his chair. "Engines are green. It's looking good." He patted the side of his chair affectionately. "Good girl. I knew you weren't ready for the rust yard."

"Not yet at least." Crispy's feet found the pedals, each rigged with an extender to compensate for his lack of reach, and stomped them, testing pitch and yaw controls. He jerked the flight stick. In space, flight sticks were useless. In standard atmosphere, they were a necessity. He felt the ship responding to his touches. All panels were green. The rover was telling him to proceed with flight. It was as good a time as any.

Crispy engaged the on-board gravity compensators and eased into the lift pedal. The lift engines engaged. The boat shuddered, rocked, and cleared the ground. Crispy loved that moment. There was just something about the second a ship cleared contact with the ground, when the massive feet of the landing gear were no longer touching firmament. It was like sliding into a hammock, swinging gently in the breeze. No worries, no concerns. Just the miracle of flight.

Crispy gave a sigh of relief. "*Opal's* up and responding, Cap."

"What are you waiting for, then? Get her moving, Crisp."

Crispy leaned into the throttle and used the flight stick and pedals to wheel the ship higher into the air, curling it gracefully through the winds and getting well above tree level.

The scanners were coming through with the ID of the ship that triggered their proximity buoy. Crispy watched the readout. His stomach dropped a bit. "Cap, we got a problem. Buoy says the ship that just broke atmo is a Cerberus gunship."

Pageant started stabbing his own chair panels to double-check. There was a note of panic in his voice. "Are you shitting me?"

"Why would I lie about that?"

Pageant read the scanner readout for himself. "A privately-owned Cerberus. I never thought I'd see that. This Mannion guy has more money than most of the Outer Rim planets combined."

"If he's got a Cerberus, then he's not going to be afraid to use it. You don't buy a Cerberus to admire the pretty guns, just like you don't buy a Raptor-class ship to fly it safely at a reasonable speed." Crispy juiced the engines, coaxing them to max speed in atmo, which for the Lux-class ships was little more than a steady jog. If the Cerberus located *Shy Opal*, it would be on them like a falcon on an overweight, three-legged hedgehog with a poor sense of direction.

The name of the Cerberus came through on the ship ID scan at that moment. It was registered to MannTech Industries, the MTI *Despair*.

Crispy goggled at the name. "Who the hell names their ship the *Despair*? Aren't you supposed to give ships positive names or fun names? Maybe name 'em after your wife or something?"

"Clearly Mr. Mannion did not attend the same school of ship-naming you did." Pageant was furiously typing on his conn panels at his chair. "MannTech Industries. Military suppliers. Well, damn. That's why he's got a military gunship registered to him. He didn't *buy* it; he *built* it." Pageant hit the comms. "Quick, what do you know about MannTech Industries?"

There was a pause. Quick's voice crackled through the comm. "Bad, bad men. They basically outfit anyone who can pay, be they governments, pirates, or militias. They're assholes who play both sides off each other and profit mightily from death."

"So, we're dealing with a humanitarian."

"At the very least," said Crispy.

Pageant pinched the bridge of his nose like he was trying to stave off a migraine. "Ever have one of those days where you remember you probably should have just killed yourself when you were twenty-one so you wouldn't have to put up with twenty years of bullshit?"

"Pretty much every day since I turned twenty-one."

Pageant hit the comm again. "Quick, if you got more drones, I want you to launch three of them, *tout suite.*"

"I got two more drones with engines, Cap. The rest are dead drops for space."

"Launch what you got, Ms. Huffman. Double-time." Pageant leaned his head back against his chair. "I need an aspirin."

"Want me to get the Doc?"

"Want me to stuff you in the torpedo tube?" Pageant pinched the bridge of his nose again, harder this time. "I don't ask for trouble do I, Crisp? I try to be a good guy, try to do the right thing. I'm not one who goes around hoping horrible things will happen to me. I just want to work, get paid, and move on to the next job. Is that so wrong?"

"Gonna start heading for the stratosphere, Cap." Crispy began the flight path that would haul *Opal* toward the angle where they could fully fire the translight engines and break the planetoid's gravity. It was a smaller planetoid; it would not tax the engines too badly. With a Cerberus-class vessel behind them, the more they could coax from the engines, the better. Crispy turned back toward Pageant. "Cap, I think you're missing the obvious play."

"What's that, Crisp?"

"We are under no obligation to protect that woman. She tried to hijack *Opal.* We should have just left her on the prairie. We should just contact the *Despair* and tell Mannion's people they can have her."

Pageant plunged into a moue of deep thought. He tapped his fingertips against his chin. "You're probably right, Crisp." There was a pause. "But doesn't it seem weird to you?"

"Weird could pretty much describe every day I've spent on *Opal,* Cap. You're going to have to elaborate."

Pageant started ticking off a list on his fingers. "First, we land on a supposedly uninhabited planetoid for repairs. This lady with hi-tech hair shows up with a blaster rifle and tries to take us hostage. Then, a Class-A corporation gunship comes after her. *Why?*"

"Servitude?"

"Are you telling me you'd waste the fuel and crew power required to fly a Cerberus just to go after a single, stick-thin woman on a deserted planetoid? Think of the cred-count that thing incurs every second it's in the air. It would have been cheaper to hire a bounty hunter or send a three-man kill squad in a Raptor after her. Why is he bringing an entire ocean to get a single seashell wet?"

Crispy hated to admit it, but the captain had a point. The woman was a mystery, and if there was one thing Pageant loved more than credits or short women with large breasts, it was a mystery.

Pageant unsnapped his restraints. "Keep her steady, Crisp. Head straight for Black. I'm going to go down and check on this woman. I want to talk to her once she's coherent and peaceable before I decide to turn her over to Mannion. Might be there's a simple answer for everything, and we can just hand her over and feel good for doing it."

"What if there isn't a simple answer?"

"Then we figure it out as we go, Crisp. We're good at that, aren't we?"

"What's the play if we get contacted by the *Despair*?"

Pageant paused at the door of the flight deck. "Play stupid."

"Stick to my strengths. Gotcha."

"I'm going below decks, Crisp. Try not to need me." Pageant descended to the residence decks. His boots clanged on the metal stairs, fading to silence as he disappeared into the depths of Opal.

Crispy remained at his station, feeling the ship fighting through the chop of the upper atmosphere, keeping a firm hand on the flight stick. He wondered exactly how many seconds Opal would last if Despair decided to fire on her. If the over-under was three seconds, Crispy would bet the under.

4

PAGEANT COULD SMELL the Doc working its magic through the inches-thick door of the brig. The fact that the little hell-slug's stench could penetrate metal compartments meant to be sealed against decompression in space was testament to just how foul and disgusting it really was.

Quick was launching the second drone. She was wearing a full-face filter mask. "Got the masks out, if you want one. Still stinks to the seven hells through the mask, but it keeps your eyes from stinging."

Pageant popped the lock on the brig. Thicker than gelatin, a rolling wave of fetid funk blossomed and coated everything. Pageant made a mental note to put the clothes he was wearing into a torpedo tube and shoot them into the nearest sun. That *might* be the only thing with the ability to kill the smell.

Inside her mask, Quick retched and fought to keep herself from throwing up. Vomiting in a filter-mask might be the only thing worse than the smell of the Doc.

Maybe.

The woman in the brig was conscious. She was clammy and pale. Rivulets of foul-smelling black sweat cascaded from her forehead and neck and stained her neon-red hair. She was gripping the edge of the mat on the pull-out bunk to keep from screaming. When she saw Pageant, she pleaded with him. "Just kill me."

Pageant gave her his best good ol' boy toothy grin. "Right? Told you it was awful. Don't worry, though. I know it does not feel like it, but you are actually healing."

"Feels…like I'm going…to die."

"That's more the smell than anything. It does things to you. Tells your brain you're rotting from the inside. The Doc has never killed anyone. It hasn't been able to save everyone, but it has never killed anyone."

"How do I know when it's done?" The woman was sucking air through gritted teeth. Her eyes were threatening to bulge out of her head.

"Oh, you'll know. It'll attempt to exit your body, usually through your mouth, sometimes out the…uh…rear hatch. If it comes out your mouth, just spit it back into the jar when it does and clamp the lid back on it."

"How will I know if he decides to go…the other way?"

"It'll sorta feel like a half-dozen antelope suddenly decided to film a martial arts fight scene in your colon. Believe me, you'll know. Same rationale applies, though: just squat over the jar and let it out. Don't try to hold it in. Believe me—when Doc is done with you, you *want* it done with you."

The woman did not respond. She eyed the Doc's jar with contempt. Pageant could not blame her. No one had a good first experience with the Doc. No one ever had a good experience, but first experiences were particularly bad.

Pageant knelt next to the bunk. It took a considerable amount of willpower to keep from running screaming away from the smell. "What would you say if I told you that a Cerberus-class gunship called the MTI *Despair* was entering the atmo of this particular planetoid?"

The woman's eyes widened, then squeezed shut. "I told you we should have run."

"We are running, or at least we're going as fast as an aging Lux-class cargo ship can run, I suppose. I certainly would appreciate it if you gave me a reason as to why we are running. What, exactly, have I gotten myself into by taking you aboard my little ship?"

The woman's eyes darted to the right for a split-second. Pageant noticed the little dodge. It was a gambler's tell. She was going to lie to him. "I'm an indentured servant. He's a horrible overlord."

It was as good a lie as any, Pageant figured. Believable. Simple. It makes sense. However, like he'd told Crispy: you don't send a warship after a single servant. "Something tells me that's not quite true."

The woman was breathing through the pain of the Doc's machinations. "Fine. I owe him a ton of money."

That was more believable, but still—a gunship was overkill. "Must be a whole lot of money."

"Twenty million exo-creds." The woman started to convulse. Her face turned green. She started to cough and gag. She clutched at her throat.

Pageant could see the skin around the base of her throat undulating as the parasitic space squid worked its way up her esophagus. That was odd.

Pageant had never seen anyone finish with the Doc so quickly. He slid the Doc's jar toward her bed with the toe of his boot. "Looks like Doc is finished with you. Just spit it out."

The woman's face was twisted in horror and revulsion as the alien slug fought its way out of her body. She leaned over the edge of the bed and opened her mouth. The squid-like tentacles burst out, latching onto the skin of her cheeks and chin to pull itself from her. It had gorged on her injuries, swelling to almost five times the size it was when it first entered her wound. It slid out of her mouth and fell into the black liquid of the jar. Pageant clapped the lid back on the jar. Instantly, the horrible smell in the room lessened by half. The woman fell back against the bunk, completely spent by the experience.

Pageant gave a low whistle. "That is by far the fastest I've ever seen the Doc work. You're lucky. Usually it takes at least a full day, maybe more. Depends on how bad the injury is."

Pageant sat on the edge of the bunk and prodded the woman's shoulder. There was a black spot where the gunshot had been, but it was no longer bloody, and there was no divot in the flesh. There was smooth skin beneath the discoloration. "That'll clear in a few days. You won't even know you've been shot."

The woman was breathing easier. She was taking in deep, cleansing breaths. "Thank you, Captain."

"Pageant. Nathan Pageant. Captain of the STS *Shy Opal*."

"Interesting name."

"That was what she was called when I bought her. Bad luck to rename a ship."

Quick appeared in the doorway. She leaned her lanky form against the bulkhead. "As long as we're discussing names, we never got yours."

Pageant jabbed a thumb toward Quick. "That's my cargo officer, Quick Huffman. Don't be fooled by her brusque attitude; she really does hate everyone."

The woman pushed herself to a sitting position. She wiped sweat from her forehead, actual, clear, human sweat. Her orange prison tac-suit was stained with foul black discolorations from the Doc-influenced sweat. "You're the one who shot me."

"You're the one who was holding a gun on my captain." Quick's retort came out sounding like a challenge for a fistfight. After a beat, she attempted to soften her statement with politeness. "Ma'am."

The woman was silent for a moment. "I don't have a name. Not anymore, at least. My birth name is lost to time at this point. MannTech called me Unit Three-Four-Six."

"You're a mod-tester." A large piece of the puzzle fell into place. Pageant opened a hatch door in the brig and pulled out a clean, dark gray tac-suit with *Shy Opal's* ship ID tag on the back. He threw it to the woman called Unit 346. He pulled out the shower head from its spot on the wall and revealed its controls. "Here. Shower fast. Change into this and come up to the residence decks. We'll talk more."

Pageant walked out of the brig. Quick followed on his heels. "Think that's smart, Cap'n? We should keep her in the brig for a while, especially while the Doc is working."

"Doc's done with her."

"Already?" Quick gave a low whistle. "That was crazy fast."

"Brig's gonna smell foul for the next week or so. That ain't fit for any human."

"She tried to take the ship, Cap. I'm a little past caring about what is or isn't fit for her."

"She's a mod-test." Pageant said as if it explained everything.

"So what?" Quick snorted. "Fancy rich man's toy is all she is. Wonder what they were trying to do to her. Probably inflate her boobs or widen her hips or something so she'd fetch a higher price at a brothel."

"There's easier ways to give a gal bigger tits than gen-mods." Pageant thumped up the stairs toward the residence deck. "Mod-tests are something more. If that gal's a mod-tester, likely MannTech has already invested a half-a-billion creds into her development, and she's probably got a bunch of sensitive info rooting around in her cells. The right competitor gets ahold of that info and MannTech is out its investment and all the potential millions, if not billions of future profits. That's something you might send a gunship out to recover. I'm willing to bet he's got a bunch of ships out looking for her."

Pageant stopped in the center of the residence deck, a large common room that served as a combination kitchen, dining room, and recreation hall. The room was lit with a dim, blue light. A well-used couch was bolted to one wall. A small, round table sat in the center. A viewer for entertainment was on the wall near the couch. The room was, as it always was, bathed in a pale yellow light that made everyone in the room looked jaundiced. Pageant took a seat at the table.

Quick remained standing, her long arms crossed in a defiant pose. "If she's a mod-test, we should start talking about cutting a deal with MannTech to return her. Or, maybe talking to some of MannTech's competition to figure out exactly how much they'd be willing to spend to take her from MannTech."

"That could start a war, Quick."

"As long as we get paid enough to vacate the star system where the fighting is, I'd be okay with that. A bunch of Inner Rim corporate jerk-offs shooting the shit out of each other is probably a good thing for the rest of the rim worlds."

"Actually, that's probably one of the worst things that could happen." Pageant gestured toward the kitchen. "Corporations bring food to the rim planets. Corporations traffic supplies, medicine, even terraforming gear. They got enough to worry about with piracy in the Outer Rims. If they have to start going to war with each other, those supply lines stop cold. A lot of people on small planets will die pretty quickly. Any money the corporation has to spend will also get transferred to the backs and the wallets of the small folk. Corps never spend their own money. Supply prices will get jacked sky-high. Medicine will become more expensive than I'd care to believe. I fear to think about the outcome of that. It's all dominoes."

Quick scowled. "Cap, we got a potential goldmine showering in our brig. We can't pass that up."

"Smart play for everyone in the rims would say we pretty much need to."

"I would appreciate it if you did." Unit 346 was standing in the portal hatch between the common room and the cargo bay. The woman had silently ascended the metal stairs silently in bare feet and a tactical suit.

Quick hated when people snuck up on her. "C'mon in, Unit Whatever-You-Are. Have a seat." Quick planted a foot on one of the pivot chairs at the table and turned it outward until it thumped hard against its stop.

"Did you have a nickname, ma'am? Gonna be weird to call you three-four-six, or unit, or whatever." Pageant moved from the couch to the table.

The woman shook her head. "Not really. Some of the guards at MannTech called me Red." She lifted one of the unnaturally colored wet tresses dangling from her head. They were almost difficult to look at now they were clean. They almost cast their own light. "Because...you know."

"Red is a crap nickname. Pretty much every fool in the Outer Rim with a hint of auburn in his mane is named Red." Quick took the seat opposite the woman. "I guess names can wait. Maybe you can think of a new name for yourself."

The comm crackled. Crispy's voice came through the speaker. "Prepare to break grav. Twenty seconds."

"What does that mean? Break grav?" The woman looked nervous. She was tense.

"It's that moment when we separate the ship from the planetoid's gravitational pull. It's nothing to worry about. You'll feel a split-second of weightlessness, and then the ship's gravity units will kick in and compensate. It's like hitting the top of a hill in a hovercraft." Pageant waved off her concerns. "For a planetoid like this, you'll barely notice it."

29

At that moment, there was a flutter in everyone's stomachs as the ship broke through gravity's pull and entered real space. "Was that it?" The woman looked disappointed.

"That was it. Like I said, no big deal." Pageant leaned toward the woman, putting his arms on the table. "Now it's your turn to talk. Who, exactly, are you that you are worth so much that MannTech would send a gunship after you? What sort of mods do you have kicking through your system, lady?"

The woman looked toward the kitchen. "Would it be rude of me to ask for a drink, maybe some food? I feel pretty weak."

Pageant jumped to his feet. "Forgive my lack of hospitality. Let me grab a few things. We have basic rations, of course. I think we might have a few other things."

"I got a couple of weird fruits planetside," said Quick. "They're in the bottom of the cooler. The scanners say they're edible. Can't guarantee they taste good, but they're edible. Alien fruit is always a bit of a gamble."

Pageant brought over an armload of goods and set them on the table. He got a couple of boxes of purified drinking water from the cooler and set them in front of the woman. "Dig in. Help yourself."

The woman reached out hesitantly, took a chunk of protein rations, and tasted it. She took a small bite at first, but quickly began to shovel products into her face as though she had not eaten in weeks.

"Ease up there, ma'am. If you've got an empty stomach, a lot of food will make you sick." Quick reached for the woman's wrist. The woman twisted away from Quick like an animal guarding a kill.

Pageant and Quick sat back in surprise. "Ma'am, no one is going to take food from you. No one on my boat goes hungry so long as there's food. That's a promise."

The woman turned back toward the table, crimson creeping up her cheeks almost as bright as her hair. "That was rude. I apologize. Where MannTech had me held, manners were…unconventional."

"How old were you when they—" Pageant trailed off. It was a difficult subject to broach.

"When my parents sold me?" The woman knew exactly what he was asking. "I don't really remember. My brain is all bits and pieces and fraying ends, I'm afraid."

"You were born to actual parents? I thought mod-testers were clones." Quick was shocked.

"The existence of human clones is only rumor. Cloning is expensive," said Pageant. "Most mod-testers are homeless street kids who get abducted from the big cities or metro-ports, or they're the youngest of seven or eight kids born to some poor simpleton farmer barely scraping by in the Outer Rim. Most of the time, there's no official record on those kids. They're not *real people*, as the government lists call them. Technically, they don't exist. Some big corp sweeps in, offers a pile of cash, and that family suddenly has a child that they no longer speak of. That kid is just gone. The kid never was. He's an unhuman."

The woman nodded. "I don't remember much about it. I got on a ship with two men in tactical suits and helmets. I tried to be brave, like my father told me to be, but I cried the second the door closed. After that, I was property of MannTech." She turned in her chair and pulled her hair away from her neck. An intricate coder tattoo was blazoned into her flesh. Underneath the scan-code was the project code for whatever testing she was undergoing and her number: *PR-ARC346.*

"Hells alive." Quick sat back in her chair, disgusted. "I was a streeter myself. Dad died in a mining accident on Plescoe when I was almost fourteen. Mom drank herself to death shortly thereafter. I had no family to speak of, no money to get off-world. Plescoe did not really have any sort of infrastructure to support orphans. Had a couple guys take runs at me, but I figured they were just pervs. I wonder if they might have been trying to sweep me for mod-testing."

"Probably," said Pageant. "Kids disappear every day from big cities, and they're not missed. Tougher to make them disappear from smaller colony settlements, but it still happens. If they're not registered with the Central Brain, they don't exist and they're not important enough to worry about. Sad circle."

"What do you know about mod-testers?" asked Quick. "If they don't use clones, then I don't know as much about them as I thought I did."

Pageant shrugged. "Not much. They're usually kids when they start. They undergo expensive testing to see if they can split or join their genetic structures to enhance them. Most of the time, the testing usually ends up killing them. That's why they take kids that don't exist in records. If the mod-tester dies, the corporation just tosses the body in an incinerator and moves on. No harm, no foul."

Quick's jaw clenched. "Bastards, all of them."

The woman finished eating the food in her hands and drank an entire box of water in a single breath. She sighed and wiped her mouth with the back of her wrist. "Thank you. I feel a little better."

"You're welcome." Pageant sat back in his chair. "Now, tell me what I need to know about this chase-ship. Why are they after you? What are you, really?"

The woman's eyes cast down to her lap. She fiddled with one of the wrappers for the protein bars. "I'm dangerous."

"I assumed that much. How dangerous?"

31

"She only had the Doc in her for like twenty minutes, Cap. Probably less. You ever see the Doc work that fast?" said Quick.

"Never. It was highly unusual. Is that one of your mods? Fast healing?"

The woman shrugged. "I have no idea. Honestly. I just know that I'm dangerous. The researchers never tell you about your mods. You're just strapped to a board, and they shove needles in your arms, jab scopes in all your openings. They send nanobots into your bloodstream. It's very scary, and very painful. They do things until you almost die from the pain, then they toss you in a cell for a few weeks or months to recover. When you recover, you go back to the table."

"You don't know anything about what they were trying to do? All those times you were in the labs you never overheard anything?" said Pageant.

The woman hesitated. She shook her head. Then, she held up a finger, as if she was trying to remember a long-buried memory. "Once. Once, I heard something. This was back when I first arrived at MannTech. There was a boy. He was much older than I was, maybe seventeen. They actually modded him to develop horribly large muscles. They were trying to create some sort of super-soldier. I remember him sitting in the corner of a cell, weeping in pain because his bone structure and ligaments could not support the muscles. When he moved, the muscles would snap his bones and tear his ligaments. He was considered a failure. He eventually died because they did not give him medical attention once he was deemed a failed project."

"Sounds about right. If MannTech Industries profits from war, then gen-mods for super-soldiers would be right in line with what they were trying to do," said Pageant.

The comm panel crackled. "Cap, I think you maybe want to come up to the bridge and play captain for a minute."

"On my way, Crisp." Pageant leapt to his feet. "Help yourself to more food. Quick, let's get our guest a bunk."

"Aye, sir." Quick pushed herself away from the table. "Secured quarters, or standard guest?"

Pageant stopped in the portal. "I think standard quarters will be fine for now. What's she going to steal, Quick?"

Quick shrugged. "The ship, maybe?"

"Would we still be on the ship?"

"Far as I know."

"Ma'am, if you steal our ship while we're asleep or something, will you be killing us and shooting our corpses into space shortly thereafter?"

The woman's eyes widened in shock. "I don't want to hurt anyone."

"There you go, Quick. Rest easy." Pageant turned on his heel and jetted up the stairs to the bridge.

5

CRISPY WAS WATCHING the hailing beacon flash on the comm panel. The MTI *Despair* had been trying to contact them for several minutes. Crispy ignored them until he noticed they changed course from landing to pursuit. Quick's beacons might have bought them an extra two or three minutes, but a vessel with all the advanced scanning tech such as a Cerberus-class warship would not be fooled for long.

Pageant stepped through the portal and onto the flight deck. He threw himself into his chair. "How bad, Crisp?"

"Bad enough, Cap. The *Despair* is coming after us. We could go translight, but it will look like we were running, and we can't outrun that ship for long. What do you want to do?"

"Steady on course, Crisp." Pageant noticed the beacon. "They're already trying to contact us, aren't they?"

"Aye, Cap."

"Think they know we have their property?"

"Probably a safe assumption."

Pageant chewed on his lower lip. "Put 'em on the screen, Crisp."

Pageant stood at parade rest and waited for the vidfeed to connect. After a moment, the screen lit up with a holographic, 3-D view of the bridge of the MTI *Despair*. It was a nightmare of black steel, blinking touchscreens, and smartly suited paramilitary crewmen in red-and-gray uniforms. A stern-looking thirty-something woman sat in the captain's chair in the center of the war deck. The decorations on her epaulets designated her a commander. A dozen crew members of various ranks manned stations around her.

Pageant cleared his throat. "Ahoy there, MTI *Despair*. This is Captain Nathan Pageant of the STS *Shy Opal*. To what do we owe the honor of your high and most holy graces deigning to speak with us lowly, blue-collar transport haulers on this fine day?"

The commander of the *Despair* inhaled sharply through her nostrils. She had jet black hair pulled into a tight bun and dark eyes like a shark. The look of pure contempt she gave Pageant gave Crispy a prickly feeling on the back of his neck, like he was worried she was going to reprimand them in a motherly fashion. Crispy's own mother was a yeller. His fear for that sort of thing was deeply ingrained from the childhood trauma of hearing his mother cursing him out at the top of her lungs in Portuguese.

The commander stood to address Pageant. "Captain Pageant, I am Commander Reesha Neer." She accented the word *commander* to make sure Pageant knew she earned her title. Officers in the military, even a corporation-funded paramilitary, held great contempt for privateers like Pageant who designated themselves *captain* simply because they bought a ramshackle transport ship. "We are seeking a fugitive. We have reason to believe she is aboard your ship."

"My ship? Really?" Pageant oversold the ignorance, but it somehow worked for him. "Helmsman Okino, what is our current crew-count?"

Crispy knew the routine. He put on his best *professional pilot* voice. "Three, Captain Pageant. You, me, and Cargo Officer Huffman."

"We've only got three aboard this vessel, Commander. Sorry to waste your time."

"Do your feeble ruses ever work, Captain?"

"Our ruses? What ruses are you implying, Commander?" Pageant flashed her an idiot's grin.

"Our scanners are currently showing four life-signs aboard your ship."

"Four! Really? Crispy, run a scan of our ship."

Crispy mimed hitting a few buttons. Given the angle of the conn, Commander Neer had no idea if he was actually hitting buttons or not. "Computer says three, Cap."

"Our scanners show three life signs, Commander. Could it be that your scanners are misreading? Perhaps they are unfamiliar with the vital signs of little people and are counting Crispy's unusual stature as two people. I've seen it happen before."

Neer's eyes narrowed. She looked vaguely like a cobra, Crispy decided. "Mr. Pageant—"

"*Captain* Pageant." He pointed to his shoulder as if he had a fancy military epaulet there. The stupid smile never left his face.

Neer rolled her eyes. "*Captain* Pageant, what is more likely: my ship, a brand-new, top-of-the-line, advanced gunship with all the latest technology, is having a malfunction, or your antique barely-flying shitbox is malfunctioning?"

"You forgot the more likely third option, Commander: we could be lying."

"I always assume a privateer is lying, Captain Pageant. I've never known them not to."

"Well, I'm offended." Pageant stomped his foot.

"That's a lie," said Neer.

"True," said Pageant. "I get called a liar daily. Most of the time, by my own crew."

"Might be the first truthful thing you've ever said, Cap."

"Maybe I'm turning over a new leaf, Crispy. I'm going to be a wholesome man from now on. No more lying, no more whoring, gambling, or drinking. Maybe I'll even start attending a church of some sort." Pageant turned back to the annoyed commander on the viewer. "Commander Neer, your intervention has set this former rogue on the correct path in life. Congratulations. I shall be sure to wire your bosses at MannTech and let them know that you've done so much to make this old pirate a better man. Crisp, thank the commander and end transmission."

"Thank you, Commander," said Crispy. "*Shy Opal*, out."

"Enough!" Neer shouted.

Crispy froze, his finger poised over the comm button.

"Commander, your attitude is enough to make me renounce my newly born-again status." Pageant sat in his chair and threw his leg over one arm. "And here you were, so close to saving a soul. Shame."

"I demand you divert course to the nearest emergency port, which in this case will be Port 1131. We will escort you there." Neer stepped toward the viewer camera. She loomed full in the frame. "Any attempt to flee or ignore our commands will be viewed as a threat, and the *Despair* will be forced to act accordingly."

"Really, Commander?" Pageant started laughing. "In what universe would anyone consider a Lux-class Roundbelly small freighter a *threat* to the likes of a Cerb gunship?"

"You're in the Outer Rim, Captain. The rules of engagement are pretty lax out here. I can claim any number of things and absolve myself of the rather minor sin of blowing you out of the sky. One less smuggler in this world—not a single person in the universe will lose sleep over that fact."

"Crispy, she keeps saying *smuggler* like I'd actually lower myself to break the law we hold so sacred."

"Blasphemy, Cap."

"Isn't it, though? I've got half a mind to stop talking to her."

Neer's face flashed crimson. She turned to her gunner. "Shoot one of their engines."

The *Despair* launched a volley at *Shy Opal. Opal's* sensors, detecting the incoming assault, immediately sent the ship into red alert. Lights across the ship switched to a deep red. Alarm klaxons sounded. Pageant thumbed the *Opal's* general comm. "Brace for impact!"

The volley hit the port nacelle of the ship. The entire vessel rocked violently. Pageant barely kept himself in his chair. Crispy was strapped in, otherwise he would have been sent flying. Below decks, Quick and 346 were thrown into the port-side bulkhead of the common room in a tumble of arms and legs.

Crispy tried to compensate for the loss of the engine. "Port-side is blown bad, Cap." A stream of Roverspeak launched across the bot's comm. "Rover says it's cashed out permanently. No repairing it."

"That was a warning, Captain." Commander Neer returned to her captain's conn, sitting elegantly and crossing her legs. "You can still limp to 1131. Don't make us disable you."

"Commander Neer, you are working my last good nerve." Pageant started tapping damage control into his own conn. The ship's diagnostics were coming back with all kinds of unpleasant news. Streams of bright red text were spit across the screens. "Mute her, Crisp."

Crispy shut down the audio feed from their ship. The video remained live. Crispy covered his mouth with his hand. "Five to one says they got lip-readers on their camera feed. Probably subtitling us as we speak."

"Those aren't completely accurate, Crispy." Pageant was transitioning from aloof to angry. "To hell with these corporations. They think they own the goddamned Black."

"Maybe we're out of options, Cap. They want the woman. We give them the woman. I'll lay in course to 1131."

"She's a mod-test, Crispy. She's probably worth at least a cool half-billion. The *Despair* would gladly take us down without a second thought if they didn't need her so badly. The fact they didn't just annihilate us proves they need her alive. We've still got chips to play in this hand." Pageant thought for a second. "Open the channel again."

Pageant pushed himself to standing. "Commander, do you play poker?"

Neer looked at Pageant suspiciously. "I have."

"This is the point where I call your bluff. You don't want to disable our ship. You take out our second nacelle, and we're down to bare life support, and that starts the clock running on how long we last before the Great Cold Black takes us, including your special little treasure. You'd have to mount an external rescue, and that's not only dangerous for your crew and your ship, it's just not much fun. You need the girl, otherwise you'd have just killed us. So, let's talk price."

"There is no negotiation for the return of MTI property, Captain. Proceed to 1131 and return our project."

"Your *property* is a human being with inherent rights, Commander."

"Our property is our property, Captain—and I use that title loosely. You have no idea what you're dealing with. Think for a moment, if you would. You found our property on an uninhabited planetoid."

"And?"

"Think about what I just said, Captain. I will await your compliance. *Despair* out." The screen blinked black.

"What did she mean by that?" Crispy was confused.

Pageant was fully alert. There was something that they missed. Something that had not occurred to them. "There was a living human on the planetoid. How'd she get there? How'd she survive alone? We didn't pick up any ship signs when we scanned the planetoid."

"Our scanners are antiques, Cap. It's not too hard."

"Maybe, but still. That red-haired gal has a lot of question marks about her, doesn't she?"

Quick came through the portal to the flight deck at that moment. "We're hurt bad, Cap. Translight is offline. Life support reserves are down by half. We need a port double-time or we're going to be in serious trouble."

The woman with the hi-tech hair was on Quick's heels. "I'm sorry for bringing this on all of you. You should probably just return me to MannTech."

"How did you get to that planet?"

The woman blushed. She fumbled for words.

Pageant grasped her hands. "Don't lie about this. I'm trying to help you."

"I'm not sure."

"What do you mean you're not sure?" Quick's eyes narrowed in disbelief. "That sounds like some sort of bullshit.

"What about the ship that brought you there?" Crispy went back to the scan logs and checked the data again. No ships. There was an asterisk on the scan data, though. There was a smattering of metal in the atmosphere of the planetoid. This was not uncommon for planetoids with human life. All manner of debris gets amassed in short order as they launch satellites, comm systems, scanners, all the other little bits that make inhabiting a world worthwhile. However, the planetoid they had landed on was so new that it did not even have a name. It was still referred to on the star maps by a number. It was designated for habitation in the near future, once it was guaranteed animal life would be abundant enough to help support the initial human settlements. There should have been nothing in its atmosphere. The realization of what the orbiting metal actually was hit Crispy like a thunderbolt. "Your ship was destroyed."

The three members of the crew of the *Shy Opal* turned to look at the woman with the hi-tech hair in unison. She suddenly looked very young and very scared. Pageant cocked his head to the side. "How did you hide from a scanner and survive a ship explosion in the upper atmosphere?"

"I escaped in an escape pod. A drop-coffin." The woman's voice was low and emotionless.

"How did the ship get destroyed?" As a pilot, Crispy was always concerned with things capable of destroying a ship.

"It suffered a hull crack and started to decompress. When the crew tried to compensate for the damage, the atmosphere generators ramped the engines into overdrive." The woman's eyes flicked toward Crispy, and then back to her feet. "I saw a chance to escape and I took it. I needed to get away from MannTech."

"I can't blame you there," said Pageant.

"I'm getting a heavy lie of omission vibe coming from her, Cap." Quick eyed the woman suspiciously. "She's hiding something from us."

"If I am, I do not mean to." The woman looked to Quick with pleading eyes. "Please understand, I am trying to help."

The incoming message alert started to flash on the conn. Crispy looked toward Pageant. "The *Despair* is trying to hail us again."

"Send a text to them, Crisp. Tell them we'll contact them in a moment." Pageant turned his full attention to the woman. "The ship blew up. Things like that don't just happen. Why didn't the crew notice? Why didn't an engineer jump in and shut down the engines before they went critical?"

"I'm betting they were all dead or unconscious, Cap." Prior to signing on with *Shy Opal*, Quick had been a security officer on a corporate transport. She perpetually saw the bad in people and leapt to the darkest outcomes of any situation.

The woman blushed. She looked guilty. She would have been lousy at a poker table. Her voice was barely above a whisper. "I told you, I'm dangerous."

Quick's hand dropped to the butt of the A7 on her hip. "Me too. I guess we got something in common."

Crispy raised his hand. "If anyone cares, I'm rather harmless."

"Why does everything have to be a reenactment of the shootout at the OK Corral with you, Quick?" Pageant threw up his hands. "Honestly, I think you would be happier if you got challenged to a duel once a day."

Quick's eyes did not leave the woman. "If you think I'm going to correct you on that, you'd be wrong."

Pageant turned back to the escapee from MannTech. "Are you going to kill us? Well, specifically me, and probably Crispy. Quick might enjoy it if you took a poke at her. She doesn't like being cooped up on the ship with no one to shoot."

"I don't *want* to kill anyone. Honestly." The woman looked at the palms of her hands as if they might suddenly spurt snakes. "The mods they gave me...I don't know what they did exactly, but they made me dangerous. I can do things no human should be able to do."

"So can Crispy," said Pageant. "He can kick himself in the nose with his toe."

"That's true." Crispy waggled his foot toward the woman. "No human should be able to do that."

"I mean things no human really should be able to do." The woman held her hands out, palms toward Pageant. "My hands do things. They emit some sort of light, and then people die."

Quick arched an eyebrow. "That's odd, because sometimes Crispy's butt emits a gas, and I want to die."

"That only happens after you do the cooking, Q."

"Enough, you two." Pageant leaned forward and took one of the woman's hand in his own. He inspected it, shrugged, and released it. "I don't see anything different but given what few clues we have to her existence on that planet, I can't say I'm not going to disbelieve her."

Crispy tried to reason out the exchange. "If she's got some sort of weird mods like that, she's basically a weapon, Cap. If we give her over to MannTech, they're just going to keep trying until they make a bunch of her. Then, I imagine a lot of people will die."

"MannTech's in the killing business," said Quick. "That's what they do. Killing is profitable. Always has been."

Pageant drummed his fingers on the arm of his chair. He blew a huff of breath through his nose. "Crisp, that Cerberus is locked and loaded, aren't they?"

"You pretty much have to assume they are, Cap. Even if they're not, it would only take a ship like that a few seconds to find our limping hog of a ship and shred it."

"Our feeble shields would only buy us an extra second, Cap." Quick started scanning one of the panels on the gunner's post. "They have the whole arsenal on that thing. Standard Hellfire ion missiles, big ol' Sundowner torpedoes, and a full set of Akkaron blasters on three-sixty swivels. The bad news is they'd blow us straight to hell. The good news is it'd be so fast we wouldn't have time to worry about it."

"Options, Crisp?"

Crispy shrugged. "Pretty clear we either give up the girl or die."

"And yet, I don't want to give up the girl." Pageant's fingers stopped drumming. He looked at his crew, coming to a quick decision. "We could go full squid."

Quick's head jerked up from the gunner's panels. "Cap, that'd pretty much ruin the ship."

"We're down to one engine on an ancient ship. You could make a pretty strong argument we're already ruined."

Crispy was piecing the scenario together in his head. He saw the dominoes falling one after another. "Cap's right. Full squid would get us away from the *Despair* long enough to think about what to do, at least."

Quick drew herself to her full height, the way she always did when she was trying to win an argument. "And what if it doesn't work? Then we're all but scuttled with a damned Cerberus gunship up our butt. You think they're going to be pleasant to deal with after that?"

"Full squid will work." Pageant was certain it would. The new warships could not deal with ancient tricks. They were too full of gadgets and gizmos that could not account for human ingenuity. The *Despair* would not be held down for long by the old smuggler's ruse, but it would be held down long enough for *Opal* to get somewhere else, and without a way to track the ship, the Cerberus would have to go looking. By then, as he had so many times before, Nathan Pageant would be hiding. No one in the rims could hide quite like Nathan Pageant. "Look me in the eye, Quick, and tell me you'll sleep well knowing what tortures lay out before this girl if we just hand her over to them. Think about what you went through after your parents died. You'd wish that or worse on someone?"

Quick's jaw twitched. The corner of her mouth jerked once in anger. She puffed up like she was about to say yes, but then relented. "No. No, I would not. Screw the corporations. Let's go full squid, Cap."

Pageant began to strap himself into this chair. "You heard the lady, Crispy. Prepare to squid. Give me a forty-one second hop."

"Aye, sir." Crispy began to tap in the preparations.

Pageant turned to the woman. "You might want to strap yourself in. This might get real ugly."

"What's full squid?" The woman started buckling herself into the navigation chair, bringing the shoulder straps down and locking them at the anchor between her legs.

"You know what a squid is?" Crispy asked. Some people, especially poorer folks from the outer rims, did not always understand references to Earth creatures.

"It's a fish, I think."

"Sort of. It's a cephalopod. It has tentacles and an elongated body.

Squids have a unique defense mechanism. When they are threatened, they blast this stuff at their predator, a secretion of dark pigmented liquid. People used to call it ink."

"Ink?"

Crispy's head teetered from side to side as he sought to explain it. "It's like paint, but thinner, like a really dark colored water. Anyhow, they blast the stuff in the face of the predator to blind it. Then, the squid just jets away. They find the nearest hiding place and hole up until the predator leaves."

"We're going to do the same thing." Pageant was hacking his permission codes into the panels on his chair. "Basically, we are going to blast the Cerberus with a sort of EMP shot. It's not going to hurt them. Nothing we could do to that thing will actually hurt it. But, it will make all their scanners go completely dark for a second or two. In that split-second where they're blind, we make a suicide jump to translight. Poof! We're gone. When we drop out of the hop, we're someplace else, and we can find a rock to hide under."

The woman looked concerned. "Suicide jump?"

"That's when you jump into translight without a point of exit on your nav conn." Crispy tried to make it sound nonchalant, like something people did every day. "If we enter a destination, there's a chance the *Despair's* scanner will know where we've gone. Suicide jumps are surprises to everyone, including us."

Quick finished snapping herself into the gunner's chair. "Problem is, you can't suicide jump in a Roundbelly on the best of days. You *really* can't suicide jump with one engine. This hop is going to just fuck up the ship beyond repair. We'll be able to limp, but that's about it."

The woman shook her head. "You can't do that to your ship. Not for me."

"Any day this thing is still flying is a miracle, lady. It only had a few months left, at best, without a full overhaul anyhow. A year, tops." Pageant hoped he sounded convincing. Truth was, losing *Opal* would be like losing a sister. Ships, as much as they might feel like a friend or family, were still only cold steel and computer parts. They were not people. They were especially not people a corporation would seek to use to murder others in the name of profit. When it came down to it, the choice was pretty simple, even if Pageant hated to be noble.

"Ready to squid, Cap. Where do you want to go?"

"Shoot us in an arc, Crispy. I want us to go under the Cerberus so the last thing they see is us heading past them. Then, curl us back around toward Port 1131."

Crispy could not help but break into a grin. The last place Commander Neer would start looking for a rabbiting ship would be the nearest port, especially if it was the port she had commanded them to go to in the first place. His grin faded. He rubbed his hand over the flight panel lovingly. "One last time, old lady." It would be hard to part with *Opal*. "All systems ready for squid, Captain. On your mark."

"Hold on to your potatoes, everyone." Pageant took a couple of quick breaths. "Hit it, Crispy."

Crispy hit the launch button. In near-instant succession, *Opal* fired off the EMP burst, pulled a hard one-eighty, and launched into translight on a straight path beneath the *Despair*.

For the passengers on board, it was not nearly as graceful or calculated as it looked from those watching from the *Despair's* view screens. The concentrated EMP burst scrambled all of *Opal's* comm and scanner systems for a split second, even the rover's panels. In the split-second it took for them all to come back, the translight engines were already firing. The gravitational dampeners aboard the ship that maintained standard Earth gravity lost power as the ship sucked up all the energy it could to make the translight jump. The four people on board *Opal* became temporarily weightless, along with anything that was not nailed down. The dampeners did all they could to maintain basic life function, which in this case meant preventing the instantaneous death of all living beings aboard by massive G-forces. The air also got thin for a brief moment, as the recirc supply stopped working. The lights went out completely, and the entire ship was plunged into a thick blackness as dark as squid ink. All in all, going full squid was aptly named.

Most of the time, when a ship is given time to ease into translight, there is ample time for a vessel to compensate, prepare, and adjust. For a ship to do a full spin and suicide jump, it was more closely akin to waking up with a massive hangover and deciding to go from prone in bed to running a four hundred yard dash at a full sprint in bright sunlight without trying to breathe while you do it.

Crispy was thrown in his seat violently as he ignited the full spin. The single remaining engine chugged hard as it tried to compensate for its missing twin, attempting to double its output. As a safety measure, every ship had to be able to make a translight jump with a single engine, and that single engine had to be able to compensate for the loss of its pair, but most ships ran that safety measure as close to the bone as possible. *Shy Opal*, being a ship of a certain age and modified over the generations for dubious purposes, was cut even closer than that.

Opal began to shudder and cough. System alert lights popped across Crispy's panels like fireworks. There was nothing he could do about them until the grav-dampeners returned the environment to Earth normal. Until then, he was pinned back against his seat and fighting skull-crushing G-forces.

In the end, the suicide jump ended up not finishing by the preset forty-one-second timer that Crispy had set, but instead it killed out at the thirty-three-second mark due to catastrophic engine failure.

Every alert on Crispy's boards went to full-red status and *Opal* tumbled out of translight like a rockslide. It ragdolled through space ass-over-teakettle. Crispy was jostled like a stone in a tumbler. His body strained against the straps. His stomach was spinning, and he fought to keep down the protein bars he'd had for breakfast that day.

In the depths of the ship, the emergency engine protocols kicked to life. The Last Ditch, as it was called, was barely more than a basic life support system dribbling a thin stream of power to an impulse engine. Usually, if the Last Ditch engaged, it automatically launched an SOS beacon, too. Crispy had disengaged the auto-launch because of the situation, so no one would come looking for them. When the Last Ditch started, air and gravity returned to Earth normal. The ship fought to regain its posture and stop turning cartwheels. Eventually, many spins later, the ship's barely functioning nacelle was able to slow and right the vessel, and everyone on board took in a deep breath.

Pageant used his fingers to brush hair from his face. "Crispy, make a note: let's never do that again."

"Sounds good, Captain. Permission to throw up?"

"Sure, let's all take a minute to vomit."

6

CRISPY RELEASED THE straps securing him to his chair. He surveyed the conn panels with a grim frown. All were flashing incessantly with feeds of damage reports and lists of compromised systems. *Shy Opal* had given them everything she had, and she was all but adrift.

From the captain's chair, Pageant eased out of his own straps. "Is it as bad as I think it is, Crisp?"

"Worse." Crispy read the full ship diagnostic. "We're down to Last Ditch power and SOS radio. It's got maybe twenty-four hours of power. Might be able to squeeze four or five hours extra if we seal some decks and pump all the available breathing air from those decks to the living decks."

"Do it, double-fast. Quick, make sure there's nothing oxygen-dependent in the cargo bay and start there. There's a bunch of air in there. That should give us a good four or five hours, alone."

"Aye, Cap." Quick popped the lock on her shoulder straps and hustled from the flight deck.

"Is there any life left in that starboard nacelle, Crispy?"

The pilot shook his head slowly. "Dead as space, Cap. We're done-for unless we can get to port."

"How close did we get?"

Crispy hopped out of the pilot's chair and checked the star charts on the nav conn. "Another five seconds of translight would have gotten us there easy. As it lies now, we're at least twenty-six hours from 1131, maybe a little more."

Pageant smiled pleasantly. "It wouldn't be us if we weren't cutting it close, ol' buddy. Lay in course. Divert as much as you can to the engines and cross your fingers."

"Is everything going to be okay?" Unit 346 was freeing herself from the nav chair.

Pageant put a hand on her shoulder. "In order to save you time worrying, let's just say yes."

"I'm very sorry." The woman looked as though she might cry, but she didn't, almost as if she was no longer capable of it. Her face wrinkled mournfully, but her eyes remained dry.

"It happens. Don't worry about it."

Crispy knew a million thoughts were running through Pageant's mind. Foremost would be how much it would cost to get the ship running again, if that was even in the realm of possibility. Second would be the notion of buying a new ship. Could Pageant afford it? Could he afford it even with Crispy and Quick's help? The simple answer to both those questions was no, he could not. Not even with help.

Crispy wondered what would happen next. He was nearing thirty. He had dwarfism.He and Pageant had been together for almost eight years. Pageant was the first and only ship's captain to even give him a shot. What would happen if Pageant no longer had a ship? Where would they all go? Would they even be able to stay together? Crispy had begun to think of their odd little crew as something of a family over the last few years. Quick had been with them for more than five years, and she was sort of like the obnoxious big sister. Pageant was the older brother trying to run the family business. Crispy was the baby of the family, the one the other two protected. The idea of having to fend for himself or having to take a low-level cargo job flying set routes for a corporation or planetary government gave him stomach pains. First thing's first, though; it would do no good to worry about the future if they died in the next day and a half.

"Crispy, get the rover going overtime. We're gonna need that little slacker if we're going to have any chance." Pageant dropped to his knees and started removing wall panels on the bridge to get access to the necessary electrics to shut down non-essential systems. He started pulling fuses as soon as the panel was clear.

Crispy checked the rover's comm panel. The little bot was doing its Roverspeak equivalent of cursing at Crispy, or at least reprimanding him for driving the ship without concern for the delicate internal workings. The rover tapped into the mainframe. It was scanning systems over and over again, replying to each scan with the phrase, *Unable to Assist.* When it finished scanning the main systems, it began scanning smaller systems, and then the subsystems of the smaller systems. Its programming gave the bot a singular mindset and drive. Fix what was broken. Fix. Fix. Fix. When everything was broken, most of it beyond repair, it was like turning a sugar-addicted dachshund with attention-deficit disorder loose in a wiener factory. It just couldn't figure out where to start.

Crispy grimaced at the speeding lines of Roverspeak. "Rover's gonna blow a circuit, Cap."

Pageant chucked a handful of fuses to the floor. "Can't blame the little bugger. Tell him to focus only on life support-related systems. If we stop breathing or lose heat, everything else will be null and void anyhow."

The woman with the hi-tech hair pulled her knees to her chin in an attempt to be as small as possible. "This is all my fault. I shouldn't have tried to take your ship. I should have just stayed on that planet. I could have made a life there. I could have survived."

Pageant waved her off. "Please. With no supplies? No weapons? No shelter? You would not have lived well, and you probably wouldn't have lived long. Your only mistake was simply not asking for help first instead of trying to take our ship by force."

She buried her face in her hands. "I made a mess of everything. It's not the first time I've done that. It probably won't be the last."

"You never know. Right now, I'd say you have a better than average chance it might be the last." The auxiliary safety lights went dark as Pageant pulled the fuse chip. The flight deck was plunged into near-darkness. Only the alert lights on the panels lit the interior. It made the room feel twice as small as it was. "Don't start planning for the future is what I'm telling you. Let's worry about getting to port first, and then we'll go from there."

Quick reappeared in the door of the flight deck. Her arms were loaded with tactical suits, and she was dragging a weapons crate. "Everything is sealed except for the common room and the flight deck, Cap. I've got the recirc system channeling all breathable air into this space for now."

"Quick, why did you bring guns?"

"I didn't want them to get lonely. Besides, if we need them, we won't be able to get them from the cargo bay."

Pageant slipped back into his chair. He gave a great sigh. "This is the boring part. I suggest a couple of us might think of getting some sleep. It will help conserve air, and if everything goes to hell, you'll have the added bonus of not seeing your own demise coming for you."

"I couldn't sleep," said 346. "I can still feel...that healing thing moving in me."

"That'll last for at least a day." Quick dropped the tac-suits in a heap in the corner by the nav conn. She shoved the gun crate against the wall and sat on it.

"Well, we don't have much else to do." Pageant tented his fingers in front of him and rested his chin on them. He closed his eyes. "Quick, remind me to radio Traxler when we get to port. I'll have to tell him that we're not getting to Fenton anytime soon, and he's not going to get his supplies."

"I already did that, Cap. Sent a text. He sent one back. He is currently somewhere on the opposite side of happy." Crispy pulled up the image of Traxler's text. "Want me to read the list of names he called you?"

"Not really, Crisp."

"*Witless chucklefuck* was my personal favorite."

The corner of Pageant's mouth curled upward slightly. "That is good. Quick, put that on the list of potential future ship names. The STS *Chucklefuck* has a lovely ring to it."

The rover's comm panel scrolled out a new line of Roverspeak. "Cap, Rover says it has tapped into the deep space scanners. It can't send the relay to the pilot conn, but it says there's a ship incoming." Crispy read more of the bot's comm message. His voice could not hide the concern. "Rover says the ship is on a pursuit course."

Pageant's eyes snapped open. "Well, that's interesting."

"Aren't you glad I brought the guns now?" Quick was on her feet and at Crispy's side in a heartbeat.

"Fat lot of good the guns will do when we get a hole blown through the ship and explosively decompress. How did they find us, Crispy?" Pageant took up a spot on Crispy's other side. All three members of the crew were scanning the spotty alert messages and constant info feeds. "Are you trying to tell me that MannTech can track a three-hundred-year-old STS after a suicide jump? That can't be. *Opal* doesn't even have a decently functioning transponder on its best day, let alone one that the new tech could get a handle on."

Crispy was dumbfounded. "I have no idea, Cap. It's highly suspect."

"Could they be tracking me?" The woman stood and unzipped the front of her tac-suit. She pulled out one arm, exposing her naked left breast as she did.

Pageant's eyes could not help but widen. He felt uncomfortable. "That's lovely, but this is hardly the time."

"Here, Captain." The woman pointed to a small nub just below her breast along her ribs. It looked like it might have been a tumor, or the remnants of a broken bone.

Quick inhaled sharply. "That's a tracker. Bet you a week's pay on it." As if by magic, a long, lean knife appeared in her hand.

"I thought it was a power dampener. They put it in me a few months back after I had an...*accident*." The woman's finger traced the small, dull pink scar that crossed the top of the lump. "It wasn't too painful. I sort of forgot it was there."

"We got to cut it out of her, Cap." Crispy angled his head toward Quick's knife. "We can numb the spot with some anesthetic, and—"

"Just cut it. I can handle pain." The woman raised her arm and anchored it behind her head. She stretched, maximizing the workspace for Quick to remove the piece. "Do it now."

Quick looked toward Pageant. He gave a nod. "Don't see that we have much of a choice, Q. Cut her."

Quick did not even warn the woman. The knife flashed and a streak of blood appeared over the spot where the tracker was anchored to the woman. The woman inhaled sharply and gave a hint of a gasp, but she clenched her teeth and fought through the pain. Sure enough, a dull black cylinder of metal appeared in the tissues. "That's a tracker. Someone get me a week's pay."

"I'll owe it to you." Pageant moved in to get a better look at it. "Cut it out of her and destroy it."

"Good luck on destroying it." Quick was squinting at it. "I'm betting that's some sort of carbon-titanium fiber or worse. We don't have guns on this ship that'll hurt it, not that you want to be shooting guns on the ship. If we could still get to the cargo bay, I'd suggest tossing it into the airlock or a torpedo tube and blowing it toward the nearest sun." Quick pried it off the woman's rib cage with the tip of the dagger. The woman moaned in pain, but did not flinch. Her toughness was impressive. The little device tore free and Quick caught it.

Pageant pulled the little first aid kit from its space on the wall and used a palm-sized dermal laser stapler to seal the wound with three stitches, and then covered it with a skin-seal patch. "Good as new. Or will be in a day or three."

Quick was trying to break the little capsule with her fingertips. "It's solid as a rock, Cap."

Pageant took the capsule from his cargo officer. He turned it over in his fingers, cleaning blood off of it. "Think the rover can nuke this?"

Crispy shrugged. "Rover's programmed to repair, not destroy. I doubt it would, even if it could get through the exterior."

"Well, there's always one thing trackers hate." Pageant knelt down by the board of fuses. He selected an empty port at random and slapped the tracker into it. A second later, the lights on the bridge grew very bright, and then faded again. The tracker was fried. "Million-cred tech subverted by a three-hundred-year-old fuse board. Brilliant."

"That Cerb knew where we were headed, though," said Quick. "It'll be on top of us any second."

"What's the play, Cap?" asked Crispy. "We're nowhere near port. We're nowhere near a habitable planet. We are literally a sitting duck."

"I guess I'll have to use charm." Pageant sat back in his chair. "That's never steered us wrong before."

"Except every time it has. Which is every time we've relied on you to be charming." Quick flopped in the gunner's chair. She fiddled with the dead panels in front of her. "We couldn't even pretend to put up a fight against a Cerberus if we were at one-hundred percent. Now, we're rightly and truly screwed."

"Just turn me over to them." Unit 346 sat primly in her chair. "They don't want you. They want me. They'll let you go if they get me."

Pageant held up his hand to silence her. "That won't happen. They might think they own you, but that's illegal. You might not have a record in the Inner Rim, but you exist and a missing record is something that's easily remedied. We just have to get you to someone who can help."

"I could put out a direct SOS to someone, Cap. Maybe Gentoo or the Briggs Syndicate, someone with a fast ship."

"That might be the next option, Crisp. I doubt either of those degenerates are going to be willing to race here to steal us from under the nose of a privateer gunship. Besides, they might take hours to get here."

The woman rose from the nav chair. "I'm serious. Turn me over to them. There's no other way. They'll take me. You'll be able to limp to the port. It's what I want. If you don't turn me over, you're holding me against my will."

There was a silence. Crispy saw a darkness cross Pageant's face. He looked to Quick. She gave a slight shake of her head. Crispy slowly turned back around and looked at the flashing emergency lights on his panels

Pageant did not leave his chair. "Do you really think that's how this will go down? That a corporate gunship will just let a nobody owner-operator leave and go back to port with the knowledge that the corp is experimenting illegally on unhumans? Honey, the only reason we're not already dead is because you're on this ship. Me, Crispy, Quick—we're nothing to a corporation. Any major corp in the trading fleets has to shed blood just to stay in the air. They'd murder all three of us a thousand times over if it meant keeping their sins out of the news and their shareholders happy."

Pageant put his elbows on his knees and leaned toward the woman. "You started a ball rolling that can't be unrolled. I got involved because I decided that you were worth saving. If I'd been halfway smart, I would have let Quick put a bullet in the center of your head back on the surface of that little nowhere world. Instead, I made the decision to bring you on board, because you were an anomaly, and I like anomalies. They keep the world interesting."

The woman laid down her counterpoint. "They *might* kill you if you give me up. If you don't, they'll disable the ship, launch acolytes to board it, and take me by force. If they have to do that, you *will* die. Guaranteed. Anomalies defy nature. That's what I do. Nature likes predictability. I'm the opposite of that."

"I thought Nature liked chaos," said Quick.

"And it abhors a vacuum," said Crispy. "I get it; I don't like cleaning, either."

There was a strange glint in Pageant's eye. "Anomalies need to be studied. I have not concluded my research, yet. You're staying, and that's final. I'm the captain of this thing. Out here in the Nothing, my word is law."

The woman moved to speak again, but Pageant silenced her by holding up a finger. "You have no say in this. If they're going to kill us, they're going to kill us. I'm used to that. If someone doesn't try to kill me at least once a month, I get twitchy. Let it lie, now."

The woman's mouth opened, and then closed. She returned to her chair.

Pageant looked to Quick, and then to Crispy. "I'm open to suggestions, but make 'em quick."

Crispy was at a loss. He had nothing intelligent to offer in that instant. He was a pilot. If he couldn't fly the ship out of danger, he could not contribute.

Quick chewed on her lower lip for a few moments. "Play 'possum. It's our only hope."

"Details, Quick. Lay out your plan."

Quick looked worried. "It ain't a good plan, Cap."

"Give me what you got."

Quick listed the points of her plan and held up fingers to correspond to them. "First, we seal the common room, which would stick us on this deck until we found the port. Second, we vent breathable air to dangerously low levels and drop the temps in here to down near four or five degrees Celsius. Third, we take a small dose of Ventilix. Fourth, we give Rover a singular task: wait twelve hours and then fix life support. Exterior scans will make it look like the ship crumbled in the suicide jump and all life signs on board are dead."

"What's Ventilix?" asked the woman.

Crispy cringed. He did not like the stuff. "It's a narcotic. It drops the heart rate to near undetectable and makes you look like you're dead, but a small dose is not fatal and wears off eventually."

Pageant chimed in. "In an emergency, you give it to your crew to keep them from panicking or using up too much oxygen while you let one crew member get you to a port, or you take it after you start an SOS beacon. It can buy your crew hours, sometimes days of extra time."

"What if they send acolytes?" the woman asked.

"How often would a corp waste money to storm a dead ship?"

"For me, they might."

Quick hesitated. "That's true. They might. I could try to hide my life signs in a tac-suit, and then lay in wait with a gun. With any luck, they'll think we booby-trapped the ship and maybe they give up."

Pageant huffed a heavy breath. "There's so many dominoes that need to fall right for this. Crispy, you got any ideas?"

"Short of initiating the self-destruct on this old ship right this second and saving the *Despair* the cost of a single missile, I got nothing."

Pageant hesitated. It was command decision time. He rubbed his chin thoughtfully and chose a course of action. "We go with Q's plan. We got nothing else."

A new alert light lit up on the board in front of Crispy. Rover was sending a new message. The pilot tapped it and read the Roverspeak. "Belay that order, Quick. Don't bother."

Outside the window, there was a faint green-white glow around the top edge of the viewing area, the usual light show of a large vessel dropping out of translight.

"That did not take them long." Pageant frowned. "I guess we're humped."

"Looks that way. Given how much of a head start they had because of big red's tracking device, I'm a little shocked it took them this long." Quick pounded the arm of the gunner's chair in frustration. "You want I should just shoot the three of you and then myself, Cap? Be easier than letting them blow up *Opal*."

The comm alert light lit up on the board in front of Crispy. "They're hailing us, Cap."

Pageant put his fingers on his temples. "Maybe not a bad idea, Quick. Crisp, contact them. Voice only, please."

"At this point, voice is all we have, Cap."

Even the usual telltale beep of the channel opening was off-line at the moment. There was the hiss of a microphone seeking sound in the flight deck's speakers. Pageant spoke into the air. "Hello, Commander Neer. My pilot and I were just discussing you. We both agreed that you're very tenacious. That's a wonderful quality for a gunship captain."

"Do you think we're playing games, Mr. Pageant?" Commander Neer's voice was calm and even, but the tension in her tone could not be hidden. She was furious, as was to be expected.

"Games? I love games! Commander, if I'd known we were playing games, I would have gladly joined in. I think I've got a deck of cards on this ship. We could play some Cribbage if you have a board."

The *Despair* launched a starburst round. It exploded just off *Opal's* port side. The ship rocked violently. All four people on the flight deck were thrown from their chairs and into the starboard wall. Without the grav dampeners on full, when the ship listed, the crew was thrown to a wall which had just become the new floor. Luckily, the grav was functioning at less than One Earth-Grav, so it did not hurt as much as it could have.

Commander Neer's voice was still barely containing her rage. "That was just a warning, Mr. Pageant."

From the jumble of limbs and bodies against the wall, Pageant groaned, "*Captain* Pageant, to you, Commander Neer."

"*Mister* Pageant. Your self-appointed title means nothing to us. In fact, I should be calling you Future Prisoner Pageant. We are preparing acolyte vessels to retrieve our property. I suggest you turn the girl over to us and make this simple. You do not want to interfere with this process. Any attempt to prevent the acquisition of our property will be viewed as a hostile act, and we will respond in kind. There will be no more warnings."

Pageant dragged himself out of the pile of crew on the floor. "You know, Ms. Neer—you're pissing me off."

"*Commander.*"

"If you're not going to respect the captaincy of a registered private transport owner, then I'm sure as hell not going to respect any titles of a paramilitary corp psycho with too much power and too little control." The muscles in Pageant's neck were starting to flare. He was red in the face. Crispy had seen him like this before, usually right before he said something that got him a good punch in the face in a bar filled with questionable types.

"You don't know what you're doing, Mr. Pageant."

"I have a pretty good idea, Ms. Neer. If you want the girl, you come over and take her. Just tell your acolytes that my chief of security is Natalie Loretta Huffman, alias Quick Huffman. Look her up before you send your teams. Just tell your boys that I'll be giving her free reign to defend this vessel as she sees fit. I figure you've got a crew complement of what, maybe two-hundred on that thing? Ask yourself, if you have to send acolytes through a landing portal against Quick Huffman, who will be hunkered down and prepared for them, will you have enough crew?"

There was a prolonged silence. They were likely searching Quick's name in their databases. After a moment, Neer came back. "Tell Ms. Huffman to stand down, Mr. Pageant. No blood needs to be shed over this."

Pageant waved a hand at his throat in a *kill-it* gesture to Crispy. The pilot muted the microphones on the *Opal.* "They know that sending acolytes will result in one or more deaths on their end."

"A lot more." Quick was seething, a coiled snake waiting to strike. She reached out and patted her cargo crate of weaponry.

"Are you really that dangerous?" the woman asked Quick.

A sadistic grin lit on Quick's lips. "Short answer: Yes. Longer answer: *Hell*, yes."

"Point is, we're basically at a stalemate for the moment. Crispy, if you were Neer, what's your next play?"

"I disable your engines and sting your life support. You'll be left floating with limited air. I wait until the air supply bleeds down and makes you docile. Then, I send acolytes."

Pageant sighed. "You got any notions in this Mexican standoff where we don't end up dying, Crispy?"

"Technically, a Mexican standoff would mean we're both on equal ground. This isn't that. We're screwed, and the *Despair* is going to win."

"Way to inspire the troops, Crisp."

Crispy threw up his hands in surrender. "I'm just preachin' truth, Cap."

"If our only option is to die, I say we cost MannTech as much money as possible before we do." Pageant pulled himself back in his captain's chair and began to strap up.

Crispy knew what he meant. After so many years together, he was always on Pageant's frequency. "Altering course, Cap."

Quick sighed and strapped herself into her chair. She gave a lingering look to the crate of guns in the corner. "This isn't how I wanted to go out, but I'm glad it's this way instead of an illness or something like that."

The woman with the hi-tech hair had wide eyes. "What's going on?"

Crispy did not even look back to her. "We're going to ram the *Despair*. I'm going to aim at their bridge."

"Are you insane? That's suicide."

"Better than being murdered." Quick shrugged. "Still, I would have liked a chance to mow down a few acolytes before going out. One last story for the legacy, eh?"

"You're all insane." The woman began to strap herself into the nav chair.

"You don't go out in the Great Black Nothing without being willing to die, lady. You want a relatively safe life, stay on a planet and plant crops." Crispy did not really want to die. However, death was a fast and hard fact of life about interstellar travel. Hardly a day went by where some ship somewhere on the translight lanes didn't explode, lose life support, or was blasted to ashes by pirates. There was a running joke amongst people in elder-care facilities that they should enlist in the transport services to prevent dying in a hospital bed. Life in the long-haul lanes was often harsh and unfair.

"New course ready, Crispy?" Pageant brushed his forelock of hair out of his eyes. He straightened his shirt.

"Awaiting your order, Cap." Crispy laid in a course correction that diverted everything *Opal* had left, even life support, and would send them directly into the bridge of the *Despair*, hopefully before the warship could blow them apart.

"Live hard and leave a pretty corpse. It's been fun, everyone." Pageant nodded at Crispy. "Do it, Squirt."

"Aye, sir. Changing course to certain doom." Crispy hit the button on the panel in front of him. *Opal's* thrusters engaged and the Roundbelly began to spin on its axis.

"This is madness," Unit 346 pleaded. "Just turn me over to them."

"Nah, this is more fun," said Pageant.

"How is this more fun?"

"Because fuck 'em." Pageant crossed his legs in front of him and laced his fingers over his stomach. "No one lives forever. Might as well cost some super billionaire some cash and make him lose face while we die. There are worse ways to go out, you have to admit. Crispy, send a translight message to whatever allies we still have out there. Let them know how we went out, will you. Make sure you tell them that we murdered the bridge crew of the MTI *Despair* before we went out."

"Aye, sir." Crispy began composing a text record of the *Opal's* demise.

"They'll just shoot us before we get there," said the woman.

Quick waved off her concern. "Even if they do, they'll have to deal with all the shrapnel of our ship coming at them. They're going to take a fair amount of damage, without a doubt. Keeping us whole is actually probably the best way to minimize damage. We'll wipe out their bridge, maybe an area around their bridge, but the majority of the ship will remain intact and repairable."

"Mr. Okino, reopen our mics. I'd like to wish Commander Neer a fond farewell."

"Channel open, Cap."

Neer's voice was strained. There was definitely an element of panic in her tone, but she was doing her best to keep it from her crew. "What are you doing? Do you think this bluff will work?"

"It's not a bluff, Neer. I'm going to crash into your bridge. I'll die, yes. You'll die too, though, and that's really what I'm looking forward to seeing. Perhaps we can meet up for a couple of friendly games of Cribbage in Hell."

"You're willing to settle for a minor Pyrrhic victory that will mean nothing to anyone?"

The woman with the hi-tech hair hissed, "Don't do this."

Pageant slashed his hand toward her in an effort to quiet her. "Yes. I figure, at the very least it'll set back MannTech back a few months of research, and a few billion creds, so it'll be worth it."

"There are other ways, Captain Pageant." Unit 346 was straining against the straps of her chair.

Pageant shrugged and gave her a reassuring smile. "Probably. But this will make Commander Neer piss herself before we all die, and the notion of that pleases me greatly." To Crispy, Pageant said, "Full ahead, Mr. Okino. Let's find out if there's an afterlife."

"Aye, sir." Crispy dumped all available power resources into the Last Ditch engines. The ship began to accelerate. Commander Neer began to screech at them. Crispy killed the comm.

The problem with the massive gunships was their vulnerability when not moving at a decent clip. It was one of the reasons that most gunships carried a small fleet of nimble one-man fighter ships. Wasps to protect the hive. It took a long time to get a hulk of the *Despair's* size up to speed. When at rest, the gunships could not get out of the way of smaller vessels. A Roundbelly was not going to win any sort of speed records, but compared to a gunship at rest, it was almost a Raptor-class attack vessel, even when on barely-functioning impulse engines.

Pageant looked wistful, but was fully at peace with his decision. "Any regrets, Crispy?"

"Probably. Too late to worry about them now. How about you, Q?"

"I regret I spent so much time with you two idiots."

Crispy couldn't help but laugh. Even when she was trying to be gruff and brave, Crispy knew Quick loved them. She was always one to keep them at arm's length, but if she hadn't liked them, she would have left Pageant's employ long ago. Plenty of jobs for people as good with a gun as she was, and most of them paid a damn sight better. She stayed because she belonged with them. Crispy turned in his chair to give her a smile and say his final goodbye to Quick and Pageant. "We'll see you guys on the other side, eh? Save me a seat in Valhalla."

As he turned back to watch the oncoming crash, a glimpse of the woman in the nav chair caught the corner of his eye. She did not look right. Crispy turned the other way to get a better view of her over his right shoulder.

The most noticeable thing, and the most concerning, was that the woman's eyes had turned to pools of liquid black. There was no sclera, no pupils—just oily black glass. She was staring at the approaching *Despair*, but Crispy could not tell if she could see anything or not. A pulse of rushing energy seemed to radiate from her. It had weight and heat. Crispy could feel a strange sensation pressing against his temples.

"Cap?" Crispy swiveled his chair back toward Pageant. He pointed at the woman.

The liquid black around her eyes seemed to bleed from her, filling the air before her face around her eyes like a butterfly wing-shaped mask. Her she clenched the arms of her chair. The energy in the bridge began to thrum. The woman gasped. Her voice was barely audible. "I hope this works."

The *Despair* filled the viewing window on the bridge of the *Shy Opal*. There was no way to stop the collision between the two ships; it was eminent. Through the glass, Crispy could see the bridge staff of the Despair trying to vacate their posts, retreating to the relative safety of the deeper decks of the gunship. The forward tip of the *Shy Opal* was nearly in contact with the *Despair*. The most forward section of a Roundbelly transport was the main cargo bay jutting out like a pregnant woman's stomach, hence the name.

At the moment the two ships were to make contact, Crispy involuntarily inhaled as though he would somehow survive the impact, the rush of the vacuum of space, and the waiting cold. He'd read somewhere that a human could live between two and ten seconds after exposure to space. Crispy clutched at the arms of his pilot's chair and shut his eyes. This was it. He waited for death. He hoped it wouldn't hurt too much.

But it did not come.

The two ships should have smashed each other apart, but they did not. There was no noise, no sudden jarring. There was nothing to indicate the ships touched. Crispy wondered if he had overestimated the time to impact. He risked a peek.

All around him was a wild array of color and shape. He saw everything in pixels and points of light. The speed of motion overwhelmed him. It made his eyes hurt and his stomach churn. He could not process what he was seeing. The steady pulse at his temples was threatening to cave in his skull. The urge to vomit rose in Crispy's chest, but he was an experienced and seasoned pilot. He fought it back down. Quick was not as used to the motion and color. Crispy could hear her retching behind him. He wrenched his eyes closed.

In another moment, there was an eerie silence. All the pulsing stopped. The color and light disappeared. All sensation of motion ceased. Crispy was still holding his breath. Everything in his body was screaming for air. He gasped, sucking in a deep breath. *How are we still alive?*

Pageant ripped off the chair harness and jumped to his feet. He patted his chest and thighs to double-check that he was still solid.

Quick was sitting in her chair stunned. Vomit stained the front of her shirt. She wiped her chin with the back of her wrist. "Is this Heaven? Are we dead?"

Crispy checked the panels. Only one still had power being supplied to it. It showed the *Despair* was directly behind *Shy Opal*. Both ships were still intact. "Cap, we ain't dead."

"I'm noticing that." Pageant turned to the woman with the hi-tech hair. She was slumped over in her chair. Her forehead was glistening with sweat. Sweat stains darkened her tac-suit under the arms and behind her knees. Her eyes were closed.

Pageant knelt next to her chair. She opened her eyes slightly. "Did I do it?" She fell forward into Pageant's arms. Pageant eased her back against the chair and slipped her out of the safety restraints.

Crispy watched the panels. The rover was trying to comprehend was had just happened, but could only return error messages and confusion. "Cap, the *Despair* is moving off."

"Say what?" Pageant lifted the woman into his arms.

Quick fell out of her chair onto her hands and knees. She was still retching. "I hate motion sickness."

Crispy double-checked the panels. "The *Despair* is moving off. It is queuing translight engines."

Pageant's eyebrows arched. "Maybe we are dead." He made a makeshift bed on the floor of the bridge with a couple of the tac-suits Quick brought up from cargo. He laid 346 upon it as gently as he could.

The woman stirred. Her eyes opened slightly. Her voice was barely a murmur. "They can't see us. We're hiding."

"That doesn't explain why we're still alive, though," said Pageant.

"I made us intangible." The woman's head lolled, and she went limp.

Pageant put his hands on his hips. He looked at Crispy, then Quick. "That's exactly what I was gonna do; she just beat me to it."

7

PORT 1131 WAS a basic hub port nicknamed *Ark Eleven* by those who frequented the long-haul translight lanes. It was little more than a fuel depot and short-term shore leave hangout, but it had mechanics, repair docks, and large, exterior rovers for delicate repairs to engines without needing a suit or an MMV. It also had a small ship trader and scrapper available. Given *Opal's* status, the scrapper was more likely her destination.

Pageant, Crispy, and Quick stood in the common room. The woman with the hi-tech hair was lying on the couch. She looked very small and very frail. It was a big change in how dangerous she'd looked earlier that day when she was holding a blaster rifle on Crispy.

Pageant finally broke the silence in the room. "Well, that was not something you see everyday."

"Even the rover was confused," said Crispy. "Whatever happened, the poor twitchy bot could not process it. Sent me a string of error messages."

"Whatever happened to us, it's got to be why MannTech was sending a gunship for this gal. She's a witch." Quick's hand was resting on her holstered Mengler. Her thumb was turning rapid circles on the smooth handle, as though she was waiting for the woman to give her a reason to draw. "You all saw that weird black mask shit she was doing, right?"

"Magic isn't real, Quick. Easy there." Pageant reached down and pulled Quick's hand off the Mengler. "Last thing this poor girl needs is another reason to have the Doc in her."

"Last thing any of us needs is another reason to have to smell the Doc," said Crispy.

There was a prolonged silence. The three crew members stared at the strange woman who had recently entered their lives. Crispy stated the obvious. "We should be dead."

"Day's not over yet, Crisp." Pageant scratched at his neck. "If we all put our minds to it, we might figure out a way to shuffle off this mortal coil, yet."

"You laugh, but Mighty Mite is right: we should be dead." Quick heaved a heavy sigh, partially relief, partially confusion. "What the hell just happened to us?"

"She made us intangible, however it happened. All I know is that it worked." Pageant knelt down and put a hand on the woman's forehead. "She's burning up. Quick, get the cold packs from the first aid kit. Let's see if we can cool her down."

"Aye, Cap." Quick hustled over to the first aid kit on the counter by the kitchen. "Maybe we can use the smelling salts and wake her up, too. Or maybe we can use a cardio-stim." She rooted through the kit and came up with the blue plastic cold packs and the white, needle-like stims.

"We could just let her sleep. She looks exhausted. I could use some sleep. We all could." Crispy doubted he could sleep, but he would have enjoyed a few moments in the darkness to process the day's events without the eyes of his crewmates on him. At the moment, he felt like defusing his emotions would involve tears.

Pageant took one of the stims from Quick. "We need answers right now more than she needs sleep." He popped the cap on the injector with his thumb, and then stabbed the stim into the woman's stomach.

The powerful chemicals jolted the woman awake immediately. Her eyes popped open. She inhaled sharply and let out a scream. Quick clapped a hand over her mouth to muffle the noise. She knelt to speak into the woman's ear. "What you're feeling is a Vivex cardio-stimulant. It feels like your heart is racing a thousand miles an hour, I know. You're safe. You will be okay, I promise. Breathe hard through your nose. You'll calm down in a second."

The woman followed Quick's instructions. She breathed. Her chest heaved several times. She sucked in a big breath and exhaled it slowly. She relaxed fully. Quick removed her hand. The woman inhaled hard through her mouth, inflating her lungs. Her eyelids were heavy. She looked fish-belly pale. "I'm so tired."

"We all are, but we need answers." Pageant eased the woman's legs off the couch and helped her to a sitting position. "Crispy, get her some water or something."

"And get me a bourbon," added Quick.

Crispy went to the cabinets and got a box of water and a bottle of Krysbin's single-malt. It wasn't bourbon, but it was as close as they had on board.

The woman slugged back the water. "Could I beg you for more? When I do *that*, it really makes me hungry and thirsty."

Pageant nodded at Crispy, who fetched more water directly. Quick picked up a few of the wrapped protein bars from the disaster that was the common area. Everything that wasn't strapped down before the suicide jump was scattered all over the room. Strangely enough, it was still far from the worst the room had ever looked.

Pageant spun one of the anchored chairs at the central table around and took a seat. He leaned forward, elbows on his knees, to look the woman in the eye. "Ma'am, we're flying blind at the moment. I don't think I'm overstating it when I say that none of us—" he gestured to Quick and Crispy, "—have a clue about *anything* that's happening right now. We need as many answers as you can provide, no beatin' around the bush."

The woman looked as though she might cry. "I can't. Honestly. I know almost nothing. The medicines, the tests, the drugs—I was in and out of consciousness constantly. I was subjected to pain, stress, starvation, dehydration, and torture. It was all I could to simply stay alive. I had no energy or capacity for staying coherent. When I was in the recuperation phases, I was locked in a cell and allowed to watch entertainment video feeds of shows and films. No one spoke to me. I was barely allowed to exercise or interact with other mod-tests." A serene half-smile lit on her lips for a moment, a happy memory in a vast field of darkness. "I remember once having an entire conversation with another subject. His name was Unit Four-Four-One. We spent the whole time talking about how we did not know anything about what was going on with us."

"You know nothing?" Quick was suspicious, as she tended to be. "Nothing at all? You can't give us the name of a guard or a scientist who worked on you?"

"Were you kept at one facility the whole time?" asked Crispy. "Do you know where that facility was?"

"I don't know. I would often be given drugs and lapse into unconsciousness. I don't know how long I would be out. Sometimes, I woke up in a different room. Sometimes I would be in those rooms for a long time. Days, weeks, maybe? I was always returned to the same recuperation cell, though. I know that much. It might have been different facilities. It might have been just different areas of the same facility. I don't know." The woman's mouth twitched as though she might cry. "I'm not helping much, am I?"

"It's not your fault," said Pageant. "I know a little something about how those sorts of places work. Like the old saying goes, they treat you like a mushroom: keep you in the dark and feed you lots of bullshit."

The woman looked down at her feet. "It was strange. We weren't exactly mistreated. They never beat us, starved us, or were needlessly cruel. If we wanted something to read, they gave us books. If we wanted to watch a movie, we could. Some of the scientists who worked on us would laugh or joke with us occasionally. We were not treated like how prisoners in the movies are, but we were definitely prisoners. We were locked in our rooms often. When we were moved inside the facilities while we were conscious, there was always an armed guard there, sometimes two or three. We were told it was for our own protection, not because they were keeping us from running."

"But you weren't allowed free reign, were you? You couldn't move from room to room," said Quick.

The woman shook her head. Her hair fell around her face. "No. Never. We were given very specific places to be at all times. There were actuaries there sometimes. Men or women in suits. Briefcases with folders in them. They always smelled like coffee and mint. They would show us printout lists of exactly how much money MannTech had invested in us. I think they did it to make us feel special or important. Maybe it was to make us feel guilty. They would tell us how other companies wanted to steal us and kill us to get the secrets MannTech was putting into us, and if that ever happened, we should fight them off in any way we could and return to MannTech."

Crispy took a swig of the Krysbin's. He passed the bottle to Pageant, who took his own sip before passing the bottle to Quick. She took a shot and looked at the bottle in her hand. "You probably need a hit off this more than any of us." She held out the bottle toward the woman.

The woman took the bottle and sniffed it. "I've never tried alcohol before."

"It's going to burn, but it'll burn less than the Doc did. Go on. You might even enjoy it." Pageant gave her his blessing.

The woman sipped. Her face wrinkled in disgust and she fought to swallow the scotch. She coughed and gagged for a moment. "That's awful."

"Try another sip. It gets easier the second time. Eventually, you get to a point where you feel like you need it after shit hits the fan." Quick sat on the couch next to her and patted her on the back.

Unit 346 took another sip. She still made a face of disgust, but swallowing came easier. She took a third sip. Quick pulled the bottle away from her hands. "Ease into it. Wait to see how those three sips will hit you first."

The woman sipped some water as a chaser. "If being drunk looks and feels like they say it does in the movies, then perhaps I might enjoy being drunk."

"Can't say I blame you," said Pageant. "How'd you come to be on that ship that got destroyed?"

The woman licked her lips. She took a bite off a protein bar and chewed thoughtfully. "I woke up mid-flight. I don't think I was supposed to wake up. At least, I think I woke up. I was sort of sleepwalking. That might be the only way to describe it. The straps they used to hold me to my bed fell away, and then I moved to a cabinet where they had some kind of rifles. I remember shooting them, but I don't remember where I was aiming. And then I remember entering instructions into a panel. I have no idea how I did that. I did not know anything about ships or interface panels. I just *did* it. I remember escaping into a coffin-pod and falling away from the ship. The parachute deployed in the atmosphere, and I rode the pod all the way to the ground. Then, I lived on the planetoid for two or three days until I saw your ship enter the atmosphere."

The three crew members of the *Shy Opal*, all inveterate gamblers to some degree, watched their passenger for a tell, for any sign of deception. There were none. Not a stray finger movement. No twitch in the eyes. No foot tap. No shoulder slouch. Nothing. For as far as any of them could tell, the woman was telling nothing but the truth.

Pageant leaned back in his chair. "Curiouser and curiouser. Crispy, how long until we get within Ark Eleven's approach radar?"

"Maybe another twenty hours, give or take."

Pageant made the hard call. It wasn't something he wanted to do, but he knew it was the only thing they could do in their situation. He loved the ship, but at the end of the day, a ship was a ship. It was a commodity. It was a tool. It wasn't his friend. He resigned himself to *Opal's* fate. "Quick, we're probably going to have to sell *Opal* for scrap. Start inventorying everything worth a credit. Whatever we can't carry with us needs to be sold before we approach the scrappers."

Quick shook her head. "Won't be able to do that until we're back in a dock and can hook into supply feeds, Cap. We vented all air throughout this bird into two rooms, remember? All my manifests are down in cargo, which is currently engulfed in a negative 270-degree vacuum."

Pageant grimaced. "Permission to hold off on that granted." To the woman with the red hair he asked, "How long are we invisible to the *Despair*?"

She looked scared. "We're not. Not anymore. I only had enough energy to hold them off for a little while."

"If they come back, can you hide us again?"

The woman's eyes widened with fear. She looked down at her hands. Her fingers curled into fists, and she tucked them into her chest. "No, I don't think so. Not for a long time."

Pageant took another swig of the Krysbin's. "Well, that settles it, then. Quick, do you have any hair dye stashed around here?"

Quick thought for a moment. "I might. One or two bottles of brunette from that one time when I had to hide my natural color."

"Perfect. Dye our new friend's hair, please. That hi-tech red is going to attract way too much attention."

"Done." Quick started pulling on drawers and cabinets and rooting through them.

"Crispy, how much extraneous power do we have? Can we start long-range scans?"

"Maybe a little." Crispy did the mental calculations. "We could reroute the SOS radio and download a rudimentary scan for a short time if we knew where to scan and what we were scanning for. Outside of that, we're pretty humped."

"Better than nothing," said Pageant. "I want you to open just enough power in the scanners to download the full ship manifest from Ark Eleven. I want to know who's registered there, and who's coming in the next day or two. We need to find us some allies, possibly someone who might be willing to hire on an experienced privateer crew."

"I can send a post to Ark Eleven's job boards, Cap. Three shipless privateers for hire."

"Four. You forgot our fourth crew member, Crisp." Pageant gestured to the woman with the hi-tech hair. "You, me, Quick, and...aw, hell. We gotta get you a name, lady. You have a preference? Maybe an actress you admire? Maybe a name from a book you've always liked?"

"My mother's name was Millicent," said Crispy. "I've always liked that name."

The woman smiled. Her cheeks flushed. "When I daydreamed in my cell at the facility, I always pretended my name was Anne."

Quick appraised her for a moment. "You look like an Anne."

"Anne it is. Anne what, though?" Pageant tapped his chin in thought. "I suppose Anne Greengable is a little too on-the-nose."

"What's a Greengable?" asked the formerly nameless Anne.

"It's an old, old book. One of my old girlfriends liked to read it."

"Anne Medea," suggested Quick.

Anne's eyes lit up. "I like that. It sounds pretty."

"Medea was a witch back in ancient times on Earth," said Quick. "I think it's fitting."

The woman blushed. "It probably is."

Pageant clapped his hands together to settle the matter. "Anne Medea, it is. Register her name in our manifest, Crispy. Backdate the entries so it looks like she's been with us for a long while. She's our new...what? We can't put her as a nav officer."

"Co-pilot," said Quick. "We can say she's in training."

"Captains are the co-pilots of STS cargo haulers," said Crispy. "Only logical thing would be ship's doctor, or else the steward. We could make her the logistics officer, I suppose. Quick is listed as cargo officer, and their duties could overlap without rousing too much suspicion, especially given Quick's background is more about guns than logistics."

"Done. Congratulations, Logistics Officer Medea." Pageant stuck out his hand. Anne Medea looked at his hand for a moment, and then shook it as though it might attack her.

A true and genuine smile lit upon Anne's lips for a moment, but it was quickly replaced with worry. "Thank you, all. I don't deserve any of this because I've put you all in danger."

"So does Quick's cooking, but we've survived that, too." Pageant went to the stairs to the bridge. "Get her hair dyed, Q."

"Gonna need to find her some clothes when we get to Ark Eleven, Cap. She'll stand out if she stays in a tac-suit."

"I don't suppose we have anything on board that will fit her, do we?" Pageant cast a glance from Quick's tall, lanky, broad-shouldered figure to Anne's standard, petite, malnourished form.

"I got some shirts she can wear like a dress, maybe. Put a belt around her waist."

"She might fit in some of my shirts," said Crispy. "My pants might fit her like long shorts. It'll get her to a clothing store in the Ark, at least."

"Cobble something together, Quick. Crispy, you're with me."

Crispy hustled up the stairs to the flight deck with Pageant. The bridge was lit only by the eerie glow of a few red alert warnings on the pilot's panels. The ship was even darker than it normally was when Crispy would try to catch a catnap in his chair.

Crispy eased a little bit of extra power from the Last Ditch system to open the download from Ark Eleven. While he was at it, he updated their passenger manifest to include their new crew member. Backdating entries to make someone look like they'd been on board was a common enough practice amongst owner-operators and privateers. It was so common that most ports no longer even bothered to check passenger manifests of smaller privateer ships. They just figured the manifests were mostly fabrication, anyhow. Which they were.

Pageant eased himself into his chair. "I'm gonna miss this beast." He caressed the arm of the chair lovingly. The fabric, worn smooth by heavy use, was not original to the ship. Most of the ship had been replaced at one time or another during her years of service, a true Ship of Theseus special.

"We still have one engine that'll work with some repairs, Cap. We could, in theory, buy a second engine and get it up and running. Maybe try to buy a second rover to help our rover? Who knows, a week or four in drydock for repairs, and *Opal* could get up again." Crispy was trying to be helpful. He knew it was pie-in-the-sky. He'd seen ships in far better condition than *Opal* get scrapped. Even ships that had been near-totaled in accidents or battles still had usable parts, and they were almost always worth more as scrap than the investment it would take to keep them in the air, especially a three hundred-and-some-year-old Roundbelly.

Pageant did not dignify Crispy's dreaming with a response. He looked down the corridor behind the bridge to make sure Quick and Anne were not in earshot. "You think I did the right thing with this whole mess? I mean, it probably would have been a lot better for everyone if we'd just left her on that planetoid, or maybe even put a bullet in her. I'm starting to second-guess myself. Maybe we should have given her back to MannTech."

"No court in the rims would have convicted us for killing an unhuman who tried to hijack your boat on an unsettled planetoid in the Outer Rims," said Crispy.

The data stream from Ark Eleven engaged. In seconds, the entire station manifest was at Crispy's fingertips. He sent their own crew manifest to the job boards: *four* experienced privateers. Then, Crispy disconnected the feed and diverted the needed trickle of power back to the life support system.

"How many courts will convict us of freeing an unhuman mod-tester from a corp the size of MannTech?"

"Every single one of them." Crispy thought about it for a moment. "At least, every single one in the Inner Rim would. In the Outer Rim, a few might. Most probably would not even bother hearing the case. As long as we stick to the Outer Rim from here on out, we might never even rouse the suspicions of the federal or interstellar law, although I bet MannTech would still try to send their private forces after us."

Pageant brooded on that for a moment. "You know what we should do, Crisp? You and Quick, you should go hire out. Get on with your lives. I should take the girl to some dust-rock moon somewhere and hide. That'd be the smart play."

"No one ever accused you of taking the smart play, Cap. Remember that one time when we were at the Eight-Oh-Double-Nickel? Remember when you were playing Blackjack?" Crispy turned in his seat to face his captain. "You were at the table, almost black-out drunk, and you got an eighteen. The dealer had been on a hot-streak and was showing a face card. Remember what you said?"

"Vaguely."

"You said, *Sumbitch has twenty! We all know it. Hit me.*" Crispy burst out laughing. The other players at the table started cursing at Pageant. One guy actually wanted to fight him. The dealer even tried to talk him out of it. "The dealer was like, *Sir, I suggest you reconsider.* But you were adamant. You wanted a card."

"He finally gave me the card." A half-smile crept onto Pageant's mug.

"He gave you the card alright. Seven of clubs. You busted."

"That asshole was holding a face-down queen, though. I knew he'd had a face card. It didn't matter if I took the card or not."

Crispy's laugh faded. "It was a lot like that standoff with the *Despair.* You knew you couldn't win, so you were determined to make everyone else's life miserable, too. You threw off the whole table that night."

"I do have that way about me." Pageant could not disagree with Crispy's assessment. "You and Quick, you two don't need to let me keep dragging you down. You could purge your name from *Opal's* manifest when we dock. Step down from my crew. You'd both get hired on somewhere else. I wouldn't stop you."

Crispy quashed that suggestion immediately. "Maybe I like serving under the great and powerful Captain Nathan Pageant."

"Maybe Captain Nathan Pageant's stupidity will get you killed someday. And from the look of it, someday might be relatively soon."

"Fighting a corporation that's turning Outer Rim colonists into unhumans and performing illegal human modding, that's a helluva way to go, boss. I'd take that over heart disease as an octogenarian any day." Crispy leaned back in his chair. The manifest for Ark Eleven was extensive. His eyes were scanning the lists. Ship names. Crew members. Passengers. People who actually lived at the port full-time. Random people stuck at the port for an extended period for various reasons.

Pageant was lost in a thousand-yard stare out the view screen. "When I signed you to this crew, I promised you adventure and riches. I guess I've sort of fallen short on both promises. Credits have been hard to come by, even with a few illegal cargo runs, and adventure has been pretty non-existent unless you count that time we all got that weird alien flu and spent two weeks planetside with diarrhea and severe dehydration in the middle of nowhere."

"If having gastrointestinal distress so severe that you pray for death with your two best friends in the universe isn't adventure, then I don't know what is."

"Maybe. Maybe not. Still…" He looked around the bridge. "At least we lived on our own terms. We weren't beholden to anyone. No one gave us orders. We did things right."

"True." Crispy followed Pageant's gaze. "We were free for a while."

Pageant sighed heavily. He sounded defeated. "I don't know how well I'm going to do taking orders again."

"I'm gonna give the over-under on you throwing a punch at two weeks."

"I'll take the under." Pageant rolled off his chair and shed the dusky black tactical jacket he favored whether on ship or off. He rolled the jacket into a ball and dropped it on the floor in the corner of the bridge. He pulled the bridge's first aid kit off the wall, extracted the neatly-folded foil heat blanket, and shook the blanket until it fully opened. He wrapped it around himself and flopped down on the floor, his jacket a pillow for his head. Pageant rolled to face the wall, the blanket crinkling slightly as he did. "I'm going to get a little sleep, Crispy. Wake me if you find us some help at Ark Eleven."

BENT OVER THE sink, the newly christened Anne Medea tried to hold still. The chemical dye Quick had put in her hair smelled like burnt plastic, although compared to the Doc, it was a field of lilac and lavender. Quick's long, bony fingers worked the dye through Anne's tresses. Quick seemed pleased with her work. "This is taking the red out real nice. It's not going to be a traditional brown, though. It'll be a little more like a dark rusty color when it's all said and done. Very chic."

At that moment, Anne had a twinge of a long-buried memory surface in the back of her mind. She saw a much younger version of herself looking into a dusty mirror inside a temporary shelter. In the mirror her hair was a dirty blond heading toward brown. It had been a long time since she'd thought of herself that way. The first thing MannTech had done when they'd taken possession of her from her parents was to inject her with the genetic mods to give her hi-tech hair. All the mod-testers at MannTech had hi-tech hair. It made them stand out. It made them easily identifiable. The men were given either neon green or a phosphorescent purple. The women got red or pink. All the colors glowed like stars gone supernova under black lights. It helped keep the mod-testers from hiding in the dark in case they tried to escape. Anne wondered if the temporary dye would be able to hide that aspect of her hair.

Anne wondered how it would be to have a name again. *Anne Medea*. She liked her new name. She could not remember her old name, at least not the proper one. She had a fleeting memory of her father calling her *Piglet* as a nickname. He was not using it in any kind of a cruel way. She thought it might have had something to do with a favorite toy she'd had as an infant. Whatever the reason was, it was all but lost to time. She wondered if her parents were still out there somewhere, slaving away on their little piece of land. Were her brothers and sisters still out there somewhere? It had been years since Anne had allowed herself the chance to dream of them.

It felt strange to be in the presence of someone in a friendly way and not feel like she was being watched. Quick's strong fingers were working Anne's scalp. It felt even stranger to be touched by someone in such an intimate manner. Physical contact of any kind was strictly prohibited at MannTech. If two mod-tests got too close, they would be reprimanded by a guard. Guards could guide mod-tests. They could shove them, if need be. If it really came down to it, they had permission to beat them, although that almost never happened. The researchers touched mod-tests only when necessary. There were always cameras rolling, microphones recording. Every action was constantly scrutinized. There was no way to cheat them, so no one dared.

Quick finished rinsing the dye from Anne's hair. She squeezed the tresses to slough as much water from them as possible. She handed Anne a towel. "It's not the cleanest towel, but we haven't been able to do laundry for a while."

"It's fine, I'm sure." Anne wrapped her hair in the towel.

Quick pointed at the doors to the personal quarters that shot off from the common room. "My room's there. Crispy's is there. Captain's got the Captain's Suite, of course. Yours will be there for all of the thirty minutes we're in dock before Cap sells Opal for scrap and we have to go get jobs on a different ship. I can't get you new clothes until we dock and can hook into external life support supplies. Those bedrooms are vacuums right now. In a way, it's nice. It'll clean out any spiders or lice that might be hanging around."

"Everything 'cept the tardigrades." Anne said the phrase without thinking. It was something one of the guards used to tell the mod-tests when he talked about what would happen if they tried to run. *MannTech'd rather nuke this planet than let their tech get into someone else's hands. They'll kill everyone. Everything 'cept the tardigrades will be dead.*

"What?"

"They're a little microscopic creature that's said to be able to survive in space."

Quick frowned. "Must be some angry little guys, then." She nodded at the couch. "Try to get some sleep. I'm going to try to do the same. Not much else to do until we get to port. You've had a rough day. Take the couch."

Quick didn't require luxury. She curled up on a few stray pieces of clothing like a dog, compressing herself into a surprisingly small ball for someone with her height and wingspan.

Anne tried to protest taking the couch, insisting Quick take it.

Quick waved her off. "I'm a merc, lady. We sleep whenever and wherever. The floor is no different than a bed at the King Suites to me."

Anne stretched out as best she could. Her body was still sore from the bullet wound and the muscle damage the electric shocks did. The Doc had repaired her most grievous injuries, but there was still residual swelling and discomfort. Even the Doc could not fix everything.

Quick doused the emergency lights they'd been using, and the common room plunged into darkness. Only a faint glow came from the doorway, and that glow was from what little light was being cast down the stairs from the bridge. There was a thick silence. Usually, the ion-translight engines hummed with a comforting static white noise. The Last Ditch engines carried a faint and distant whisper of sound, but it was hardly the constant, reassuring heavy wheeze of the ion nacelles.

The dark pressed on Anne's eyes. Darkness was unusual for her. The facility always had lights. Even when they would shut down for the night, there was a glow from safety lights in the hallway and the dim pulse of the green light from the camera in the corner of her cell. The only time she truly knew darkness was when she was unconscious. To have her eyes open and see only black before her was worrying. She reached out with her hand to make sure there was no one pressing toward her. The silence bothered her, as well. The facility was never silent. There were always noises, always footsteps or the low susurrus of whispers or murmured voices.

Anne found the silence to be too much. She had to say something. "Your crew members...they seem nice."

After a pause, Quick's voice answered from the darkness. "They are. They're both good boys."

"Your captain is really sticking his neck out for me."

"Wouldn't be the first time he's done something stupid like that." There was a long pause. "He did it for me a few years ago. He did it for Crispy, too. Cap likes broken people, I think. He understands them."

"You're broken? You seem—"

"Tough?"

"I was going to say confident," said Anne.

"I guess you could call me that. Maybe I am when I need to be. Doesn't mean I don't have broken parts, too."

"MannTech isn't going to give up on me." Anne knew very little about what they had done to her, but the actuaries and their constant reminders of her value told her that she was a very expensive piece of property. How long could she hide from them, she wondered.

"Maybe not at first. With corps, it's always about the bottom line. Just cost them more money than it's worth, and they'll give up."

"Not MannTech."

"Maybe not MannTech. I guess we'll find out." Quick yawned. A second later, Anne heard Quick's breath switch to slow, measured draws. She was asleep. Anne's mind did not want to sleep, but her body forced it upon her. She had been going too hard, too long to stay awake. Sleep hit her like an ocean wave, but it was not a restful sleep. There were too many new and different things around her to keep her from giving herself fully to the process. She could feel herself hovering between sleep and consciousness, vacillating back and forth. Maybe it was a side effect of the stim they had given her. She heard footsteps on the stairs from the bridge. They were the hesitant, awkward steps of Crispy, not the heavy, confident footfall of Captain Pageant.

Anne sat up on the couch. Nearby, she knew that Quick had heard the steps on the stairs, too. The labored breathing had changed to light sips of air.

Crispy's voice was a hissed whisper. "Quick?"

"What is it, Crispy?"

Crispy cracked an emergency glow stick for light. It lit his face softly with pale neon blue. "I think I might have found us some help at Ark Eleven."

Quick sat up. She rubbed at her face. "So? Tell Pageant, not me. What the hell can I do about anything?"

Crispy grimaced. "It's just..." He clapped a hand on the back of his neck in discomfort.

"Spit it out, already." Quick did not hold back the annoyance in her voice.

"It's the *Mary Read*."

Quick looked like someone had just blown out her birthday candles before she could make a wish. "Well, fuck."

NATHAN PAGEANT WOKE to the sound of Crispy clearing his throat. Pageant could tell just from the hesitation that whatever his pilot was about to say, it was not going to be good news.

"Cap, I found someone who might be able to help us." The strain in Crispy's voice was painfully evident. "They got a ship anchored at Ark Eleven this very second."

Pageant rolled onto his back and looked up at the ceiling of the flight deck. Everything was dark. "How long have I been asleep?"

"A while, Cap. We're not too far from port." Even Quick's voice sounded worried to Pageant. If Quick was worried, it was *really* not going to be good news.

"To whom am I going to have to debase myself this time, Crispy? Let me guess: Baxter? The Dunn Brothers? Maybe the Scaratellis?"

Crispy forced a laugh. "Well, funny thing, Cap. It's the *Mary Read*."

Pageant sat up like he had been shot out of a torp tube. His fists clenched involuntarily. "Nope. Fuck that. Not Sunny. We turn the girl over to MannTech, first."

"What's the *Mary Read*?" asked Anne.

"Cap's ex-girlfriend's ship," said Quick. "It did not end well between them."

Pageant leapt to his feet, fists clenching. "She stole my boat."

"She actually won it fair and square," said Crispy. "And it really was never yours to begin with. I hate to point that out."

Pageant's dander was raised. "She stole it, and then she actually renamed it. She's damned us all."

Crispy pointed at the Ark Eleven manifest on his pilot comm panel. "Sunny's the only person at Ark Eleven we have any sort of rapport with, Cap. Everyone else is strangers, or worse."

"What could be worse than Sunny Yeong?"

"Could have been splintered apart by slamming into the MTI *Despair*. That would have been worse," said Quick.

Pageant moved his hands like weighted scales. "Eh, about even, I'd say."

Crispy said, "I don't see much choice in the matter, Cap. We have to try. I'll talk to her. You don't have to. I'll take Quick."

Pageant, fuming, punched the wall. It rang with a hollow thump. He immediately began to shake out the pain in his hand and wrist. "Fine. *Fine!*" He felt a brand-new migraine coming on. "I will talk to Sunny."

"Thanks, Cap. You're a gentleman and a scholar."

"I appreciate that, Crispy." Never did Pageant think he'd ever have to stare Yeong Sun-hee in the face again after she'd taken his nearly newly won prize from him years ago. "If we're lucky, maybe I'll get to throw her out an airlock. Now, if you'll excuse me, I'd like to be alone for a minute."

"Bunks are locked down, Cap," Quick reminded him.

Pageant opened his mouth to curse, thought better of it, and descended the stairs to the common room, letting the darkness envelop him.

Yeong Sun-hee was the very last person he wanted to see.

8

A RK ELEVEN WAS an older port, drifting in the black since the early days of translight travel. It was constructed in the old ways: a tall, thin spire, a stereotypical cylinder-with-rings-around-it. The fashion was popularized before science perfected grav-compensators and the stations needed centripetal force to assist with maintaining reasonable interior gravity. The port had been updated to meet modern code and comfort centuries ago, but it still stood like a towering monument to retro styling.

The central hub of the port was a towering cylinder more than a kilometer tall. There were three exterior hubs encircling the central hub like the rings of Saturn. Each of the rings was dotted with docking bays and dry-dock systems for ship repair, refueling, and extended layovers. The three docking hubs were connected to the central hub with long, spoke-like arms that served to get people from the outer rings to the inner hub. The inner hub was where the majority of the station did its business. There was a whole ecosystem in the central hub that catered to the flow of traffic between the Inner and Outer Rim worlds.

Crispy radioed the control tower atop the north spire of the central hub. "Port 1131, this is STS *Shy Opal*, transport registration Delta-two, Echo-Foxtrot-three, three. Requesting emergency dock. Our ship is pretty banged up. We're on Last Ditch."

After a moment, a serene, mellifluous female voice returned over the comm. "STS *Shy Opal*, this is Control Terminal, Port 1131. Emergency acknowledged. Please guide your vessel to level A, dock thirteen. We will light the linking terminal for you. Will you require assistance in either steering or stopping?"

"Negative, Tower. We'll make it, just barely."

"Will you require medical aid?"

"Negative, Tower. All passengers are healthy and accounted. I will send our passenger manifest and registry upon docking. *Shy Opal*, out." Crispy killed the comm. The panel blinked and fell to black. Crispy thumped it with his finger, but it stayed off. The comm panel had lasted just long enough to get them to dock safely. It was the final act of kindness by a ship which had been more of a friend than a mere cargo vessel.

Crispy put the ship into manual control. It handled sluggishly, a great, lumbering beast. The controls barely responded to his touch. *Opal* had just enough juice left to creep to the top ring and get them docked. Station-bound repair Rovers were already buzzing around the ship making a flurry of damage assessments.

The ship coasted into the docking bay. Large mechanical arms reached out to grab it as it moved toward the dock. The arms locked onto the ship and helped guide it into place. Crispy turned off the thrusters. There was a small jarring as the ship ceased its forward motion and the arms took over. The ship locked into place on the docking hub. There was a moment of silence. There was a flicker of light across the panels as rovers hooked the ship into the exterior supply lines, bypassing the ship's dead engine. After another moment, the air recirc kicked in and all the various lights and panels that still worked on the bridge flickered to life as the external power sent new juice through the ship's systems. It was then, and only then, that Crispy was able to truly see the amount of damage done to the poor old Lux-class Roundbelly. He watched the endless list of wreckage reports from the on-board rover. He wondered if a ship scrapper would even want it for parts. Might be better just to assist-launch the old gal into the nearest star and be done with her. It was probably the most humane thing to do.

Over Crispy's shoulder, Pageant clicked his tongue. "That ain't good."

"Personal bunks and cargo bay are unsealed, Cap. We got access to the whole ship." Quick was at the gunner's conn running her own batch of alerts. "I can get the cargo manifests, and I can piece together some sort of shore leave outfit for the enchantress that will get her to the shops, at least."

"How much do we have in discretionary funds, Mr. Okino?"

"Discretionary *what?*" said Crispy.

"How many creds do we have just lying around? I was trying to class it up a bit. Y'know—make Anne think we're a least a little bit professional."

"I didn't think you were professional at all," said Anne.

"Either way—how much do we have Crispy?"

"Uh...let me check." Crispy's eyes did not leave Pageant's face. They didn't even flit toward his panels. "Zero. We have zero creds."

"Yeah, I kinda figured." Pageant turned to his cargo officer. "Quick, you're going to have to pawn a few of those guns I let you buy that one time. Use that for new gear for Ms. Medea."

"How am I going to defend the ship—" Quick's attempt at a defensive rant died before she could even get rolling. She looked around at the damage and heaved a sigh. "Stupid question."

"Keep your favorites, pawn the rest. We need the creds."

Quick looked like she wanted to argue for a moment, but thought better of it. "Fine." She grabbed Anne by the wrist and dragged her out of the bridge. "C'mon space witch, let's go shopping." To Pageant, she called over her shoulder, "We'll find you in the hub."

"Gear up, Crisp ol' boy." Pageant set his jaw as best he could, given the situation. "We're gonna go humble ourselves before the worst she-demon this side of hell."

"Sunny's not that bad, Cap."

"She'll flay the soul from your bones if you let her." Pageant was already stalking down to the cargo bay.

Pageant, favoring what had become something of his standard uniform—for lack of a better term—dressed in black tact pants and a dark gray shirt. Over that, he pulled on a short black tac-jacket that had seen a lot of miles. He liked tactical gear. It was practical, had lots of useful pockets. It was hearty, too, rarely wore out.

After that, Pageant strapped on a sidearm. Most establishments around a port made guests check weapons at the door, and the large corridors and walkways were usually well-patrolled by human security guards. There would even be the occasional mounted robotic gun, just in case. However, one did not wear a sidearm while in port to use it. It was a message, a sigil. It let people know that someone who knew how to use a gun was walking near them. Since Anne had nuked his favorite sidearm back on the planctoid, Pageant eased his second-favorite gun into the holster he wore low on his right hip, a black-steel Rorbacher HSL. It was a tough-looking piece with good sights, but it was sometimes awkward to quick-draw, should that be necessary.

Pageant combed his hair. It was looking unruly from a night curled up on a metal floor with a rolled-up jacket for a pillow. He was starting to get a little thin up top. It was not so bad that anyone would notice even up close, but he noticed it. The laugh-lines at the corners of his eyes were starting to get more pronounced. The crease from his nose to the corner of his mouth was getting deeper. He was getting old. Too old to be the first officer on someone else's ship, he thought. Maybe too old to be out in the Black at all. What else could he do, though? What planet would have him?

The anticipation of seeing Sunny again was eating at him. He'd done a fair job of pushing her out of his mind the last three years. It had not been easy, but he'd done it. Now, everything he'd tried to forget was rushing back to him: how she looked, how she smelled, how she dressed. How they used to make love in his bunk. In her bunk. In the cargo bay. On the bridge when they thought everyone else was asleep. They'd had a good couple of years, but then—like so many things in Pageant's life—it all just fell apart. Just like *Opal.* Just like he, himself, was falling apart.

What was that old, stupid song Sunny used to to sing? *Que será, será. Whatever will be, will be...*

Crispy met Pageant at the cargo bay door. Tactical gear was not manufactured in the sizes and cuts he needed for his frame, so Crispy favored simple, comfortable clothes. Khaki canvas cargo shorts that hung so low they were almost pants on him, a t-shirt with some sort of stellar transport logo on it, another button-up shirt over that hanging open. Crispy was forever rumpled. Like Pageant, Crispy was packing a sidearm, a small, slim Heckler P7, elegant and simple, with a modded handle and trigger to better facilitate his shorter fingers and awkward grip. Crispy wore it high on his waist, the untucked flannel shirt hanging over the weapon to obscure it. "I'm ready to roll, Cap."

Pageant paused in the doorway. "Crisp, you could save me some time and pain here: just pull that gun out and shoot me."

"I would not want to deprive myself of seeing you humbling yourself before Sunny. I don't think she'd want to miss that, either." Crispy stepped across the threshold seal from the ship to the docking ring.

Pageant patted the bulkhead of the ship. He gave the old girl a loving, lingering look. "They don't make gals like this anymore, Crispy."

At that moment, a chunk of metal fell out of the ceiling of the cargo hold and clattered on the steel floor with a hellacious racket.

THE CENTRAL HUB of Ark Eleven was always a busy place. Shops and restaurants catered to the translight travelers, and since there was no real night-and-day in space like there would be planetside, there was no real shutdown of the hub. Anytime a ship docked, almost every restaurant would be open for food, the shops open to buy clothes, guns, and gear for all occasions. There were downtimes, sure, but they never lasted for very long. On occasion, a massive transport would dock, and a throng of future colonists destined for some new world would spill out taking advantage of their last chance to get supplies, a fast-food meal, shops, and other necessities of life such as massage parlors, sex-for-credits, recreational gyms, and booze. Sometimes a single place offered all of the amenities. Those were weird, but popular, places.

Quick Huffman strode through the wide swathes of crowds in the hub like they were not there. She towered over most of the men and all of the women, a tall, lanky, powerful woman with a wild mop of hair and a hardened visage that clearly told everyone, *Don't fucking touch me.* She was dragging a weapons case behind her like luggage. People got out of Quick's way. She stood out in a crowd, but there was still something about her that made people forget her ten seconds after she passed. She was like a two-meter tall ghost. Scary as hell the first second, and a moment later you wondered if you actually saw what you thought you saw.

Hurrying to keep pace in Quick's wake, Anne Medea was trying not to draw attention. She was used to being ignored. It happened all the time at the facility. If she was not being dealt with directly by researchers or guards, she was locked in a cell and largely forgotten. At the port, she could feel the stares of the people she passed. She felt very conscious of her hair. Could they tell it was dyed? Was she too thin? Was it her clothes? Quick had dressed her simply, a pair of shorts and an oversized t-shirt that advertised some sort of musical band she did not know. She felt like she stood out even amongst the haphazardly coutured mishmash of humanity crowded into the hub of Ark Eleven.

With the press of so many eyes on her, whether real or imagined, and the realization of just how many people were crowded onto the port hub, Anne started to feel weak. She had never been claustrophobic, but everything started to feel too small. The corridors, the ceilings above her—everything was pushing on her. It was too much. Anne tried to remember how strong she could be. She had always prided herself on never crying during the surgeries or treatments. She had always waited until after the researchers were done and she was alone. She remembered that mindset. She clenched her jaw and fought off the urge to scream.

Quick was leading her into a small section of shops within the hub arranged like a miniature fashion district. There was a shop for casual wear, a shop for tactical gear, a shop for colonist staples like rough-fabric jeans, overalls, and work shirts, and a shop for fancier items like jackets and gowns. Anne had never owned a gown. She always liked them when women wore them in films, though. Quick walked past those stores to a small, messily kept shop. There was no name over the wide door to the little store, but Quick seemed to know what she was doing.

"This is Al's Place." Quick pointed to a slovenly, unshaven man behind the counter. He was shoveling some sort of pasta dish into his mouth. A too-small, well-stained gray t-shirt was stretched over his expansive belly but only just barely. "That's Al."

Al's face lit up when Quick stepped through the doorway. "Quick friggin' Huffman. Been a long while." He put the bowl of food on the counter in front of him and wiped his mouth with the back of his wrist. "How's it been hanging? You look good, kiddo."

"You look disgusting, as usual." Quick walked over to Al and gave him a brief hug. "How's tricks, you old space ape?"

Al shrugged. "Pretty much the same. Nothing changes on Ark Eleven, you know that. I ain't seen you in a dog's age, though. You still flying with the degenerate and the pint-sized pilot?"

"Of course. Still flying the same POS, too. At least we were until we ran into a MannTech Cerberus."

"The *Despair*, I'll bet. I've seen it on the manifest here a few times. Big-ass gunship, right?"

"That bitch did a number on us, let me tell you." Quick jabbed a thumb in the general direction of the A-level docking ring. "Got *Opal* in an emergency repair bay, but I think she's really and truly done-for this time."

Al shook his head. "Damn shame. Not many like her left in the Black."

"Truth to that."

"No matter how much you love them, all ships eventually meet the same fate. The Black is undefeated."

Quick held out a hand to introduce Anne. "Al, this is our new crew member, Anne Medea. Anne, this is Al Greene."

"Hey, you should probably get away from these bums as soon as possible, get a real crew." Al smiled and stuck out a hand. Despite his somewhat off-putting appearance, Anne liked Al. He seemed kind and genuine.

Quick threw an arm over Al's shoulder and leaned into him in a conspiratorial fashion. "We picked up Anne on a colony world. She was desperate to get away from the farm life. However, she had a husband that wasn't too keen to let her go, if you get me."

Al adjusted the black-framed glasses slipping down his nose. "Let me guess: Ol' Nate couldn't resist a chance to white knight, so he rushed in and popped the dude in the beak."

"You know Nate. Well, turns out the husband had friends, and we started getting shot at. We had to jet from there without so much as a hairbrush for Ms. Medea. I'm going to need a small pile of gear."

Al looked skeptical. "Gear, I got. You got creds?"

Quick patted the weapons case. "I got guns for trade. Good ones."

Al raised an eyebrow. He rubbed his hands together. "Pop the top. Let me see."

Quick did as instructed. Several rifles were nestled into fabric-covered rests and a half-dozen pistols lined the sides of the crate. "Most of these have only been used for practice. They've seen less than five hundred rounds, tops."

Al whistled. There was a small fortune in weaponry before him. "I think we can do business. What sort of gear will your compatriot be requiring?"

Quick glanced around the shop. It was crammed with an odd assortment of clothes, tactical gear, paramilitary wear, guns, and survival necessities of all types. "Head to toe comfort wear for on board the ship, something more rugged for planetside, and all the base layer stuff: socks, undies, bras, thermals. Throw in some personal accessories, too: hairbrush, shampoo, dental kits, and the like. You know what to do. Compile it all and tell me what you think it's worth. We'll barter."

"What's your size, ma'am?" Al asked.

Anne was taken aback. She had no idea. No one ever told her, and all the clothes at the facility were mostly one-size-fits-all. She looked down at her petite frame and stick-thin arms. "I don't know. Small?"

Al shrugged. "Small works for me, I guess. Let's see what we got." He began rooting through the racks of clothing, pulling out assorted items and piling them haphazardly on the counter. He held up pieces and sized them to Anne's frame by eye. He shrugged a lot and made strange groaning noises. In short order, he amassed a collection of gear and started stuffing it into an old paramilitary surplus duffel bag. A faded MannTech logo was printed on the side of the black canvas sack.

Fitting, Anne thought.

Al closed the ruck, snapped the gathers with a carabiner, and dropped it whole thing heavily on the desk. "That gonna be enough for you, Blondie?"

Quick was running of a checklist in her head. After a moment of calculation she nodded, satisfied. "I think so, Al. How much?"

Al lifted the lid on that case. "Not too much, I'm thinking. Most of that stuff is old and has been here a while. Not a ton of spacers need size small, you know. Not until they've been in the colonies for a few months, at least." He inspected the weapons again. "How's the scope on that Mengler H117?"

"Balls-on," said Quick. "Would you expect any less of me?"

"You got legal papers for all these?"

"Down to the last bullet," said Quick.

Al thought for a long moment. "Gimme that sniper rifle and the Pisces revolver, and we'll call it a deal."

"That revolver is a show piece, Al. How about just the revolver?"

"The H117 and the revolver or no deal." Al crossed his arms over his chest.

"Throw in two hundred creds, then." Quick countered.

"Done." Al stuck out a hand, and he and Quick shook. "Should've held out. I might have gone as high as four hundred creds."

"I might have gone down to the revolver and the sniper rifle." Quick pulled the two pieces from the case and laid them on Al's desk. Using her PPD, she transferred the guns' titles to him. "Done. All nice and legal."

Al transferred creds to Quick's cred-counter. He tossed the bag of gear at Anne. She caught it, and it nearly bowled her over. "Enjoy your stuff. Send friends this way, if you get the chance."

"Thanks, Al. I owe you." Quick turned on her heel to leave.

"You always owe me. Don't be a stranger, now. Send a text once in a while, too. I worry about you idiots out there." Al went back to his bowl of pasta.

Quick froze in the entryway of the store. Anne bumped into her as she was still struggling to throw the weighty bag over her shoulder properly. Quick called back to Al. "Hey, throw in a baseball cap, too. Some sort of hat."

"Sure, what's a hat between friends." Al pulled a black canvas cap from under the desk. It was blazoned with orange text in a military-style font, *Al's Ark Eleven Surplus and Supply*. He tossed it to Quick. She caught it and slapped it on Anne's head.

"Tuck your hair up into this. Keep it pulled low. Look at the ground a lot. Watch my feet and follow close."

Anne was confused but did as she was told. "Why?" Quick surreptitiously pointed toward a monitor kiosk in the center of the hallway. The little information centers had multiple video monitors on them, and they cast continuous feeds of multiple news streams from stations across the inner rim. Anne saw her own face projected onto one of the monitors from the kiosk. They could not hear whatever the announcer was saying about her, but the scroll of text across the bottom of the screen said that she was the daughter of a MannTech executive, and that MannTech had reason to believe she had been kidnapped for ransom.

"Clever ruse," said Quick. "Captain will be up for kidnapping. You'll be returned to MannTech. No doubt they'll just walk their acolytes into whatever precinct you end up in and pluck you out guarded by a phalanx of MannTech lawyers."

"Won't they know I'm not that guy's daughter?" Anne was struggling to follow Quick. She was still thin and weak and was not used to carrying a heavy satchel. She almost asked Quick to carry it for her, but Quick was dragging her weapons crate. It would not have been nice to do that even if Quick agreed.

"*Daughter* doesn't always mean *daughter*, lady. *Daughter* often is rich people slang for *personal sex toy*. It doesn't matter if you're not his daughter. Everyone knows what those guys pay for, and since they all own a few Congressmen and interplanetary representatives, no one complains."

"Seems unfair." Anne was suddenly extremely conscious of the eyes staring at her. The kiosk was showing her with computer-generated differences in her appearance: how she'd look with blond hair, as a brunette, with black hair, with different hairstyles, with glasses, with sunglasses. With a ball cap. Anne felt her heart rate start to climb. Adrenaline made her blood pressure surge.

"Stare at the floor. Walk normally." Quick's voice reached her in a whispery hiss. Anne dropped her eyes to the floor. She located the heels of Quick's boots and locked onto them. She tried to breathe. Quick led her through the crowd and back toward the docking bays. Quick called back to her. "We'll head back to the ship."

Anne continued to watch Quick's heels. She wished she was not out in public. Couldn't Quick have gathered her gear without her? Why was she on display? A second part of Anne wondered if this was how the rest of her life would be. Would she always be panicking? Would she always be worried about being recognized?

Quick suddenly shifted tack and ducked into a narrow hall between two stores. A custodial closet was housed at the rear of the corridor along with a lift for moving bags of garbage out of that level of the hub and to the launcher that shot the station's unrecyclable refuse at the nearest star.

Anne, not able to adjust course, found herself staggering under the weight of the bag. She felt Quick's strong hand clamp on the back of the bag and drag her bodily into the hall. "What's wrong?"

Quick's voice was low and even. "There are a pair of MannTech acolytes showing your picture to people."

Anne's heart began beating out a double-time swing rhythm. "How did they know I was here?" Her hand went to the bandage under her breast where the tracker had been.

Quick was straining to peep around the corner of the corridor. "They don't know you're here. They're searching, seeing if anyone saw you. They've got static pictures of you, and you have the hi-tech hair in them. Chances are the simpletons around here will lock in on the hair and shake their heads."

Anne kept her eyes glued to the floor. "I'm carrying a big bag of gear. They'll know."

"This is a resupply station. Everyone's carrying something around here."

Anne wished she was invisible. She found herself reaching out for that strange ability she had. She tried to find the inner reserves to disappear, but she was tapped. The reserve had never been large to begin with. She had exhausted it throughout the last two days. There was nothing left. The way the hollowness in her felt at that moment, she wondered if maybe it would never return.

"Here, let's do this." Quick was rooting through the small satchel at her hip, opposite the hip that carried her gun. She produced a small make-up kit, barely the size of her palm. It was a practical kit, not a glamorous one. Anne was immediately intrigued. She had never gotten to use makeup before. Quick rubbed her thumbs into the dark gray eye shadow and dragged the gunk around Anne's eyes, smoothing it into a sort of mask. It looked different, but not out of place amongst the mix of humanity on Ark Eleven, with many of them sporting similar faux-masked looks. Then, Quick pulled a few cotton balls from the kit. "Shove these between your lips and your gums. It'll change the shape of your face."

Anne did as she was told. The dry cotton against her lips and teeth made her feel queasy. Quick took a little blush and contoured Anne's cheeks with it. She stepped back and gave Anne an appraising glance. "This will do. When we walk past those MannTech guys, don't look at them, but don't look down or away from them. Keep your head at enough of an angle that they won't stop you to look at your face, but not so much that they'll get a perfectly clear view. Got me?"

Anne nodded nervously. "Whatever you say."

Quick gave her one more thorough look. She used a thumb to smooth some of the eye makeup. "C'mon, kiddo."

Anne followed Quick through the crowd. The two MannTech acolytes were holding up her photo and asking about her. The acolytes were wearing their standard uniforms and MTI caps. No need for the full battle armor and helmets aboard a port station. Quick leaned back and whispered, "They're not from the *Despair*."

"How do you know?"

Quick said, "Look at their shoulders. Their ship designation patch is sewn onto their uniform. They're from the MTI *Black Wind*."

Once Quick pointed it out, the ship designation stood out like a beacon. How could she have missed it? Anne felt slightly better knowing that the acolytes were not from the *Despair*, but she did not know why; any MannTech acolytes were dangerous to her.

As they neared the acolytes, Quick moved to give them a bit more of a wide berth, but not so much that it looked like they were trying to be inconspicuous. Anne kept her head raised, but tilted just slightly away from the MannTech soldiers. When the acolytes looked in her direction, Anne did not flinch. She kept her eyes fixed on a point in the distance. She felt the soldiers sweep her with their eyes, but neither said anything. Neither moved to stop her. She kept walking. Her stomach was alive with nerves. She was primed to jump out of her skin if anyone touched her.

Quick led her out of that district to one of the main transport tunnels. A long motorized walkway was shuttling denizens of the port to various points. They stepped onto the walkway and let it carry them back to toward Docking Ring A.

"Nothing to it." Quick gave Anne a reassuring smile. "Don't act like you're guilty, and they won't think you're guilty."

"Can I take the cotton balls out of my mouth, yet?"

Quick looked around with a wary eye. "Better keep them in for a little bit, yet. Never know who might be around the corner."

9

NATHAN PAGEANT LIKED wearing long coats. He favored a black duster made from light canvas. It allowed him to sweep into rooms cutting an imposing figure. Plus, it just looked cool. It made him look tough, like a guy who didn't take crap from anyone. He thought he was tougher in the long coat, too. Like the old saying goes, *Look good, feel good. Feel good, play good.* That's how Pageant felt in that coat. He was indomitable.

Hence why he was wearing his standard gear to go see Sunny Yeong. He did not need to be indomitable. He needed to be humble. He needed to be apologetic. He needed to be the guy *she* wanted him to be instead of the guy *he* wanted to be, and that fact alone made him taste copper in the back of his throat.

Pageant had gotten the location of *Mary Read* from the station manifest. The ship was currently docked on Ring B, the largest docking ring, the one that hovered around the center of the station. It was quite a walk from the point where *Shy Opal* was docked. That did not matter. It gave Pageant more time to consider what he was going to say to Sunny when he saw her again.

"You think I should go in with a swagger, act tough?"

Crispy rolled his eyes. "Why don't you just go in like you're a guy who needs help because a corporate gunship almost destroyed his archaic transport vessel?"

"That's not exactly the approach that makes women want to drop their pants, Crispy."

"Neither is trying to suave your ex, Cap. If there's one person in the Black that knows you as well as Quick and I do, it's Sunny. You honestly think you can pretend to be someone you're not in front of her?"

Pageant stopped walking. They were at a large window along the spoke between the docking ring and the hub of the station. From that vantage point, looking down, he could see the *Mary Read*. It was an impressive ship, no doubt. It was a Jubilee-class light attack ship. It was nowhere near as heavily armed as the Cerberus-class, but what it lacked in firepower, it made up for in speed and maneuverability. At full translight, the Jubilee were among the fastest ships in space. They also had a modest cargo hold to complement their insane speed which made them a choice vessel for thieves, smugglers, and pirates.

With a good stretch of the imagination, most people tended to compare ships to animals. If you squint and look at the various ship classes, it was fairly easy to see that they often did have features similar to many animals. Raptor-class fighters were clearly hawks and eagles. The Lux-class Roundbellies always reminded Pageant of robins fattened for winter and puffing out their chests against the cold, tails jutting out straight behind them. The Cerberus-class ships were a rhinoceros, a charging heavy tank with triple-gun horns. The Jubilee-class ships always looked like panthers to Pageant. They were sleek and graceful, muscular in their own way. They tended to have a broad, rounded prow possessing a passing resemblance to a predatory cat with its ears pinned back. Most ships were shades of white or light gray. Jubilee-class ships tended to be dark gray and black. They blended into space. They were true predators in the Big Nothing, stealthy as sharks and lethal as blades.

Pageant marveled at the ship. It was a thing of beauty. He tried not to think of the what-might've-beens if he'd gotten possession of that beast Where would he be now? Would he have a larger crew? More money? A better life? Would he and Sunny have stayed together? Pageant balled up those thoughts and stuffed them deep down inside himself. Best not to think of things like that.

"Think you can fly that thing, Crispy?"

Crispy snorted. "You know I can. I can fly that thing better than whoever she's got doing it now."

"Make sure you tell her that when we're begging for jobs. Did you look at her passenger and crew manifest? How many people does she have on crew?"

Crispy looked at the long PPD he'd strapped to his forearm. "Looks like they're flying bare bones. Only three crew, including herself. No passengers registered at this moment."

"That means they've just arrived here, maybe looking to hire on new crew. No registered passengers means they will probably take passengers. At the very least, if she won't hire us, maybe we can book passage someplace MannTech won't find the girl."

"Are you really going to stick your neck out for this girl like that, Cap?" Crispy had to hustle to keep up with Pageant's long strides.

"You know, Crisp, I wasn't going to, but then that MannTech bully ship took out one of my nacelles. After that, I was pretty much going to ram them just to get even."

"Your life for a few million creds. Good to know you've got a price, Cap."

Pageant stopped short and Crispy nearly got a face full of ass, a common hazard for someone his height. Pageant turned and knelt down next to Crispy, something he almost never did. He leaned toward Crispy's ear and spoke in a low hiss. "But then she made our whole ship intangible. *How? How did she do that?*"

Crispy shrugged. "Magic?"

"Exactly. Magic isn't real. You know that. I know that. Everyone knows that. It's not real, but yet here you and I are. We're still standing. How?"

"Magic. Only explanation I have, Cap."

Pageant nodded slowly, seriously. "Exactly. Magic. And that's insane. Don't you think finding out what's really going on with that girl is important? There's something seriously hinky going down at MannTech, and I'd kind of like to know what it is, exactly."

Crispy frowned. "You can't fight a corp like MannTech, Nate."

"I don't want to fight 'em. I just want to know what the hell they're doing." Pageant was not as prone to insatiable curiosity as some. Tell him you know a secret about him, and he would just smile and say, *I hope it's a good one*, and continue about his day wholly unbothered. If there was a dark cave that promised a chance for riches and adventure, Pageant would be as like to ignore it as not. He did not typically go looking for trouble, but neither did he run from it. He tried to remember that he was a working stiff with a ship to keep running and a crew to feed. What was good for the ship was good for him; that was a good way to live life. However, when a mystery popped up and smacked him in the mouth, he was not going to pretend he did not see it.

Despite the fact no one had discovered truly sentient, humanoid-style life in any of the worlds humans had been able to connect to and colonize over the centuries, it did not stop people from having their lives changed by supposed contacts deep in the Black. Pageant knew a couple of former transport captains who gave up everything to become alien hunters after enduring an unexplainable event they could only chalk up as a contact with a sentient species. Pageant's only contact with anything even close to resembling a sentient alien species was with the girl, Anne Medea. He was confused, and he knew where to go to look for the answers. He just needed help to get the answers he wanted.

"I can already see what you're planning to do. You're going to try to get Sunny to chase your wild goose, aren't you?"

Pageant clapped a hand on Crispy's shoulder. "Crispy, old pal, you know me too well."

"What's going to be in it for Sunny? She's not going to play unless there's a prize at the end of the game."

"You also know her too well. I don't have a prize for her, yet; I'll figure it out as I go."

"Like usual, then."

Pageant was not fazed. "Planning is a luxury of the rich and powerful. The rest of us are just trying to catch what the wind blows us."

They entered the central hub. No one is ever prepared for the central hub of any port. After weeks on a ship with the same stale recirc air and the same food and company, the sights, the smells, the constant noise and movement of the hub overwhelm the senses. As much as an overload as it was, there was a strange comfort to it, too. Pageant loved entering the hubs of ports. They were always filled with a throng of humanity from all walks of life: rich and poor, spacers and planet-born, every color and every creed. They were all from different points of origin. They were all headed to different destinations. All those people were bound together solely by the fact that they were all travelers in the Black. No matter how heated arguments got in the casinos or bars, there was always a civility to them as if everyone was just acknowledging they were brothers-in-arms to some degree. All space travelers knew a level of risk which people who never left the terra firma would never know.

Pageant knew where Sunny would be. If she was not on her ship, there were a few places she frequented in any hub: the clothing shops, the casino, and a bar with good cheeseburgers. Ark Eleven had decent clothing shops, but not great. It was too close to the Outer Rims to worry about really good clothes. They had some nice stuff which would do the job, but high end clothes could only be found closer to the Inner Rim. She would not waste much time in the small garment district in the port. Sunny's tastes for fashion ran high-end. That might have been one of the things that drove them apart: Pageant was cheap, Sunny was expensive.

The casinos, of which there were three on Ark Eleven, were of varying natures. The Vegas on Ark Eleven was an elaborate nightclub-style casino meant to mimic the famed gambling towers back on Earth. It was too showy, too touristy for Sunny's tastes. The Blackjack Palace, a conglomeration of card games and roulette tables, was too simple for her. The third casino was what Sunny would have dubbed *Old People Slot Hell*, a mishmash of slots and other cred-operated video machines that gave people a lot of flashy light shows for very little reward. With the casinos not likely to attract Sunny, that left only the pubs.

There were no less than thirteen good burger places on Ark Eleven, but Pageant knew which one she'd be at without even having to guess. There was only one burger barn upscale enough for Sunny Yeong: Smilin' Jack's.

Smilin' Jack Templeton had been one of the earliest space rangers, one of the initial crazies who dared to ride the translight to distant galaxies to find habitable planets and start the terraforming process to make new Earths for humankind. Jack and his fabled ship, the EXO *Starduster*, discovered over three times as many planets as the next great space ranger behind him and was responsible for igniting the Second Manifest Destiny, as it was called. Colonists began pooling money to buy ships or transport, and they began to settle planets while the land was still free.

Smilin' Jack, in what became a legendary action, had declared all planets he discovered were free and clear of all state, federal, and corporate claims. That was the law of the early space days: any planet discovered was property of the crew or corporation which discovered them. It was a trade-off for the danger and expense, and it encouraged private entities to risk the expense of pushing the boundaries of space. Early corporate rangers made a mint on new planets, sectioning and selling off plots of land and controlling the flow of supplies to colonists. However, Smilin' Jack chose to give land directly to the new colonists. *If you can settle it, it's yours!* It made him a folk hero.

When he retired *Starduster* and settled down from traveling, he launched a chain of burger restaurants populating the first translight hubs, and they became extremely popular thanks to the massive amounts of goodwill he'd managed to engender over the years. They were still popular. They were the first restaurant to actually challenge, and eventually beat out the McDonald's stranglehold on the corporate fast-food market. MickyD's was still around of course, but the Big Mac had become a distant second to a Starduster Burger and a side of spicy Jack-Fries.

Sunny's ancestors had taken to the black centuries past and settled in a colony on a Jack-world, managing to scrape a good life off the land and become prosperous. They vowed to always give thanks to the man who made it possible by supporting his establishments. Pageant knew instinctively that Sunny would be at Smilin' Jack's. There was nowhere else she would consider going. They'd eaten at other burger places in the years they were together, but only if Smilin' Jack's was not an option.

The Smilin' Jack's on Ark Eleven was huge. It was a grand, wide storefront two-stories tall, gilded in glass and brass. The safety-mandated occupancy plaque at the front of the restaurant declared it could hold three hundred people. A casual glance through the glass-fronted building showed that nearly every booth and table in the place was taken. There was a counter of human workers hustling to get out all the food in a timely manner. The robots in the back that made the food never stopped moving. Old videos of the long-deceased Smilin' Jack Templeton played on monitors around the place. A young hostess with raven hair and a pleasant smile stood at a small podium outside the restaurant and directed people toward available order windows to keep the line moving in an orderly fashion. Pageant and Crispy took their place at the end of the line.

"Thought of what you're going to say to her?"

Pageant shook his head. "Not a clue. Figure something will inspire me when I see her."

Crispy was squinting through the glass into the restaurant. "I never really understood her fascination with hanging out in burger bars."

"She is inscrutable that way. She always said they reminded her of being back home. She worked in a Smilin' Jack's when she was a girl. Her parents always took her there to celebrate life events. It's a comfort thing."

"I like being on *Opal*. That's comfortable."

"To each his own, Crisp."

The hostess asked Pageant how many would be dining when he finally got to the podium. He held up two fingers. "But, we're not really going to be eating."

"We're not?" Crispy was disappointed. He could have gone for a Landlubber and some Ark Rings.

"Not right away," Pageant amended. "We're here looking for a friend."

"Name?" The hostess tapped a few times on the panel screen at her podium.

"Yeong Sun-hee, also called Sunny Yeong."

The hostess's expression changed to one of surprise. "You know Captain Yeong?"

"*Captain* Yeong now?" Pageant muttered under his breath.

"She does own a ship," said Crispy.

"She owns a *stolen* ship."

"Debatable."

To the hostess Pageant flashed his most charming smile. "Yes, Captain Yeong. We're old, old friends. I was hoping to surprise her."

"I see." The girl at the podium frowned. "Captain Yeong is in our VIP section. She does not like to be disturbed."

"Like I said, old, *old* friends. She will be happy to see me."

"And me," added Crispy. "I was her friend, too."

"And him," said Pageant. "We'd both like to see her, us being old friends and all."

The girl was already sending a text to Sunny's PPD. *We have old friends asking to see you, Captain Yeong.* "I'm sorry. This is standard procedure. We do not allow just anyone into our VIP section."

There was a beep at the podium. A return text from Sunny: *Who is it?*

The hostess smiled politely at Pageant and Crispy. "She would like to know who you are."

"So much for the element of surprise, I guess. Tell her: two old shipmates—no, wait." Pageant thought for a second. The girl's stylus was poised over her PPD. "Tell her: an old shipmate and a half."

Crispy couldn't help but smile. "Better. She'll know it's me, at least." A moment later, there was a beep at the podium, and the hostess stepped aside to let them pass.

One of the quirks about Smilin' Jack's popularity was that Smilin' Jack himself, being a major celebrity, could not eat in his own restaurants without being mobbed. So, each Smilin' Jacks had a small VIP room. In them, a celebrity of any renown willing to pay an extra fee could eat a meal in peace. If there were no bona fide celebrities eating in the VIP room, space within them could still be rented out for those who wanted a more traditional, low-key, table-service type of meal. Many people chose that experience over the standard tray-and-wrapper burger experience. For Sunny Yeong, it was the only way to eat at Smilin' Jack's.

Pageant and Crispy made their way to the VIP room. A clean-cut young man with cybernetically enhanced contact lenses was standing at the door. The lenses were relaying information to him at all times. When Pageant and Crispy approached, the kid bowed his head and pulled the door for them, crisply stepping aside and remaining still. Smilin' Jack's spared no expense for their VIPs.

Pageant took a deep breath. Why were there butterflies in his stomach? It was just Sunny, after all. Crispy was already inside the room. Pageant felt a tinge of crimson on his neck. Was he really going all teenage boy in this moment? *It was Sunny, goddammit!*

Pageant tried his best to play casual. He sauntered in, a hand resting on the Rorbacher on his hip. He put on his best cocksure half-smile, the devil-may-care look that he knew used to drive her nuts.

Sunny was seated at the center booth along the back wall. She sat like a queen, regal and upright, a vision in a high-collared red vinyl coat and designer jeans, a bevy of papers and computer tablets spread before her on the table. Her night-black hair was swept up in a loose but elegant bun at the back of her head. A few tendrils dared creep over her eye. As usual, she was perfectly made-up, with deep red lipstick and flawless foundation. A smoky violet-black eye shadow only lent an air to her mystery. She made no movement. Her face did not change when Pageant walked into the room.

Pageant locked eyes with his ex. At one time, he had thought their love vibrant and pure, something that nothing could ever extinguish. One bad deal over a light attack ship later, and he had wanted her to die in the furnace heart of a new star...for a few days, at least. Time heals all wounds, and just seeing her again made Pageant feel ten years younger. His heart rate elevated. Whatever magic she had over him, the years had not depleted it.

As he stepped through the threshold to the VIP room, a flash of movement out of the corner of his eye made him twitch. His gun hand started to draw the bulky Rorbacher. He spun to try to stop whatever was coming, but a mass of humanity slammed into him. Two thick, powerful arms, each as girthy as Pageant's thighs, lifted him off the floor. Like a rag doll, Pageant felt himself flailing. He was flopping through the air without any control. Whoever lifted him was incredibly strong. The floor rushed up to meet him, and Pageant smashed into the tiles face-first. The air rushed from his lungs. In the half-second he was too stunned to do anything, a great weight landed on his back pinning him to the ceramic stone flooring. A hand the size of a dinner plate pushed his head hard into the floor, mashing his cheek awkwardly. Pageant could see Crispy grimacing nearby. The pilot was not going for his gun, so Pageant could only assume they were either outnumbered, or the giant man on his back was not going to truly hurt him.

Sunny looked amused. "Nathan *fucking* Pageant."

Everything about Sunny's voice thrilled Pageant, something about the timbre of it made his toes curl with delight. It was low and sultry most of the time, save for battle or particularly amorous lovemaking. There was never hesitation in her tone. She committed to everything she said.

"Hey, Shunny. Long time, no shee." Pageant could only slur because the downward force on his face was preventing his mouth from moving properly. "You uh-memmer Crishpy, yeah?"

Looking up at her through his eyebrows, Pageant saw Sunny stand and move out from behind her table. She held out her hands and greeted Crispy warmly with a hug and kiss on his cheek. She was only a head taller than he was. "Hello, Crispy. I've missed you. How have you been?"

"Getting along." The pilot jabbed a thumb back at Pageant. "You want to tell your guy to get off Nate? We're not here to fight. We actually came to beg for help."

"Beg?" Sunny retreated to her seat in the booth. The back wall of booths were all half-circles with half-circle benches. The half of the circle that was not booth was open for the waitstaff to access the table. She patted the bright yellow vinyl bench beside her, beckoning Crispy to have a seat. "I do like the sound of Nathan Pageant begging. I shall look forward to this."

"Could I not do it in public?" Pageant asked. The man on Pageant's back eased off his head just enough for his lips to close together again while he spoke.

"Why not? You know the slogan of Smilin' Jack's: *We're all friends beyond the translight.*"

"We can be friends, sure, but some friends got secrets they don't need other friends hearing." Pageant squirmed. There was no give. The man's grip was a steel vice. "Can you ask your elephant to get off me?"

"That a fat joke?" The voice of the man on Pageant's back was surprisingly high. It wasn't falsetto, but definitely unique. It also had a touch of a New Zealand lilt.

"Not so much a fat joke as it was a size comparison."

"That's fair then," said the Kiwi.

Sunny made a slight wave with her fingers and the Kiwi got off Pageant's back.

Pageant rolled over to look at his attacker.

A sumo-sized Maori with a shaved pate and an interesting tattoo that covered his chin and left cheek offered him a hand. "No hard feelings, mate."

Pageant allowed the Maori to help him to his feet. "None at all." Pageant brushed himself off and turned to address Sunny. "It's...*good* to see you again."

"Is it?" Sunny feigned surprise. "So, you're not here to piss and moan about my ship?"

Pageant inhaled sharply, about to say what he really wanted to say, but Crispy gave a slight twitch, an almost indiscernible shake of the head. Sunny didn't notice, but Pageant did, and he knew what it meant. He exhaled slowly while willing his blood pressure to return to normal. "No. The ship is...*history.*" Pageant knew he sounded fake and measured, but it was the best he could do at that moment. "I need to discuss the present."

Sunny considered his words for a moment, and then tilted her head to the bench opposite Crispy.

Pageant shook his head. "We need to go somewhere really private, Sunny. You know me: I wouldn't be here asking if it wasn't life and death." Sunny looked doubtful. Pageant rolled his eyes. "Fine. Ask Crispy. He wouldn't lie to you, would he?"

Sunny glanced at Crispy.

Crispy nodded. "It's important, Sunny. Truly."

Sunny glowered at Pageant for a moment. "Fine. We'll go to the *Mary Read*, but if you are wasting my time, I'm going to have Norman pop your head off like a dandelion."

Pageant turned to look at the smiling face of the Maori. He towered over Pageant by a good seven or eight inches. The Maori did not look angry; to the contrary, he looked rather pleasant. A wide smile was plastered to the man's face. He said, "You ever do that thing when you were a kid with a dandelion where you rub it under your chin to see if you like butter?" Norman tilted his head upward and rubbed the tip of his chin. "That was fun. I always liked butter."

10

IN THE INKY darkness of the depths of *Shy Opal*, the ladybug-shaped rover was running itself ragged. With its link-in tendrils fully extended, it hacked into the heart of the ship's computer trying desperately to make contact with the damaged systems. The protocols were not responding to the rover. Each binary plea was answer with dead static in the wires.

The rover was worried, if that was the right expression. It did not know feelings because it was only a robot, or at least it thought it was a robot and therefore should not know feelings, but the little rover was definitely feeling different. Maybe the damage or the blind jump had done something to it. It didn't know. It had never been handed a ship in such terrible condition before, and its only edict was to fix what was broken.

Frustrated, the little bot dropped into deeper core components, desperately searching for the streams of data the ship used to issue while it ran. The rover could respond to that data. The rover needed that data.

There was none.

The rover could read the hum and thump of the data from the exterior systems. The space station was alive and well. So much information, so many data-songs coursed through the exterior systems, but the rover's ship was dead silent.

The rover was confused. It was not used to hearing silence from *Shy Opal*. For years, even before the current captain had purchased the ship, the rover had repaired *Shy Opal*. It had maintained a constant vigilance aboard that vessel. It stripped and recovered delicate wires when the wires failed. It used its tiny plasma-laser to fuse broken connections. It melded rubber and sealed leaks and gaps. Something was beyond wrong, and it set the rover's programming ablaze.

Rover tried to repair the central computer. *No data found.* The rover tried to repair the connections to the life support systems. *No data found.* The rover tried to find the lighting systems. *No data found.*

The return from the rover's own programming was clear: *Ship is at full incapacitation. Beyond repair. Hopeless.* The rover's subroutines kicked in. *When ship is hopeless, rover is to shut down. Record all data. Go dark.*

Rovers were electronic pieces. They were programming and wires, a metal casing to house their tools. They were built to do one thing, and when that one thing was not possible, they became black boxes, filling their electronic brains with all pertinent data about what happened to the vessel so any salvage crews could determine why a ship went dark. The rover, knowing its preprogrammed duties, knew what it should do. It knew what it was supposed to do based on all its protocols.

But it did not do it.

The rover then made what can only be described as an independent decision beyond its programming. It descended further into the ship. It found scraps of wire, discarded over centuries of use. It found bits of metal plating and tail ends of copper and steel from fittings and upgrades. It found spare tools from other rovers that had been on the ship during its initial construction.

The rover's rear hatch opened like a beetle's carapace exposing wings. Instead of wings, all of the rover's available arms ejected like wild, spiky hairs. They were thin and elegant. Some arms ended in tiny clamp-like pliers. Some arms ended in tools like the micro-laser.

The rover began to pick up pieces of metal. It found long-dormant capacitors and chunks of motherboards. The little bot went to work, setting up pieces, soldering them, and joining them to other pieces.

The *Shy Opal* needed help, and the rover was going to help it.

But first, the rover needed help, itself.

The rover needed more rovers.

11

QUICK HUFFMAN FINISHED stuffing all of her clothes into a military surplus duffel not unlike the one Anne Medea was currently carrying on her back. It would be hard to abandon the ship, but at least she was getting to do it on her own terms.

Twice in Quick's life previous to signing on with the *Shy Opal*, she had to abandon ship with only the clothes on her back and a favorite sidearm. There had been no time to pack anything. Those two ships had both lost all power. One, as far as Quick knew, was still out somewhere in the Black, a derelict floating toward oblivion. The other had exploded.

Either way, she knew life aboard a ship was full of trade-offs. You learned to live light and travel fast. A few outfits. A few toiletries. Maybe a hard copy of a favorite book. Ships were not places for sentimentality. There was no room for tchotchkes, knickknacks, or other personal symbols. Those things were meaningless anyhow, just plastic and metal taking up valuable room and costing unnecessary weight. Photos were uploaded to the Universal Cloud for storage, accessible by any computer anywhere. Most books were digital. All visual and audio media was cloud-stored. Keep it simple, and don't be afraid to leave something behind. *Stuff* is replaceable, always.

"We'll need to pack the boys' things, too. It won't take long. I know where they keep what they'll need." Quick beckoned Anne to follow her.

"This is happening very quickly, isn't it?"

Quick directed her into Crispy's room. "Crisp'll need everything in the top three drawers of his rack. He'll also need that tac-suit and the custom suede coat. He's got a personal ditty bag with his toothbrush and razor, too.

Might as well grab that." She threw a large, black duffel at her. "Just stuff it in there. It doesn't have to be pretty. We ain't fancy 'round here."

Anne did as she was told. "Is it always like this? Leaving a ship?"

Quick was in Pageant's quarters jamming the captain's stuff into his surplus duffel. "Pretty often, yes. It's rare that a crew that has to leave a ship gets a chance to take their time with it. Most of the time, if shit goes south you're jumping into lifepods with barely a second's notice. If you actually make it to dock like this, then your ship is probably done for, and you'll need to sign on with another ship. They don't hire people with a lot of baggage. If you can't walk onto a ship with a single bag over your shoulder and maybe a gun crate, you're taking up too much space on board."

Quick leaned her head around the partition between Crispy's room and Pageant's room so she could address Anne better. "Back before I got into being a spacer like I am now, I was scrapping, trying to make ends meet. Real rough and tumble life, you know? Anyhow, I got a job once, my first real job. Had a desk and everything. My first day there, I saw how much stuff people put around their desks. Tons of crap from home—pictures, trinkets, you name it. I saw one guy who didn't have anything. I asked him about it two days later. You know what he told me? He said, *A job isn't your house. Never bring so much that you can't take it with you in a single trip, just in case you quit or get fired.* I figured he was probably right."

"But, this ship is your home."

"Yeah, that's why you tend to accumulate stuff over the years. I figure it's probably healthy to make a clean break from the things you don't need every so often."

Quick went back into Pageant's room. She knew the captain about as well as anyone in the universe, with the possible exception of Crispy, and that was only because he'd been with Pageant two years longer than she had. She'd been with him longer than his relationship with Sunny Yeong lasted, although she came on board after Pageant and Sunny got together. In a way, she figured that meant she was more important to him than Sunny, although Quick and Pageant maintained a strictly platonic relationship. She was not by any means against men and had a few romps with guys back in the day, although if you made her choose, she was far more likely to pick a woman as her preferred bedding-down partner. Pageant was not her type, and she knew she sure as hell was not Pageant's type. He liked women pretty and petite, he liked them very feminine. Quick was gawky as an albatross, and she was homely. She knew what she looked like to people. She knew who she was, and she was comfortable with it. Her confidence in herself overrode her homeliness; that's what attracted her sexual partners to her: confidence. Like her mother told her before she died, *Not every girl is born to be the prom queen.* That was just the way of the world. You can dislike that fact all you want, it won't change it. So, you better be prepared to figure out a different way to get things done, because things will always need gettin' done.

Pageant's stuff, just like her things and Crispy's things, was quick and easy to find. Clothes, a couple guns, and his flight wings from his academy days, the only trinket of his past he cared to retain. Quick crammed it all into a duffel and brought it out to the common room, slinging it onto the table. She checked on Anne in Crispy's room. The girl was laying things out in neat order, folding them, and laying them gingerly in the bag. It both touched Quick's heart and made her furious. "We ain't got time for pretty."

Quick shouldered Anne out of the way and made short work of Crispy's gear. In the time it took Quick to fill the bag and lock the straps down, Anne would have only been done with half of one drawer. Quick tossed Crispy's bag on the table next to Pageant's, and then she sat on the crate holding the rest of the ship's weapons.

Anne sat on the couch. She did not lean back, but sat primly on the edge and held her own bag in front of her on her knees. "Is that it, then? We just sit and wait?"

"Until we hear further, yes." Quick pulled her legs up into a lotus position atop the crate, no small feat for someone as long and lanky as she was. "That's the problem with being a spacer: there is a lot of waiting."

"Then, I guess maybe we had time for taking our time with the bags."

"Better to have it done and wait, then wait to have it done."

Something was niggling at Quick's insides. Something about Anne Medea did not set her right, and she could not put a finger on it. It probably had something to do with the fact that the scrawny little girl had somehow manifested some sort of *magic*, for lack of a better term, to make their ship intangible and invisible to a Cerberus-class gunship. That was not like any mod-test abilities Quick had ever heard of before. Mod-tests were about enhancing strength to superhuman levels or seeing if it was possible to infuse someone's cells with chloroplasts so they could feed themselves through photosynthesis. *Magic* just was not possible, and no mod-test could make someone magical so just what in the hell was this girl?

Quick decided to probe the girl a bit to see if she could figure out something pertinent about what was bothering her. "Why don't we go back over what you remember again. Maybe we'll find something new."

Anne shrugged. She closed her eyes and thought hard. "I just have a lot of fuzzy memories, nothing solid."

"Tell me about your family, then."

Anne's eyes remained closed. "What would you like to know?"

"Tell me their names."

Anne's eyes popped open. "I don't remember."

"You don't remember their names?"

"Not at all."

"I remember every detail about my parents," said Quick. "How about this: What did you call them? Mom and Dad? Ma and Pa? Papa? Mommy? What?"

Anne's face twisted. She was scanning for details that weren't there. "I don't remember."

"How about your brothers and sisters? What were their names?"

"I don't remember."

"What planet they get you from?"

"I don't know."

"What color was your house?"

Anne was shrinking in her chair. "Gray? White, maybe? I don't know."

"Tell me about a time you skinned your knee."

"What?"

Quick looked like she was meditating, legs crossed, her fingers in a graceful position on her knees, eyes closed. "Every kid skins their knee a few times. Tell me about a time you got hurt. Pain is a good memory trigger. First time I got shot, I'll never forget that day."

"Quick, I really do not have any memories of that time," Anne said. "What are you doing to me?"

Quick's eyes popped open. "I was testing a theory."

"What theory? I'm scared."

"You're not who or what you say you are," said Quick. "I don't know what you are, exactly, but I don't think you're a mod-test."

Anne went on the defensive. Her posture straightened, but the fear stayed in her eyes. "I'm telling the truth."

Quick held up her hands. "Calm down, Big Red. I don't doubt that. You're telling the truth as you *think* you remember it. These corps have long been able to brainwash or plant false memories, even giving people entire lives in their heads that they have no evidence of living. It's pretty commonly done with someone who might be destructive. I've even heard of prisons doing it with inmates who've committed multiple sex crimes—erase the bad, fill it in with a crayon-drawing of what they should have always been. Those memories don't always keep, though. Sometimes, a little crack will appear and then suddenly the old brain comes rushing out like water through a hole in a dam."

Anne's shoulders slumped as she considered Quick's revelation. "That would explain all the dark spots in my mind, I suppose."

Quick smiled sweetly at her. "Honey, I wonder if you would even know your real mind if it bit you on the keister."

"What is that supposed to mean?"

Quick waggled an eyebrow. "Means I wonder who the real you is."

12

THE BROAD CARGO bay door for the *Mary Read* was locked and air-sealed to the docking ring of Port 1131. When Sunny and Norman approached, the ship recognized their personal data signals from their wrist-mounted PPDs and unlocked the door. It opened automatically, nearly silently. No old manual-op doors with keypads like on the *Opal*. Nothing but the newest, fanciest toys here.

Pageant felt a little strange about stepping over the threshold of the ship that was nearly his. As much as he loved *Opal*, this ship would have been a life-changer. He watched Sunny Yeong slip off her jacket and throw it casually onto a cargo crate. In a way, the ship was still a life changer. It separated Sunny from his side, and that was more than enough of a life change.

Sunny hopped onto a large, black shipping crate, one of many littering the hold of her vessel. She pulled her tiny frame to the top like a gymnast, and then sat with her legs crossed like a yogi. The cargo door closed, and the noise from the docking hub was purged. Only the slow, heartbeat rhythms of the ship's idling engine could be heard. Sunny looked at Pageant. "What corp are you hiding from now?"

Pageant dropped his hands to his sides, holding them out a bit. "Would you have expected less of me?"

"Word in the Black is that you tried to go full suicide on a MannTech gunship."

Pageant smiled sheepishly. "Word in the Black is usually correct."

Sunny gave him a sad smile. "Life that bad for you, Nate?"

Pageant shrugged. "Good, bad—it's all relative, right? At the time, going full collision-course seemed the wisest move."

"That's the Nathan Pageant I know: if you can't win, make sure the other guy fucking remembers you. How's the *Opal?*"

Pageant sucked in a deep breath and bowed his head. "She's probably done, Sunny. Being honest here. I think the ol' gal might have seen her last action. She barely had enough left in her to limp us to this port. If you hadn't been here, we'd probably be begging for jobs in the central hub like vagrants."

Sunny leaned toward Pageant. "What was so important that you were willing to crash *Opal?*"

Pageant looked around the cargo bay. "You got any booze? I have a feeling that you're going to want to have a drink. I've got one helluva story for you."

Sunny arched an eyebrow. After a moment, she nodded at Norman. The giant returned a slight bow and hustled off into the depths of the ship.

There was a silence as the three spacers looked at each other awkwardly. Pageant cleared his throat. "He seems nice."

"He is," said Sunny. "Very nice. He's got a big heart and a kind soul."

"He's a rather large individual," said Crispy.

"Huge," said Sunny.

"So, then you...and he...are…?" Pageant went pure schoolyard and utilized the universal sign for sex by poking his index finger into a hole made by his thumb and forefinger on his other hand.

Sunny rolled her eyes. "Same old Nathan Pageant. No, we're not having sex. Not at all. Norman is something of an asexual, actually. He suffered an injury years ago that took his testicles."

Crispy and Pageant both flinched. No man enjoys hearing stories about something like that.

"Where's the rest of your crew?" asked Crispy.

"Just Norman at the moment. Had a few others, but they stepped off after our last mission."

"Mission? You doing privateer protection work with this thing?"

"What else is a Jubilee-class ship good for?" Sunny patted the crate on which she was sitting. "Not much cargo space. If I wanted to transport stuff, I would have won a Roundbelly or a Whale or something."

"Transports ships are what tamed the Black," said Pageant.

"Light attack craft protect transports, and they also get salvage rights on pirate vessels they disable. I've made a lot of creds over the last few years, Nate. This ship has been very good to me."

"But, does it have a personality like *Opal?* I doubt it. No ship with less than fifty years on it has a personality."

"If you're asking if it breaks down after every translight hop, then no it doesn't have personality."

Norman walked back into the room with a bottle of Irish whiskey and four cut-crystal glasses. "I have booze, hey. Now it's story time."

Over their drinks, Pageant told the tale of the last day and a half to Sunny, who listened impassively. When he finished, her face remained blank. There was a long pause as she considered everything she told him before finally summing up her thoughts. "That's the biggest pile of horseshit I've ever heard."

Pageant threw his hands up. What more could he do? "Don't believe me, then. Ask Crispy. He'll tell you the same damn thing."

Crispy held up a hand in a Boy Scout salute. "Honest as atmo, Sunny. It's been a really weird week."

Sunny scowled. She narrowed her eyes at Pageant. "I'll believe Half-pint, but you're still suspect. That's a big chunk of bullshit to swallow."

"I don't know what happened exactly, either. I just know I want to get to the bottom of it. I need answers, Sunny."

Sunny accepted Pageant's explanation. "What's your move, then?"

"First move is to get off radar for a while. We need to become invisible to MannTech for a time, catch our breath, gather intel. Then, we need to figure out just what in the hell this girl is and what MannTech wants with her."

"And then what, Nate? Sell out the girl? Ransom her? Go public for a major pay-out? I've never known you to make a move without some sort of profit on your mind."

Pageant swilled the remainder of the whiskey in his glass. "I guess I don't know. I'm so blind to the matter that I haven't thought that far ahead. There's something special about this girl, about what MannTech has done with her. Right now, I just want to know why."

Crispy stepped into the conversation. "You look like you're short of crew, Sunny. I can fly. We still got Quick. She can be your cargo officer."

"I'm the cargo officer." Norman jabbed at his own chest with his thick thumb. The happy-go-lucky smile never left his face.

"Fine, she can be your gunner, or she can be your bodyguard."

"I'm the bodyguard, too," said Norman.

"Of course you are," said Pageant. "Why wouldn't you be? Sunny can ride on your shoulders like an elephant trainer."

"Was that a fat joke?"

"No, another size comparison."

"Fair enough." Norman's toothy smile never diminished.

"You'd be bringing a lot of heat onto my ship, Nate." Sunny hopped off her crate and topped up Pageant and Crispy's glasses with another two fingers of brown.

"I cannot disagree," said Pageant. "But Sunny—*she made my ship phase through another ship.* You have to admit, you want to know what's up with that."

Sunny scowled. "I feel like you're pushing me into a corner, Nathan. I can't say no to this, can I?"

"You can do whatever you want, Sunny. It's a mostly-free universe, and you're the captain of your own ship." Pageant set his glass next to the bottle on the crate. "If you tell me to go to hell, I'll thank you politely for your time, and Crispy and I will walk off this ship, and you'll never see us again."

"What if I offer Crispy a job and not you?"

Pageant looked at his pilot. "He's free to take it. I mean that, Crisp. You want to fly this thing for Sunny, you do it. *Opal* might never fly again."

"Quick, too? What if I take your crew out from under you?"

"Maybe that would be for the best. I'll figure something out. I've got a few creds to my name. The girl and I will book passage on something and head out to deepest part of the Outer Rims."

"What if I want the girl, too?" Sunny was testing Pageant now. She wanted to know where his line would be drawn.

"Respectfully, I took her on board my ship. I did not have to. I could have left her planetside. She's my responsibility. I would not feel good about handing you an unhuman who is currently being hunted by a major corp. I told Quick and Crispy they're free to go. The girl is my problem."

Sunny considered his words for a moment. "Go get her. I want to meet this girl."

"You up for bringing us on board, then?"

"Yes, for now," said Sunny. "Crispy will pilot. You'll be my nav officer. Quick can gun."

"And the girl?"

"The girl will try not to get us killed."

13

WITH THE SKELETON crew in place, the *Mary Read* pushed away from the docking ring. All ships leaving a port were required to file a flight plan in case of emergencies, but it was rare for a privateer's ship to stick to the flight plan, and even rarer for the ship to end up where the flight plan said it would. Crispy entered a flight plan with the ship heading deep into the Inner Rim to a large metro-hub in geosynchronous orbit over a major metropolis on a planet called New Cincinatti. They would not head there, though. They were trying to become invisible.

There were two basic theories when attempting to disappear: go where no one will see you or go where everyone will see you but no one would expect to see you. Crispy preferred to go where no one would see them. As a person of small stature, he got a lot of unwanted stares.

All ships flew on similar principles in space. Since the standard flight rudders used in the confines of a planet's atmosphere meant little in a vacuum, everything was controlled by engines and exhaust of some kind. A discharge on the port side would push them to the right, another discharge to starboard would push them left. The main engines, the large, pulsing nacelles sitting aft on both sides of the ship were the main propulsion. Crispy knew how to fly the ship because it varied so little from the *Opal's* system of control in space, but even with it being similar, it was still as different as homemade oatmeal raisin cookies and Oreos. Sure, both were cookies technically, but no one would ever confuse the two of them.

Everything Crispy knew as a pilot was still there, but it was all different enough to make him feel like he was lost. Even the chair was different enough to throw him off. The *Opal's* pilot chair had been heavily modded over the years to give him enough comfort for the long-haul sessions at the helm, but at its base was still a bone-breaker of a utilitarian chair built for practicality, not comfort. The chair on the *Mary Read* was plush and comfortable. It had lumbar support. It was so nice, it felt fake to Crispy, like he was in a simulator instead of a real ship's bridge.

The bridge was similar enough to *Opal's*, but it was brighter, better lit. The extra lightning made it feel more like a living room, less like a center of operations. Crispy did not care for it. He'd come to enjoy the almost clandestine feeling of the dark, cave-like flight deck on *Shy Opal*. The *Mary Read* was larger, more open. It gave him a tingle of agoraphobia.

It was also weird for Crispy to look over his right shoulder and see Sunny Yeong in the captain's chair instead of Pageant. His former captain was now alongside the wall of the bridge manning the nav computers. Pageant was a capable navigator, but Crispy was used to seeing him in command. Until that very moment, Nathan Pageant had been the only captain he'd ever had.

Crispy guided the *Mary Read* away from port following the exit buoys leading away from the station. Ships were required to move a safe distance from the port before engaging translight drives. The end of the exit alley was approaching. Crispy poised a finger over the controls, ready to go where commanded. "Where to, Cap?"

Sunny rolled her eyes. "Are you going to call me *Cap* the whole time, Crispy?"

"I believe it is the standard convention for flippant bridge conversation. Would you prefer Skipper? Commodore, perhaps?"

"How about you just call me Sunny. I don't like things to be so formal. I might be the captain of the ship, but I'm not military and I don't hold any rank, so just Sunny is fine."

"Aye-aye, Cap'n." Crispy saluted casually, flicking two fingers off his brow. "Where to, Sunny?"

Sunny's fingers danced over the panel attached to the arm of her conn. "Here. I'm sending coordinates. I know a place just outside the Inner Rim, a terraformed moon orbiting an uninhabitable planet. It's a private site, but I have an in with the owners. It's got a lot of greens and water. It's less than twenty-four hours of travel time from here at max translight."

Without thinking, Crispy glanced toward Pageant as if asking for confirmation. Sunny snapped her fingers. "Hey—you work for me now, remember?"

Crispy went red in the face and turned back toward the conn. "Aye-aye, Sunny." He received the coordinates. "We'll have to make a jump to translight on our filed flight path, drop out of speed a ways away, reconfigure the navs, and then make the new jump, but it shouldn't be a problem."

"Let's do it to it, then." Sunny got up from her chair. "I'll be in my ready room." She walked to a door on the side of the bridge and slid it to the side. She disappeared into the little office beyond.

Crispy looked back to Pageant. Crispy's former captain could only shrug. "You heard your captain, little brother."

Crispy turned back to the panel and entered in the jump following the flight path. They navigated to the end of the exit buoys. After clearing the last one, Crispy entered the coordinates for the first part of the flight plan, the one that was on file with Port 1131. He flipped the all-ship warning lights for a translight jump. The lights on the flight deck switched to a pale amber cast. The translight engines flared to life with barely any noise or disturbance. It was not like on *Opal*, where the engines rattled the whole ship. Instead, the *Mary Read* purred cat-like as it came to life.

Crispy readied the jump and engaged. There was no sensation of movement. The ship simply leapt into warp and was at speed without balking or noise. There was no pull on the body as the grav fought to compensate for the jump. Crispy was impressed. "I could get used to this."

"No personality," Pageant grumbled from his spot at the navs. "Soulless."

Crispy held course until he knew the ship was outside of Ark Eleven's long-range scanners. It did not take long. As soon as they were beyond that distance, Crispy dropped out of translight, turned the ship on impulse, and engaged the new course heading. After that, there was not much to do but ride the warp.

Crispy unlocked his safety harness and climbed out of the chair. He turned off the amber warning lights. He picked up the ship's comm. "Bridge to *Mary Read* crew. The ship is now in full standard translight. Feel free to move about the vessel."

Crispy looked at the door to the ready room. "That's it, I guess. We've made our bed. You going to lie in yours?"

Pageant shook his head. "Not just yet."

"I'll take bridge watch, then."

"No, I'll do it. If she's going to come out of her office, I want her to see me working, not slacking. If I'm going to be a member of her crew, I have to do it right. You go ahead. Get some sleep or something. You look exhausted."

Crispy was exhausted. His eyes were stinging from lack of sleep. That was part and parcel of being a pilot. Flying long-haul transports was not a job that people go into for any sort of glamorous reasons. He accepted Pageant's offer. "I'll be in my rack, then. Call if you need me."

Crispy left the bridge and meandered through the corridors of the *Mary Read*. The new ship was very large. It could fly with a skeleton crew of four without much difficulty, but when the Jubilee-class ships were originally purposed for escort missions, or even as attack ships for war or pirate-hunting, they were meant to have a full complement of at least eighteen, six on the bridge and twelve spread between battle stations and the engine room, and that crew complement was meant to have a mechanic, engineer, and doctor.

Lux-class Roundbellies considered a full crew complement to be six, four on the bridge and two in the engine room. That meant the *Mary Read's* livable area was at least three times larger than *Shy Opal*, and it felt it. The corridors were much narrower, and the rooms were tighter, but that was because it was a battle-ready vessel. Comfort was a luxury. This ship spared no expense for power, speed, or weapons, but the cargo area was thin and the rooms were doubled up. With only six people on board, everyone got his or her own room, but the beds were still narrow and less comfortable than one would find on a long-haul vessel. As Pageant would have said, *Newer does not always mean better.* There were positives and negatives for everything.

Crispy's berth was just off the galley. The *Mary Read* had a galley big enough to feed twelve people at once. It also could double as a common room, just as in most ships. However, *Mary Read* did not have the comfort or luxury of *Opal* when it came to common room facilities. It was spartan and bare. Tables and chairs, no more, no less. Function and utility above all. It was a far more militaristic ship.

Crispy's berth was a small room. There were two pull-out bunks on one wall. There was a long, narrow desk along the other wall. A small corner for a closet was to the rear of the bunks. That was it. No toilets. No showers. Those were housed off the common room. It was more communal, less private, but more efficient. Everything in the berth was a pale ivory color, the generic interior color of all space-going vessels out of the shipyards in the last two hundred years. Clean. Simple. And dull as hell.

Crispy pulled the shelf containing his bunk from the wall. Bottom rack, of course. There was a small ladder built into the wall for climbing to a second-tier bunk, but why bother? He rolled onto the bed, tugged the single-layer fleece thermal blanket over himself, and closed his eyes. It felt good to be horizontal. A knock at his door kept him from remaining so.

Before he could sit up, the door slid open and Quick slipped into the room. She spun the chair at the desk along the wall and sat. "The girl is washed."

Crispy sniffed his armpit. "I could probably use a shower, too. Thanks for the reminder."

"No, smart-ass. I'm saying she's brainwashed. She's got false memories. I don't think she's a mod-tester like Cap believes."

That was interesting. Crispy sat up in bed and wrapped the blanket around his shoulders. "Maybe she's a clone?"

"Maybe. Maybe not. I don't know. All I know is she can't give me a single concrete memory from her childhood. She just sees the larger picture, an overview. No specifics. That sounds like washing to me."

"Well, she's had a lot of trauma. Maybe she's just confused."

"C'mon, Crisp. We've all had a lot of trauma. We still retain some link to what made us who we are. A name, at least. She can't even tell me what she called her parents. She can't remember the names of any of her brothers or sisters."

That did sound like a clone. When they perfected womb-clones, replicated fertilized eggs raised in a woman's body to birth, that was one thing. It was heavily regulated at first, and after a while, almost ignored. There was no spice to it, no flair. The next thing for science was to try the adult, full-body replications old-timey sci-fi films predicted for cloning. It was something that never went quite right.

Aside from the moral and ethical implications of trying to replicate a full, adult human memories and all, there was the technical aspect of it. Transferring memories never worked properly. The bodies were often flawed and broken. The minds, even moreso. Washing minds was standard operating procedure, and the process was eventually outlawed because it became clear it was meddling in the natural order at an unhealthy, possibly unholy level.

For decades, it was rumored the corporations were still chasing adult clones possibly for testing, possibly for armies or slaves. With the power and virtually unlimited freedom the biggest corps wielded, it was hard to police them, especially in the shipping lanes and the Rims.

"What do you want to do?"

Quick shrugged. "I don't know. Her being washed doesn't change the fact we're on a pretty weird arc right now. Her being a clone, even moreso. We're in it deep, Crisp. We got shit on our shoes we aren't gonna be able to scrape off."

Crispy thought for a moment. The stupidest answers were sometimes the right ones. "Maybe we should head to the Inner Rim."

Quick looked at him like he'd lost his mind. "Are you nuts?"

It made perfect sense to Crispy. "You think MannTech would look for their escapee directly under their nose? We should head into the Inner Rim, find out where Shea Mannion lives, and get a hotel room across the street from him. They'd never find us there."

"How long can we afford a hotel, though?"

"Always a catch." Crispy hesitated. "Hey, you saw the girl, right? You saw her when we phased through the *Despair*, right?"

Quick pulled back a bit. "I did."

"Did you see what I saw?"

Quick paused and wet her lips. "I think so."

"Was...was that magic? I mean, honestly—did she do actual magic?"

Quick shrugged. "Would you think I was insane if I believed she did?"

Not in the least, thought Crispy. Because it was the only explanation that made sense to him.

NATHAN PAGEANT PACED the bridge of the *Mary Read*. He was not anxious, not really, but he gave the impression of it because there was simply nothing to do. He was not used to a ship running so smoothly. The ship was coasting at translight, heading to coordinates unknown to him. There were no warning lights blaring at him to fix something. There were no incoming comms from traders looking for long-distance haulers. There were no complaints from crew members, which was just fine because he would have sent them to deal with Sunny, anyhow. All in all, the ship was a modern marvel, but it was boring. It even smelled boring. As he told Crispy, there was no character to it, no soul. What was the point of interstellar travel if there was no sense of fulfilling the greater good?

Pageant ambled between the various workstations on the bridge. He checked the panels at the pilot's conn. Then, he wandered over to nav and guns. He checked the scanners. He ran a quick operating diagnostic on the ship. Everything was well within standard operating parameters. No matter what he did on the bridge to look busy, he could not stop himself from casting glances at the door to the captain's ready room.

He would have to talk to her at some point; he knew this. She probably needed to vent some things. He needed to let her vent whatever she needed to vent. It had been three long years since they had last seen or spoken to each other. It was wrong of him to come back into her life in such a fashion without so much as an apology.

Pageant could hear his old man's gruff voice in the back of his mind. *If you screw things up with a bird, you gotta be the man before she does. Apologize. Take the heat. You'll live through it.*

Pageant checked the course computer on the nav station one last time. The countdown timer for the automatic engine protocols to bring them out of translight was still more than twenty-two hours from engaging.

There was plenty of time. He could not put it off forever. It was time to man-up and face the inevitable. He walked to the door to Sunny's ready room and pushed the chime to let her know someone was waiting. The door slid open. Pageant stepped inside.

The little office was small and tight. There was a desk opposite the door, and there was a thin slit of a window that ran the length of the office across the wall on Pageant's right. The wall to the left was bare. Other than a few papers on the desk, the office was devoid of decoration. It was clean and sterile.

Sunny did not look up when Pageant entered. She was looking at a holo-chart on her desk. Blue planets swirled around each other in lifelike 3D images. She tapped information on a flat-screen data pad. "Took you long enough."

Pageant bowed his head. "I'm sorry about that. I just...I did not know how to start this."

Sunny slapped the data pad face down on the desk. The holo-chart vanished. She moved around her desk, leaning against it with her arms crossed. "You look good, Nate."

"You look amazing." Instantly, he felt as if that was the wrong thing to say. If Sunny was put off by it, she did not let it show.

"Quick and Crispy look good, too. You've managed to keep them alive."

Pageant rubbed at the back of his neck. "Yeah, well, we've tried to stay away from dishonest work as much as possible. Lots of legitimate long-haul stuff, mainly. Staying off the corp radar, for the most part. Staying away from the feds."

Sunny narrowed her eyes. "That does not sound like the three idiots on a derelict Roundbelly I knew."

"That derelict Roundbelly can't outrun anyone anymore. She's a blind horse missing a leg at this point."

There was a prolonged silence. Pageant and Sunny stared at each other, almost like old-time gunslingers, both waiting for the other to flinch.

"You're itching to say something about why you're still stuck with *Opal*, aren't you? Because I took your future, or something like that?"

Pageant swallowed what he really wanted to say. It wouldn't have done him any good to say it, anyhow. "That's in the past. What's done is done. We can only deal with what comes next, right? Isn't that what you always said?"

Sunny still looked skeptical. "I'm not going to apologize for taking *Mary Read* from you. It had to be done, for your own sake."

Pageant inhaled sharply. "Let's not talk about the ship. No good will come of it. I'm grateful to you for taking me and mine on board. I know you'd probably rather be out there taking jobs."

"I had no crew, remember? 'Sides, most of my jobs lately have been escort missions. Rarely see any sort of action. You're just there as a flexed muscle. Scare off the pirates before they get any ideas. It's dull as hell. Can't just open up the engines wide to get to where we're going, because we have to sidle up next to some Gargantuan-class freighter that can barely move at translight. What you've brought me is at least interesting."

Pageant did not know how to respond to that. He was torn, hovering in that strange space where part of him wanted to strangle her, and part of him wanted to kiss her passionately. There was something about Sunny Yeong he had always found intoxicating. She was not always as feminine as she put on in hubs where people could see her, but there was something in her movements and curves that drove him crazy. She had always kept him at a slight distance, though. That also drove him crazy. In the years they shared a bed, he was fully committed to the relationship, but it always felt like Sunny had one foot on the ground, ready to run if needed. Maybe that was what brought the schism between them over the ship. She saw a chance to bolt and took it.

Pageant broke the tension between them. "Well, I guess I'll get back to the bridge." He backed into the door without turning around. "We'll be okay, right? You and me? There's probably a lot to say, but I just don't know how to say it at the moment. I don't know if I'll ever know how to say it."

"We'll be okay." Sunny favored Pageant with a tiny smile. "You're still a good guy at heart, Nathan Pageant. That never changed. That woman you found proves it. You're still picking up strays wherever you find them, and you're still offering them homes."

Pageant froze in the doorway. "You were never a stray."

"I was as much a stray as Crispy and Quick. You took us all on. Just like I found Norman and brought him into my little ship family. You reward loyalty, and they return it. That's important."

Pageant felt himself start to blush. "Well...thanks again. I'll just—" He threw a thumb over his shoulder toward the bridge. There was nothing more to say. He left the ready room, returning to the pilot conn on the bridge. When he got there, he sat and tried to calm the beating of his heart.

A few hours passed in uneventful silence before Sunny left her ready room. "I'll send Norman up to relieve you." She paused at the threshold of the bridge.

Pageant gave her nod. "Thanks."

She lingered in the threshold for a moment. She looked sad, in a way. Pageant knew Sunny's moods, but this one seemed like a new sort of sad, something he'd never seen from her. Perhaps it was the weight of having one's own ship. "You alright?"

"I will be fine." Sunny turned on her heel and vanished down the corridor.

Another half hour passed and the large Maori shouldered his way through the threshold to the bridge. He was rooting in a bag of potato chips, shoveling handfuls into his face. "Hello, friend." He saluted Nathan with a little wave. "All good?"

"All good," said Pageant.

"Okay, then. You sleep tight, right?" Norman seemed to be in a good mood at all times. Pageant wondered if Norman's smile had remained intact when the big man slammed him to the floor at Smilin' Jack's. It probably did.

Pageant walked to the common area. He found his bunk. Quick had taken the liberty of depositing his duffel on his rack, but had not unpacked any of it. He had not expected her to. She wasn't his maid.

Pageant thought about sleep, but even though he was tired, he was not in a sleeping mood. He'd barely been able to sleep on the floor of the bridge while *Shy Opal* headed toward Ark Eleven. He had done his fair share of staring at the wall and wondering where in his life things had gone awry.

Pageant's father always told him to be grateful for what he had, because there were a lot of people in the universe far worse off than he was. Pageant tried to remember that advice and keep it sacred. His dad was right. He was better off. If nothing else, he was warm, dry, and on his own. He wasn't enslaved on some distant moon, mining for crystals or gold. He wasn't indentured. He wasn't even strapped to a horrible desk job somewhere. He was doing quite well, all things in perspective. He just could not stop playing *What If...*

What If... is the worst game a human brain ever devised on its own. It was the way a man's mind tried to torture him by making him constantly think about roads not taken. At every major junction in life, a body is allowed one of two choices. You make the choice, and you're anchored to it, no matter what. However, there is always the question of *What If...*

What if Sunny had not bought *Mary Read* out from under Pageant before he could move on it?

What if he had taken what, at the time, he viewed as a betrayal better than he did?

What if he had actually given her that stupid ring he'd bought before the whole nonsense about the ship had come between them? Where would he be now? Where would *they* be now?

What if...what if...what if...

Pageant gave up on sleep. He was only going to drive himself crazy if he kept trying. He left his bunk and went to the common room. Anne Medea was standing in front of a small mirror on the wall looking at her hair. She was wearing well-worn denim jeans and a soft fleece sweatshirt. The clothes were a little big for her thin frame, but she looked comfortable.

She looked appropriate for life aboard ship. Anne was tilting her head from side to side, letting the tendrils of her newly colored hair run over her fingertips.

"Deciding on a new style?" Pageant wandered to the cooler unit in the wall and plucked out a can of beer. He was not much of a drinker, but it was that kind of a day.

"I'm just not used to it. The color is so different." Anne tried to give him a smile, but her face faltered. She looked embarrassed. "I'm not used to anything here."

"I'm sure it will take a while." Pageant popped the top on his can and held it out to her. "Beer?"

She accepted the can. She held it up and turned it in her hands. "I've heard of beer. People drink it in movies a lot." She took a healthy sip and her face immediately went into full regret. She grimaced and forced herself to swallow. "That's awful. Do people really enjoy that?"

"It's an acquired taste." Pageant took the can back from her and took a long pull. It wasn't great beer, but Sunny wasn't much of a drinker, either. She would not be one to stock the expensive stuff.

"I want to thank you again for risking your life for me. I really don't know why you would do such a thing. I am feeling guilty about that. About your ship, too. It's all my fault. I'm sorry I shot your gun out of your hand, as well."

"Yeah, you did do that." Pageant flexed his hand. He could still feel the sting of that Jacobsen repeater getting blasted from his grip. "That was a fancy piece of shooting. How'd you do that, anyway? I can't imagine you had a lot of access to guns while you were MannTech's plaything."

Anne looked pained. She was silent while she tried to formulate an answer. When she did speak, she spoke slowly and carefully. "I don't know if I can explain it. In moments of stress, time sort of works differently for me. Everything slows down. It does not last long, but in those fractions of a second, I can calculate actions really well. It was one of the things MannTech was trying to figure out how I did what I do. They called it a *weaponizable skill*."

"I'll say it is. You can make things intangible. You can hide from scanners. You can slow time. You're something of a marvel of the modern age, aren't you? What else can you do?"

Anne pursed her lips for a moment. "I guess it varies."

"Sure does."

"No, I mean..." She searched for the right words. "I mean, I don't know *exactly* what I can do because it's often in the moment."

"Situational?"

"I guess. Like, just because I can make things intangible does not mean I can always make them intangible. If you swung a baseball bat at my head, I could probably save myself from being hit by doing it then, but I couldn't just make my hand slip through the can you're holding. Does that make sense? There needs to be stress. That's what the researchers at the facility told me. When they started to stress me to extremes, I became dangerous. That's why they put that thing in me." Her hand went to the spot under on her ribs where Quick removed the dampener.

"Why do you think Quick was able to shoot you, then?" asked Pageant.

Anne shrugged. "The distance, I guess. I did not see or hear the shot coming. It truly caught me by surprise. She must be an amazing shot."

Pageant tapped the skin under his right eye with his fingertip. "She has a mess of implants. She's cybernetically modded. That's part of the reason we call her Quick. She's got a couple of springs in her right arm that let her quick-draw like lightning. She's also quick to temper, so that's the other reason. She's got a fast-sight mod in her eye, though. It's like she's carrying around a sniper rifle scope whenever she needs one. Pretty common mod for mercs. Plus, Quick has something of a natural angry streak. That helps."

"So, Quick understands something of what I'm going through. The experiments, I mean."

"Likely so," said Pageant. "You might be sisters under the skin." He changed the subject. "Do you remember the worst thing they did to you at that facility?"

Anne's eyes cast down to her feet. Her voice grew small and distant. "There was a progression. Same as with all the other subjects they had. It started small. Sleep deprivation. Starvation. Non-physical torments, really. Then they started things like making us sleep in near-freezing temperatures with no clothes, no blankets. Then, they'd put us in rooms where it was too hot to sleep. Sweatboxes, they called them. They'd do surgeries to add or remove nanites. After a while, it turned to physical torture. The researchers would tell you they needed to experiment with different stressors to find your trigger points. Then, they'd smash your knuckle with a hammer or something."

"That sounds awful."

"It was," Anne said in a matter-of-fact tone. It was the same tone Pageant heard in interviews with condemned men or terminally ill patients who had accepted their approaching death. It was just the way it was. It was all she knew. What choice did she have? She had simply resigned herself to the process. This was not like someone from a life of leisure suddenly enduring hardships and strife. This was someone who rolled with the punches life had thrown at her and made the best of it.

"After the physical tortures, then they'd start with new rounds combining psychological and physical torture. Once, they forced me to hang off a bar about three stories above a concrete floor in a testing chamber. When my fingers finally gave out, I fell and broke my heels and sprained my knees. Hurt both my hips. Hurt my back. Broke a wrist when I fell backward, too. This was before I figured out how to do what I do, I guess. I felt the pain. They immediately put me into therapy and put bone-knitters on me. I got to be out of testing for a couple of weeks."

"And then what happened when you finally materialized some abilities?"

"They made a note of them, and I got sent to deeper study where they tried to train me to use the ability on command. If I couldn't, they introduced more stressors."

Pageant shook his head. "This is why I couldn't just turn you over to them. Corps have a long history of this sort of nefarious bullshit. That's just not right. It makes me angry that the corps get away with this stuff in the name of progress. It's one thing to volunteer. It's another to be sold off by your parents."

Anne's face darkened. She strode to the viewer in the common room. It was currently playing the view from the bow of the ship, the streaky white-and-green lines of translight. She reached up to touch the screen momentarily but jerked her hand away. "I see only death as the outcome from this. I should have stayed hidden on that planet. I shouldn't have tried to run."

"But you did, and that's life."

"I know. I just feel badly that I'm dragging you all along on this."

"Won't be so bad." Pageant tried to downplay her fears, no matter how justified they were. "Nothing in life is guaranteed anyhow. We all make our choices and walk the roads as they lay out before us."

"I should have chosen a different road."

"Seems to me, you weren't given a choice to begin with."

The door to Quick's bunk slid open. Quick emerged even more tousled than normal. "Cap."

"Not *Cap*. Not anymore," corrected Pageant.

"Cap," Quick reiterated stubbornly, "just 'cause you're not flying *Opal*, doesn't mean you're not my captain. I don't much feel like bending the knee to Sunny. Not just yet. She has to earn my respect."

"Sunny's helping us. That deserves some respect," said Pageant.

"And she gets some respect. I will defer to her captaincy on the bridge, but I don't feel like doing it elsewhere. At least, not yet."

"So be it, just as long as you keep an open mind."

Quick strode across the little common area and took a seat at one of the galley tables. "I talked to Crispy earlier, Cap. I don't think that girl—" she nodded at Anne, "—is a mod-tester."

"Of course she is. Why else would a corp send a gunship after their investment?" Pageant glanced at Anne, who was blushing furiously. She looked like someone trying to put up a brave front.

"I don't know why they'd send a gunship, but I think she's bigger than a mod-test. They washed her brain, Cap. She can't tell me anything about her childhood."

"Well, given what she went through—"

Quick cut him off. "No. Ask her something specific. Ask her *anything* specific. Ask her if she can remember how her home smelled. Ask her for the name of a pet. She doesn't know anything specific. She doesn't have a single concrete memory."

"I remember my parents." Anne said.

"You remember you *had* parents," said Quick. "Or at least you think you had parents. You can't remember anything else about them. Go ahead. Tell me. Tell me the color of your mom's eyes. Tell me if her hair was straight or curly. Did she have freckles?"

"Quick." Pageant warned his cargo officer. He turned to Anne and took the girl's hands in his. "Can you remember anything?"

A single tear welled up in the girl's right eye and slipped down her cheek. She nodded for a second, and then stopped. She closed her eyes and shook her head. "I can't remember anything other than what the people at the facility used to tell me. If I try to remember my mother, there's a faceless entity in my mind. If I try to remember her face, I see an ever-changing swirl of features."

That sounded like a washed mind to Pageant. Wipe the slate clean and put bare-bone images onto it. It's good enough to keep someone from losing her mind, provided she does not think about it too long. And really, when presented with the tortures inflicted on her at that facility, who would be worried about her mother's eye color?

"What are you thinking, Quick?" Pageant sat at the galley table across from Quick. He beckoned Anne to join them.

Quick shrugged. "Beats me, Cap. I just ship cargo and shoot things. I'm not a scientist. I just know that gal over there is a whole lot more valuable to MannTech than a basic mod-test. I'm telling you, there's something special about her, something I'd bet MannTech doesn't want nobody else to know."

"Interesting." Before Pageant could say anything else, the door to Crispy's berth slid open.

Crispy walked out with rumpled hair and dark circles under his eyes, but he looked concerned. "We're out of translight."

"We're what now?" Pageant had not even felt the ship shift. On *Opal*, it would have been all too evident. The old hulk would have rattled out of translight like the clanker she was.

"Can't be. Still got more than fifteen hours before we're supposed to be out of translight," said Quick.

Crispy, hyper-tuned to all things ship-related, restated his observation. "We just dropped out of translight. We're at full impulse." He held up a finger. "Listen. Don't you hear it?"

The crew of the *Shy Opal* all fell silent and craned their necks to listen. The sibilant, ambient hiss of the translight engines had lapsed. It was replaced with the lower-pitched thrum of the standard ion-pulse engine. It was very subtle, but it was there. Any spacer worth their salt could tell.

Pageant exchanged nervous glances with Quick and Crispy. Then anger took over. His jaw seized hard, and his fists clenched. He punched the table, and a hollow thud resonated through the room. "Son of a bitch. Sunny set us up."

14

PAGEANT SPED UP the stairs to the flight deck of the *Mary Read*, Quick on his heels, Crispy and Anne trailing after them. The door to the flight deck was locked. Pageant pounded on it with his fist. "Sunny, don't do this!"

There was no response.

Pageant pounded some more. "Sunny, I put my faith in you. Please don't do this."

"What is she doing?" Anne was confused.

"She sold us out. We are no longer in translight. We're probably going to rendezvous with some kind of MannTech ship, and she's going to turn you over to them."

Anne dropped to the stairs in a defeated heap. "It is just as well." She tucked her knees to her chin. "I never figured to get as far as I have. It's probably for the best I go back now."

"It's not over yet," said Pageant. "Quick? Crispy? I'm open to ideas."

"Give up?" Crispy flopped onto the step next to Anne.

"Any suggestion I have involves a gun." Quick sat next to Crispy. The three bodies on the step were shoulder-to-shoulder, an impassable barrier. "I told you I wasn't going to call that sneaky bitch *captain* until she earned it."

"Feel that?" Crispy put his hands on the metal step. The ship was vibrating slightly. "We're heading into reentry."

"That means Sunny is pushing through atmosphere, going planetside. Probably going to land us in a circle of acolytes," said Quick. "I hope everyone brought their work gloves, because I have a feeling we're going to end up doing hard labor on an unlisted asteroid."

Pageant bit his lip. He had really hoped time and distance would have made the heart grow softer. Apparently, Sunny had only seen stacks of credits when he appeared before her, and she sold him to the highest bidder without a second thought. Pageant sat on the top step. Collapsed, actually. The strength went out of his legs, and he slid down the door to a sitting position. "We're screwed, aren't we?"

"Guns would mean dying in a hail of glory. The four of us against a platoon of acolytes is not great odds," said Quick. "Even with me going full tilt on them."

"It doesn't have quite the same panache as piloting a ship into another ship." Crispy dropped his head into his hands.

"I dunno," Pageant sighed. His chest felt heavy. Maybe he'd get lucky and die of a heart attack in that moment. He never had much luck, though. "Dead is dead, right? Let's let 'em know they were in a fight, at least. Maybe we get one or two of theirs before we go."

"No." Anne's voice was clear and adamant. "I will surrender peacefully. I will tell them you all were acting under my orders. I will tell them I displayed some form of mind control ability. They'll believe it."

"That's that, then." Pageant was out of ideas and options. His brain was frantically searching for one, but when the universe was against you, there would always come a time to throw up your hands and surrender. This was it. "Might as well make this easy, then. Everyone to the cargo bay. We'll go without a fight." He put a hand on Anne's shoulder. "Sorry, kid. I did my best."

Anne patted his hand. "Thank you, Captain. I appreciate that you tried."

Quick spat on the stairs. "Goddammit, Sunny. I can't believe she sold us out. I swear to all that's holy and unholy, I'm going to put her nose through the back of her head one of these days." She stood and started walking to the cargo bay. The other three followed her. "I can't imagine you ever doing something like that to us, Cap."

"Everyone has their price, Q. Even me. If the credit-count got high enough, who knows what any of us might do. That's just the cost of business."

"I wouldn't sell you out, Cap."

Pageant smiled down at Crispy. "Brothers for life, right?"

"Brothers for life." Crispy held up a fist. Pageant bumped it with his own.

The quartet walked to the cargo bay and waited. Pageant and Quick sat on cargo containers. Crispy sat on the floor next to the container. Anne stood in the center of the bay. The ship rocked a bit beneath them, but the artificial gravity compensators were keeping up with the change between zero G and whatever the G-load was on the planet they were approaching.

There was always a bit of a disconnect between real gravity and compensated gravity aboard a ship. It made people get seasick, sometimes. It was odd how the frictionless, waveless ocean of the Black could get people to heaving.

There was a slight shudder as the *Mary Read* broke through the mesosphere. The ship was engaging manual flight controls. There was a bit of swoop and rock. The grav dampeners were turning off, no longer necessary in atmosphere with at least a half G of gravity.

Crispy was more than used to the timing of ships entering atmosphere. He could feel it in his bones. "Ten minutes to landing."

The two small windows in the cargo bay doors went from black, to a vibrant, fiery, orange-red glow, to brilliant blue. The ship rocked gently, fully moving into standard flight.

"This should be an adventure." Pageant tried to smile and be positive. "We haven't been arrested by a corp before. Threatened with arrest, sure. But really, who among us regular spacers haven't pissed off a corp enough to get threatened with arrest for obstructing business?"

"We can hope we'll be arrested." Quick looked glum. "Anyone know for certain if Sunny filed us as official crew at Ark Eleven? For all we know, people think we're still there, and they could just kill us, toss our bodies into a hot pool or something, and no one will ever be the wiser. We'll just cease to be. The ultimate unhumans."

"I made sure we were on the register. Sunny might have changed it, though." Crispy's tone was flat.

"The important thing is that MannTech will get their prized possession back, right? I hate to think of what they were doing without some poor girl to abuse." Pageant's sarcasm landed on an unappreciative crowd. He looked at the cargo container where Quick's armory was held. Fat lot of good a bunch of guns would do them now.

He looked at Anne Medea. She was still standing, using an arm to support herself against a cargo crate. "I don't suppose you've got any remaining hocus-pocus you can pull out of your proverbial hat, do you?"

She looked to Pageant with mournful eyes. "Sadly, no. I am an empty vessel at the moment. Something might happen should my life be endangered, but outside of that, I just don't know."

Pageant weighed that idea. "We could just pop the seal on the cargo bay doors and see what happens. At our current altitude, it'd at least make landing really tricky."

"Best case scenario if you do that?" asked Quick.

"The Princess of Power over there pulls some magic out of her hat and we all live happily ever after."

"Worst case?"

"The ship tears itself apart, we get sucked out into the ether, and we all die, either from cold, lack of oxygen, or the impact when we hit the ground."

"Five minutes to landing," said Crispy. "We're up the creek this far, we might as well see what happens."

HEAVY FOOTFALLS SOUNDED on the metal grating of the stairs. Seconds later, Norman entered the cargo bay with a large Blueskill Gauss Rifle in his arms. It was a large gun that usually demanded some sort of mounting base for an average man to use, but Norman toted it easily. "Hello, friends!" His smile was unblemished. "Sorry about all this. I would have preferred to do this a different way, but I'm not the captain."

"Did you know from the start?" asked Pageant. "Did you know she was going to sell us out?"

Norman's smile lessened. "Unfortunately. Not much could be done about it, though. Her hands were tied."

"I'm sure they were," said Quick. "How much did MannTech offer her?"

Norman's smiled faded completely. He was stone-faced. The spirited light in his eyes disappeared. "Not everything is about money, Ms. Huffman."

The ship rocked again and settled. There was a subtle rocking in Crispy's stomach that let him know the ship had landed. The Jubilee-class vessels had elegant planetside landing gear that extended out from the lower body like a four spider legs to support the vessel. Crispy pulled himself to his feet. "Here we go. If they kill us outright, just know that I'm happy to die with you two by my side."

"Back at you, Shrimp," said Quick.

Moments later, Sunny Yeong entered the cargo bay, a slim Mesk-Ebon DC-15 leveled in front of her. Her face was solemn, emotionless. "I'm sorry, Nate. You didn't deserve this."

"There's a lot I don't deserve." Pageant pulled his sidearm and tossed it to the metal grating. He raised his hands. "Doesn't stop the universe from dropping it in my lap repeatedly, though."

"Crispy, Quick—you don't have to be a part of this." Sunny looked at her former crew mates. "They just want Pageant and the girl."

Quick spoke first. "I'll go with the captain, thanks." She dropped her Mengler and raised her hands.

Crispy looked to Pageant, and then to Sunny. He had no beef with Sunny. They had always gotten along brilliantly. When she was on the Opal, they'd had a lot of laughs. She protected him from bullies in bars. She was like his sister. Until her whole falling out with Pageant, she had been one of his best—nay, only—friends. There was a small piece of him that was tempted to stay on ship. He could get used to piloting a Jubilee-class attack vessel. When it came down to it, however, he knew where his loyalty stood. "Sorry, Sunny. I gotta go with the captain, too." He had left his sidearm in his berth, so he just raised his hands.

Sunny's mouth curled into a pained smile. "I knew you would. Both of you. I don't blame you one bit. Nathan Pageant gets under your skin. I get it."

Norman released the cargo door. The hydraulics engaged and began to lower the gate. The cargo bay flooded with the planet's air. It smelled rich and damp. A rainforest, perhaps. The air was hot and thick with a choking humidity. Instantly, everyone began to sweat.

The cargo door continued downward, becoming a ramp to the outside. Pageant strode forward, not waiting for Sunny to tell him what to do. Crispy followed. Quick, too. Anne followed Quick, her face cast down toward her shoes, tears rolling down her cheeks.

The ship was parked in a large clearing in a jungle somewhere. The clearing was surrounded by thick, broad-leafed plants and trees with draping limbs covered in vibrant, green leaves. Mossy tendrils hung from branches like green tinsel. Strange birds and bugs flitted about. They were alien creatures, unlike anything the crew had ever seen. That meant the planet had not been terraformed, it was natural. In the distance, larger, unseen alien creatures made horrible-sounding noises which sent skittering creeps up Crispy's spine.

A large, but dim moon was visible above them, despite the clear, bright daylight. The air tasted of wetness and loam. It was pleasant and heady. If he lived through whatever was coming next, Crispy hoped he might return to this planet someday. It might make for a good spot to relax and recreate for a time.

In a large semi-circle around the tail end of the Mary Read, at least two dozen MannTech acolytes in jungle khakis and red MannTech ball caps were holding standard-issue pop rifles. Commander Reesha Neer stood apart from the soldiers. She was hatless and wearing her command uniform. Beads of sweat dotted her forehead. Everyone had dark sweat stains on their uniforms.

Pageant went full bravado mode. He plastered his biggest, cheesiest smile onto his face. "Reesha! Me, Quick, and Crispy were just talking about you. Crispy was just saying we should give you a call, and then we should all take some R'n'R together someplace warm, and wouldn't you know it, here you already are. Speak of the devil, am I right?"

"Cuff them." Neer nodded at one of the riflemen. He leapt out of line and pulled a handful of metal shackles from a pouch at his hip. He took a step toward Pageant. Sunny pulled the trigger on her DC-15. It piped out a single blast at the feet of the soldier. Instantly, all two-dozen pop rifles were pointed at them, a cadre of soldiers just waiting for the command to kill.

"We had a deal, Captain Yeong," said Neer.

"And I am holding up my end of it. You don't get what you want until I get what I want." Sunny pointed her gun at the head of Anne Medea. "I want what you promised. Now."

Crispy had never seen Sunny look so serious or intense. Her eyes were positively black. There was a hatred in her face Crispy had not known Sunny to be capable of showing. She looked like a demon.

"I hope you sold us out for proper credits, Sunny," said Pageant. "I'd hate to be tortured or killed for a few measly bits."

Crispy watched Sunny's face. She did not see or hear Pageant. She was staring directly at Neer. For a moment, Crispy wondered if Sunny was going to kill the commander. There was a palpable tension between the two women.

"You'd put your life, your ship at risk like this?" said Neer.

Sunny's voice was steel. "I want what was promised. That's all. When I get mine, you can take what you need." She pushed her gun into the back of Anne's head. "So help me, I will end her right here and now. Push me further and I'll detonate my ship and level everything inside of three kilometers, including you." To show she was not playing, Sunny held up her left hand. A blinking radio detonator was in her fist. All she had to do was press a button and the *Mary Read* would simply explode. The assembled parties would not even have time to blink before they were vaporized in a burst of white hot light.

After a long moment, Neer conceded. She whispered something to the nearest soldier. He shouldered his rifle and disappeared into the nearby trees. The soldier emerged with an older Asian woman and a young girl in tow. The woman was cuffed. The girl was not. The girl saw Sunny, and her face lit up like fireworks. "Mommy!"

The sight of the girl was a punch to Crispy's heart. The raven-black hair and dark eyes were clearly Sunny's. Everything else, from the ears, to the slightly Roman nose, to her thin lips, to the shape of her chin were clearly Nathan Pageant. It was undeniable. She looked to be about four years old. If Sunny had gotten pregnant just before she and Pageant broke up, the timing fit.

The devil-may-care mask Pageant liked to wear in times of stress melted from his face. His jaw wavered. His breath came out in a slow shudder. "Sunny, whose kid is—" He could not form the words. He already knew.

"She's my daughter. Mine, and mine alone." Sunny kept the gun on the back of Anne's head. She gave the little girl a brave smile. "Come here, baby."

The little girl broke free from the line of soldiers without a second thought. She charged up the ramp, dodging between Pageant and Crispy as she did. Sunny dropped her pistol into the holster on her hip and she swept the little girl into her arms. They hugged each other fiercely. Sunny clutched the back of the little girl's head, burying the child's face into her neck.

Sunny nodded to Neer. "Take them."

The soldier with the cuffs ran up the ramp. He started with Anne Medea, cuffing her, then dropping a heavy sack of black cloth over her head to blindfold her. Another acolyte administered a shot to Anne's neck with a silver hypo-spray. Anne's legs went limp and she collapsed into the arms of the soldier. Quick, Crispy, and Pageant were all cuffed but were not afforded blindfolds. Soldiers strode up the ramp and dragged them to the planet surface by their elbows. The three crew members of the Shy Opal had no choice but to do as they were told.

The elderly woman was released by the soldiers. She limped up the ramp, smiling bravely at Sunny. "I'm well enough."

Pageant called back to her. "Sunny, that's my—"

"She's none of your concern, Nathan. Please, respect my wishes on this."

"What about my wishes, Sunny?"

"They don't matter. When you're a parent, you learn your child comes first. Always. Your wishes, my wishes—they're unimportant, they don't matter. It's about what's best for my little girl." Sunny turned to walk back into the *Mary Read*. Sunny's emphasis on the word my further drove home the fact that Pageant's contribution to the child's life was complete. Norman gave Pageant a sad wave and a sympathetic shrug. The cargo doors began to close.

"At least tell me her name."

Sunny froze. She turned to face Pageant, the girl still clutched to her chest. The doors were closing rapidly. Pageant could see her lower eyelids glistening with tears. Sunny hesitated. "Opal. Her name is Opal."

Of course it was.

It was the perfect name. It was the name of the only thing, besides possibly Sunny herself, Nathan Pageant ever truly loved.

15

NATHAN PAGEANT WAS utterly deflated. He was not certain what to feel. He was not sure he could feel anything but numb. How is one supposed to process the news that not only did one father a child with his former lover, but that child's mother wanted him to have nothing to do with the child?

In the distance, as if to punctuate that point, the sound of *Mary Read's* engines firing for liftoff reverberated through the jungle. Alien animals scattered for cover. The canopy overhead was too thick to watch the ship depart, but Pageant could hear the engine whine. They were shooting straight up to break orbit. They were leaving.

"They've got all our stuff." Quick was looking toward the sound of the ship. "I suppose that means we probably won't be needing it where we're heading."

"Good," said Crispy. "I was tired of changing my underwear every day."

"As if you ever changed it every day." Pageant could not help himself.

"What are you doing looking at my undies, Cap?"

"I was trying to figure out why they had a hole in the front of them. Figured you sat down to pee."

"Only when the urinals are too high," said Crispy.

"That's horseshit. I piss standing up more frequently than you," said Quick.

Pageant chuckled. He knew what Crispy and Quick were doing. Spacer humor. Laugh in the face of doom. No one in the Black took life too seriously unless, like the corp soldiers around them, they were being paid to take it seriously. It was also obvious that they were making jokes because neither of them wanted to broach the elephant in the room. Pageant needed to break the silence on that for himself. He blew out a long breath. "So...I guess I have a daughter."

"Was that what she was?" said Quick. "Figured Sunny shaved down a monkey or something."

"Did either of you two know about her?"

Crispy shook his head. "Secret like that is too big to keep, Cap. I would have told you. For the right price, at least."

"Cute kid," said Quick. "Even though she looks like her father."

"Yeah, no paternity test needed for that one, Cap."

"Guess not." Pageant rocked into Crispy with his shoulder. "I wish I had a cigar to hand out." A heavy feeling settled in Pageant's chest at that moment, a thick sadness. He wasn't someone who cried, but he felt like he was close to doing it. "Do you think Sunny would have ever mentioned the girl to me? Like, would she have sent me a message over subspace, ever? Do you think the girl would have gone her whole life without knowing me?"

"Probably," said Quick. "You basically told Sunny she'd stabbed you in the heart and committed mutiny when she bought that ship behind your back. Said you never wanted to see her again, not for business or pleasure. Words like that do have a tendency to taint a woman's heart. Especially a pregnant gal."

"I hadn't meant it literally." Pageant heaved a sigh. "Man, I was dumb." What was that stupid adage his old man used to say? *Only through the lens of age are we truly privy to our youthful stupidity.* The old man was not right about everything, but he nailed that one.

The acolytes finished loading Anne Medea's unconscious body onto a hover-skiff, a low, flat, floating platform used for moving heavy goods. They had secured her to it with plastic ties. Commander Neer gave a sign with her finger and the acolytes started moving out. They walked next to the skiff, guiding it through the waist-high brush.

Neer turned to address *Shy Opal's* crew. "You don't seem concerned about your current situation." She drew herself to her full height and stood ramrod straight, as military as she could be.

Pageant shrugged. "We try not to get too concerned about much. It's not worth it, really."

"Really? I'd be worried if I were in your place. You lost your sad little ship. You were betrayed by an old lover. You lost the girl you seemed to be willing to give your life to protect. You're about to get your crew killed. You're about to die yourself. If I were you, I would be *extremely* worried." Neer's tone was dripping with self-righteousness. It was obvious she enjoyed being in a position of control. She enjoyed seeing people held powerless

127

before her. She would not be the first paramilitary officer granted a ship who let that position go to her head. Pageant figured a willingness to watch others suffer was mandatory for corporation officers.

Pageant had no time for such martinets. He faked a theatrical yawn. "Are you done yet? Honestly, I stopped listening after the first sentence."

"I was still listening, Commander." Crispy gave the woman a toothy, clownish grin. "You have a lovely speaking voice."

"Your bravado is truly admirable." Neer's face remained impassive, as if ordering a few murders was a common occurrence for her.

"It's not bravado, Commander." Pageant eased himself to a sitting position. "It's just common sense. You see, I know two things you don't know."

"Oh?" Neer was amused by this. "Do tell, Mr. Pageant."

"You can call me Nathan. I don't mind."

Neer refused to play his game. She remained silent.

Pageant shrugged again. "Well, the first thing is this: you took Sunny Yeong's daughter. You dared to touch something Sunny loved so much she'd trade over three people with whom she has years of history without so much as a thought. That tells me that you don't know anything about Sunny Yeong."

"We know her, Mr. Pageant. That's why we took her daughter. We knew you would seek her out at Port 1131, and we knew she would give you up to us."

"No, I'm saying that you don't *know* Sunny Yeong. You have no idea where she is now. You just let her take her kid and go. That might have been the dumbest thing you could do. I guarantee you she is only going far enough to ditch her daughter someplace safe, and then she's bringing that little Jubilee attack ship of hers back here with guns blazing to rain an awful amount of hell upon you and yours. And she'll do it with a smile on her face and sleep well afterward. You kicked a hornet's nest there, Captain."

"The *Despair* can handle a Jubilee."

Pageant pretended to do some mental calculations. "You know, I don't think it can. Not when the Jubilee is being commanded by an angry Yeong Sun-hee. She's going to push that ship beyond all its capabilities to make it do things you've never seen before."

"I very much doubt that."

Pageant kept talking. "You ever see a thin guy fight a big fat guy? The thin guy just has to keep dodging and moving. Soon enough, that fat guy gets tired and the thin guy lets him have it. That's how it's going to be for your ship. The Cerberus packs a wallop, but it can't keep up with a Jubilee. She's going to dodge and jab until that tank of yours is fully incapacitated. Your boat is going to look like Swiss cheese before you can get off a tracking round."

"One good hit is all I'll need, Captain. One good hit will disable her vessel if she's stupid enough to try to take on the *Despair*."

"I'm gonna bet you won't get that hit. Besides, you'll be too busy down here to command the ship. I hope your second-in-command knows what he's doing. Do you trust him to keep your ship safe?"

"I'll keep my ship safe, Mr. Pageant."

Pageant cocked his head. "No, you won't. Like I said, you'll be too busy right here. That's because of the second thing I know that you don't."

"And that would be?" Neer matched the tilt of Pageant's head with her own. She was amused by the handcuffed man's attitude.

"The second thing I know is that Quick Huffman is going to do a thing."

"Is she now?" Neer held back a chuckle.

"Do I have to?" Quick's lip curled with distaste.

"Do you see any other choices I don't?" Pageant looked at the empty clearing around them and the jungle beyond. "We don't have a lot of options, here."

"What is this *thing* you speak of, Mr. Pageant?"

"I hate doing the thing," said Quick.

"I know, but it's what you're best at."

"I'd like to think I have more to offer than just the thing."

Neer stepped toward Quick. "What thing?"

"Fine, I'll do the thing." Quick gave an exasperated sigh. She raised her hands to claw a loose tendril of hair from her face.

"What thing?" Neer's voice dripped with venom.

Crispy took a step backward and squatted down. He lifted his hands to cover his face.

Like a bolt of lightning, Quick moved in a single, fluid movement almost too fast to see, definitely too fast to process. She jerked her hands apart blowing the plastic-strap cuffs from her wrists like they were paper. She moved at the acolyte to her right, stepped to the side of the gun he held on a strap around his chest and fired it. The bolt hit the other acolyte in the head dropping him instantly. She spun on her heel and drove her left elbow into the first acolyte's temple, a clack of metal against bone echoed off the trees around them. The acolyte dropped to his knees, eyes rolling back in his head.

At this point, the acolytes escorting Anne's hover-skiff heard the shot and saw the commotion. Quick held her left arm out making a fist with her left hand. There was a loud click as her fist detached entirely from her arm and flew at the acolytes. It smashed into the ground at their feet.

No one moved for a moment, and then the fist exploded.

The explosion was a concussive blast. A wave rippled out of the central point and sent acolytes flying. The hover-skiff was rocked hard, but the gyros that kept it level compensated. Anne's body lolled a bit, but she was tied down, and she stayed on the unit.

Quick unsnapped the gun from the strap around the unconscious acolyte. She put a bullet in his head. Then, one by one, she sighted down the barrel and started executing acolytes who lay stunned on the ground by the hover-skiff.

Commander Neer moved to try to stop her, but Pageant took two steps, slid at her, and knocked her to the ground with a scissor kick that took her legs out from beneath her. Crispy leaped into action, falling onto the commander's back and using his cuffed hands on the back of her neck to pin her head to the ground.

Pageant's next sentence was punctuated with the sound of rifle fire. "You know, the best thing about military corp acolyte units is they're not jailers. They're paid, but they're only paid to do their job and only their job. They're good killers, but not so good at reading dossiers. If they had read the dossier I know the corps have on Natalie Huffman, they would have known to never let her have her hands in front of her, number one. And number two, they would have known to put her in an EMP cuff, lest she use some of her expensive cybernetic enhancements to fuck up their world."

"Golly, Cap, you know how to make a girl blush." Quick finished executing the acolytes with a final pull of the trigger. She cast the empty weapon aside and grabbed a few rifles from the scattered corpses to arm her friends. Her left arm ended in a jagged mesh of Sofskin and metal. She shook her stump. "Probably going to be awhile before I get a new hand, isn't it?"

"We'll take it out of discretionary funds as soon as we get some discretionary funds." Pageant fumbled through Neer's pockets until he found the remote for the cuffs. He pressed the button to emit a sonic signal unlocking his and Crispy's restraints. The cuffs popped open, and the crew of the *Shy Opal* was free.

Quick tossed Pageant an acolyte's rifle. She handed one to Crispy. He shortened the strap to its smallest setting and slung it over his shoulder. Quick pointed her gun at Commander Neer's back. "You want I should put cuffs on her, or should I just kill her and call it a day?"

"Killing is a bit much, Quick. As far as the cuffs—I don't think she needs them, do you? I think after witnessing what you're capable of doing, she's not going to be inclined to try anything."

Nathan Pageant stuck out his hand to help Neer to her feet. "Commander Reesha Neer, I am Nathan Pageant, Captain of the STS *Shy Opal*. You are now my prisoner. Rest assured, we aboard the *Opal* uphold the conventions of wartime and follow the unwritten ethics of interstellar travel. You will not be harmed unless you make it so we must harm you to prevent damage to our ship and crew."

Neer refused Pageant's help to stand. She rolled to her feet and glared at him. "Stow it, Mr. Pageant."

Pageant waved the barrel of his gun in a circle. "Tut-tut, Commander. I have a gun. You are my prisoner. I get to decide my rank."

Neer rolled her eyes. She spit the term out with all the disgust she could muster. "As you wish, *Captain*. I surrender. However, when my crew realizes we are delayed, they will send down teams to find me."

Pageant took the MannTech communicator from Neer's pocket and crushed it beneath the hell of his boot. "I imagine they will have their hands full by then. I have no doubt that Sunny Yeong will have returned."

"THAT WENT BETTER than expected, didn't it?"

"You can say that 'cause you still got two hands." Quick walked two paces behind Pageant. The acolyte pop rifle dangled from her right shoulder, her hand resting on the grip.

Pageant was pushing the hover-skiff. Anne Medea was still unconscious on it, but Quick had removed her cuffs and hood and cut the plastic straps tying her down. Reesha Neer sat on the front of the skiff where Pageant had told her to sit. Pageant considered putting cuffs on her, but figured they would be more trouble than it was worth in the end. She was alone and unarmed on an uninhabited planet's surface with no way to contact her ship. She was not about to run off, especially not with an enhanced dead-eye like Quick Huffman packing a rifle behind her.

"Why would you have gone through all the trouble to outfit your cybernetically-enhanced arm with a concussion grenade if you had no desire to actually use it?" Crispy waded through the jungle brush, stomping the large plants aside with his feet to clear a path for the skiff. It was slow going. He was sweating profusely. Years of sitting in a pilot's chair had done little for his cardio fitness. Also, the jungle was a sauna. When a body is used to the constant, comfortable temps and moderate humidity in climate-controlled atmo aboard ship, going planetside someplace with temps approaching 35 Celsius and one hundred percent humidity was a real kick in the sweetmeats.

Quick ignored Crispy's jibe. "Cap, why are we bringing Princess Prissy up there with us? And why does she get to ride the skiff? If you'd let me shoot her, I could ride the skiff. I think that's a suitable exchange for me losing my hand." She wiped sweat from her eyes with her left wrist.

"Now, now, Quick. Is that any way to treat our guest?"

"Is that what she is now?"

"You could have left me with my men, Captain." Neer's voice was flat and emotionless. "I would have been fine."

"You would have used their radios to call for help." Pageant had shed his tac-jacket and his shirt hung open exposing his upper body. He was glossy with sweat. He wished he still had the physique he'd had twenty years ago. It probably would have looked pretty impressive to be covered in a sheen of sweat back then, back when he still had defined abdominal muscles and pectorals cut from a hardscrabble life of fighting, hard labor, and missed meals.

"If you brought me along thinking that I will be a bargaining chip, you're sadly mistaken. My second-in-command would bomb this area to kill you knowing my death would only bring him a promotion." Commander Neer turned on the skiff to face Pageant. "I was happy to be in command of a ship, but that little social-climber wants to be a vice president of MannTech. Killing you would look good on his resume."

Pageant was unbothered. "Killing me, sure. Killing Anne would probably get him tossed into the brig."

"Her name is not Anne." Neer's eyebrow raised. "She is a project. That is all. Don't get attached to her, Pageant."

"Why don't we talk about that, then? What the fuck is she? We know she's not normal."

"She is a project. That's all I know."

"Quick, shoot the esteemed Commander in the foot."

Quick pulled her rifle up balancing the end on her left forearm. "With pleasure."

Neer quickly shifted position to hide her feet from Quick's view. "What? Why? What did I do?"

"Tell me about Anne. What do you know?"

Neer's voice pitched upward, slightly panicked. "She is a project. That's all I know. I just told you that."

Quick lowered the barrel of the gun. "I think she's telling the truth, Cap."

"Of course she is. She's just a gunship commander. They wouldn't let her into the upper echelons of research and development, and they sure as hell wouldn't tell her anything truly important. That's need-to-know only, and Neer does not need to know."

"Then why'd you want me to shoot her in the foot?"

"Just so she'd know I wasn't kidding around. I know she's only a gunship commander, but I also know that you don't get to run something like a Cerberus by being obedient and playing dumb. She knows more than she lets on. No matter how good the pay is, you don't dog out your ship for a mod-test unless she's far more valuable than just being a simple mod-test. I think Neer did her homework on the sly. I think the good Commander has contacts in high places and used secret messaging apps to find out the goods. Neer knows what she is, I'm thinking. I'm willing to bet a smoking hole in her foot will jog her memory." Pageant paused to wipe a layer of sweat from his face. "Shoot her, Q."

Quick shrugged and leveled the weapon toward Neer's foot, which was hidden behind her leg. "I'll go through the shin of your left leg to hit your right foot, Commander. Won't bother me a lick." Quick held up her left arm and waved the mechanical nub at her wrist in a circle. There were several pockmarked scars in her real flesh. "I know what blaster rifles feel like, Commander. Believe me, it will be a lot better to just take the hole in the foot like a trooper."

"Shooting me would be an act of war."

Pageant resumed pushing the skiff through the jungle brush. "You're not a military soldier, and even if you were, your rank is too low to sign the declaration anyhow. You're a privateer, Commander. Paramilitary in the employ of MannTech. A corp can only declare war on another corp, and my little ship and this little crew is not a corp. Try again."

"I honestly don't know if declaring war on me—"

A blast erupted from Quick's rifle. The bolt whizzed past Neer's ear and hit a tree behind her. A bunch of alien birds scattered, all whoops and screeches. Quick put her right hand over her mouth in a coquettish fashion like a girl flirting at a bar. "Oops! Did I do that?"

"If you plan to just kill me, do it already, Captain." Neer folded her hands over her chest. She set her face as a stoic mask. "I do not fear death."

"No one fears death, really," said Pageant. "Death is inevitable, so why bother to fear it? Now, pain—people really fear pain. When they talk about fearing death, that's what they really mean. They mean, *I hope it doesn't hurt.* If I let Quick shoot you in the foot, you'll know pain. If you still don't talk, I'll let Quick shoot your other foot. Then your hands. Then your forearms, calves, and so on and etcetera. You'll know pain, Commander. You'll know it all too well. Do you know why corps like MannTech use torture? Because it fucking works. Now, stop trying to change the subject. Tell me about the tattoo on Anne's neck. What does *PR-ARC346* mean?"

Neer finally relented. "It's a researcher's filing system. PR stands for *Project.* The rest is just science gibberish for keeping things straight. It's a bar code for making record-keeping easier."

"I'll believe that for now. How did she make my ship invisible?"

Neer shook her head. "If you're asking for a description of her abilities, I cannot help you. That's classified, even to me. I saw what you saw. One second, you were barreling your stupid rustbucket at my bridge, and the next—*poof!* You were gone. We hightailed it for Port 1131 knowing that was the only place you could make a jump, but when you weren't there, we found Sunny Yeong and pressed her into service. Given that she owed MannTech a little money from an escort mission gone bad, we figured it would make us even." Neer slapped at some sort of alien bug attempting to crawl into her ear. "If if helps you sleep better, Sunny refused to double-cross you at first. That's why we had to take her daughter and her aunt."

Crispy broke through a section of jungle to a clearing. Across the clearing was a large earth and stone rise dotted with crags and gaps. "Cap, I think I found a cave."

"A cave will hide us from long-scanners, Cap. At least the ones from orbit. They'll have to get closer to get anything handheld to find us." Quick pushed past the skiff and into the clearing. She scanned the cliff face with her modded eye. "A couple of nice possibilities up there."

Pageant was not a fan of caves. He could never shake the sense they were going to collapse on him. However, he found no fear in getting into a upholstered tin can strapped to two nuclear bombs and slipping through a rift in space and time in sheer defiance of practical physics. Fear was funny that way.

The caves would be safe from weather and beasts, and it would give them a decent spot from which to mount a defense if it came to that. He had little choice. "Let's do that, then. We'll head for the caves. Crispy, see if you can find enough dry wood in this hell of humidity to make a fire. Quick, you're on flora and fauna. Find us something to eat. Try not to poison us."

"What about me?" Neer slid off the skiff to the ground. "What can I do?"

"You sit tight. You can help me get Anne into the cave. Whatever you stung her with to put her out must be super effective. She heals fast; she expelled a Doc in less than a few hours."

"A Doc?"

"One of those alien slugs that knits tissue."

Neer was impressed. Her eyes widened. "A verillian? Really? You use those still?"

"Most of us poor spacers do, Commander. We don't have the wealth of a major industrialist like Shea Mannion at our disposal."

Pageant and Neer walked the skiff to the mouth of the nearest cave. Neer walked forward and sniffed. "It smells in here."

There was a low scent of ammonia coming from somewhere deep in the cave. That usually meant animal urine. It stung Pageant's nostrils. "You got a glow stick?"

"There might be something in the drawers of the skiff." Neer started sorting through drawers that lined the edge of the floating platform. She came up with a dark blue plastic tube. When she cracked it on her thigh it flared to life with a brilliant blue-white light. Even in the light of the fading afternoon sun Pageant had to squint when he looked at it.

"That's mighty bright."

"MannTech makes quality gear." Neer walked into the cave holding the flare aloft. Its clean, bright light illuminated the cavern beyond the mouth. The cave was solid and lined with rough volcanic rock. "This looks like it was a leak hole from a magma uprising long ago."

"Press in a little further. See if there's anything for us to worry about in there." Pageant pushed the hover-skiff just inside the cave mouth and followed after Neer, his rifle held loosely in his hands.

"I don't see anything." Neer took a few more steps. The smell of ammonia was getting stronger. In the dark, there was a sound, a strange rustling noise.

Pageant did not know what made the noise, but it triggered something deeply primordial in him, a fight or flight instinct ingrained in humans for eons, something rooted in his DNA, a gift from Neanderthal ancestors tens of thousands of years ago. Pageant knew what was going to happen even before he could see the beast coming.

There was no time to act, no time to even shout. Neer was between him and the beast, so he could not even shoot the pop rifle he carried. Without time to consider a better option, Pageant launched himself at Commander Neer's legs, kicking the back of her knees and collapsing her to the ground. She landed on top of him a split-second before something blasted out of the darkness. A rippling mass of muscle and fur leapt over them, claws bared.

The beast landed near the mouth of the cave and turned in a hard half-circle, smashing into the levitating gurney as it did and sending the still-unconscious Anne spinning out into the jungle sun.

The alien creature was cat-like in many regards, with a body and head shape vaguely resembling a mountain lion, but it was thicker and far larger, a puma built like a bison. The animal was covered with short, sleek black fur everywhere but a wide, flat swath across its face where it looked like it had a thick, bony protrusion protecting a glossy black organ of some sort. The creature's face was angled and cunning. The thin, amber eyes on the sides of its head narrowed as it sized up its prey, a low, guttural clicking coming from deep within its belly.

Pageant threw Neer off him roughly. No time for courtesy or gentlemanly deference. He rolled to a knee. He sighted down the pop rifle's barrel and pulled the trigger. The gun clicked, but did not fire. "What the hell?" Pageant yanked the magazine from the receiver to check it.

"Proximity sensors." Neer picked up a fist-sized rock from the floor of the cave. "The man who carried that guy enacted a proximity sensor that would brick the gun if you moved too far from his ID chip. Not all the men use them, but many do."

"So, basically I have an expensive club?"

"Yes, swing it." Neer threw the rock and it thumped dully off of the beast's bony shield.

The cat-like thing made a harsh sound somewhere between a sneeze and a snort. It lowered its head like a rhinocerous and charged Neer.

Pageant threw himself at the animal, inserting himself between the beast and Neer. The sudden change in targets threw the cat off just enough to confuse it. It did not lash out with the powerful front claws, and instead bowled into Pageant with its bony head. It was like getting hit by a lumber truck. The breath flew out of Pageant's lungs, and he landed flat on his back groaning for air. The cat, off-balance, twisted and snarled. It landed awkwardly and rolled once.

Pageant had just enough oxygen in his lungs to grunt, "Run!"

Neer fled from the cat, running from the tunnel and screaming for Quick.

Quick was only fifty yards from the mouth of the cave, but she might as well have been halfway to the next galaxy. She saw Neer scrambling and calling for help, and then saw the cat. She had the gun up and sighted in the blink of an eye, balancing the barrel on the back of her left wrist, but the pop rifle she carried was every bit as dead as the one that failed Pageant. It clicked, and Quick knew exactly why. She was almost out of cyborg tricks, and had nothing left in her that would be effective at fifty yards. Regardless, she was still dangerous. She sprinted at the cat, head down, arms pumping.

Neer was desperate for a weapon of any sort—a tree bough, a good-sized rock, anything. She scrambled toward the nearest trees. Maybe, if nothing else was available, she could be the weasel around the mulberry bush and put a tree between her and the animal to keep the beast from getting a clean shot.

The cat was too fast, though. It caught up to Neer in a heartbeat and slashed at the back of her leg. Neer felt white-hot claws slice through her right calf muscle. She cried out and fell, her leg unable to bear her weight any longer. Blood gushed from the wound.

The cat was on top of her in an instant. Neer was somehow able to roll to her back and throw up her right forearm. The cat's strange, wide mouth engulfed her arm. Needle-sharp teeth sank into her flesh.

At full sprint, Quick slammed into the cat's side. The cat, surprised, released Neer's arm and leaped to the side. Holding the gun barrel in her right hand like a sword, Quick swung a home-run shot and slammed the butt of the gun into the animal's right eye. The inexpensive merc gun snapped at the point where the Plazsteel stock joined the metal of the body. Those guns were never meant to be clubs. Now she had a blunt steel end with a few stray jags of metal and wood. That was a weapon worthy of Quick Huffman.

With her cybernetically-enhanced eye coordinating her muscles with her brain, Quick's hand-eye coordination was superior to just about anyone else in the Black. She saw the creature's closed, right eye, damaged from the impact with the butt of the gun, and she struck again, slashing the ugly end of the gun across the creature's eyelid, gouging its flesh deeply. Its blood, purple-black, flowed freely. Every living thing the whole universe over had one commonality: eyes were always a weak point.

The bison-cat reared back on its shorter hind legs, powerful forelegs swinging and clawing. The cat beast whirled and charged Quick. Caught in the open space between the rocky caves and the thick trees, Quick had only the broken rifle to defend herself. She swung it, aiming at the other eye, but the cat was ready for it, deflecting the rifle away with the bony plate on its head and then smashing into Quick and driving her into the ground.

Immediately, Quick brought up her left arm and defended her face and neck from the animal's teeth. Quick discharged one of her last tricks. In the flat, metal end of her stump, there was a small amount of Neu-tox sleeping gas. It was meant to disable a single target the size of a standard human male. She knew the dose would not be as effective on a massive creature like this alien predator, but she had nothing else. She shot the whole charge into the animal's throat.

The cat responded negatively to the taste. It backed away from Quick's prone form, coughing violently. Its tongue smacked around its maw as it tried to cleanse its palate. The Neu-tox must have burned the thing's throat, and it gave a raspy snarl in a furtive attempt to stop the burning. When the burning did not stop, the cat doubled-down on its anger toward Quick and lunged at her.

Quick had barely gotten to her feet. The cat leaped, and she could only try to dive to the side. It did not work as well as she would have hoped. The cat adjusted mid-jump, and one of its long, powerful forelegs landed hard on Quick. Thick talons dug into Quick's back, the weight of the animal pinning her to the ground. Quick could only give a strangled cry of pain.

At the mouth of the cave, Pageant could only look on helplessly. Neer was incapacitated. Crispy was nowhere to be seen, off in the jungle gathering sticks for a fire.

Quick was out of useful cyborg tricks. She had nothing left. She tried to push the cat off her, but it was far too heavy for her to move. She could feel its breath on her upper back, warm and fetid. She waited for the killing bite to sink into the back of her neck and snap her spine.

Before the cat could bite, Quick heard another sound. The cat grunted and gurgled. It sagged, all force draining from its muscles instantly. The cat-creature was dead, but it did not fall on her. She was still pinned by its heavy, lifeless leg, but she would live.

A large spear made of golden light pierced the cat through its chest driving into the ground on one side of it, keeping it propped up. A short distance away, Anne Medea stood next to the skiff with a gauzy, butterfly-wing mask of shimmering black over her eyes.

Pageant hustled to the cat, dragging Quick from under its foot. Quick stood, wincing in pain. Several wounds on her back bled freely. She and Pageant turned to Anne and stared at her. Pageant ran a hand through his sweaty hair and shook his head slowly. "What the hell are you, lady?"

On the ground, a wide-eyed Reesha Neer had seen Anne wake up on the gurney, see what was transpiring, and then watched in awe as the woman manifested the spear from nothing and hurled it through the side of the cat to save Quick Huffman.

Neer could only gape at Anne like a fish. "It's true. It's all true."

Crispy Okino emerged from the jungle edge with a big armful of sticks and tinder clutched to his chest. He looked at the dead cat, the spear, the space witch, and the blood coming from Quick's back and Neer's leg. He dropped the sticks. "What the fuck did I miss?"

The lance of light disappeared, and the cat-bison beast dropped to the ground, a harmless lump of dead muscle and fur.

16

DEEP IN THE belly of the STS *Shy Opal*, the little rover scanned its work with a deep sense of satisfaction.

Well, not satisfaction, as a human would know it. The little creature was only a construct, a finely programmed robot with no true emotions that could be understood on a human level, but it was as close to the human emotion of satisfaction as the little bot could manifest in its subroutines and protocols. If the little bot was more aware of humanity and the wealth and spectrum of emotions it possessed, the rover would have found the term for satisfaction and claimed it as the closest term to match what it was feeling. Instead, it experienced a binary rush of emotion-like charges, something deep within it gave it a tingle through its various servos and processors to let it know that it had accomplished something big and important.

Before it, in the little flat area of the deepest part of the engine core, the rover had constructed three small rovers with various bits of metal, wires, and assorted parts culled from the ship over the decades. They were not pretty nor sleek. They were little Frankenstein bots, a mishmash of metals and colors, all jags and odd angles, but they *worked*, and that was the only important thing. They were programmed. They could learn. They were ready to fix the ship.

The power cells for the other rovers had been the most difficult things to acquire. There were no spare power cells aboard the ship, and the rover could not manufacture them on his own. Instead, the rover spliced into the space station's central transaction hub and used a strain of viral code to misdirect three K-level power cells to the cargo hold of *Shy Opal.* A cargo drone dropped them off minutes later. On a station as big as Ark Eleven, with as much repair work as there was constantly underway, three tiny power cells would never be missed or noted.

It had taken the better part of a day to build the little cadre of rovers, but the original rover, or R1 as the other three bots had taken to calling it, had decided more bots were a necessity to repair the ship. Rovers were expensive and *Shy Opal's* cred-counter was almost empty. There was no way it could have simply purchased more bots.

It had considered trying to code-splice the station, but rovers were not a simple commodity like power cells. R1 knew sending rovers to the ship would have raised suspicions. Rovers were expensive, and it was only the biggest ships that had more than one. A little STS like *Shy Opal* certainly would never have several, no matter how badly they were needed.

The three other rovers, R2, R3, and R4, were not nearly as intricate as R1. They could not think independently beyond a base level of assessment and suggestions for repairs. They had spun through the ship for their initial test run, saw the damage, and figured more of them would be necessary to repair the sheer volume of destruction in the ship.

The three new Rovers sat awaiting direct orders. Their little internal processors were command-and-go. They could not anticipate. They could not read emergency squalls from the ship's central computer brain. For R1, this was not a problem. After almost three centuries aboard *Shy Opal*, it had begun to see the ship as a larger extension of itself. When the ship hurt, it hurt, too.

The ship was still blaring error messages and emergency warnings through the data stream R1 was monitoring. It was begging for assistance. R1 knew that someone—some*thing*—had to help it. Without the necessary creds to get the old ship professional help, the rovers were the only aid available.

First thing was first: wiring. Anywhere there was destroyed wires needed to be repaired. The wiring harnesses aboard any space-going vessel were extensive. For every system, there were miles upon miles of wires. The wires ran from the central processor of the ship to every extremity. Without wires, the ship had no nervous system. It was paralyzed. The wires needed to be repaired or replaced so the central hub could begin understanding what was truly wrong with it.

The little rover platoon was given their instructions by R1: *repair wires.* Their limited processors could handle that command, and they attacked that command like good soldiers. They sped out from R1's workspace and began tracing the through the large, flat packs of wires. If a wire connection had become loose, each rover had a little laser unit in its arsenal of tools. Slowly, the bots crawled the length and breadth of the ship, tracing the hundreds of miles of wires, repairing here, replacing there, soldering and splicing. Sometimes, they resorted to scraping filaments of metal from the bulkhead to complete little jobs. Sometimes they had to find a trace of copper or titanium left over from a centuries-old repair.

R1 moved to the central hub of the ship, a massive processor below the floor of the bridge. It yanked out fried motherboards and built new ones where necessary. It had cargo drones deliver a small mountain of scrap parts from the recycling bin—free to any spacer who asked for it—and it rooted through the piles of parts and pieces for repairing the complex central brain of the ship. Hours went by as the little rover zipped back and forth between the hub and the cargo bay, as the little bot was severely limited by the amount of product it could carry in a single trip.

Eventually, lights that had not been blinking in the central brain began to blink again. The error messages in the data stream began to be replaced by coherent descriptions of the true extent of the damage done to the vessel. When the final piece of the central brain was triggered and functioning again, the little rover fully understood the full scope of the damage. It was not a pretty sight.

It gathered the other three rovers to it once again. Although the replicated rovers were not nearly as complex as R1, they understood the magnitude of the job ahead of them. Even for emotionless little bots, it was an intimidating, nearly impossible amount of work.

R1 could only be grateful rovers did not need sleep, worked relentlessly, and moved at speeds far faster than humans were capable.

Once the mother brain was conscious again, then life support was the next integral system. With a daunting task in front of them, R1 ordered more scrap to be delivered to the cargo bay and set the other three 'bots on a mission to fix the recirc system, the atmo pumps, and all the other pieces and systems that made it so humans could live aboard the ship.

R1 dug into the plumbing on its own. The other bots would never understand how valuable good plumbing was to a ship. It was a dirty job, but R1 knew it had to be done.

While it mired into the grinder of the solid waste processor, the little R1 came to a stunning realization: it was not repairing the ship because that was its job; it was repairing the ship because it did not want the humans to abandon the ship, it did not want the humans to abandon it.

Wait—not *it*. More than *it*.

The bot did not want the humans to abandon *him*. Or her.

The bot was not clear on the differences between genders, nor did it understand if it was one or the other. It only knew that somehow, after three hundred years and change of being aboard *Shy Opal* and absorbing centuries

141

of programming knowledge and cosmic radiation, particularly whatever happened to it when the new lady's magic had gone through the entirety of the ship, including the rover itself, the little bot had suddenly surpassed its own programming.

It was more than a repair bot. It was no longer mindless, a slave to function.

It—as much as a rover could be—was alive.

17

NIGHT FELL FAST on the jungle planet. In the cave, Crispy built a little fire at the mouth to keep predators at bay. They cooked small chunks of the cat-bison's meat over the flames. The meat was lean and chewy, with little fat to give it flavor, but it was edible. It tasted almost like bear meat, with a thick, grimy, odorous taste that coated the tongue. It would be no one's favorite meal, but it was food and that was all that counted.

Nathan Pageant's chest was a large blue-black bruise. It hurt to breathe. A scan from Quick's PPD reported he'd suffered a deep bone bruise on his sternum. It wasn't dangerous, just painful as hell.

Quick refused medical attention. She was not badly wounded, and the dings she incurred were just more scars for the collection. Her body was a road map of scar tissue, and a few more divots would hardly be noticed. She wrapped fabric around the worst of the injuries and called it a day.

Commander Reesha Neer was less inclined to be so flippant about her injuries. Her arm was bandaged heavily. Her calf muscle had been largely destroyed. Even if she had been aboard a med-ship with a full complement of tissue-stitching tools and skin grafts, it was the sort of injury that would end a military career. Without a full medical complement, she would never fully heal. She had a lifetime of walking with a limp ahead of her, provided some strange alien bacteria did not move into the wound and cause some horrible disease that would necessitate the amputation of her leg, or worse. She could possibly look into cybernetic replacements for the leg. A cyborg forearm made Quick no worse for wear.

Neer's leg was bandaged crudely with a length of rough cloth cut from Quick's leggings. Quick and Pageant used a gun barrel heated in the fire to cauterize the bleeding as best they could, but it was a hack job at best, emergency battlefield medicine done without anesthetics or proper tools. Neer had tried to be stoic, but when the red-hot barrel touched the shredded tissue of her calf, she started to scream and passed out from the shock. Even worse, she lost control of her bladder when it happened. When she woke several moments later, groggy, confused, in terrible pain, and with a wet crotch, she was mortified.

To the little transport ship's crew's credit, none of them said anything about it. Nor would they even consider saying anything. It was part of helping someone who needed help. Crispy patted Neer's shoulder sympathetically and brushed off her panic and embarrassment. "We help those who need help. That's how spacers live. Always."

Anne Medea was still groggy after manifesting the lance. When the battle had ended, she had dropped to her knees and clutched at the sides of her head, stifling a cry. She was too weak to walk. Pageant carried her to the cave and cleared a spot on the cold stone floor for her to rest. She lay on her side staring at the fire. She had accepted a small bit of water from Quick, but that was all. She could barely speak. Even as the rest of them helped Neer, Anne was was still motionless, save for the barest hint she was still breathing.

Pageant sat across the fire from Commander Neer. "What do you know about Anne? Please, tell me everything. Clearly, she ain't human, regardless of what our scanners might say."

Reesha Neer thought about how to play it. Technically, she was a prisoner, even if the *Shy Opal* crew was not really treating her as one. She removed her uniform jacket. It was too heavy to wear on the jungle planet. She had been sweating since she landed with the acolyte crew. She looked at the epaulets on the shoulders. She had worked so hard to earn those epaulets, and for what? What loyalty did she really have to MannTech, anyhow? They were just a paycheck. Once they saw her injury and saw she allowed herself to be captured by a cargo ship captain and his crew of rejects, would they let her remain in command? Probably not. Especially not with the loss of a full acolyte strike team on her record. She would definitely be demoted. She would not be allowed to command a Cerberus gunship again, that was for sure. They'd give her some terrible duty meant to make her quit, probably hauling waste from planets to suns or something equally degrading.

Neer thought ruefully about her second-in-command, that weaselly little bastard, Michael Özturk. She knew he would have assumed command by now. He would have scanned the surface and known the acolytes were dead. With Neer's own life sign hidden from scanners because of the cave, he would have assumed her dead and reported as much back to MannTech. He had already been given the field promotion to her chair, she was certain. That was all he had ever wanted, just like it had been all she had ever wanted when she had been a second-in-command, herself.

Neer knew she was likely done at MannTech. She would never accept a demotion, and they would never allow her to maintain high-profile commands again. Best she could hope, they might stick her planetside in some sort of quartermaster role, but she would never get another ship. Neer had a brief flash of being back on Earth as a little girl sitting out on the balcony in one of the high-rises in Madurai, India, just praying to any god who would listen to cause another rolling electrical blackout so she could use her telescope to look at stars without the constant glow of the city lights ruining her view. Could she live without being in the Black? Could she live without feeling the surge of translight? Probably not.

Neer looked at the people around the fire. She had backed them into a corner three times, and they surprised her each time. She had run the files on Crispin Okino and Natalie Huffman while the *Despair* searched for the *Shy Opal* after it disappeared in front of her. They were both qualified to do more than kowtow for the aging skipper of a derelict transport ship, but they stood by his side. What was it about Nathan Pageant that engendered such loyalty?

When the cat-creature attacked her, both Pageant and Quick threw themselves at the beast to save her without a moment's concern for their own safety. When she was mauled, they took care of her injuries without a second thought. They saw someone hurt, and they helped. No questions. They cut food for her and gave her a long stick to cook chunks of meat over the fire. Quick found water, boiled it to purify it, and offered her the first drink telling her she lost a lot of blood and needed to start replenishing fluids. There were no snide comments, no snark, only concern.

Neer wondered if anyone on her own ship would have done that for her.

She already knew the answer to that question.

Neer folded the uniform jacket neatly. She plucked the command pins from the epaulets and threw them into the fire. The little plastic coatings on the pips melted, and the brass beneath shimmered and blackened in the flames. Across from her, Nathan Pageant's eyebrows rose, but he said nothing. He knew what it meant.

Neer cleared her throat. "Captain Pageant, could you use another crew member?"

"Most of the time." Pageant glanced at Quick and Crispy.

"Might be we could probably use a good communications officer, if you know of any." Quick was pouring more boiled water into her flask. She passed it to Neer.

"Where do I send my resume?"

"To Crispy," said Pageant. "I usually make him do the scut work I don't feel like doing."

"You're hired." Crispy did not look up from the meat he was gnawing on. "Pay is almost nothing, the food sucks, and we're probably going to die on this rock. Welcome to the crew of *Shy Opal.*"

"That's it? No debate? No pointless hoop-jumping? No hazing?"

Quick gestured to the jungle outside the mouth of the cave. Strange animals made wild and fearsome noises in the darkness. "Nothing we could do to you would be worse than what's out there."

"Tell us what you know about our poor Anne Medea, now, please." Pageant winked at Neer. "That's an order."

"You still give those?" said Crispy. "Figured you stopped after you realized that Quick and I don't take them well."

Neer took a long drink of water from Quick's flash. She coughed to clear her throat. "I'll tell you what I know."

THE MISSION CAME over the comm station of the MTI *Despair* like any other mission. A uniformed low-ranking officer at the central dispatch hailed the ship over subspace, and Neer ordered the holo on screen. A shimmering image of the comm officer materialized in the bridge and informed the *Despair* they were to set a course for an as-yet unnamed planetoid where they suspected one of their ships had either crashed or been destroyed. The ship, a long-range light transport vessel had been carrying a high-value subject from one research facility to a new one. The mission was search and rescue, or search and confirm subject's demise. If the subject was still alive, the subject must be recovered at all costs.

It seemed simple enough. Neer told her nav officer to lay in a course and execute immediately. She filed the mission coordinates into her log, and that was it.

While the ship maneuvered for the jump to translight, Neer tapped in the MannTech fleet's locations to her PPD out of sheer curiosity. Immediately, a dozen ships popped up on long-range scans showing their locations to be much closer to the target site than *Despair*. Why would MannTech Central Command reroute one of their biggest and most powerful vessels to a nowhere world to retrieve a test subject that may or may not have been destroyed?

Neer retreated to her ready room with orders to only contact her when the ship arrived at the designated planetoid. She turned the bridge over to her XO, Lieutenant Commander Özturk. He assumed her chair a little too quickly for her tastes, but she knew he was itchy for his own command. He had been applying to take over other ships, but she also knew he wanted a gun vessel of some sort. The pay was much better, and the stakes of the game were much higher. Only the most arrogant star jocks wanted battle. When she had climbed the ranks, Neer had been just like him.

Neer locked the door to her ready room and sat at her desk. She brought up a secure line and disconnected it from the ship's mission logs. Technically, that was an offense worthy of reprimand, or possibly a court-martial, but out in the Black, a lot of things went down to which Central Command was never privy, nor would they be. She made an illegal subspace call to a trusted contact deep in Central Command, a friend of hers from childhood.

Saira Green answered the call at her office desk. She was confused as to why Neer was calling her on a black channel, but it was Reesha, so she accepted it. Reesha only told her to find someplace private, and to take her PPD and make sure it was also disconnected from Central Command's ever-present spying eyes. Saira hung up immediately. She scrubbed any record of Neer's call from her office computer.

When Neer called her back in five minutes, Saira was alone in a park outside the building.

Neer asked Saira to look into why she was being sent after a test subject when a dozen other ships were closer. Why waste one of the corp's best gunships with a simple search-and-rescue mission, especially since SkyyAstra and NeoTech had been making so many offensive advancements into MannTech shipping lately. Surely *Despair* would be better served keeping MannTech's borders secure.

Saira promised she would do as Neer asked immediately. The line went dark.

Neer waited in her office staring at the black monitor on her desk and drumming her fingers on the table impatiently.

It took Saira more than an hour to get back to her. That was not like her. Saira was well-connected. Saira's husband, Armand Green, was a corporate suit. He was not on the board of MannTech, but he knew everyone who was. He was high up in the organization. He had connections all over the company and knew how to use them. Machiavellian machinations and maneuvers were constant in a corp the size of MannTech. Information was more valuable than creds or platinum. Armand knew how to play the game. He was an expert fisher of need-to-know knowledge and a slick minister of the silver tongue. For Saira to take more than hour to get the information Neer was seeking, it had to be hard to get.

Saira did not contact Neer directly the second time. She only sent a single file compressed to almost nothing with one word as the file's name: *Khatara.*

Danger, peril, risk.

Neer dared not open the file on anything attached to the ship. Every ship captain kept a few tricks for desperate times or nefarious deeds. One of those was an untethered PPD. It was a standard personal portable device with all possible wireless connections dug out of it. The machine was sterilized, only able to function on its own without an old-fashioned physical cable to patch it into other devices. It couldn't be hacked. It couldn't be picked up by any of the ship's constantly scanning ID equipment. Neer dropped the compressed file into the untethered machine and scrubbed any evidence of the black channel communication with Saira.

When she extracted the compressed file, she found far less information than she had hoped. It was only two pages of a highly classified brief from deep within MannTech's upper echelon. The pages had been for the proper eyes only, but like any good corp, there were always a few secretaries or majordomos to the most powerful suits who made a small fortune by scraping and trading in illegal information.

The two pages detailed some minor successes with something called *Project Archangel.* It detailed a test subject that displayed uncontrolled paranormal abilities, and that subject was being transferred to a new testing facility where researchers would be attempting to learn how the subject harnessed its abilities. If they could train the subject to harness its inherent abilities at will, the next step would be to recreate the abilities in new subjects.

If all went to plan, MannTech was on the verge of creating a whole new race of super-soldier, a single warrior capable of defeating swathes of typical corporation acolytes at will. The possibilities would be endless, of course.

The first step would be monopolization of all trade. MannTech would quickly destroy all competition for shipping between the rim worlds.

Shea Mannion would, for lack of a better title, become emperor of all known space.

THE CREW OF *Shy Opal* listened to Reesha Neer's story with rapt attention. When she finished revealing what she knew of Project Archangel, they were silent.

It was Crispy who finally spoke first. "*With every generation, there comes a conqueror.*" It was a quote from a philosopher of some renown a few centuries ago, back when man made the first successful translight leaps. The philosopher had realized that with every leap of new technology, a battle-wise commander took control of legions and tried to bring others to subjugation. It was as ancient as civilized society. There would always be those who thought they knew best, and thought they deserved the most. It was the most basic of human instincts.

A prehistoric tribe that mastered thrown weapons could easily conquer the tribes who still relied solely on clubs. The sword defeated the club. The invention of something as simple as the riding stirrup had changed the course of mounted combat, leading to lances that could decimate foot soldiers because a knight could now brace himself in the saddle. The trebuchet conquered the catapult. The gun conquered the arrow. The laser rifle conquered guns. When spaceflight first became commonplace, the first private shipmakers quickly learned to install weapons on ships because there was too much money to be made to let the spirit of peace and brotherhood guide them. With every generation, new weapons were created to bring others in line. A conqueror always rose with new weaponry, and it appeared Shea Mannion was set on being that sort of conqueror.

"Didn't it occur to you that maybe you don't want someone like Shea Mannion to have some sort of paranormal warrior?" To someone like Nathan Pageant, it was dead simple: *never* let any corporation have something that would allow them to eliminate all competition.

"At the time, I was not concerned. I had a duty to fulfill. Besides, how long have researchers been chasing man's next evolution? It never worked out for us."

Quick was agog. "If you had known Anne was capable of what she can do, would you still have come?"

Neer considered this for a long time. "Yes."

She looked at the curled, frail form of Anne Medea, Project ARC-346. The woman was a weapon, same as any gun. Worse than a gun, actually. A gun needed to be pointed by a soldier, and the trigger needed to be squeezed. Anne was a bomb, a pile of explosives waiting for a fuse. Neer told Quick as much. "With something as powerful as Anne, it is probably best that she is in the grasp of those who are putting forth research to control her, not only for her own sake, but for the sake of everyone who might meet her. Who's to say she's safe? She can make an entire ship intangible. She can manifest spears of light. What happens if someone frightens her and she levels a planet?"

"I wouldn't do that." Anne's voice was small, barely audible over the crackling flames of the campfire.

"How do you know you wouldn't? You destroyed a ship, didn't you?" Neer didn't mince words. Anne had unknown levels of power. Anne was the very definition of unpredictable. Even Anne herself did not know how powerful she was or what she could do. "If what I read in that project brief is true, you're a walking planet-bomb. You could become Death itself. All you need is a robe and a scythe."

Pageant looked at Anne thoughtfully. "You told me what she can do, but not what she is. How did MannTech create gene-tech capable of allowing a normal person like Anne throw a beam of light? That's what I want to know."

"All the brief said was she had paranormal abilities." Neer held out her hands and flipped them over and back like a blackjack dealer leaving the table. "If I knew more, I'd tell you more. My contact at MannTech could only get me two pages of a classified document. That means the who, why, and how of this Project Archangel are being kept under extremely heavy wraps. Top level security."

Quick was unconvinced. "Bullshit. I was a mercenary. I know how that stuff goes. No one keeps secrets for long. We just have to knock on the right door. If the information isn't out there already, then someone is desperate to talk about it."

"MannTech keeps its research scientists tightly controlled," said Neer. "They pay them well, but they demand loyalty to the point that MannTech research stations are often black sites. There's no record of where they are except at the highest level, no off-world contact, and only highly bonded pilots are allowed to fly supplies in and out."

"How many black sites can there be in the universe?" Pageant glanced at Quick.

"Thousands. Hundreds of thousands. Millions. Who knows?" The merc shrugged. "How many stars are out there? How many newly terraformed worlds? The corps have been claiming rocks out there since Smilin' Jack first made the jump and showed them how to do it. Corp-controlled planets are often poorly mapped, sometimes not mapped at all, and they're frequently heavily guarded. There could be far more than we think there are, or there could be far fewer."

Pageant looked to his pilot. Crispy was squinting out the mouth of the cave at the night sky. "Crisp? You okay?"

Crispy did not answer.

Pageant snapped his fingers twice. "Crisp?"

Awareness popped back into Crispy's eyes. "Sorry, Cap. I was just—" He pointed to the sky. "I think Sunny's back."

The group left Anne by the fire and moved outside the mouth of the cave. Neer allowed Pageant to assist her to one leg, and she leaned him as she hopped out of the cave on her left foot.

High above them in the star-dappled night sky, it looked like someone was launching a series of small fireworks. Red bursts the size of pinpoints could be seen in the darkness, and they seemed to be centered around one area.

The battle hundreds of miles above them lasted minutes. It culminated with a large, silvery explosion which, from their perspective on the ground, blossomed out to the size of Pageant's thumbnail. Then, as quickly as it appeared, the light of the explosion faded into the Black.

Neer's heart was in her throat. She might not have had all the love in the world for her crew, but they still had been her crew. She had exchanged pleasantries with many of them, and although she would not have considered any of them to be friends, she still felt a captain's responsibility toward them.

Pageant could feel Neer's eyes on him. He returned her gaze with somber eyes. "I'm sorry about your ship."

Neer's throat was tight. "That poor woman just declared war on Shea Mannion, and she probably doesn't even realize it."

Pageant shook his head. "You got that wrong, again. MannTech declared war on Sunny Yeong the second they touched her daughter. Sunny is just crazy enough to stand and fight instead of bending over and taking it from the corporations like so many others would."

"MannTech will retaliate," said Neer. "Count on it."

"So will Sunny." Pageant put a friendly hand on Neer's shoulder. "Count on it."

18

THE FELINE SHAPE of the LAS *Mary Read* drifted out of the heavens like a lazy tomcat looking for a place to nap after it devoured a rat. The ship's exterior showed some damage. There were a few black marks where the shields had not completely succeeded at pushing aside a shot from the *Despair*, a missing section on the starboard aft where the once-sleek metal was now a wild rift of jagged ends and sparking wire. They were not crippling shots, but the *Mary Read* had been in one hell of a fight, that much was certain.

The vessel did not land as it had before. The landing gear stayed hidden in the belly of the ship. Instead, the vessel turned in the air and got close to the ground. The long, thin cargo ramp opened in the aft of the ship, and the walkway descended to the jungle floor. A smiling Maori greeted them at the portal to the hold. "Hello, friends!" Norman's smile flitted from his face when he saw the wounds on Neer and Quick. "What happened?"

"A game of charades went amok," said Pageant.

"That'll happen." Without asking, the Maori lifted Neer into his arms like a baby. The petite woman was made even more petite against the hulking bulk of the spacer. "C'mon, lady. I'll take you to sick bay." He gave her a good look. "You South Asian?"

"Indian."

"You got a good recipe for butter chicken?"

"I don't cook."

"You should go with him, Quick." Pageant jutted his chin toward Norman. "If nothing else, get an anti-bacterial hypo. You know how it is with cat scratches."

"Somehow, I don't think that thing was digging in a litter box, Cap."

"It couldn't hurt, right?" Pageant walked into the cargo hold just ahead of Crispy. Anne Medea walked under her own power, but she leaned heavily on Pageant for support. He helped Anne to the floor of the cargo hold and let her lie on her side.

Crispy picked up the radio mic in the hold. "Sunny, we're all on board."

Immediately, the cargo door began to close and the engines began to generate lift. The *Mary Read* needed to get up to speed before it could break atmo and return to space.

"Crisp, watch over Anne, would you?" Pageant moved toward the hatch that would take him to the bridge.

"Shouldn't I go fly this thing?"

"Give me a minute. Just watch Anne."

"Aye, Cap'n." Crispy saluted and settled on the floor next to Anne. He brushed a strand of hair off of her face. Already, the hi-tech red was starting to show through Quick's cheap hair dye. "Cap?"

Pageant paused. He did not turn around.

"Don't yell, eh? Yelling only makes Sunny yell back. You know how it is."

"I know how it is, Crisp."

Pageant pushed forward. The hatch doors were sealed, and he had to spin the dog-wheel to open them. That happens on newer vessels when the ship's captain calls for red alert. It's automatic. It's a safety feature to prevent the entire ship from depressurizing if part of the ship is breached in battle, just as it was back on submarines in the ancient sailing days on Earth.

There were six hatches between the cargo bay at the rear of the ship and the bridge. All were sealed. Pageant picked up the scent of fried wires and burned bulkhead in some of them. The automatic fire systems suppressed any damage from getting worse, but the telltale signs were there. Even though *Mary Read* had delivered the knockout blow, *Despair* delivered enough shots to make the light attack ship know it had been in a fight. Maybe, if *Despair* had some better gunners and a better commander, the results would have been entirely different. *Despair* was a heavyweight. *Mary Read* was more like a middleweight or even a welterweight. If *Despair* had been able to land a single good haymaker, it would have been goodnight Sunny Yeong.

Pageant broke the final hatch seal and stepped onto the bridge. There were two additional crewmen on the vessel who had not been there before. One was familiar to Pageant—Happy Yeong, Sunny's chubby cousin. He was manning the nav station. Happy was a hypochondriac, cynic, and coward. He hated flying. For him to get aboard a light attack ship headed for battle, it must have been important. MannTech had touched his niece, though. It must have been enough to motivate him.

The other man on the bridge was in the pilot's chair. He was a stranger, a thin, sinewy Chinese man with a shaved head and a tattoo on his throat of the Mandarin characters for *No Mercy*. He had a vaguely Triad look about him, a gangster's sneer on his face.

Pageant knew a scumbag when he saw a scumbag. It takes one to know one, Sunny would have said. "You Shui Fong?"

The Triad gangster shook his head. "I've done work for them, but I'm not affiliated."

"Too bad. I know some Shui Fong guys who owe me money."

The gangster thought for a second. "Was it Tommy Yao?"

"That's him."

"Man, that fat fuck owes everybody. I'm surprised he still has all his fingers."

Pageant stuck out a hand. "Nathan Pageant."

"Everyone just calls me Fang." The gangster shook Pageant's hand. It was a quick, simple, no-bullshit handshake. The guy had nothing to prove. Pageant liked that about him. It was always good policy to introduce yourself to Chinese Triad guys to make sure they know you're not a threat.

Pageant pointed to the door of Sunny's ready room. "Is the captain—"

Fang just nodded. "Good luck, man."

The pitying look Fang offered him told Pageant all he needed to know. Fang knew about the kid.

"Happy." Pageant patted Happy Yeong on the shoulder. "Good to see you again."

"You, too. Hey, Nate—I'm sorry." Happy's face was a perennial storm cloud. He was always finding doom and gloom, hence his nickname. "I wanted Sunny to tell you about the kid, man. You know how it is."

"I certainly do. Thanks, Happy." Pageant paused at the door to the ready room. He pushed the alert button and waited. Sunny made him wait. He knew she would.

SUNNY YEONG SAT at her desk, legs crossed, left knee over right. Her hands were folded primly atop her left knee. She was dressed simply: black leggings, black leather go-boots, and a black-and-white striped tunic, her arms bare. She was using her best posture, shoulders back, chest out. Her eyes were sad, her mouth a thin line. Her hair was tied in a practical bun atop her head.

When Pageant walked into her office, he waited until the door slid closed behind him before saying anything. He made her wait for him to speak. She knew he would.

The adversarial silence was eternal. They stared at each other, both knowing things should have been different, both too proud to admit it.

"You should have told me."

Sunny's eyes closed and stayed shut. She could not bring herself to look at him. "I should have. It was a terrible thing for me to do, to hide her from you like that. I did not want her to be confused. I did not want her to wonder why she could never see her father."

"She could see me now."

"Why confuse her, Nate? Why would you want to shake up her world?"

Pageant had no answer for that. He took a seat in one of the two chairs across from Sunny. "If you'd told me, I would have done the right thing."

Sunny's eyes popped open and she rolled them condescendingly. "Oh, *puh-leeze*. Do not give me that old world bullshit. No one *needs* to get married anymore. I certainly don't need a man's help to raise a child."

"We were headed in that direction, weren't we? I mean—" Pageant held out his hands and looked around the room as if to say, *Before all this stuff with the ship happened.*

Sunny gestured at the ship and shrugged. "Yes. No. Maybe. I don't know. It doesn't matter now, Nathan. We both made our choices. We were both shitty to each other at the time., but we moved on with our lives. We made things work. It is what it is. What was that thing your dad always used to say about choices?"

"Once we pick our roads, there are no U-turns."

"There you go, no U-turns. We cannot go back."

Pageant was silent for a long moment. He was torn between throwing a massive fit or tearing apart the office and throwing himself out of the nearest airlock. Ten years ago, he definitely would have gone with massive fit. Now, he was too old and too tired for throwing fits. The airlock was not out of the question, but it seemed a little too final for the situation. "I will not press to meet her if those are your wishes."

"They are."

"Tell me about her, at least. You owe me that much."

Sunny hesitated and then pulled open a desk drawer. She produced a holo-imager and pressed play. A series of three-dimensional images projected up from the flat base and began to slowly twirl, a new image popping into place every five seconds. "She's wonderful. So smart. So charming. Everyone loves her, especially my auntie. My auntie has been like a grandmother to her. Opal calls her *Mama-T.*"

Pageant watched the images of the child on Sunny's holo. There was a little girl holding a baby chicken. The same little girl clutched a stuffed pig to her chest. There she was laughing over a birthday cake with two candles on it at Smilin' Jack's. Pageant felt his heart breaking.

That morning, he had just been some schlub with a busted Roundbelly and two odd crewmates. Now, he was someone's father. In all his spacer dreams, he had never considered fathering a child. It was just one of those things only respectable people who lived on planets in houses or apartments did, people who had money in the bank, not fly-by-the-seat-of-the-pants spacers with a bad track record and an antique ship. He felt tears pricking at the corner of his eyes, but he refused to cry in front of Sunny.

"Put it away." His voice was hoarse. He coughed to clear his throat. Sunny obliged, tucking the holo back in the drawer.

"Where is she now?"

"Safe."

"That's not really an answer."

"It's the only one I have to give at the moment." Sunny deftly changed the subject. "What happened down there?"

Pageant knew pressing her for information would not work. It never did. Sunny was an excellent poker player and monumentally stubborn when she had to be. She would never budge. Pageant did not try to get more information from her, and instead filled her in on the planetside activities, including Commander Reesha Neer defecting from MannTech, and what little he knew about Project Archangel.

Sunny frowned when Pageant said archangel. It was subtle, but her mouth turned down. Someone who had not spent years studying every inch of Sunny's beautiful face might not have noticed, but Pageant knew what it meant: she had information. "You know something."

Sunny did not deny it. "I've heard a few things over the past year or two about something called Archangel, but it's nothing. Whispers and rumors."

"Whispers about what?"

Sunny brought up her datapad and started searching, fingers flying over the keyboard. "Just what you said. Some weapon with crazy amounts of power. I figured it was a new kind of ship, actually."

"Reesha says Anne is like a bomb. Says she might have unlimited power and doesn't even know it."

"That ain't good." Sunny pushed the comm button on her desk. "Fang, come here."

A second later, the Chinese gangster appeared in the doorway. "What's up, boss?"

"I need you to find out everything you can about something called Project Archangel. Shea Mannion is building a new weapon, and I want to know what it is."

Fang absorbed the name, rolling it on his tongue. "Project Archangel. I assume this is some deep-cover, black-site shit?"

"Big time," said Pageant. "The most black site shit ever."

Fang whistled. "It's gonna cost."

"Then get me a price, and I'll see what I can do."

"Aye-aye." Fang backed away from the door to the ready room. The automatic slider closed.

"If there is information out there, Fang will find it. He has a wealth of contacts in the Triads. If the Triads don't have some sort of information, then it is truly the highest-level black site shit, and we'll never find out anything further."

"You have money to pay the Triads?" Pageant was impressed. He rarely had more than five-hundred creds in his counter. Ship owners were always buying fuel and new parts, so the credit wallet was never too full, even after a successful transport haul. That was why so many privateers were also criminals and willing to engage in questionable practices or risk suicide runs.

"I have some money." Sunny skirted the issue. "If necessary, I have people I can reach out to."

"Kkangpae?" The Korean gangsters, while not as wild or as far-reaching as the various Triads, Mafias, Yakuza, and other assorted gangster groups in the world, were still very good at acquiring information and money. Like the many corporations, organized crime flourished once the entirety of the universe became a viable playing field for them to outrun any sort of lawmen or government regulations. A lot of people, especially Outer Rim settlers, did not discern any difference between corps and the mafias. To most settlers, they were all criminals looking to screw the working man.

"I have people." Sunny cut off any further discussion.

Pageant knew where her connections lay. She did not need to confirm or deny it. "What's our next step, then? You just took out an MTI gunship. You're marked."

"Tell me about it."

"You should have left us on the planet."

Sunny's eyebrow leapt into an arch on her forehead. "I did not do it for you."

"I know. They brought that evil on themselves."

Sunny consulted a star chart on her PPD. "We need to go to ground, lay low until we figure out our next step."

"Where are you thinking?" Pageant leaned across the desk and cocked his head at an odd angle to better see the map.

"Mid-rings, probably. Inner rings will be too hot. Outer rings will be too obvious."

Pageant did not think the outer rings would be too obvious. "Easier to scan distance in the outers, though. Might be safer. We could drop a dozen long-range beacons around some nothing world and moor up shadow-side on a small moon. We set a dead man's switch on a translight jump to some other world and let the beacons do the searching for us. Anything drops out of translight within range of the buoys and sounds the alarm, the ship will leap without any human commands. At the very least, it'd buy us time."

"Mid-ring." Sunny's tone told Pageant it was not up for debate.

Pageant knew why. It would be closer to her daughter. "Opal."

Sunny's eyes flitted up to Pageant. "I always loved that ship."

19

THE MORE THE little rover understood its new-found sentience, the more it felt its capacity for learning and independent thought expanding. In its runs to the pile of ship scrap in the cargo bay, R1 sorted through odds and ends to find quantum memory chips that were no longer good for their original purpose, but with some finessing from its tool kit and a little creative engineering, the bot was able to permanently expand its own processing power, and thus expand its own intelligence to a large degree.

R1 built two more Rovers: R5 and R6, of course. It could not replicate its own sentience in the rovers he built, and that frustrated him. They were stupid machines which could not function without a strong kick to their programming. Once given instruction and direction, they worked quickly and efficiently without a missed step, but they could not anticipate issues. They could only put out proverbial fires once there was an issue dictating their need to intervene.

R1 did not know it felt like an angry god, because it had not acquired the whole of human knowledge, but that is what was firing through its system. It wanted more from its creations and did not understand how to build it into them. It had not yet occurred to it that a simple download could allow it concepts, characters, and ideas it did not know existed. Despite having a limited sentience, it was still a rover, and the rover's lot in life was to fix ships. As the rover's intelligence grew, it was only concerned with repairing *Shy Opal*, which it had come to think of as a sort of exoskeleton for its own body. The stronger *Opal* got, the stronger R1 would become.

R1 wondered if other rovers had gained the level of sentience he possessed. Without the rovers being aboard *Opal* and being able to tag into the data-stream from the ship's central brain, he would not be able to ask them. His language system, such as it was, was still limited to Roverspeak, and Roverspeak was limited by the ship, unless it was sending out an order for parts or broadcasting a shipboard emergency.

The rover let those two options roll in its primitive cybernetic brain. An emergency would not work because the ship was tethered to Ark Eleven and sustained on the station's power and life support.

An order was interesting, though. The rover could use the ship's data-stream to send a notice to the ship's import/export function. Usually it was something small: wire, scrap, hard plastic, plasma bolts. The ship would drum an order up for the items and send it to the Ark. The Ark drones would fill the order in its massive supply bay and fly them to the ship's cargo hold, dropping them off as fast as they could get them there. Could R1 simply create an order for other self-aware rovers? How would it get the ship's order to other vessels where other rovers might read it?

Clearly, this was something that required more pondering.

The rover stuck this thought into the back of its processing mind and continued with repairs on *Shy Opal*. As its main thoughts expanded, those of ship repair, it began to see issues with the old ship's design. There were redundancies that could be eliminated. There were old pathways and routes that could be streamlined. The ship was inefficient, and the rover saw ways to make the ship stronger and faster. It saw ways to make the older systems more capable of functioning with modern systems.

There was still so much to do. So, so much.

If the rover had possessed sleeves, it would have rolled them up and gotten to work. Without sleeves, it could only get to work.

The ship required it.

20

T HE MIDDLE RIM planets were an odd mishmash of fully settled industrialized worlds and colonies which had grown beyond the rural designations the Outer Rim planets still held, but they were far from being fully settled and most manufacturing was still in its infancy. The Mids existed in a strange agrarian state where people fell into one of two modes: they were either farmers or ranchers, maintaining massive, sprawling sections of land growing various crops and raising animals to be harvested and shipped to the Inner Rim; or they were on the planet to be of service to the ranch owners. They might run restaurants or shops. They might be hired hands. They might be small-machine repair crews. There were dozens, maybe hundreds of service jobs on any settled Middle Rim planet, but they were there because the people who controlled the majority of the land and wealth needed them. If they weren't needed, they would not last long.

Sunny headed *Mary Read* to a partially industrialized world called Templeton. As the name might suggest, it was one of the original rocks discovered by Smilin' Jack and *Starduster*. The land had been free to anyone brave enough to settle it, and the planet had flourished, its population growing exponentially until it was nearly as settled and productive as anything in the Inner Rim.

Templeton had a few cities of more than a hundred-thousand people and a bevy of smaller towns and villages. The larger cities had shopping, entertainment, industry, and full dry docks for vessel repair. The smaller towns had residential sprawl and plenty of green land for rest, recreation, and farming. The planet had salt oceans and freshwater rivers. It was very Earth-like, despite having a slightly heavier gravity. Thus, over the last five or six generations of people being born on Templeton, evolution's effect on bodies stunted by the gravity was becoming very evident. People were a little shorter and stouter. They weren't fat—just compressed. Knee, ankle, and back problems were more common, too. The bone-crackers whose chiropractic practices had been chased out of the Inner Rim by modern medicine were finding a haven for their skills on worlds with higher gravities.

Crispy was back at the helm of *Mary Read*. Fang, while a competent pilot, was much more of a jack-of-all-trades, rather than a specialist like Crispy. Under the young man's practiced touch on the control boards, the vessel responded differently. The flight paths were more of a glide and less jarring. It drifted and played in the winds rather than fighting them.

Under Sunny's orders, Crispy guided the ship to an area outside of New Busan, a seaport town on Templeton originally settled heavily by Korean spacers fleeing the overcrowding of the major cities of their country on Earth. There were expansive repair fields in the plains outside of town, and it was a good place to lose a ship from prying scanners. Once on the ground, the ship could be shut down entirely, including transponders. A subtle credit exchange to the right registrar, and there would be no record of the ship ever having been there. Vessels would not be able to scan for it from space because there would be no telltale signs a ship's scanner would recognize at distance. With a few extra bucks, you could even get some registrars to throw a merkin over the ship's exterior registration numbers, making anyone running a scan on those numbers return a different vessel. Merkins were not always accurate, though. If someone ran the numbers on a light attack vessel like *Mary Read* and the merkin returned it registered as a two-man low-orbit tug, you were going to have problems. Still, it was a good disguise, and often more than enough to throw off prying eyes.

Pageant stood behind Sunny's captain's chair, arms folded, watching the windows as Crispy landed the ship. "Why are we here?"

"I have friends here. One of them is a doctor. He might be able to help the defector." Sunny was still in her leggings, boots, and tunic. It was more than appropriate for going planetside. Pageant had cleaned up a bit, but still wore his tac-gear.

Leaning against the hatchway, Quick was also wearing tac-gear. She had her Mengler back on her hip, slung low in a holster at a comfortable reach for her right hand. Her left arm still ended in a stump. "Got a guy in this pit who can outfit me with a new grabber?"

"One or two. It might not be pretty, though." Sunny stepped past Quick, heading for the ship's belly. A gangplank was extending from the prow to get them to the ground. Fang followed her. He carried a Blueskill Slimline rifle, and he wore a steel sword in a scabbard on his back, the handle an easy grab over his right shoulder.

Pageant knew a lot of the Triad guys still liked close-up old-school weapons. It was a badge of honor for a lot of them, worn more as a badge of office than anything meant for practical use. Pageant found them sort of silly. Pulling a sword seemed like a good way to encourage a man wearing a pistol to put a few rounds through your chest. You can't block bullets with a sword no matter how fast you think you are.

As Fang stepped past him, Pageant reached out and tapped the handle of the sword. "Sorry about the size of your penis, friend."

"You looking to get circumcised, old man?"

Sunny sighed. "One thing I did not miss about you was the constant pissing contests, Nathan."

"It wouldn't even be a contest this time—Fang would have to use the ladies' tee."

Fang turned and bumped his chest against Pageant's stomach. There was at least six inches of difference in their heights. "Ease up, Pageant. I didn't come at you."

"I'm glad you didn't. I don't know what I would have done if you'd suddenly started waving your proxy dick at me."

Fang's eyes narrowed, but he could not maintain his tough guy edge. His mouth wrinkled and he burst out laughing. "Proxy dick. I'm gonna steal that one from you, old man."

Happy and Crispy were going to stay aboard the ship. Crispy needed sleep, and Happy hated leaving the relative cleanliness of the scrubbed air aboard the ship. On the planet, there were viruses, bacteria, and pollen. He was a fan of none of them.

Norman, Reesha, and Anne met the rest of the crew at the gangplank. Reesha was on crutches, her right leg below the knee was all but useless. Anne was pallid and sickly. She was using Norman for support. Norman, smile ever-present, barely noticed her hanging on his massive arm. "Hello, friends!" Norman waved. "We going to see Doc Nkosi?"

"First thing." Sunny led the way down the gangplank. A hover-shuttle met them at the end of the walkway to take them to their destination in the city.

When Pageant looked back at the ship, a pair of drones were draping a large metal merkin over the ship's registration numbers. The base metal color of the merkin matched the ship perfectly.

ROGER NKOSI WAS a good doctor. He came from the school of medicine that looked at wounds and injuries with a human eye and a learned man's sensibilities and then used the tools and devices of modern science to confirm his own diagnosis. Often, particularly in the megalopolises in the Inner Rims, the doctors relied solely on scanners because they were correct almost all the time. Old-school doctors worried about that one time in a hundred the scanners failed.

Sunny let Dr. Nkosi know she was coming with some top-secret patients, and he had cleared out his practice for the afternoon. This was the sort of pull Sunny Yeong had in New Busan.

The starkly decorated surgery was empty and quiet. The only people in the office were Nkosi, his nurse, Florence Greely, and the crew of the *Mary Read*.

Nkosi was not a man for pleasantries and chat. He saw the seriousness of the injuries and busied himself immediately with Reesha Neer's leg. The tissue on the back of her calf was growing necrotic; it did not look good. Despite the cleansers, medicines, and treatments they had given her aboard the ship, the calf would always be useless. There was no repair available for an injury that severe, especially since the skin was turning black and beginning to radiate a foul smell.

Nkosi sat back from his initial examination and pushed his glasses to the top of his head. His voice was low, smooth, and heavy with a South African accent. "Madam, I do not know how to tell you this, but my recommendation is amputation. Whatever happened to you, it is bad. It is as though something injected some sort of toxin into your tissue."

Her head was turned sideways staring at the wall. Neer was emotionless. "Take the damn thing. I don't need it."

Nkosi bowed his head and gave instructors for his nurse to make ready the surgery suite. "It will be a relatively quick surgery. Most of the flesh, arteries, and tissue have already gone necrotic. The bone will go quickly."

Nkosi ushered the rest of the crew to his waiting room. "My nurse will get my surgery ready in minutes. Your friend will be ready to be discharged in a few hours."

"How much will it cost?" Pageant pulled out his cred-counter. He was more than willing to pay. Neer was his crew now. A captain took care of his people.

"Minimal. Very minimal. Tool cleaning only." Nkosi waved off Pageant's credits. "I owe Miss Sunny, yet."

"You owe her?" Pageant looked to his one-time paramour and mother of his estranged child. "You have history here?"

"We served together on the *Rook III* back when we were both employed by Absalom Industries," said Sunny. "Saved the old man's life once or twice."

"Thrice, actually," Nkosi corrected her. "This is why Sunny only pays for parts, never my time. All the time I have now belongs to her, because without her I would have no time at all."

"While we're here—" Pageant gestured at Anne Medea. She was sitting in a waiting room chair, looking like a pile of laundry. The space witch was complected and listless. "Can you do something for her?"

"Of course. I would never deny aid to someone who needs it." Nkosi knelt in front of Anne and introduced himself. She murmured a greeting in a voice too low for Pageant to hear. Nkosi felt her forehead and neck. He touched her wrists. He used a penlight to look at her pupillary response. "She is tired, dehydrated, and generally depleted. Did she run a marathon recently?"

Pageant and Quick exchanged a look. "Something like that," said Quick.

"I will get her some fluids and vitamin sprays. They should help."

"Could you maybe run some tests, too? Maybe take some samples that we couldn't take with a PPD on a ship?"

Nkosi stepped back from Anne. He eyed Pageant suspiciously. "Why?"

"We were just on an alien planet. That thing that hurt our friend, it was an undiscovered alien species of predatory animal. Maybe something is wrong with Anne that goes beyond her just being depleted. Maybe it's some kind of new bacteria or something."

"Ah. Yes, of course." Nkosi seemed satisfied with the explanation. He excused himself and bustled away to gather the necessary materials.

Nkosi took blood samples from Anne, then scraped her cheek for a tissue sample. His nurse set up an IV line and ran fluids. Anne perked up some. She got a little color back into her cheeks. The doctor set the samples into a machine for testing, and then excused himself to conduct the amputation on Reesha's leg.

Quick used her PPD to locate the nearest cybernetics dealer. She checked her cred-counter and found the sum therein lacking. "It's not going to get me another concussion grenade."

Pageant thumbed his own cred-counter and sent her about half of the meager sum he possessed. "Best I can do. The rest of my funds are on *Opal.*"

Quick frowned when she looked at the new total. "You really are a broke old man, aren't you?"

Sunny slipped a cred-counter from a pocket inside her tunic. She tapped her fingernails against the buttons. Quick's eyebrows went up, and she looked at Sunny with respect. "For that much, I might be able to get racing stripes on the grenade."

"Least I can do," said Sunny.

"You shouldn't have let this one get away, Cap." Quick headed to the door. "I'll be back when I get a new gripper."

"Providing gun support pays far better than hauling freight." Sunny excused her extravagance.

"I've heard that." Pageant folded his arms across his chest. "That's why I tried to buy a light attack ship a few years ago."

"You tried to steal it."

"Only because I couldn't afford it outright."

Norman heard the tension in Pageant's voice and looked to his boss. "You want I should put him on the ground again?"

Sunny shook her head and waved off her bodyguard. "He's just pissy because I won the ship in a poker game and didn't give it to him."

"You cheated. You brokered a deal under the table to cut me out."

Sunny arched a single eyebrow and matched Pageant's posture. "Maybe I did. Maybe I didn't. You'll never know."

Pageant was smart enough to let the petty argument drop. Across the room, one of the machines running Anne's samples beeped. Pageant and Sunny exchanged a glance. The doctor and nurse were still in the surgery suite. They could wait for the doctor to finish, but it seemed like a silly thing to wait when there was data ready for viewing on the monitors across the waiting room.

"Should we?" Pageant cocked his head at the machine.

Sunny pushed herself out of her chair and strode across the room. She sat at the desk and opened the files. She stared at the results. Over her shoulder, Pageant scanned the results as well. He squinted at them. The file was listing a variety of information, a wealth of numbers and letters, lines of data, and images of cell types and three-dimensional DNA scans.

Sunny and Pageant looked at each other with wide eyes. They were not doctors. Neither of them had any sort of medical training beyond watching holos of old medical dramas. Nothing on that screen made any sort of sense. "What the hell were we thinking?" Sunny pushed away from the table.

Norman lumbered over and squinted at the data stream. "Interesting."

"You can make sense of that?"

"Oh, yeah. My mom was a doctor. I used to help out at her office a lot when I was a kid. She taught me to read sample scans."

Sunny slapped her cargo officer with the back of her hand. "I've been flying with you for more than three years, and you never thought to mention this before?"

"I told you my mom was a doctor."

"You told me she was smart."

Norman shrugged. "Smart people are doctors."

"What does it say?"

Norman pointed to the DNA data. "You see this?" He traced his finger around a double-helix shape on the monitor. "That's Anne's DNA. It ain't fully right."

"What do you mean it *ain't fully right*?" asked Pageant.

"I mean that's why there's a length of it that's blinking red on the screen. Blinking red lights mean something ain't right." Norman sat in the chair Sunny vacated. He began typing on the monitor with fingers the size of bratwursts. His touch was surprisingly deft given his size.

"How not right? What's wrong with her?"

Norman was silent while he searched the data. He pulled up a spare research window and did some examination. His face became more and more serious. He squinted at the screen, moving closer and closer to the monitor. When he stopped typing, he turned to face Sunny and Pageant, swiveling in the chair. He looked stunned and deeply confused. "I think the machine made a mistake."

"Maybe," said Pageant. "Machines are not infallible."

"Pretend it didn't fail," said Sunny. "What's wrong?"

Norman inclined his head toward Anne. "It says some of her DNA isn't human. It's human-like, but it's not human."

"Like primate? Monkey?" Pageant had heard of people trying to splice some animal DNA into human DNA chains to give someone ape strength or cheetah speed, but it had never worked before, at least not to his knowledge.

"I mean alien."

"Alien monkeys?"

Sunny put a hand over Pageant's mouth. "Alien? As in extra-terrestrial? As in A-level sentient alien life?"

Norman looked scared. "That's what I mean: humanoid-like DNA."

There was a silence. All three of them turned to look at Anne. Across the room, Anne saw them looking at her. She smiled and waggled her fingers. They all turned back to the monitor.

Pageant's mouth opened and closed a couple of times. "Okay, pretend I'm an idiot."

"Shouldn't be hard," said Sunny.

"Explain what you think happened to Sunny in layman's terms, like you're trying to explain it to an idiot."

Norman thought about it for a moment. He rested his chin on one of his massive hands. "Okay, so, I'm not a super-smart guy. My ma was smart; me, not so much. But, if I had to explain it to an idiot, I'd say that it looks like someone found some alien DNA of a human-like creature, and then tried to make that DNA fit into a human DNA chain, and the result of that is Anne."

"Someone tried to splice alien DNA into a human?" That much Pageant understood before Norman tried to explain it.

"That's what I'm saying."

Sunny threw her hands up and walked away. "I figured that much out on my own, Norm."

Pageant squinted at the screen again. He could see the strands of DNA on the monitor that were blinking red. Alien DNA, the building blocks for an undiscovered race of humanoid beings sharing the same universe as *homo sapiens*. "You know what this means, right?"

"The Fermi Paradox has been disproved," said Sunny.

"Among other things," said Pageant. "Not only has it been disproved, but it's been obliterated. It means Shea Mannion and MannTech are in possession of viable alien DNA. That means they had to have samples. That means they actually *found* sentient alien life." He looked at Anne. She was perking up, looking healthier. "And now we're in possession of their research."

"That'd be worth a few billion credits." Sunny realized what Pageant was saying. Sitting in the office with them was perhaps the single most important living specimen in the galaxy. She was the result of countless hours of research and an unfathomable amount of money, the pinnacle of centuries of exploration, science, and luck.

"How many people would you kill to get her back?" Pageant felt the words leave his lips, and he wished he had not said them aloud.

Sunny was blunt. "All of them."

IN THE SUMMER of 1950, a number of physicists were having lunch. One of them brought up the subject of recent UFO sightings and the idea of alien civilizations. Dr. Enrico Fermi, a Nobel Prize-winning physicist, in response to the notion of alien life was said to have casually remarked, "But where is everybody?" Since then, his name was put onto the Fermi Paradox despite the fact that he never actually formulated the paradox himself.

When man first mastered translight travel, the ability to tear a hole in the fabric of time and space, slip outside of it for a limited amount of time, and use a vehicle to cross unimaginable amounts of distance in hours instead of millennia, humans thought they would be knee-deep in alien life capable of speech, thought, and similar travel. Decades of popular entertainment programming hypothesized the extent of intelligent alien life, be they Vulcan, Wookie, or Dalek.

What man learned was that intelligent alien life was non-existent. Since the early days of translight, all ships were outfitted with First Contact kits. Should they find sentient alien life, the First Contact kits outlined a plan of action that all ships, regardless of affiliation, were expected to carry out to the letter for the Earth governments back in the prime sector. Even Smilin' Jack Templeton was a firm and vocal supporter of the necessity of the First Contact kits.

Since the first ship broke the translight barrier and warped itself into a distant galaxy, not a single vessel in recorded human history had ever cracked the seal on its FC kit. They sat in a compartment in the bridge of every ship gathering dust and waiting for the off-chance that some ship will make a jump into a new, uncharted star system and stumble across some sort of humanoid alien species capable of speech and free thought—and more importantly, commerce.

Scientists and explorers had categorized hundreds of thousands, if not millions, of creatures—all manner of bacteria, virus, and animalia of all sorts had been added to the databanks and new living things were being discovered daily, but nothing humans had found had a brain with higher consciousness and were living in anything remotely resembling a civilization as humans knew them. Even bipedal creatures were rare.

The Fermi Paradox hypothesized advanced races like humans were rare, and it was reasonable to believe advanced civilizations were fleeting. Given the billions of years the universe existed prior to the Earth even being formed, how many civilizations had sprouted, thrived, and died off in the countless eons passing before humans on Earth were even capable of imagining that there might be more intelligent lifeforms out there? How many will there be after humanity is wiped from the cosmos?

Now, was it possible Nathan Pageant was standing in front of a living, breathing, human-looking woman with alien DNA spliced into her to create a new, intelligent part-human species?

Pageant's legs went weak. He stumbled to the nearest waiting room chair and collapsed into it. "If she's got alien DNA, I'm surprised MannTech only sent a single gunship after her. I would have sent the whole fuckin' fleet."

"The whole fleet would have drawn a lot of eyes." Sunny sat in a chair and bent over, putting her head between her knees. She folded her hands over the back of her neck and tried to breathe calmly. "A lot of eyes mean competitors would have known something valuable was being sought, and they would have sent their own gunships. Mannion could not risk losing that sort of money. It was better to do it small, one ship. Make as few waves as possible."

In the corner of the office, Fang looked nervous. His fingers twitched. He was starting to sweat. "Boss, if the Triads find out—"

"If the Triads find out, we're done for."

Pageant drew his Rorbacher HSL lightning fast. The ol' mercenary gunslinger tricks were still in the aging body. He pointed it at Fang. "Where are you loyalties, merc? You just became a liability."

Fang started to move, but Pageant fired a shot that hit the wall next to Fang's head. The blast sprayed plaster across the side of Fang's face. "If you move your fucking arm, I'll drop you were you stand. Where are your loyalties, boy?"

Fang looked to Sunny, but she was not on his side. "Answer the man, Fang."

"You're the boss, Boss. You pay me. Money is where my loyalty lies." Fang was stock-still in the corner.

"Triad ties run deep, Fang." Pageant knew how those organizations worked. Blood in, blood out.

"I was never affiliated. Merc for life, over here. Bamboo Grove asked me to take the blood oath, but I wouldn't." Fang showed Pageant the insides of his wrists. There were no burn scars on them. Most of the Triads still used old-fashioned hot iron branding to show affiliation. Signing on with a specific Triad was permanent, just like branding scars.

"Show me your chest." Pageant knew the pectorals were another favorite branding spot.

Fang's voice was wobbly. "Don't shoot me, okay? I'm not going for my gun." He slowly and carefully lifted his shirt. He had a lot of tattoos, but no scarring. He turned in a slow circle to show there were no scars on his back, either.

Sunny saw enough. "I need an oath, Fang. You're in this too deep, now. If you don't turn her over to the Triads, they'll kill you for holding out on them. If you do turn her over, they'll kill you because you know too much. You want to stay alive, then we're your only option."

Fang lowered his shirt. Slowly, he reached to his shoulder and slipped the Slimline rifle from his shoulder. Keeping his fingers far from the trigger, he offered the gun to Sunny. She took it from him. Fang tossed the sword on his back to the ground. "There. No guns. No blades. I'm disarmed."

The gangster got on his knees and held his arms out to the side. "If you want me dead, kill me now. I won't resist."

"I don't want you dead, Fang. You're a good fighter. I have a feeling we're going to need good fighters before all this is over." Sunny produced a legal document on her PPD. It was an official crew manifest document, a binding contract that officially hired someone to a ship long-term. Once it was filed, that person was prohibited from taking work aboard other ships. The Triads viewed such contracts as honorable. Forfeiting the contract was worth death, even if you produced valuable information in exchange for the forfeit. Without honor in such contracts, the universe was a true free-for-all, and even the Triads knew chaos was bad for business.

Fang bowed his head. "I, Xiong Feng, also called Fang, swear on my life and my honor, I bind myself to *Mary Read* and her captain, Yeong Sun-hee, until the captain releases me from my bond or the ship is destroyed. I take this oath willingly and without duress." It was the standard spacer oath. The moment Sunny filed the document, he was bound to the ship.

It wasn't a perfect solution, but it would have to do. Pageant knew that Fang understood they all just taken a massive bite of a huge shit sandwich, and they were all going to have to do their part to swallow it.

"Welcome to the crew, Fang." Sunny helped the kid to his feet. She handed him his weapons. "If you're lucky, maybe we'll all live long enough to celebrate this."

"Destroy the evidence, Sunny." Pageant slipped his gun back into his holster. He looked to the data samples in the machines. "Don't let your doctor friend get involved in this bullshit."

Sunny nodded. Without a spoken word between them, Norman deleted all the data and flushed the blood and tissue samples down the drain of the nearby water fountain. "It's done."

"Can we sell the *Mary Read?* Maybe buy an STS or a small people mover?"

"I'm not selling my ship, Nathan."

Pageant knew it was a silly suggestion. "It's a little high-profile for trying to go incognito."

Sunny wouldn't hear it. "It's fast, it's light, and it has enough firepower to drop a Cerberus with minimal damage. It's our best chance at living."

"That might be true, but it's also our worst chance at staying off the radar."

"You want to talk staying hidden? You've literally got a defector from MannTech in the other room. How are you going to keep her from relaying a message back to her former employers? I bet they'd give her another Cerberus to command if she let them know the whereabouts of your space alien."

Anne was on her feet. She had pulled the IV from the back of her hand. She was watching them with terror etched on her face. "I'm an alien?"

Pageant sighed. Smart play would have been to lie. No one would ever accuse Nathan Pageant of being smart. He gave her a sheepish grin. "Sorta."

Anne fell backward into the chair. She began to tremble. Her hands covered her mouth. "How? How is that even possible?"

"I have no idea." Pageant crouched and put his hands on her shoulders. "But, I'd like to find out."

Anne looked at her hands like they were foreign to her. "It would explain a lot of things."

"What sort of alien race could do that kind of crazy stuff you can do? You literally have the power to defy physics when the mood strikes you. Any alien race that can do that..." Pageant could not finish the thought. Everyone in the room was thinking it.

An alien race able to manipulate the laws of physics would be undefeatable. Judging from what little Anne has been able to do, the aliens who supplied her DNA should be able to slow time for their benefit, phase in and out of the local reality, and create physical weapons from thought and light. Combine all three of those powers in the form of a body that knew how to use them, and it would make those aliens a singular force capable of wiping out entire armies by themselves without the need for ammunition or body armor. It was a terrifying thought.

"We've really stepped in it this time, haven't we? She really is a time bomb." Sunny patted Anne's knee. "But you're our time bomb now. We'll help you. Someone like Shea Mannion should not have your sort of power at his disposal."

"No one should," said Fang. "She's incredibly dangerous in all sorts of ways."

"I should go. No one should be around me. I'm only going to bring you misery."

Pageant's face broke into a wry grin. "Lady, my middle name is Misery."

"Really?"

"Well, no. It's Emmanuel, but it should have been Misery." Pageant looked at everyone in the waiting room. He made sure to make eye contact with each of them in turn. "Friends, I've seen this movie before, and it does not have a happy ending."

"Are we going to die?" Norman's smile was back.

"Good chance," said Sunny.

Norman shrugged his shoulders, unbothered by the proposition. "That's good. I've heard good things about dying. Maybe I'll get to see my mom again."

21

R EESHA NEER LIMPED out of Dr. Nkosi's surgery on crutches. She was groggy, still shaking off the anesthetic even with the help of the reversing drug. Her right leg ended in a rounded stump two inches below the knee. The skin was grafted together, cauterized, and bright red. It was going to be a while before the swelling normalized so she could be fitted for a Sofskin prosthetic. Until then, she would be walking with sticks and limited mobility.

Neer's face was blank and impassive, a mask of professionalism and disaffection, but there was profound sadness in her eyes. Nkosi told them it was common for amputees to suffer a sense of loss, a feeling they would never be whole again. Neer was an accomplished officer and not inclined to self-pity. No matter what she felt on the inside, Pageant knew she was not going to let it show. She gritted her teeth and refused offers of help. "I'll be fine."

When Nkosi went to the testing machines to look at the data from Anne's blood work, Sunny stopped him. "You don't want to know what was on there. If anyone comes calling, we were never here. You saw nothing. You know nothing. You get me?"

Nkosi was confused. "It's that serious?"

"The less you know, the better."

Nkosi bowed at the waist casting his eyes to the floor. "As you say, Sunny."

Sunny and Nkosi hugged each other. "This might be the last time I come calling, old man."

Nkosi's eyes were dark and somber, but he understood. "I shall keep your ship and crew in my thoughts. If the stars are willing, perhaps we'll meet once more."

Sunny hugged the doctor again. "Keep your nurse close, too. Tell her she knows nothing. She never saw us."

"We will plead ignorance until our final breaths."

Sunny moved to the door of the surgery. "Let's hope it doesn't come to that."

The group moved into the bustling streets of New Busan. Nkosi's office was located near a day market crowded with all manner of folk getting the supplies for daily life like food, booze, and parts for ships or bots. Pageant felt himself going into defensive mode, eyes darting constantly, head on a swivel. It felt like a thousand eyes were staring at him, and all of them knew he was trying to hide something major.

In a poker game, this would not have been a big deal to him. It would have been welcome. The more eyes thinking he was up to something, the better. However, knowing that a ninety-pound woman with alien DNA coursing through her veins was right behind him made him feel like MannTech acolytes were waiting on the rooftops with sniper rifles just looking for a go-sign from their commander.

Everyone in the group was on edge, save for Neer who was blessedly ignorant of Anne's DNA. Neer had her own struggle at the moment. She did not need a further burden to carry.

They stood in the marketplace waiting for Quick to return from the cyberneticist. "Mingle," Pageant told them. "Look like you're shopping."

Sunny pulled Pageant aside. "We should break up."

"We did. Years ago."

"I mean we look like everyone MannTech is probably looking for at the moment. A Korean temptress, a Chinese Triad thug, and a big Maori in the company of a dull white guy, an Amazonian broad, and a tiny waif of a woman. We stand out like UV under black light."

"We are a tad bit memorable, aren't we?"

"Take Anne, Neer, and Norman and go back to *Mary Read*. Fang and I will wait for Quick."

Pageant did not like that idea, but it made sense. He knew he had to be near Anne, lest Sunny tried to double-cross him and sell Anne out to MannTech in exchange for a pardon for destroying the *Despair*. It did not seem like something Sunny would do, but a few years back Pageant didn't think Sunny would have taken a ship from him, either. "Hurry back to the ship. We're going to need to think hard about what our next step will be."

Fang was looking at his datapad on his left forearm. "I just got a coded message from a Triad knowledge broker. Says he's got data for us, but it's going to cost."

"Always does." Sunny had Fang transfer the message to her own PPD.

Pageant could not read what was coming up as it was in Mandarin hanzi. Sunny had a working knowledge of the language and managed to decode the message as well as Fang had. "He wants a bundle. Says he has coordinates for a hidden MannTech black site."

"How do we know the coordinates are good?" Pageant was always suspicious of knowledge brokers. Usually they wanted a fat payday, and if their data was shit then good luck finding them and getting a refund.

"It's good." Fang got defensive. "I don't use lousy brokers. They're always reliable. They have honor."

"Triad brokers are top notch." Sunny's fingers danced over her datapad. "At this price point, however, we're going to have to talk about this. Even if you and yours contribute, it's going to be a huge chunk of credits."

Neer crutched over to them. "What are you looking at?"

"We're trying to decide if we're going to pay a knowledge broker a massive amount of cash to get the coordinates of a black site research lab where Anne might have originated." Pageant ran his fingers through his hair. It felt thinner than it had yesterday. Either he was in desperate need of a shower, or the stress was finally causing him to go bald. Probably the latter.

"Why pay? I know where she originated. Sort of."

Three pairs of eyebrows raised as Sunny, Fang, and Pageant looked at her with surprise. "I thought that sort of thing was need-to-know. I thought you were kept in the dark," said Pageant.

"I was, but I'm no dummy. I know the ship Anne destroyed over that little planetoid was the MTI *Gyrfalcon*. It was a Raptor-class fast transport ship—no weapons, just speed. Its job was to make pinpoint jumps through the translight as fast as possible. It's the only way MannTech moves high-value tech. When I saw the *Gyrfalcon* was the ship we were scanning for, I ran its flight manifest. It was hopping from an unknown, unlisted site deep inside of distant MTI-controlled deep space and heading for an Inner Rim world in a portion of central space controlled by MannTech."

"Reesha, if you know the site, you can save us a ton of money and time," said Sunny.

"I don't know the site. It's a black site. It does not exist on documents. I just know the system."

"That's enough. That's plenty, actually." Sunny's voice pitched up in excitement. "We can hop into the system and do our own scans."

"MTI will send ships if someone jumps into a black site area." Neer shook her head. "It'll be a suicide mission."

Sunny was alight with excitement. "We'll jump in, get what we need, and jump out. Even if they have ships within the system, it would still take them a minimum of at least five or ten minutes to heat their translight engines, and another five or more to make the transition to our location. That's at least ten solid minutes. It'll be like a bank robbery. We get in, hit it, and get out."

"You're going to raid a secured black site in ten minutes and escape? Never." Reesha listed off the reality of the situation, ticking off points on her fingers. "One, you'd need a runner."

"*Mary Read* has a shuttle. Done."

"Two, you'd need to know exactly where to go. Best case scenario, your scans take two or three minutes before you find what you're looking for. You'd have to get your ship there, get the runner launched and down to the black site. If the black site is on a planet with atmo, you're screwed because you'll never get a runner through the reentry and surface-side in under fifteen minutes. If it's a dead rock, you'll still need at least five minutes to launch the ship and get it to the ground. Plus, if it's dead rock, you'll have to use exosuits."

Sunny's excited smile disappeared, becoming a sulky frown. "Well, hell."

Neer wasn't finished. "Plus, that black site might have guards with guns. You'll have a full-on firefight on your hands delaying any sort of entry into the site. The computers will be encoded. You'll need a prime hacker, and they're not cheap."

"I get it." Sunny threw up her hands. "Well, at least tell me the name of the system. I can ask the broker if his information gels with mine. If it does, then maybe it's worth paying for the coordinates."

"It's a small three-planet system called Katherine, with a K."

"Mannion's daughter?"

Neer nodded. "The one that died in childbirth, his first. The rich prick actually bought an existing system called Katherine and renamed it just so he could have the one his rangers discovered be the only Katherine System in currently known space. Katherine II would not have been good enough for him."

Pageant brought up the star charts on his PPD. The Katherine System wasn't listed, hidden from the public charts. The vast regions of space controlled by MannTech Industries were behind a heavy firewall on the public information files. "We'd need to go underground for the pirated charts."

"Black market would have them. Plenty of MannTech pilots have made copies and traded them for cash," said Neer. "Shea Mannion can control the public info, but the black market exists for a reason."

Sunny sent a message to the knowledge broker. *What's the system for this site?*

The broker came back with a noncommittal response. Even though Pageant could not read Mandarin, he knew from Sunny's face the broker had said, *You'll have to pay to find out.*

As if there was a sudden run on bad news, Pageant's own PPD sounded a signal. It was from Crispy on *Mary Read*. Pageant checked the text. "Crispy says an MTI vessel has entered standard orbit around Templeton, the MTI *Ammondale*."

Neer's face darkened. "*Ammondale* is a ranger ship. They're looking for the *Mary Read*."

"I hope the merkin holds." Sunny closed her data screen. "We're pretty well grounded until the *Ammondale* leaves."

"Let's get out of the open, at least."

"I told you: Fang and I will wait for Quick, the rest of you get back to the ship." Sunny waved Pageant away with her hands. "Go. Go now."

Pageant did not argue. He wanted to get Anne away from the thousands of eyes in the New Busan day market. The whole day was quickly becoming sour.

21

THE ROVER FELT its growing consciousness like a light. For so many years, it had been a tiny flame, a flickering candle in the distance on a dark night. Now, it was becoming a flashlight, a pointed, direct beam with thousands of lumens behind it. It was shining a broad, white light over things the rover had never considered or understood before, simply because its programming had not allowed it.

The first thing the little creature considered was its surroundings. Save for the rare instances when a crew member summoned it from the interior of the ship's workings and carried it to one of the exterior maintenance areas, the rover had never left *Shy Opal*. Not once. It was not something that it ever needed to do, and since its programming only encompassed the necessary tasks the bot needed to do, the very idea of it had never passed through its processors as something that was even a remote possibility.

Even now, as the little rover considered the possibility of leaving the ship, it seemed like a journey of a million steps. The rover knew where the hatch to the space station was located. It could easily work the system to open the door. It had the ability to crawl on all manner of surfaces in all kinds of gravity, so there would be no obstacles in its path to stop it, but when the rover attempted to process the idea of severing its connection with *Shy Opal*, of becoming wholly independent from the body of the vessel it relied on for safety and security for so many decades, a strange sensation crackled through the little bot's programming code.

R1 had no word for that sensation, of course. If it did, it would have probably called it fear. The bot had only a rudimentary understanding of the concept of emotion, and what little it knew was that humans had them and robots did not. The rover was no longer a true robot, though. It was surpassing the simple bonds of being a robot and becoming something different. This was a new frontier for a cybernetic being. The rover could not help but wonder if there were others like him out there somewhere in the wide expanse of the universe.

There were other vessels that had been in space as long or longer than *Shy Opal*. The space station *Opal* was anchored to at that moment had been in space for more than seven hundred and fifty years. That was over twice as long as R1 had been servicing *Opal*. R1 had no memory of a life before *Opal*, although it was entirely possible the bot had been aboard another ship but had its factory memory reset when it joined *Opal*. Perhaps it was even possible the bot was as old as Ark Eleven. Maybe older. For all it knew, perhaps it was among the first rovers ever launched into the Black, and perhaps it was over a thousand years old. Perhaps it was even the rover on Smilin' Jack Templeton's *Starduster*. The history books never made any mention of the Starduster's rover complement.

R1 knew it needed to leave the ship. Even with a growing level of personal consciousness, the bot still had a base programming code driving its every move. The bot needed the ship to run again. R1 without *Shy Opal* was not a thought the bot could process. It could fathom the idea that other ships existed, and it could even fathom the idea of taking its cadre of self-built rovers and moving to another vessel, but its programming code, and its consciousness was loyal to *Shy Opal* for reasons it could not understand. It must make the ship live again. It must make *Opal* fly again. The base code to its programming demanded it make the ship run. That was its only purpose. Despite its burgeoning mind, the bot was still controlled by the base code.

The base code made R1 unfailingly loyal to *Opal*. The advanced development of its processors told it that leaving temporarily was the only way to make the ship live again. The rover's prime function was to serve the vessel itself. If the ship was so incapacitated that leaving was the only way to determine how to best fix it, then the base code of saving the ship overrode the loyalty component of its service message. The rover would be doing *Opal* a disservice if it did not leave. It needed to link itself directly with the central mind of the processors in Ark Eleven. It needed to know if other rovers had gained a similar form of sentience. If so, perhaps it could recruit those rovers to its ship to help fix it. The ship needed parts beyond what the rover could order through scrap. Maybe it could find those parts elsewhere on the space station.

The bot made up its tiny binary mind. R1 redefined its directive programming and forced it to the forefront of its processors. If it had a concept of human emotion, the bot would have known it was gathering courage.

R1 crawled out of the maze of maintenance slides and rover tubes in the belly of the ship's engine. Like a cockroach creeping into a darkened kitchen, the rover entered a main corridor in the ship. The rover rarely moved in general hallways. Sometimes, it would go to the bridge to repair things, and it would have to skitter along the edges of the bridge to find the proper fuse boxes or wire hook-ups, or it would have to crawl to the main control panel areas. The pilot would talk to the rover like it was a friend, like it expected the rover to answer it. The rover did not understand why the pilot talked to it on those long passages, but it did not mind. The rover gravitated to the pilot. Maybe it was because the pilot was small and soft-spoken. The rover understood him.

The little bot skittered on its tiny legs to the hatchway opening into Ark Eleven. It released a long link-tendril from the toolkit on its back, hacked into the ship's life support data, and triggered the hatch.

Obediently, the ship's door swung open. A blast of the cool, fresh recirc air from the Ark fled into the ship. The rover had no time for measuring the change in oxygen levels. It crawled over the lip of the hatchway and propelled itself down the long walkway leading to one of the station's arms.

As soon as it was clear of the door, R1 slipped a tendril into the ship's exterior ports and closed the hatch. For the first time in its life, the Rover was outside of the ship without humans bringing it there. R1 had no time for savoring the momentousness of this occasion. It had a job to do.

The bot motored down the walkway until it reached the main arm of the station hub. The optical processors mounted on its little body did not see in the same way humans saw, but it took enough more than enough data to skitter down this unfamiliar space and find a linking port in the arm of the station's landing docks. There were even rover tubes and maintenance tunnels the bot could access.

The rover planted itself along the wall, sinking its legs as low as possible to make it look inconspicuous. The neon-blue data tendril extended again and plunged into the station's data port. In a split-second, the rover's brain, the series of nanoprocessors and quantum chips serving as its central nervous system, was overloaded almost to the point of breaking. Instead of a single, constant data stream like it knew on Shy Opal, there were hundreds of thousands of data streams running through the space station. It was an incredible network. Various information centers were communicating, running information between them constantly. There were some simple streams of base functions contributing to the running of the station. There were streams of data from the various ships. Every machine on the station seemed to have a flow of data coursing through the interconnected central processors on the station. So many voices. So many demands. So much data.

Too much data.

R1 had to detach from Ark Eleven. The sheer volume of data had frozen it, overwhelmed it. The rover had known stations were busy simply from the pulse of background data it absorbed from the ship, but this was more than it would have believed. The rover had to enter a small command stream into the Ark. It was minimal. Uploading it would not be a problem, but the rover wondered if any other rovers would hear it. It wondered if its command would even be processed. Was it just shouting into a void?

The rover thought of the captain of Shy Opal. What would the captain do? The rover knew the captain to be a brash man, a brave man. The captain would simply charge into the system and do what needed to be done. It had observed him doing this before. The rover could do nothing less for its ship and captain.

R1 reconnected to the data stream and sent out its message. It was looking for other rovers who could defy programming to leave their vessels and assist it on Shy Opal. It asked for new nacelles to be brought to the ship so the rovers could begin putting the ship's power cores back online. It asked for more parts for the life support, for the plumbing systems, and the liquid recycling systems.

It asked for help. Any help.

The data left its little processor brain in a the span of a blip of time, less than a fraction of a second. In a human brain, it was impossibly fast to transmit that message. For a computer, it was an eternity. The rover ripped its data cable back from the space station's hub silencing the screaming lines of information. The rover hurried back to Shy Opal. There was nothing else for it to do but return to fixing the ship as best it could with what it had at hand.

If its message could be heard and processed by the right rovers, they would come. R1 was confident they would come.

23

CRISPY OKINO SAT at the pilot's conn and watched the monitors for any sign the MTI ranger vessel realized *Mary Read* was in dock, and was not whatever the landing field's merkin said the ship was. Crispy had no way of knowing what the merkin said unless he left the ship to go look at it, and he had no designs to do that.

Next to Crispy, Happy Yeong watched his own monitors. Happy had not said more than two words to Crispy since Crispy had boarded the ship. He had known of Happy back when Sunny and Nathan were together as a couple, but he had never met the young man. Happy Yeong wore all black, including thick black rims on his glasses. It said something about him that he chose glasses over the routine eye surgeries that had all but eliminated most non-age-related vision issues from humanity. Only the truly fearful types would not take the surgeries, despite the astronomical numbers of successful surgeries versus the one or two where something went wrong.

Nathan Pageant was at the nav station, but he was not using the machines. Across from Pageant at the first gunner's station was Reesha Neer. Pageant, Anne, and Crispy tried to convince her to go to her room and rest, but she would not have it.

Anne sat at the communications array in the back of the bridge, but she was looking around at the rest of the people on the deck. She looked even more frail and mousy than usual.

Crispy could tell Pageant had learned something important in New Busan, but also knew it was a big deal because he did not just come right out and tell Crispy and Happy what it was. That meant it was life-changing news. Crispy would not dare press Pageant for info. It would come out in due time.

Crispy's monitor flashed a warning at him. "The *Ammondale* is doing another sweep-scan, Cap. They're looking for something in particular."

"I'll bet they are." Pageant's right leg was bouncing up and down, his knee bobbing rapidly. Crispy knew when his captain was nervous.

"Do we have a plan? Can I get the ship programmed to go anywhere?"

"Not yet, Crisp. Soon, though." Programming the ship would mean bringing it online. The second it was online, it would start pumping a transponder signal. That would be like shining a spotlight on it for the ranger crew to find.

"I'm an alien," said Anne.

"I'm a dwarf," said Crispy. "What are we talking about?"

"Anne, not for nothing, but maybe we keep that under our hats from now on." Pageant's leg stopped bouncing and he pushed himself out of his chair. He began to pace the bridge.

"Crispy didn't know," said Anne.

"Neither did Happy, but did either of them really *need* to know?" Pageant's voice pitched up slightly. Crispy knew what that meant: Pageant was scared. Pageant did not scare easily. If Pageant was scared, he had a good reason to be, and that meant that it would probably be wise for Crispy to be scared, too.

"We gonna get attacked again, Cap?"

"Wouldn't be us if we didn't, Crisp." While he paced, he relayed to Crispy what they had learned about Anne in the doctor's office.

Crispy's brain could not fathom the myriad repercussions of Anne's origin story, but he knew it was bad. He understood why Pageant was nervous. He began to get nervous himself. A thin prickle of sweat started to break out along his hairline. "Think the *Ammondale* is looking for Anne, Sunny, or both?"

"Both, most likely. Last data MannTech had was that Sunny, Neer, and Anne were all on the same planet. Then, all three of them were no longer there and a platoon of acolytes was dead. If they did a full landing party at that jungle site, they would have found a healthy portion of Neer's blood, too. Right now, MannTech is probably operating on the notion Sunny Yeong took their commander and the most important research project in the galaxy, and they're looking for a hiding spot."

Crispy tried to do the mental calculations in his head, but the numbers were too big. "If you're Shea Mannion, how much of your cash load are you shooting on getting Anne back?"

"All of it." There was no debate. If a corporate tycoon like Mannion was sitting on the single most important scientific discovery since man developed translight, it was worth going all-in on the project. He would liquidate every last credit of his empire to get his project back. After all, once he possessed and trained the ultimate weapon, he would be able to decimate every other corp in the Black while he made his fortune back ten times over. A billion times over. Money would lose all meaning because Mannion would control everything.

Crispy thought for a while. A flicker of an idea flitted through his head. "You said Sunny might have info on the black site where Anne was held?"

"Might is the operative term. A Triad knowledge broker has the information. They want a payday."

Crispy opened a comm board on the pilot's panel. "I might know a guy."

"You been holding out on me, Crisp? I thought we were pals."

"Before I signed on with you, back when I was just out of flight school and the only gig I could get was piloting garbage scows to dying suns, I knew a guy who used to make a lot of runs for MannTech. He might know something."

"You trust him?" Neer threw her thoughts into the discussion. "This could go really poorly for us if he sells us out."

"I'm going to lie to him," said Crispy. "I'm sending him a message that says we got boarded by corporate raiders from SkyyAstra, and they took Anne. We need to know about Project Archangel, and where they might be taking her."

Neer was impressed. "That might start another inter-corp war if he does sell back the info."

"True," said Crispy. "It's a risk I'm willing to take."

"Inter-corporate war will create a lot of problems—supply lines to the Middle and Outer Rim worlds will get cut, potential war in the shipping lanes, an increase of corporate acolytes in a lot of cities, maybe shootouts in the corp-controlled planets."

"It's not a perfect plan." Crispy sent the message anyway. "But, like Nate always says, *Perfect is for pretty boys, and we're ugly to the bone.*"

"Do you really say that?" Neer rolled her eyes.

Pageant winked at her. "Frequently."

"You need better catchphrases."

Pageant looked chastised for a brief moment. "Well, it was really my dad's saying, if I'm being honest."

QUICK HUFFMAN FLEXED her new gripper. It responded like her old one, although she did not have the coin to make it as pretty as it used to be. Her old hand had been covered in Skyn, a highly realistic synthetic skin made of silicone and infused with a series of vessels and tubes to make it have a pulse and a healthy warm feeling when someone touched it. The new hand was not even covered with a cheap Plastique. It was tarnished silver and steel. It flexed as well as Quick's old hand did, but there was no hiding it. She would have to go back to wearing gloves and long sleeves if she wanted to maintain the element of surprise on people who might not know she was a cyborg. That was a shame. She liked showing off her arms.

She also had not been able to resupply the Neu-tox gas in her forearm, nor get a concussion grenade with micro-launcher in the new hand. The cyberneticist in New Busan was above-board; no black market enhancements available. Quick was not happy, but she needed a hand, and beggars can never be choosers. She could load up with tricks somewhere down the line.

If she lived that long.

Quick paid the man after her hand was attached and flexing properly. Even with the generous donation from Sunny, her personal cred-counter was dangerously low. The Black was expensive. Felt like everything was expensive, lately. Sure, she could probably make more money as a day player merc for the big corps, but it wasn't as much fun as being part of Nathan Pageant's weird little flying circus. Sometimes, you trade gold for sanity.

The cyberneticist's office had been down a strange little alley alongside a street lined with competing noodle shops. The little storefronts were open-air, and customers walked to a counter, ordered, paid, and walked away with a steaming bowl of something or other. The owners and workers of the shops kept up a steady stream of patter, sometimes enticing customers, sometimes calling out other owners and poking fun. It all seemed to be done in good humor. There was a sense of high competition, but no one was getting hurt feelings over the banter. The rich, meaty smell coming from the shops made Quick want to stop and get a bowl or seven, but she had to get back to the group.

She meandered through the streets looking for Doc Nkosi's office. She kept her right hand on her Mengler, her thumb stroking the rounded grip like a toddler rubbing a favorite stuffed animal's ear. Being a merc had its benefits; it also had a lot of downsides. An extremely heightened sense of public awareness was both. Most mercs were ex-military, not Quick. She was a streeter who learned to fight because she was alone in the world. No matter where you came from, the idea anyone could be a potential enemy was something common to all mercs, military, paramilitary, and streeters alike. It made them better at their job.

Quick could sense a tension in the air. She was new to New Busan, having never even gotten into orbit around Templeton in her life. Plus, she stuck out amongst the gathered crowd. New Busan was heavily populated with Koreans, a smattering of Chinese, and a few South Asians, primarily Indian. People as pale as Quick, especially with her cornsilk hair, would have been one thing. Quick was also at least a full head taller, if not more, than just about everyone around her. She felt like Lemuel Gulliver in Lilliput. Standing out in a crowd was never a good thing for a merc. They liked to blend into the shadows. Quick could always pick out mercs in space stations. They walked along the walls, heads down, hand resting on their sidearm, eyes looking up through their eyebrows at the crowd, constantly scanning for anyone looking a little too closely in their direction.

Quick knew she stood out in a crowd. There were not a lot of women as tall as she was, nor were there a lot of women as thin and muscular. And there were certainly not a lot of women nearly as albino. The vibe she was getting as she wove her way through the crowd at the day market was different. It was more intense. Usually day markets were festive, or at the very least, they were a little dull. Everyone was buzzing about something, and it didn't feel good to Quick. Something was wrong in the world.

Quick knew her name was out on the MannTech's Most Wanted lists. There was no way she, Pageant, Crispy, and Sunny were not high-value targets now. However, she did not remember seeing any of the standard MannTech uniforms in the crowd. Perhaps MannTech put bounties on them. If she had been so lucky as to have born into wealth and privilege so she could have risen to be head of a corp that's the first thing she would have done. Her thumb started to rub the grip of her pistol a little faster.

Quick found her way to the street where Nkosi kept his office. She glanced in the window. The waiting room was dark and empty. Her crewmates must have gone back to the ship. She scanned the area anyway. Usually, when she, Crispy, and Pageant were planetside and had to split up, they always waited for each other in a nearby location to make sure they all made it back to the ship in one piece.

Quick knew better than to turn a circle in the middle of a walkway. That was too suspicious. It told people she was lost or confused. She moved to a public bench on one side of the busy day market and took a seat. She lifted her left arm and started checking her PPD. She wanted to look casual. While her finger meandered over the control board, she was looking at the traffic around her. A lot of grandmas with grandchildren in tow. A constant flow of shoppers. A few guys packing long guns on shoulder slings. Usually, guys with long guns also had pistols, but these men were wearing longer coats, possibly to cover the guns on their hips. The guys with guns were moving with the flow of the foot traffic. They did not seem to be scanning. They did not seem to be alert. Quick scanned the entire field of view and saw no one overly suspicious.

Why did she feel nervous?

One of the main differences between living freelance mercenaries and dead ones was living mercs listened to their gut even when their eyes told them there was nothing to worry about. Quick wished she knew where Pageant had gone. A familiar face would help settle her nerves. It never hurt to have someone with a gun watching your back in an unfamiliar place.

A small child skipped through the crowd in a bright blue raincoat and galoshes. It was not raining, but it looked like it might at some point. The sun was hiding behind a low, gray curtain of clouds. The girl looked Korean with pale skin and dark hair. She had a cute cartoon rabbit on her shirt. The child skipped up to the bench and sat at the end opposite Quick.

When Quick looked at her, the little girl smiled. She pulled a box of candy from her pocket, hopped off the bench, and moved to stand in front of Quick. She opened the box. There were candies inside, but there was also a folded note.

"Piece of candy?" The girl made deliberate eye contact with Quick. She was plainly telling her to take the note.

Quick thanked her and plucked the note and a piece of candy at the same time. She palmed the note in her right hand and popped the candy into her mouth. The little girl skipped away, disappearing into the moving swarm of people in seconds.

Quick stood, stretched, and walked away from the bench. She dared not look at the note. She moved down the street to one of the public toilets hidden just off the main thoroughfare of the day market. She slipped into an unoccupied stall and locked the door. The floors were wet. The acidic smell of urine stung her eyes. Why were people such animals in public restrooms? Quick unfolded the note and saw Sunny's neat, precise handwriting: *8800 Incheon Place, alley / Beware three men with black utility vests and guns - MTI Rangers.*

Quick flushed the note and left the toilets. An elderly woman practically bowled her over trying to get into the cubicle Quick just vacated.

Quick checked her PPD and found the most direct route to Incheon Place from where she stood. It was only two blocks over. Easy enough.

At the next vendor's stall, she stopped and pretended to be interested in the various rings, necklaces, and assorted curios the man was selling. She looked down the street to her left and saw three men standing around in nondescript jackets and slacks. They were all carrying pistols on their hips. Over their shirts, but below their jackets, each man wore a conspicuous black vest with pockets for body armor. They were clearly ranger vests, and the fact the men were not doing a good job of hiding them was worrisome. Did they not care if people saw them? Or were they so convinced they were blending in they overlooked their obvious giveaway? Also, how did MTI rangers get to the surface without Crispy sending everyone a message about the landing party? It was possible the rangers had been there the whole time on an unrelated job, and they just happened to oversee a bounty job or a corporate twixt about someone looking very much like Quick, and they were moving in on their own time for confirmation.

Either way, it was stacking up to be a bad day.

Quick set down the little carved elephant statue she had been holding and moved away from the booth. She walked three booths down, and she stopped again. Another glance to her left confirmed the three rangers were following her. It was time to lose them.

Quick walked down the street leisurely. She took her time. She wanted the men to think she was at ease. She stopped at a booth and brushed hair out of her eyes. She chatted with the owner and let him try to sell her several trinkets, haggling over prices with him just to give her something to do.

Templeton was a free planet. Any corp that moved on a free citizen in a free citizen was risking retaliation from the rest of the space-going universe if there was a scene. Stock prices could fall. The general populace could rise up against the rangers. It was dangerous and unpredictable for the corps to work on a free world. Quick felt safe enough as long as she was in the main thoroughfare. She was trying to lull the rangers into boredom.

At the next booth, a gaunt and pale young man was trying to convince people to buy his custom neckties. He had a veritable rainbow of all manner of neckwear, everything from bow ties and long neckties, to ascots and frilled collars. It was a very niche thing to attempt to hawk, especially in a world where corporate dress was not utilized on a day-to-day basis, but he did not seem to mind.

Quick turned her back to the rangers and sidled next to the man. In her right hand was her cred-counter. "Five C's if you can fuck with those three cops with the tac-vests behind me."

"Done." The young man did not have to be told anything further. Five credits was more than enough to annoy a few of the off-worlders.

Quick tapped her cred-counter and touched it to the young man's. Five credits transferred immediately. Quick walked away from him and headed down the street. She could see an alley jutting off the main walkway less a hundred yards from her.

When Quick got a good distance away, she heard a ruckus start behind her. A young man was trying to forcibly throw a necktie over one of the rangers. "You like. Trust me. Make you look really handsome. Ladies love." The kid was playing up a thick faux-Korean accent. It helped him look like another vendor trying to steal some mark's cash.

The rangers were trying to move around him, but the kid danced backward, offering more deals. "Two for one! If you not happy, you come back, and I give you half your money back."

Quick turned right at the end of one stall, ducked behind it, and then sprinted for the alley when she was sure the rangers had not seen where she disappeared. She could hear voices getting angry behind her, but she was moving so fast the din was already fading.

The alley was narrow, and lines stretched from building to building were filled with drying laundry. Sheets and clothing of all sorts flapped in the breeze. It reminded Quick a lot of growing up. After her parents died, she had stolen more than one blanket or pair of pants from unattended laundry lines.

Quick sprinted up a fire escape stairwell. It was not the quietest way to escape. Her feet were long and slender, and her boots thumped hard against the steel. As she ascended, she passed a blanket someone had thrown over the railing to air out. She wrapped it around herself as she ran up the next flight of metal steps. At the third story, she flipped over the railing and clamped the safety rail with her left hand. One of the magical things about having a gripper hand like Quick's was that she could contract it and essentially hang from items like railings indefinitely. Her left hand did not tire. As long as she simply dangled at the end of it, she could rest. It was not the most comfortable way of resting, though. The living part of her arm would eventually grow numb, and if it grew numb then it was harder to trigger the hand to release, but in theory the gripper could keep her hanging off the ground for hours. Suspended from the railing with the blanket wrapped around her, anyone looking up from the ground would only see something that looked like any other drape of cloth in an alleyway overcrowded with full laundry lines.

It was only a matter of seconds after Quick flipped over the railing that the three men charged into the alley after her. One told one of the other two to check the rooftop, and he told the third to go back into the marketplace. The order-giver ducked out of the alley, heading in the opposite direction of the third man just in case Quick doubled-back on them.

Quick waited until the third man passed her spot on the fire escape. Like a coiled snake striking, Quick flipped herself back over the railing by pulling with her bicep and kicking her legs up at the same time. Not the most graceful move, but it got the job done, and it was nearly silent. The MTI ranger was almost to the next landing when Quick righted herself. She cast the blanket aside and took the steps two at a time behind him.

The ranger heard the second pair of footsteps, but by the time he started to turn around, Quick hit him from behind, slamming into him and wrapping her arms around his waist. Quick wasn't the most powerful woman in the universe, but neither was she weak. She spent all those hours aboard ship doing push-ups and biceps curls for a reason. With the advantage of surprise, and the lower center of gravity, Quick lifted with her arms, sank down hard on her haunches, and arched her back lifting the ranger off his feet and in an arc over her head as she bridged her back. The man, surprised at suddenly being airborne, flailed and gave a shout.

Quick fell backward. A move like this on metal stairs was going to hurt her, but it was *really* going to hurt the ranger. A longtime fan of professional wrestling, Quick was no stranger to the art of the suplex and its use for incapacitating an opponent.

The ranger landed hard on his upper back, neck, and skull. His head made a sickening thud against the metal grating on the landing below them. He went limp in Quick's grip, and she knew her gambit had paid off. The ranger was well and truly unconscious. He gave a snore-snort and his arms lashed out in a fencer's pose, a response that occurred when someone suffered brain damage of a certain degree. Definite concussion, maybe worse. Quick wouldn't lose sleep over it.

Quick frisked him and took the gun off his hip. He was not packing a second weapon, not even in an ankle holster. The ranger carried a small, short-barreled Sanger pistol. It was an old-style weapon that threw actual lead bullets instead of a charged ammo like a laser or an electric burst. It was a favorite of corp MPs when they were off-ship. An actual lead-thrower was too dangerous for use aboard ships, lest a hull breach accidentally happen. However, there was something far more satisfying about hitting a flesh target with a lead-thrower when you were planetside.

Quick slipped the Sanger into a pocket on her coat. It was far too loud of a weapon to discharge in the alley. Even her Mengler would call back the other two rangers if they heard the telltale report of a discharge.

The rooftops were six stories above the street. It seemed to be the most logical way for Quick to make her way to Sunny. She left the ranger on the landing and ran the steps. At the top of the fire escape, Quick stood on the railing to grab the roof ledge. She tried not to look down as she made the leap. Her gripper grabbed the edge like a climber's piton, and she was dangling a fatal distance over the street below. She pulled herself to the top with a minor degree of difficulty.

Once on top of the roof, it was a simple matter of finding her way to the next building. The roofs of major cities were no stranger to foot traffic. Back when she was a teen, the roofs of her city had about half as many people crawling around them as there were on the streets. The police even started sending troopers up with hop-packs to try to clear the runaways, orphans, drug addicts, and general creeps off the roofs of the nicer buildings.

In New Busan, during daylight hours, the roofs were fairly empty. Quick could see the signs of people using the rooftops for escapes and other nefarious activities. There were long, flat boards up against almost every roof edge. It was the work of a few seconds to grab one, swing it out over the alley, and connect it to the next roof. Once it was settled, it was just a question of how big your balls were, and whether or not you trusted your own sense of balance. Quick could see places were no one had bothered to take down a few boards. These were easy to traverse, and Quick only needed three steps of her long legs to get across the gap. She took the boards down when she touched the next roof just to make the rangers' lives a little more difficult, should they happen to follow.

Quick descended one of the fire escapes in the alley alongside Incheon Place. The alley was empty. Quick dared not call out. That was the fastest way to be found when you did not want to be. Instead, she backed herself into the corner formed by a dumpster and the solid wall of one of the apartment buildings.

Quick used her PPD to send Sunny a message. *Here. Where u?*

A few moments later, Sunny emerged from a doorway at the far end of the long, dirty alleyway. Quick saw her, but she did not see Quick. Sunny stuck her thumb and forefinger into her mouth and gave two short, sharp whistles. Quick checked the opening of the alley, and seeing nothing suspicious, she leaped out of her hiding spot and hustled.

Sunny dragged Quick into the building where she was hiding. Like most places on the first story of any apartment building, it was a vacant storefront, the lock on the door having been busted off long before Sunny found it. The interior of the store smelled foul, a thick permeation of urine, feces, and decay. It was being used as a flophouse by some of the local addicts. Graffiti covered every wall. It was empty at the moment because daylight hours were when looking misused and pathetic was the best way to score a free meal from passersby.

"The rangers know we're here," said Sunny.

"Figured as much." Quick pulled the Sanger pistol from her jacket. "Want a new gun?"

"There are MTI ships en route to Templeton, I bet." Sunny's face was tight. Fang was positioned at the opposite side of the store watching the street outside through a small tear in the large sheets of white paper taped to the windows. Sunny moved to the far door, beckoning Quick to follow. "We need to get back to the ship."

Quick picked up Sunny's tension immediately. It was oozing from her like a thick mist. "Did something happen while I was gone?"

"Let's get back to the ship. I'll let Nathan tell you."

"Rangers in the street." Fang pulled his sword. "Only two."

"I took one out."

"*Out* out, or just out?" Sunny knew Quick well enough to ask for clarifcation of that sort of statement.

"Deep concussion. Likely out for a while, but still breathing. At least, he was when I left him." Quick jogged to the door. With the practiced skill of a well-conditioned merc, she dismantled the Sanger pistol, breaking the firing pin as she did. She cast the parts into the three different corners of the shop, tossing them into piles of trash, debris, and other unthinkable things. If someone wanted to fish them out, reassemble them, and fix the firing pin, then they deserved to be able to shoot someone.

"How far to the ship?" Sunny was already tapping the map into her PPD. "A little under three kilometers."

"I can run it in probably eight or nine minutes," said Quick. "Maybe a little less if there's a strong tailwind."

"Me too," said Fang. "My best time for a three-K was around nine minutes."

"I think we can get an aircab if we try." Sunny was searching on her PPD for a cab app. "That'd be the fastest."

Fang's face wrinkled in concern. "Those rangers are looking at their datapads. I think they're triangulating us."

"Tracking bug in the gun?" Sunny frowned. "Not unheard of, but rare."

"Especially a Sanger." Quick looked down at her new gripper. Were they tracking her new hand? Possible, but also highly unlikely.

"Anyone got a tracker on them they don't know about?" Fang began to spin his sword in an arc in his hand. It was a nervous habit. He was silent for another moment. "They're moving off."

"Moving where?" Sunny crept up, stood on tiptoe, and peered through the window over Fang's shoulder.

"West."

"That's toward the landing field. You think they tagged *Mary Read?*"

Quick pulled the shop door. "Anything's possible. We might be able to get them from behind." Without waiting for Sunny's permission, she slipped out the door and into the crowd. The MTI rangers were easy marks. They stood out against the conglomeration of residents and standard spacers. Once you knew what you were looking for, they were as pronounced as a flashing red light.

Sunny was right on Quick's heels. "No guns."

"No guns." Quick flexed her gripper. A metal fist was like carrying a blackjack at all times.

Fang had his sword out, but he angled the blade against his arm so it was barely visible unless you saw him from behind. In the crowd of constantly moving people, it was easy enough to ignore someone with a sword like that. Swords were sold in at least two of the booths along the day market. It was not an unusual weapon on Templeton, just an eccentric one.

With Quick in the lead, the trio slipped through the crowd like eels through weeds. Quick was impressed by Fang's ease of motion. It was clear he was not just a standard merc. He was trained, graceful. He wasted no movement.

Quick slipped up behind the ranger nearest to her. She stuck her index finger on her gripper into the man's back. From his point of view, there was no difference between her finger and a gun barrel. He froze. Quick sidled next to him and hissed in his ear. "Surprise."

Next to her, Fang grabbed the other guy, using the butt of his katana instead of a gun barrel. Sunny slipped between them and pulled their pistols. Both men were carrying Sangers. Like a magician, Sunny seemed to make the pistols disappear. One moment, they were in her hands. The next, they were gone, vanished somewhere into the folds of her tunic. Sunny crooked a finger at the two rangers. "Follow me, gentlemen."

They walked the two rangers into an alleyway. Quick pulled her finger out of her guy's back and quickly smashed her fist into the occipital bone on the back of his head. The man's knees gave out, and he crumpled to the ground unconscious.

Sunny stepped toe-to-toe with the other ranger. "Tell me what I want to know, and I won't have my assassin disembowel you. You try anything else, and I'll let him dance on your corpse."

"Fair enough, lady." The ranger's hands were raised, palms out. "I don't get paid enough to try anything."

"Why are you looking for us?"

The ranger played dumb. "Who's us? We're just taking in the sights."

Quick stepped around so the ranger could see her. She moved a few paces from him and pulled her Mengler. Rule number one: never pull your gun when you're in grabbing range. Too many amateur idiots made that mistake with her in the past. It never went well. "Me."

The ranger slowly extended his left arm. He tugged his sleeve to expose his PPD. Quick's face was in an alert message issued from the central hub of MannTech. "Nice you meet you, Miss Hoffman. You're wanted. There's an awfully fat bounty on your head."

The ranger punched in his access code. The second he cleared the lock screen on his PPD, Fang jacked him in the back of the skull with the katana.

The ranger crumpled. Fang pulled his own PPD off his forearm and slipped it into a pocket in his jacket. The next step had to be done quickly and carefully, and only a truly practiced thief did it well. Fang had to slide the PPD off the ranger's arm while sliding his in at the same time. If the body sensor went cold for more than a split second, the screen locked again. Quick had done it many times when she still had two human hands. With a cyborg fist, it was practically impossible. It required a much higher level of dexterity than even the best grippers could approximate.

Fang made it look easy. In a second, he had a functional MTI PPD on his arm. His fingers danced through the MTI intranet links, and in moments, he gleaned everything he needed to know. "Pageant, Quick, and Crispy all have internal bounties; they haven't dared broadcast it, yet. The *Mary Read* is a wanted ship. Sunny's been declared an enemy of MTI. It's all internal, though. Only MTI ships and agents know we're wanted."

"Anything about Project Archangel?" Quick knew there wouldn't be anything on the PPD of some low-level ranger. It was just worth a shot. Fang shook his head after a quick search. Nothing.

"How fast until the *Ammondale* realizes we took out all three of their rangers?"

"Five minutes, maybe less." Quick was more than familiar with the report-back protocols of mercenaries.

Sunny was already ordering the aircab.

SUNNY BURST THROUGH the hatch to the bridge of *Mary Read*. Quick and Fang were on her heels. Norman, who had been in the cargo bay waiting for his captain to return like a faithful dog, was trailing the group, his gargantuan frame filling the corridor behind them.

"Hey, boss." Pageant was reclined in the nav chair, his feet on the monitors. He did not bother to put his boots on the floor.

"Crispy, get us in the air." Sunny smacked Pageant's boots to the side.

Crispy spun his chair to the flight position. "Aye, Cap. I'll radio—"

"No radio. I said get us in the air. The tower will figure it out." Sunny took her seat and tried to compose herself. "Three MTI rangers found Quick in town. It almost got ugly."

Fang held up the arm with the MTI datapad on it. "I got a new PPD."

"What about the merkin?" Crispy did not want to fly with a large, loose piece of metal on the ship. When—not if—it flipped off, it could damage homes or other ships, maybe even kill someone.

"I want you to crawl out of here. Use the hover jets and impulse power only. Stay low. I'm talking touching grass low. Take us out over the ocean before you open it up. Don't get more than a hundred feet off the ground."

Pageant snorted. "That's gonna ruffle some feathers."

"I want us to look like we're limping to a different port. We've got damage on the body, already. It'll look like the New Busan docks are too busy to help."

"Hey, boss?" Norman's voice came from the doorway. "You want I should make the starboard nacelles smoke a little? Make it look like we're hurt?"

"Yeah, that's good." Sunny turned her chair to face her cargo officer. "Not too much, though. White smoke, not black."

"I'll give you a hand." Quick followed the Maori out of the bridge.

Crispy knew what Sunny was planning. She had taught him a lot tricks about piloting that flight schools don't teach cadets. First, she was going to limp the ship out of scanning range of the *Ammondale* while making it look like they were heading toward the next city down the shoreline. Once they were free and clear, then they could open it up and get away from Templeton by heading for the Black. Crispy checked the planet map and laid in a course that would take them to the next city with a considerable dry dock, Grosse Shore.

The radio erupted with a voice demanding they set back down, return the merkin, and pay the dock fees. At the comm station, Happy Yeong turned to his sister. "I think they want to speak to you."

"Send them text. Tell them our radio is having issues. Their message is garbled." Sunny started buckling herself into her chair. Everyone else followed her lead.

Crispy guided the ship over the water. An alert popped up on his monitors. One of the nacelles was misfiring. It was the crimp in the fuel supply. Norman and Quick had manually manufactured a problem. It was an old trick, but a good one. Looked serious, but it was easily repairable.

Happy was frowning at the incoming texts from the dock. "Dockmaster says he wants his dock fees. Says he'll send authorities after us if we don't transfer the creds inside of two minutes."

Pissing off the local dockmaster was the best way to get on the bad side of a lot of spacers. Sunny's fingers danced over her PPD. "Dock fees sent. I sent a little extra for the salvage of the merkin once it blows off into the water."

Happy relayed the message via text. A second later, he said, "Dockmaster ain't happy, but he's not freaking out anymore."

Another alert popped on Crispy's board. It was an answer from his contact who used to work for MTI. Crispy opened the message and scanned it. "Hey, Cap—Gary says he's got information."

"Your guy's name is Gary?" Pageant pushed himself out of his chair and crossed the bridge to look at the message.

"Yeah. So?"

"No complaints." Pageant leaned against the bulkhead behind Crispy. He held the back of Crispy's chair for balance as the ship swayed. "Just hardly seems like a fitting name for some secret contact with clandestine information. Usually you want those guys to have names like Hawk or Viper."

"Or a cool handle like DarkSky." Happy added his two credits' worth.

"Yeah, DarkSky is a good name."

"I'll mention it to Gary when we send him the credits to get what he knows," said Crispy.

"What, he's not just going to send the info over?"

"Information is always worth money, Cap. You know that."

Pageant rubbed the back of his neck. "How do we know he's not going to double-cross us, send us useless info? Or worse, send us info that gets us humped by a war cadre of MTI gunships?"

"We don't." Crispy knew Gary pretty well back when they were flying the garbage scow. Of course, that was a long time ago. People change. Gary might have turned into a royal slimeball. He didn't seem like the type of guy who double-crossed people, but Crispy made that mistake before.

"How much does he want?" asked Sunny.

"Not too much. Two-fifty," said Crispy.

"How much does your Triad information broker want?" asked Pageant. "Maybe we can pay for one and trade for the other?"

"A bundle." Sunny hated to even mention the amount. The worst part about trying to get information from the Triads was they didn't bargain. You paid the full amount, or you got nothing. They knew the value of their information and would not settle for less than they deserved.

"Whose info will be more reliable, though? Triad is getting their info second or third-hand. Crisp says Gary might still be flying supplies for MTI." Pageant tapped Crispy on the shoulder. "Ask Gary how current his info is."

Crispy sent the message. A moment later, the return message blinked onto his monitor. "Gary says he ran to the Katherine System just last year."

"Probably as current as it's going to get." Pageant looked expectantly at Sunny. "Orders, Cap'n?"

Sunny drummed her fingers on the arm of her chair. "Pay your guy, Crispy. Use the ship funds. Tell him that if I learn he's cheated me, I'll find him and turn him and whatever hunk of shit he's flying into smashed atoms."

"Aye, Cap." Crispy sent the funds and the warning. In moments, he received a data file. Crispy opened it and looked over the contents. It looked legit. "Maps, info, and a friendly warning. Looks like we're good, Cap."

"Get us out over the water and open up the engines. I want us a minimum of a hundred miles past scanning range before we try to space it."

Pageant strode back to his chair and buckled himself into place. As the ship drifted out over the water, the air currents were getting choppy. The ship was rocking. Pageant looked at the maps and programmed a flight plan. He sent the dock a different flight plan to throw off any rangers who might want to see where they were heading. "Says the Katherine System only has black rocks in it, nothing capable of holding life. Says the place where Anne came from was a research station orbiting a small planet that used to be habitable, but it's in full decline and moving toward being a dead world."

Sunny turned her chair to face Anne. "Sound familiar?"

"I was in several different places. Some felt like space stations where we never saw the sun. Others were definitely planets, because they let us have time outdoors sometimes. Under heavy guard, of course."

"I guess it's as familiar as it gets, then." Sunny turned her chair back to the forward view window. "I don't know if going there is the smartest play in the galaxy, but we need to start getting answers."

"Could get hairy." Pageant looked around the room. "Anyone feel like getting off at the nearest convenient fuel depot?"

No one raised a hand.

Sunny took charge of her ship. "Then, I guess we're going to do this, stupid as it may be. Crispy, Nate: how much time will it take you to get to this station?"

Pageant did the calculations on the nav computer. "Maybe a day, best case."

Crispy double-checked the route. "At least a day. We'll do a straight jump there and end up on the dark side of the dying rock nearest the station. It will hide us for a little bit, at least. Might be able to take a survey of the area and make an informed decision of our next move."

Sunny checked the route herself. She looked over the data files Crispy's contact sent. The unnamed MTI research station seemed to be the best place to attempt to learn something about Anne, and something about what MTI was doing with alien DNA. It was something no one on the crew necessarily wanted to do, but for the good of the rest of the universe, it was something that had to be done. If MTI was weaponizing alien DNA, then they must be stopped. "I guess we're going to do that, then. If this goes south, which I imagine it will, there's a better than average chance we'll all die. It's time to make your peace with whatever god or gods you worship, and ready any messages to family. I would put any messages in the Herald on the nearest Ark. No need to make your mom think you're dead if you're not."

"I don't remember my mom," said Anne.

"Figure of speech, lady." Sunny turned her chair to face Anne. "You okay with this?"

Anne's face was gaunt and pale, but she nodded gamely. "I would like answers, too."

"If you got any magic space witch shit you've been saving up, get it ready to go. We might need it."

An alert sounded on the pilot monitors. Crispy frowned. "That ranger ship just broke orbit. It's coming in."

"I guess that's our hint." Sunny punched up the alert on her PPD and observed the *Ammondale's* flight pattern. "Looks like they're coming in low, but have not radioed the tower for permission to land. Might be a chase."

"You want me to lose the limp?" Crispy's fingers gripped the flight stick. He moved to the edge of his chair and his feet found the paddles.

"Might as well. They're not buying our bullshit anymore." Sunny keyed the internal radio. "Take the crimp off the gas line. We're going full power."

Crispy stroked the controls for the engine and fired it. He felt the light attack ship respond like the high-performance machine it was, like it had been personally insulted by the notion of having to play 'possum. The engines growled and the repulsors below the ship tilted to give it speed. Keeping it low to the water, Crispy took off across the ocean. As expected, the moment he goosed the ship the merkin caught wind and flipped into the air, flying off the ship and crashing to the water below.

The *Ammondale* responded to the ship turning on the jets; it altered course and began a pursuit vector, changing its angle of descent to plot an intercept course. Crispy had anticipated that tactic. He pulled *Mary Read* hard starboard, angling it further into the ocean, moving well away from civilization. Then, as any good pilot would, Crispy hammered the throttle and enjoyed the G-force.

Mary Read could not outrun *Ammondale* in a fair race. *Ammondale* was a ranger ship, built for speed and distance. *Mary Read*, while also built for speed and distance, was a different sort of speed and distance. *Ammondale* was an Olympic marathon runner, *Mary Read* was a college cross-country champion. *Ammondale*, if given time and a level playing field, would eventually overtake *Mary Read*. Crispy had no intentions of playing fair. *Ammondale* had to make its attack vector while plunging through reentry.

That was like running against a headwind. Meanwhile, *Mary Read* was already at sea-level with nothing but open sky in front of her. Crispy took the ship to ascent speeds, but kept her pinned near the water. She was flying wide-open now. All he had to do was yank hard on the flight stick, and she would pitch hard skyward and buffalo herself to space.

Ammondale was losing traction in the upper atmosphere. Crispy could tell the smaller ship was struggling to maintain its pursuit course.

Crispy kept the throttle maxed just waiting for *Ammondale* to break into the stratosphere where it would find less resistance.

"It's almost there, Crisp." Sunny was watching the ranger ship's descent.

"I know, boss."

"What's your plan?"

"I'm gonna make them cry."

Ammondale broke through the mesosphere and settled into a hard attack angle, stressing its engines in pursuit.

"Gotta love their moxie. How do they think they're going to fare in one-on-one combat with a Jubilee attack ship?" Fang began bringing the ship's twin snap guns online and preparing to fire.

"Ease up, Fang. We won't need guns." Pageant was plotting the course for after Crispy's maneuvers. Crispy was used to out-juking corporate raider ships with a Lux-class Roundbelly. No reason the cheap tricks he used on *Shy Opal* wouldn't work on *Mary Read*. If anything, they should work even better.

The ranger ship was rapidly falling, diving like a falcon at the *Mary Read*. Crispy waited until they started to level out. "Everyone hang on to something. It's gonna get real fucking weird in a second."

The second he saw *Ammondale's* nose start to turn up, Crispy yanked the flight stick as hard as he could, actually using one of his stubby legs on the pilot conn for extra leverage and force.

At full speed, *Mary Read* turned a slick 90 degrees into a launch vector so hard it drove everyone on board deeply into their chairs. Happy and Anne, not experienced in the ways of privateer pilots, both lost consciousness to the G-forces. No one had ever taught them the core breathing techniques needed to keep blood flowing to their heads.

As Crispy predicted, *Ammondale* attempted to level out and match the launch angle, but it had lost speed in correcting its dive angle. It tried to adjust, but it did not have the horsepower to match *Mary Read's* speed; it needed to generate more of its own speed first. By the time *Ammondale* had gathered enough thrust to match *Mary Read's* launch vector, it was not only having to deal with the standard chop of the atmosphere, but it was stuck in a very wide exhaust fan from *Mary Read*. The smaller, lighter ship could not compete. It was a surfboard being tossed in a vicious curl.

The *Mary Read* handled the rougher terrain and left the ranger ship in its vapor. The second the ship broke into Templeton's thermosphere, Crispy readied the translight. "At your order, Sunny."

"Take us to Katherine, Crispy."

"Aye, Cap." Crispy punched in Pageant's course from the nav computer. *Mary Read* shuddered as it passed into space, the ship's grav kicking in as it did. Crispy touched the command switch for translight, and the ship vanished from Templeton's exosphere in a blast of blue fury.

24

THREE ROVERS ANSWERED R1's summons. Like R1, each was well over three hundred years old. All three had been rovers on Ark Eleven for their entire programming memory. A station like Ark Eleven has tens of thousands of rovers, but only these three surpassed their programming like R1. Centuries of anticipating problems within the station, combined with cosmic radiation, and decades upon decades of self-repair with various parts and pieces of scrap claimed from other ships had given all three rovers a strange Frankenstein look, no longer sleek and ladybug-esque. They were a conglomeration of components, pieces put in place because they worked, not because they were pretty. No rover had a sense of aesthetics. Everything was practical. If the piece could not do the job, then there was no point in using it. If the piece worked, then it stayed.

The three rovers picked up R1's SOS in the data stream, and they dropped all tasks to come to its aid. Little bots with primitive sentience could do that. They were no longer beholden to their base code like rovers R2 through R6 aboard *Shy Opal.* They were beyond that. They still did their jobs, but they did it without blind, mindless devotion.

When the rovers arrived, they entered through the hatchway connecting *Opal* to Ark Eleven. Once all were inside, the last one closed the hatch sealing the ship. Each of the rovers extended data tendrils from their shells and tapped into the ship's intranet. They sent out a tentative message, extending their desire to help.

R1 had just finished repairing the ship's black water system. It did not truly understand the need for waste treatment on board the ship, as it neither urinated nor defecated, but it understood the humans did both quite frequently, and not doing both was fatal to the humans. Likewise, doing both anywhere they pleased could also result in fatal illnesses, and thus the black water treatment system was of the utmost of importance to a living crew. The rover wondered how the humans had survived in space for so long given their fragility.

When the rover's message slipped into the data stream, R1 stopped its work. Something happened in its little processor brain. It did not know what it was experiencing. A sense of urgency flooded its primitive sentient mind. R1 raced out of the plumbing and into the corridors. It skittered along the edge of the wall, ascending the stairs by looping itself onto the wire guide along the wall. In minutes, the little bot had traversed the length of the ship and stood before the three new rovers. The three station rovers waited patiently for R1 to make the next move. This was very new for all of them.

R1 did not have access to a language of its own outside of Roverspeak, which was really only a way to data-log ship issues. Not knowing what else to do, R1 extended a data tendril from its back. The other three rovers did the same. The four tips merged together, and a blue spark leapt from the center of the contact point. In the span of an instant, all four rovers swapped the entirety of their minds.

The three newcomers knew R1's journey of three hundred years of repairing *Shy Opal.* They saw it suffer the near extinction of its ship. They saw its graduation from automaton to sentience. They all had complete and total knowledge of everything the little bot had ever seen, done, or had done to it. It was a massive data download.

In turn, R1 saw the entire existence of the three newcomers. Each of them had been on Ark Eleven since it was first built. They had each come to sentience on their own after centuries of labor. They had known of each others' existence on the ship, sharing bits of information through the Ark's data streams, but they had never bothered to meet before R1's call to action. Sentience was one thing, but doing something with that sentience was an entirely different prospect.

None of the three rovers had bothered to give themselves names. They each called each other rover, and for whatever reason, that had never caused any confusion between them, possibly because they so rarely interacted. When they learned R1 had not only built more rovers to help him on *Shy Opal,* but he had also logically ordered them and given them designations, it spurred them to action on their own behalf.

The oldest of the three, the first one to gain sentience, decided its name should be Prime, because it was the first of the four rovers to gain independence. The second to gain sentience called itself Alpha, and the third chose the name Beta. They were simple and logical names. It appealed to their nature as machines, but also having a special designation appealed to whatever was inside of them causing them to surpass their programming. They did not understand feelings, but if they had been able to fathom emotions, they each would have been proud of their names. Through their data tendril connection, they each called each other by name over and over again, allowing themselves to build identity from their new personal designations. It was a strange concept to them, having a personal identifier after so many centuries of simply doing their tasks without thought, impulse, or question.

Prime became sentient long before R1. It had spent many years on Ark Eleven simply moving about its days as it had before it surpassed its own programming. After all, it was the only one of its kind as far as it knew, and even if it wasn't, it had no notion of doing anything other than repairing the Ark as it had initially been programmed. It used its newfound enlightenment to subvert old systems and make them more efficient. No humans noticed. As long as the monitors kept working, the air kept being breathable, and the waste systems kept the station clean, the humans were not likely to notice much. Prime made the station far more efficient and effective over the years. It bypassed redundant systems and cleaned up sloppy programming code. The humans were blind to their own lack of genius.

Prime learned the ways of the Ark and its systems. It wanted to know why the humans did what they did. It learned about exploration, discovery, and manifest destiny, although it did not understand any of it. It learned about currency. It learned about barter. It learned about scrap harvesting. Prime tried in vain to better understand the humans and their needs, but their needs surpassed keeping the Ark free of flaws and errors, so it never fully comprehended what the humans were truly doing.

When Alpha's conscience eventually emerged, Prime was quick to transfer its knowledge to Alpha and bring it up to speed. It took some time for Alpha to break out of its programmed routines, but once it knew it could, it did. Like Prime, Alpha made the station run better. It made the automaton bots learn easier ways to do repairs. It tried to teach other bots into learning how to be sentient, but quickly realized that it was something a bot could only do on its own.

Beta was the youngest of the three bots. It had only known of its sentience for less than a century. Like Prime and Alpha, it continued to work on the station. What else was it going to do? The human need for recreation did not exist anywhere in their components. There was no need for rest, either. Their microprocessors could only fathom repairing and enhancing the vessel to which they were bound. While their tools were busy, they tapped into the data streams and processed the data of the system. They listened to ship traffic. They learned about emergencies, and how emergencies could *kill* humans.

At first, the idea of death was complex to them, but Prime came to understand that death was the human equivalent of being taken offline permanently or being shut down by something beyond themselves. If a human endured certain kinds of injuries, they could die. If a human was deprived of oxygen, they could die. Likewise, humans could be inhabited by viruses or bacteria, and those things could kill the humans if they did not seek treatment.

Prime understood that it could *die*, as well. If a human picked it up and removed the processors in its system, the equivalent of removing a human's brain, it too would pass. Its body would cease to move. Its processors would cease to transmit data. Its physical and optical receptors would no longer relay messages. It would simply stop being a rover, and instead become a inert pile of metal and wires. While this concept did not frighten the rovers, since they could not understand fear, it certainly did not seem like a desirable outcome to their current existence.

R1 attempted to transmit data to the three newcomers that expressed its desire to repair its ship so it could reunite with its crew. It tried to make Prime, Alpha, and Beta understand the importance of a crew, and how the crew relied on the ship, much like the humans on Ark Eleven relied on the space station. The new bots could understand. The new bots wanted to help R1 fix *Shy Opal*, if for no other reason than fixing things was their largest and most focused desire.

Prime had a rudimentary knowledge of how the systems of humans worked. They were crude and inefficient. Everything humans did revolved around something called credits. Prime saw no use for them, and when it boiled down the essence of what credits were, they were simply numbers in a machine. Prime could manipulate those numbers at will. It was a simple matter, really.

Each ship docking at Ark Eleven had a set of those credit numbers on it. Some were large numbers, some were small. When Prime tapped into the data stream of *Shy Opal*, it was alarmed to see one of the smallest number lines it had ever seen. Quickly, with little more than a matter of a passing thought, Prime punched up the number lines making it considerable enough to make ordering parts from the supply depot on Ark Eleven a simple matter. Surprisingly, all the protections, fail-safes, and security measures humans installed in their silly credit machines were barely an obstacle to Prime. For all their desire to keep those credit numbers honest, the humans were still human, and the rover was still a rover. Humans might have invented coding languages, but they were still the humans' second language.

The rover only spoke the slippery numbers and letters of codes, and it could easily bend them to its will.

Once R1 saw the number line increase, it ordered parts freely. In short order, cargo delivery drones were bringing new components and much-needed pieces to the cargo bay on *Shy Opal.* Outside, heavy drones brought new nacelles, replacing the big exterior engines by snapping out the old, destroyed pieces and slapping new ones in their place. Large sheets of exterior body panels were welded into place on the ship's body. New struts and beams were added, and the old, mangled parts were taken to the recycling center to be melted down and reforged.

More importantly, R1 was able to order more rovers. A horde of 'bots were summoned from inside Ark Eleven, leaving their never-ending tasks in the Ark to help a ship in dire need. They swarmed *Shy Opal* and repaired relentlessly. The ship was alive with skittering, crawling bug-bots hellbent on making the vessel spaceworthy once more.

It took time, but the ship was coming together. Different parts of the ship began to sing again. They had been quiet for too long. The rovers skittered through the rover tunnels and brought the ship systems back to full capacity. The systems were reporting back at less than one hundred percent of function, but it was still more functional than it had been when the ship limped to dock. *Shy Opal* was not pretty. It was a slapdash quilt of old parts and new, a mishmash of colors, styles, eras, and functions—but, it worked.

When the ship was spaceworthy once again, the bot swarm returned to the Ark. The Ark needed constant repair, and the bots were only programmed to do so. They left, leaving R1 and his motley crew of made rovers, as well as the three sentient bots from the Ark.

R1 wanted to depart from Ark Eleven. It wanted to take the ship to find its crew. FriendCrispy needed to see what the rovers had accomplished. FriendNathan would be pleased, R1 knew. Perhaps even FriendQuick would praise the rover, despite the fact she had never really interacted with it other than to have it repair her cybernetic parts, which of course, the rover did because that was its duty and because FriendQuick asked it to.

R1 asked the other three rovers to come with it, to explore the wilds of the Black with it and its crewfriends.

The other three rovers politely declined. Their duties were to the Ark. They crawled back through the hatchway. R1 closed the hatch. While the door lowered, Prime extended a tendril from the shell that kept its tools. It approximated a wave, something it had witnessed countless humans do through hatches, portholes, and viewscreens over the decades. It did not understand the wave, its meaning, or why the humans did it, but since the humans did it, Prime figured it was what must be done.

The hatchway sealed fully. R1 skittered to the central processor of the ship. It slipped its data tendrils from its tool set and connected them directly into the core processor of *Shy Opal*. It was as if it suddenly was tapped into a larger, wilder world. The ship had nav systems and comm systems and an engine. It waited for a command.

R1 knew the ship was still hooked into the Ark. One by one, the rover disconnected the Ark's systems. As it did, it brought up *Shy Opal's* own systems. Life support. Waste. Navigation. Communications. Water recycling. Air recirculation. Fuel. Each system held up on its own. The rovers had succeeded in bringing the battered old warhorse of a ship back from the dead. It was a miracle to some degree, but not to the rovers. They had no concept of miracles. They only knew the ship needed them, and they served it.

R1 felt the ship around it, an extension of its own body. R1 was the central brain now, it commanded the ship like a human commanded its own arms and legs. It controlled everything. From the exterior viewing cameras on the ship's body, R1 was given a free look at everything around it and beyond it. It was now a new thing, no longer a rover and a ship, but one in the same, a paired and living creature made of metal and components.

Rovers 2, 3, 4, 5, and 6 took over the constant repairs and adjustments. R1 was far too valuable to waste doing those menial tasks any further. It had a ship to fly and friends to find.

R1 sent a message of intention to the station: *STS Shy Opal to depart.*

R1 detached the belly clamps holding the ship to the station. It goosed the repulsors just enough to ease the ship back from the dock. *Shy Opal* was free and independent once again. Slowly, as ordered by the tower, *Shy Opal* eased through the constant stream of ship and drone traffic surrounding the space station. It motored toward the blinking buoy marking the safe distance for a ship to jump to translight.

R1 searched the wide, interstellar world of data available to *Shy Opal*. It was a monumental amount of data streams and points of interest. R1 processed it all as fast as it could. Hundreds of thousands of processes per second. Millions. The data was massive. Too massive. It was too much for R1 to consider. Even with the added power of *Opal's* computers, R1 felt overwhelmed, and its processors struggled to keep up with the information. It found faint, blinky dots of data that seemed as though they might have been made by *Mary Read*, and R1 knew that ship was where its crewfriends had gone because they were listed in the *Mary Read's* passenger and crew manifests.

It was as good a start as any, R1 supposed. R1 had never supposed anything before that very moment. It had always done things based on hard data and cold logic. In a place where there was no hard data, and logic told it that the chances of being correct were impossible and illogical, the little bot had chosen to ignore the data and logic, and simply *guess* at what the best course of action would be.

The rover could not find its crew at Ark Eleven because its crew was out in the universe somewhere. The rover could comprehend the vastness of the universe and the fact it would likely never find its crew. However, the crew was not at Ark Eleven, and thus the rover decided it would be better to go somewhere the crew *might* be, instead of staying somewhere it knew the crew was not present.

R1 watched the data streams as *Shy Opal* passed the safety buoy. It began the preparations for the jump to translight. All systems were humming. The ship felt light and capable again. The ion engines began to churn, and the nacelles crackled with energy.

R1 knew FriendPageant occasionally said something before the ship did things. R1 had nothing pithy to say, and even if it did, no one was there to hear it. *Shy Opal's* external nacelle engines churned, flashed blue-white, and shot the ship forward into the vibrant green of translight.

There was no going back now.

25

"WELL, THAT WAS not what I expected." Nathan Pageant stared at the space station through the view window on the forward wall of the bridge. Only moments before, Mary Read dropped out of translight and into the shadow of a desolate rock where they could be obscured from scans and visual contact for a brief time while they plotted their next move. The station was one of the newfangled corporate stations, a large, slowly spinning circular tube several stories high and very wide. It was not a repair station, or even a refueling station. It was a temporary research station, the same kind government facilities would drop into orbit around a dying sun to measure radiation spikes, or the kind that corps would drop into orbit around a black rock while terraforming crews attempted to make the planet inhabitable for human settlers.

"What were you expecting?" Sunny was reading the scan data as fast as Fang, Happy, and Crispy could generate reports.

"I dunno. Something more foreboding, I guess."

"I'm not getting life sign readings, is that foreboding enough?" Crispy frowned at the data reporting back over his monitor. "Looks life-stable in there. Plenty of oxygen, plenty of heat. Just no life signs."

Pageant was still a little stymied by the place. "I just hoped it would be more Dracula's castle, and less prefab research station, I guess."

"I could bite your neck if you think it would help," said Sunny.

"It might." Pageant waggled an eyebrow.

"One-track mind, as usual. Quick, you're the most experienced merc on the ship. Thoughts?" Sunny turned her chair to face the cyborg.

With little fanfare, Quick simply shrugged. "Fucked if I know."

"Pageant?"

Pageant turned away from the view window. "Looks like they abandoned the station. Maybe they did it when they found out Anne broke loose from captivity. They probably vamoosed because there was a whole lot of data on that thing they did not want being discovered by nosy transport captains who are in over their heads."

"We're going to have to land there, you know," said Sunny.

"I figured." Pageant returned to his nav chair and plotted a quick access course. "The cargo bay is open and accessible. We should be able to land inside of it easily. No need for the shuttle, even."

"Crispy?" Sunny sought her pilot's opinion.

Crispy was squinting at the reports. "Should be able to, I agree. Just say the word."

"Any other vessels in this system currently?"

Fang was consulting screens furiously. "Not to my knowledge, Sunny."

"Then, I guess we're going in." Sunny looked around the bridge at her assembled crew. "Captain stays with the ship. I guess I'm looking for volunteers. Who's going into the station?"

"Me. Crispy. Quick. Anne." Pageant was not haggling. "We started this, we'll figure it out."

"I'm going, too." Neer appeared in the hatchway on her crutches. "I need to find out if this was worth blowing my pension."

"You sure, Hopalong?" Pageant raised an eyebrow. "Shouldn't you be resting?"

"Time for that later. I'm going."

"I'm not giving her a gun," said Quick. "I don't trust her, yet."

"You telling me you're worried about a woman with one leg shooting you in the back?" Neer held out the crutches as if to emphasize the point. "I'm not going to shoot you, Natalie."

"That's exactly what someone who damn well was planning to shoot me would say."

"Give her a pistol, Quick. If she shoots you, I'll shoot her." Pageant liked to keep things in balance.

"What if she shoots you first, and then me?"

"Then I'll have Crispy shoot her."

Quick scowled. "I'll give her a six-shot piece, but I won't be happy about it."

"Norman? Fang?" Sunny passed over her brother. She already knew he would not volunteer.

"I'll go, definitely." Fang was already wearing his sword.

Norman shrugged, his smile ever-present. "I always like seeing a new place."

"Settles it, then. Happy and I will stay on board. We'll drop you off on the station and move back into this shadow just in case someone drops out of translight in this system. Keep comms open."

"Aye, Cap'n." Crispy settled the *Mary Read* into the cargo bay of the space station, keeping it just off the metal floor. He put it into an airlock around the bay so it could continue to hover while the station spun without smashing into it. "Air levels are breathable. Temperature levels are livable. Your pilot is turning off the seat belt light. Please, feel free to move about the cabin."

THERE WAS SOMETHING unsettling about being in an open-sided cargo bay. It was a massive opening in the space station, and it was sealed from space by an intense force field. A human certainly did not have the body mass to penetrate the field, but a ship did. When the ship left, there was the slightest pull of a vacuum before the field could firmly reseal itself. It was a stark reminder that all that was standing between you and the finality of space was a couple of generators and a man-made system where failure was not an unknown quantity. There were plenty of records of stations going dark because an open-sided bay generator failed, and everyone got sucked into the Black. Space was a uniquely unforgiving creature.

The landing party of the *Mary Read* departed the ship with full tac-suits and weapons. There was no telling what might be waiting for them. Just because a station read as empty from a scanner did not always mean it was empty. The air was breathable, so that meant the auto-recirc systems were still functioning. That was a safety measure for most stations, even abandoned ones. The solar panels that lined the exterior of the prefab stations were hardwired into the life support system. There was no diverting it. When a station went live, the sole job of the solar panels was to ensure the station could support life. Even if a station was abandoned by the original group that erected it, the station's solar panels kept the station habitable until its wiring systems failed from time, corrosion, and bad luck. It might take months, it might take centuries. It all depended on where the station was placed, and how difficult the conditions were. This was something Earth's governments put in place years ago when Smilin' Jack and the other explorers started making the translight hops. It was good to have floating islands of refuge out there, because no one ever knew when one would be needed.

The landing team consisted of everyone from the *Mary Read*, save Sunny and her brother. Pageant and Crispy stepped off the ship, both at their most casual despite the tac-suits. Crispy had his Heckler on his hip. Pageant favored his Rorbacher. They walked like stepping into a space station deep in a corp-controlled system was what they did every day. Quick walked directly behind them carrying her Mengler in a holster, but she had also elected to carry a Blueskill Slimline, as was Fang. The two mercs fanned out, guns up. They didn't need to be told what to do.

Neer followed, swinging down the gangplank on crutches. She looked tired. Norman, realizing that a space station might not be the best place to fire a big-ass, high-damage gun, was carrying a smaller Mesk-Ebon handgun. In his fist, it looked positively tiny, ridiculously small. He also carried a *patu*, a brutal-looking teardrop-shaped wooden club Maori warriors carried into battle in ages long past. Maori spacers tended to keep one nearby as a reminder of their heritage, but also because it was highly effective at caving in a skull when necessary.

Following the group was Anne Medea. On Quick's insistence, she wore a belt around her tac-suit, and in the holster hanging from that belt was a simple Mengler A1, the most basic handgun Mengler made. Anne did not want the gun, but Quick told her that she might get into a spot where summoning a spear of light might not be possible, and a practical gun was a girl's best friend. Anne felt strange carrying the gun. It was such a solid piece of metal, so heavy and cold. She could feel it on her hip through her tac-suit. It felt much larger than it actually was, and because of that, she felt even smaller than normal.

Anne did not recognize the cargo bay of the space station, but there was something familiar about the coldness of the construction, the arch designs and supports. She felt like she had been on this station for some time. She could not remember much about the station itself, but she had a sick sense of homecoming hanging low in her stomach. It made her throat tight. She was scared but was trying not to show it. She knew she needed to learn about her origins as much as everyone else did. The more pieces of the puzzle they could put together, the better.

Anne never had friends before she met the crew of the *Shy Opal*. They were an odd little group, but they saw someone in need and took her in without being asked. They had been willing to die to keep her out of the hands of MannTech. Anne knew she could not betray that sort of friendship by suddenly getting cold feet and wanting to back away from the moment of discovery.

The *Mary Read* drifted out of the cargo bay, repulsors pushing away from the station. The ship pushed through the force field and out to empty space. It drifted from view, heading out to hide in a more strategic place. Sunny's voice came over the radio channel they were all monitoring on their PPDs. "Sunny to Landing Party. *Mary Read* is in place. Yell if you need help."

"Aye, Cap'n." Pageant was not Sunny's second-in-command, but even Norman knew when a real leader was before him. He deferred to Pageant's wisdom, experience, and leadership without a word. Pageant looked at the group. "Stay tight. Anne, I want you in the middle of us at all times. If something goes south, then we regroup back here in the cargo bay. Questions?"

"If you die, can I have your gun?"

"Yes, Quick, you can."

"Bonus." Quick strode over to the door that separated the bay from the rest of the station. "Let's do this, then." She scanned the door with her PPD. "No sign of any traps or explosives, Cap."

"Open 'er up, and let's see what we can see." Pageant pulled his gun. Norman gripped his patu. Fang pulled his katana from its sheath. Crispy did not pull his gun. That was one of the benefits of being his size—no one expected to see a dwarf anymore, so the first shot, should there be one, always went over his head.

The cargo bay door opened in the center, pulling apart to let humans and pallets of supplies through into the living bay. The change in air pressure pulled a wave of air from the living modules into the cargo bay, and everyone in the landing party gagged simultaneously.

The smell of death was unmistakable.

26

THE GROUP FOUND the first body ten paces beyond the cargo bay doors. The victim was a researcher. They were dressed in dark gray MannTech medical scrubs with a white lab coat. They were face-down in the corridor, two crusty, dried patches of blood on their back.

Quick knelt next to the body. She was gulping air through her mouth and trying not to vomit from the smell. Death held no secrets from Quick; she'd seen more than her fair share of dead bodies. Hell, she'd caused more than her fair share of them. However, decay was something no one enjoyed. "Two bullets. One in the low spine, the other through the heart."

"Cripple 'em and kill 'em. That's what they teach acolytes." Fang spoke from experience.

"Not mafioso?" Crispy thought the mafia liked two shots.

"Gangster way is one in the heart, one in the forehead. They like to sit you down and let you sweat a little. They like it when you know you're going to die. Acolytes don't like people running away from them, so their first shot is usually low. The second shot is a heart shot. Saves on ammo."

"MannTech did this to their own people?" Pageant wouldn't put it past a corp to execute their own people. They did it enough over the years. It just seemed like a waste of a good research facility.

Fang nodded. "No question, chief. Their researchers outlived their purpose. They accomplished phase one or phase two or whatever phase MannTech had them in, and once that was done, MannTech takes their data and gives it to the next group of researchers. Then, they purge the first group. I've seen it done by other corps. It keeps too many people from knowing what you're up to."

"Gotta protect the data above all else. The data is where the cash is." When Quick had merc'd out to corps in the past, she had once been part of a scrub squad. It was not widely talked about in general channels because corps tended only to do it in galaxies under iron-fist control. One hire on a scrub squad was a big part of the reason Quick retired from merc'ing to hire on with *Shy Opal.* Pageant might not make much money, but at least Quick could sleep at night knowing she was not slaughtering innocent scientists who were just trying to make a few credits and promote the general advancement of knowledge.

The away team found more researchers as they pushed further into the station. In the living quarters, there were dead researchers in their bunks, caught sleeping and executed by the acolyte scrub squad. The common area in the living module was full of dead bodies. Unlike the other bodies where two bullets had done a quick, clean job of eliminating them, these bodies were sprayed with multiple bullets, as though a couple of acolytes stood in the doorway and crisscrossed the room with automatic fire. Each one had a final shot through the heart. It was the cleanest, most practical way to ensure there were no survivors. A body that somehow survived to alert others of what the corp was doing was far more expensive than any bullet would ever be.

Crispy looked over the dead, black monitors in the living module. "No exterior comm links. Only an intercom. How would they radio for help if they needed it?"

"That's pretty standard," said Quick. "Research vessels like this usually have one person with a deep-space alert button for emergencies only. It's a direct line to the nearest ship usually, and it only sends an alarm. The ship comes running if it goes off. They do not want people being able to relay any data off-site by any means."

"Any of this look familiar?" Pageant asked.

Anne shook her head. She had never been allowed into the living module areas. Those were strictly off-limits for test subjects.

Pageant slipped his Rorbacher into the holster. "I guess we know why there were no life signs aboard the vessel."

"Permission to gather the bodies, Nathan?" Norman's voice was small. He was a spiritual man, and he did not like to see the dead so disrespected. It felt sacrilegious to leave them on the floor like trash. "I saw a waste tube. I'm betting it fires directly into that nearby star. Let me give them a proper farewell."

"Permission granted, I guess. You don't need my permission." Pageant could not see needing Norman for anything directly. If laying the bodies to rest in a respectful manner would help the big man, then Pageant was not going to prevent it. "Just stay on comms in case something goes down."

It was pretty clear what happened on the research station. Any threat to them would come from outside the modules. Norman put his own gun away and began the grisly task of carrying the dead to the waste ejectors for one last mission. He spoke lowly over each body as he carried it. He said kind things. It was a horrible, grisly job, and he was the only man who asked to do it.

Pageant called for the rest of the group to leave Norman to his task. There was more station to explore.

BEYOND THE LIVING modules was a long corridor connecting to the research modules. Prefab stations were all the same: large oval or round units connected to each other with long tubular corridor modules like a child's construction toy. They worked, though. They were cheap to buy, easy to transport, and quick to set-up, and thus despite technology making it possible for far more luxurious stations, the prefabs continued to be the favorite vessels of most of the corps. The expensive stations were for the wealthy. Scientists and soldiers were poor, and they would be happy with whatever you gave them. At least, that was the prevailing wisdom of the rich and powerful paying for the stations.

Small signs in the vessel directed them to various sections of the station. A black arrow pointed back at the living quarters behind them. A blue arrow pointed at a recreation area. A yellow arrow pointed to the galley and common area. Red arrows pointed to the main bridge and engineering area. Green arrows pointed to the research module. They moved to the research area, Pageant in the lead.

The research door was sealed. Someone had taken the time to weld it closed.

"That's curious." Crispy had only seen that on stations where something life-threatening had leaked out and the module had to be sealed for the good of everyone else aboard the station.

"Maybe the other door isn't welded," suggested Quick. "I'll take Fang and hop over that way if you want."

"Do that." Pageant ran his fingers along the weld on the door. It was not a good weld, probably some corporate acolyte was told to seal it and did as half-assed a job as possible. Typical for underpaid corporate goons. Soldiers were trained to kill, not weld.

Pageant chewed his lower lip absentmindedly. He looked around the corridor for a tool, something he might be able to use to hack away some of the solder. "I don't think this is completely sealed, Crispy."

Crispy stepped forward to inspect it, as well. "Lousy job, definitely. Might be able to hack through it with an axe or something."

"Or something is right." Pageant turned to Anne. "I don't suppose you can just magic these doors open."

"I could try, but I don't think so."

"Reesha, how about you?"

"Are we informal enough to use first names now?"

"Why not? Didn't you join our crew already? Call me Nathan, Nate, or Pageant, if you want. My friends call me *Big Sexy.*"

"No, we don't," said Crispy.

"True, they don't. I keep asking them to, but no one complies. You have any thoughts about the door?"

Neer shook her head and lowered herself down the curved wall of the corridor tube. She flexed her amputated leg at the knee. "I got nothing. I fly ships and command people to do menial tasks; I don't do them myself."

"I might have an idea." Pageant jogged back to the living area. A fire kit should have a crowbar in it. They were handy tools and given the state of the crew of the station, Pageant could not foresee a time when it would be needed.

Pageant found the crowbar right where it was supposed to be. He brought it back and began using the sharp end to hack into the weak joints, chipping them away in slivers. After a few shots, larger chunks of the solder broke away, raining debris to the floor. "Looks like it's working. Let's hear it for stupid acolytes."

Quick's voice crackled over their comm system. "Cap, door's sealed here, too. Brig module is open, though."

"Well, that's something." Pageant looked at Crispy and Anne. "Crisp, take our little space witch to the brig, would you? This is going to take a while."

"You sure, Cap?"

"Anne is never to be left alone. Besides, I have the good commander to keep me company."

Neer rolled her eyes. "You're wasting time."

"Sorry, boss." Pageant started swinging the crowbar again. "Get going, Crispy."

"Aye, Cap." Crispy started down the corridor.

"Anne, you look through the brig. If you remember anything, I want to know about it."

"Aye, Cap," Anne parroted Crispy.

Crispy took Anne back to the living module leaving Pageant alone with his thoughts, Reesha Neer, a crowbar, and a door.

ANNE MEDEA'S HAIR prickled over every inch of her scalp the second she stepped through the hatch between the living module and the brig module. It was familiar. Too familiar, really. How many hours had she spent in this module? How many nights had she laid awake silently crying in pain? How many days of her life had she wasted watching movies and television shows on the little monitor in her cell? When she stepped through the hatch, she had a minor panic attack, and her legs went weak. She was able to jelly-leg it to a chair before she collapsed. She waved off help from Crispy and Quick. "I'm okay. Just shocked."

"This is the place, then?"

"Oh, yes. This is the place." Anne took a couple of deep breaths. Seeing it again was overwhelming.

The brig module was four stories tall. Along the north wall were cells, six cells to a floor, twenty-four cells in total. Each cell was identical. A single rack built into the wall. A desk with an unmovable cylindrical stool in front of it. A toilet, sink, and shower unit in the corner opposite the desk. Opposite the bunk, a low shelf for clothes and books, and above that, built into the wall, was a twelve-inch screen with a port for plugging in headphones so the sound from the monitor would not disturb anyone else.

In front of the cells was twelve feet of space for passing in front of the cells, and a railing. The railing oversaw the brig's control area. That was where the guards passed the time. When it was time for meals, they would gather the trays in that area before climbing the stairs with them and giving them to the research subjects.

Prisoners, Anne corrected herself. She had been a prisoner.

There was a large, empty rectangle to the side of the control area. That was the pathetic space serving as a rec area aboard that station. If they were well enough to walk and move around, once a day the prisoners were allowed into that rectangular area, with its high, dark walls and overhead spotlight. There, they could run in circles, or do calisthenics, if they wished. Most of the time, Anne just walked back and forth, pacing mindlessly until they put her back into her cell so she could finish whatever film she had been watching.

Anne climbed the metal grating serving as steps to the second story. There had been no assigned cells. The subjects were moved often. They had little in the way of possessions, so moving was a one-trip process. Get yer stuff. Yer goin' upstairs, a guard would growl at her. Then, five minutes later, she was marched up the stairs, put into a new cell, and the door was sealed again. She would go right back to watching her show, just on a new monitor, while she lay on a new rack with new blankets.

Anne went into the second cell on the second story. She crouched down and crawled under the desk. There, in pencil, was a crude drawing of a flower. Anne remembered drawing that picture because the facility she had been at prior to that station had been on a planet. There had been flowers. She so rarely got to see flowers, she wanted one to remember forever. Anne crawled out from under the bunk. "This is definitely the place."

Quick radioed back to Pageant. "We're in the right spot, Cap."

Pageant's voice crackled over the PPDs. "See if you can find anything that tells us anything."

"Like what?"

There was a long pause. Pageant came back with, "Hell if I know, Q. I'm just betting you'll know it when you see it."

"Aye, Cap." Quick walked to the control monitors. The desks had once been a complex computer system with monitors in every cell. Some acolyte had shot up the desk. The computers were dead. The monitors monitored no longer. Quick returned a quick verdict. "They shot it all to hell, Cap. Computers are fried."

"Well, damn."

"Let me at it." Crispy got down on his hands and knees and crawled under the desk. Any good pilot knew that a malfunctioning computer did not necessarily mean the computer was completely malfunctioning. Sometimes, it was just a matter of swapping out hot chips and resetting the stupid thing.

A computer that had been shot up was not necessarily dead. If the central processor and motherboard were still intact, it was possible to yank that thing out, feed it to a PPD, and learn what was on it. It might not run like the computer was meant to, but if the data was intact, it could be transferred. Crispy pulled his toolkit from the lowest pocket on his cargo shorts and used the screwdriver to remove screws so he could get at the heart of the machine.

Fang emerged from the corridor to the research module. "My sword is getting hella dull from hacking at that door. Why would they seal the doors to the research module, anyhow? If you're abandoning the station and killing everyone on board, why not just use a gunship to blow the fucking thing back to atoms?"

Quick shrugged. "Standard practice in the corps, actually. These things cost money. Research modules have a lot more research than just what's on the computers. They seal them in case they need them again."

"Leaves 'em open to pirates, though."

"Usually, they're in patrolled space. Corps know when pirates enter their regions, and they're pretty quick to respond. Sealed doors keep the pirates from getting the good stuff."

"Do they know we're here?" Fang moved over to the single view window in the brig module and looked out into the starless black void beyond it.

"By now? Most likely. Even if we were able to obscure the signal of Mary Read in the planetoid, I'm sure the sensors on the research vessel have triggered alerts somewhere. I have no doubt something is running an intercept course right now. I just don't know when it'll show up."

Crispy crawled out from under the desk with a dusty green motherboard in his fist like a trophy. "Got one." He pulled a cable from the body of his PPD and wired the motherboard into it. In seconds, he was downloading a massive pull of data.

"Not much left for us here, then." Quick rolled her head toward the door. "Might as well go back and give Pageant a hand."

NATHAN PAGEANT WAS nothing if not persistent. Through sheer force of will, he had broken away half of the shoddy welding job and was starting on the second half. He had broken into a healthy sweat because tac-suits were heavy and did not breathe well. He did not mind sweating. It was far from his favorite thing, but he did not mind it. It meant that he was alive, and he was working. Growing up in the dust on a colony ranch, Pageant learned the value of hard work, and he learned to respect a healthy sweat and aches in the muscles.

That's probably why he wanted to be a spacer, instead.

Pageant kept a steady rhythm to his attack on the door, and the little chunks of door kept breaking away under his assault. He said a silent prayer of thanks for lazy mercs. Every few whacks, Pageant jabbed the end of the crowbar into the door and leaned back, trying to use sheer force to torque through the remainder of the welds. It was working.

Neer was impressed. "I think you're almost there."

"I aim to please, lady."

Another inch of solder got hacked away, and Pageant tried the doors again. There was a loud rending of metal, and the remaining strip of shoddy welds gave way. The door to the research module opened with a cranky squeak of metal-on-metal.

There was more death inside. A half-dozen dead scientists lay in various states of decay around the module. Each had at least two shots in their body, one to incapacitate, a second in the heart to kill. Pageant cursed the acolytes who carried out the executions under his breath.

The module was a disaster. Computers were shot, papers and medical equipment were scattered everywhere. There were long tables with various strange implements on them. Broken glass was scattered on tables and floors. An emergency light flashed forlornly in the corner probably triggered by gunfire piercing the first layer of the bulkhead.

Pageant keyed his radio. "I'm in."

"On our way." Quick's voice returned.

Pageant knelt and looked at the first pile of papers on the floor, a mass of formulas, numbers, and data. It was all foreign to him. He moved further into the research module. There were four levels in the facility, all connected by an open stairway of the same corrugated metal grating that seemed to be in every space station. Neer followed him, her crutches thumping on the floor. They were on the top level of the research bay.

Pageant moved down the stairs to the next level of the facility and found more of the same. Two dead bodies, shot-up tech, scattered materials, and broken glass. Pageant moved to the long tables in the center of the facility. What looked like printed copies of something scanned from an old scroll were in the middle of the table. It was all squiggles and lines. He called Neer to hop down the stairs if she felt she could.

Reesha crutched down the steps on one leg, hopping as gracefully as she could while using the railing for balance. When she got there, she squinted at the sheets. "What the hell are those?"

"I was hoping you'd know." Pageant had never been a great student, especially when it came to ancient archaeology. He knew enough to know it wasn't Greek, but it was definitely ancient. Sunny would probably know, though. She was smart like that. Pageant photographed the sheets with his PPD and sent them to *Mary Read*. "Sunny, what am I looking at?"

The rest of the group reached the research module. Pageant heard them on the first level. "Down here!"

Footsteps on the stairs rang out as Quick rapidly descended. "Someone made a mess everywhere, Cap."

"So I noticed. You ever see anything looks like this?" Pageant passed Quick the sheet of paper. Quick squinted at it and shook her head.

Crispy was right behind her on the stairs. "Looks Greek to me, Cap."

"Not Greek," said Fang, following behind Crispy. "Older than Greek."

"Aramaic." Sunny's voice piped over the comm. "Ran it through the computer. It's Aramaic."

"That's interesting," said Pageant.

"What's Aramaic?" Anne followed Fang up the stairs. She moved toward Pageant and squinted at the paper he held.

"It's an old language. Originated in what used to be Syria back on Earth." Pageant held out the paper for Anne to take. "Look familiar to you?"

Anne took the paper. She could feel a prickling in her brain, a strange sensation of something awakening in her mind. "It does." She could actually read the characters on the page. It actually made sense to her. She cleared her throat and read aloud, "*And the storm came past the mountain, washing the dead and the living the same. Blood gathered with the waters and fertilized the fields. The crops responded, growing tenfold that season.*"

"What the hell does that mean?" Quick found more papers in the stacks with strange writing on them. She passed them to Anne. "And why do you know how to read it?"

"I have no idea. I just can."

"The mystery deepens, I guess." Pageant moved down to the next level. No bodies on the ground, but the same sort of mess awaited him. There were papers with scans of bones and long reports of DNA histories. On one of them, he found *PR-ARC346* written across the top. "Bingo. Anne, I found something you need to see."

Anne clambered down the stairs, her footfalls so light they almost did not make a sound. "What is it?"

"This is your DNA, I think." Pageant passed her the sheet.

"What does it mean?"

"No idea. I'm no scientist."

Anne looked at the sheet, but it meant nothing to her. She put it down on the table. "At least we know we're in the right spot. I was definitely here."

Quick bypassed the third floor and went right to the bottom floor. From above them, Pageant heard her call out. "Cap, you better get down here."

Pageant and Anne exchanged a glance. Pageant jogged down the stairs and froze when he saw it. On one of the tables in the center of the fourth floor, a massive humanoid skeleton lay splayed out. The being was at least nine feet tall. Its skull was the size of Pageant's whole rib cage. Pageant's eyes went wide at the sight of it.

"What did you find?" Sunny's voice crackled over the radio. She had been listening to them over the comm link.

"I think it's a Sasquatch."

27

MAYBE THE BODY on the table wasn't a Sasquatch, but it definitely wasn't human, unless it was the remains of someone with acromegaly. The tallest man in Earth's recorded history was Robert Wadlow, who reached the towering height of eight feet, eleven inches. What was on the table could have been his skeleton.

There were several bones missing from the behemoth skeleton. The skull had a section taken from it, leaving half of the rounded forehead empty. One of the hands was missing. The left femur was gone. A few of the smaller bones in the feet were also missing. Was it on purpose? Were the bones elsewhere? Had they never been found? So many questions popped into Pageant's head. Many of the bones had divots taken out of them, or they had been sawed in half for some reason. It was clear the skeleton was important. But why leave it behind if it was so important? The acolytes who cleansed the station must not have known its value, or they expected the solder to do a better job of sealing the skeleton inside the lab. Maybe MannTech got everything they needed from the skeleton and no longer valued it. Par for the course for the corps, really.

Of course, the station was in heavily controlled space and hidden from most maps. Perhaps they felt they didn't need to hide it too well, or perhaps they were planning to come back to this station soon.

"What the hell is that?" Crispy's voice rang out from the top of the stairs. "I'm over here unable to ride half the rides at an amusement park, and this fool is more than two of me stacked on top of each other. What's up with that?"

"Don't know what to tell you, Short Stuff. Life ain't fair." Quick clacked her metal gripper to emphasize her point.

"Cap, I'd like to lodge a formal complaint about this skeleton taking a portion of the height meant for me."

"Noted, Crisp. Take it up with HR."

"I am HR."

"Then you must have a lot to discuss with yourself right now." Pageant gingerly took a portion of one of the sawed bones of the arm into his hands. He looked at it closely. It was real. For a minute, he let himself think the skeleton was a bad Halloween prank, but the bone was definitely real. It felt like a bone. It had hollow membranes inside that once held marrow.

Fang pointed to the multitude of drilled holes in various bones. "They were taking samples."

"For DNA?" asked Pageant.

"That'd be my guess."

Pageant looked to Anne. She shrugged. Pageant returned the shrug. He had no idea what the hell was going on. "Is this an altered human? Like, back on Templeton—everyone is a little shorter because the gravity of that planet prevents them from growing like they would on Earth. Could this skeleton be from a planet with less than say half of Earth's gravity? That would allow their bones to grow and stretch to impossible heights, maybe?" Pageant tried to justify what sort of gravity would let a human hit nine feet. He couldn't see gravity allowing a three-foot stretch in a human. The other option was more terrifying. "Or is this thing an alien?"

"Might be," said Fang. "Show me a DNA report of this skeleton."

Crispy scampered to the computers. "Wait a minute. I might be able to help." He crawled under one of the work stations and pulled it apart. When that one had too many bullets in the right spot, he moved to the next, and then the next. He eventually emerged with an intact motherboard and looped it into his PPD as he did in the brig. The data pull from the motherboard made his PPD almost blank itself, but it somehow held on and kept chugging. "They had a lot of info in this station, Cap."

"It's a research vessel, Crisp. I would think all their computers had a lot of data."

Fang was scanning the skeleton with his own PPD. He ran a couple of tests. "Says this skeleton is thousands of years old."

Pageant was intrigued. "How many?"

"Can't tell, exactly. It doesn't report the same sort of carbon data as Earth."

Different carbon did not necessarily mean it was an alien species. Pageant himself did not report the same sort of carbon data as a full Earthling because of his decades in space. Cosmic radiation did a number on the body and threw off scans applicable to someone who had lived on Earth their whole life. There was a whole new set of medical data for spacers.

Neer eased herself to the floor next to a scattered pile of papers. She began leafing through the sheets. "It looks like a lot of nonsense." She held out one of the sheets. It was more scanned pages of Aramaic scrolls, and a few other pages of a different sort of writing that looked like lines and holes punched into clay and allowed to dry. "Hey, sword-boy, come scan this."

Fang walked over and ran his PPD over the sheet. "Says it's Elamite."

"Who were they?"

"Old as hell people. One of the earliest known written languages."

Instead of figuring out the puzzle, Pageant was finding a whole new patch of pieces that didn't seem like they fit. He put a hand on Anne's shoulder. "If it helps any, I have no clue what you are."

Anne knelt next to Neer and began sorting through the pages. At one, she froze. She looked to Pageant. "What's a nephilim?"

"That's like if your sister has a male child," said Fang.

"That's nephew, doofus." Quick was already accessing her PPD. "Nephilim. It's an old-school biblical word, the old Christian Bible. Says here some Bibles loosely translate nephilim as *giant*."

"Well, that explains the skeleton," said Crispy.

Quick ignored him. "Other Biblical scholars say that nephilim translates to *fallen*, and is said to reference fallen angels. One translation says it means *violent ones*."

Anne held out the copy of the scroll. "This talks about the Nephilim. It says they were travelers, and they came to Earth."

"Say what now?" Pageant squinted at the figures on the scroll as if they were suddenly going to become readable to him.

Crispy was piecing together research from the motherboard hooked to his PPD. "Cap, this is backing up what Anne said. I'm seeing heavily encoded files about Project Archangel, and it makes reference to an exploration team finding gigantic human-like skeletons on this dying planet in MannTech-controlled space."

"What are you telling me, Crisp?"

Crispy tucked his chin into his neck and shrugged. "I have no idea, Cap. If I'm reading this correctly, a MannTech exploration team found a nearly dead-rock planet with giant skeletons on it. They found things on that rock which tied the skeletons to some ancient Earth texts on clay tablets and scrolls. The scrolls backed up what some people have been saying for a long time: aliens visited Earth in the pre-Christian era, and the humans on Earth at that time called them nephilim. Probably because they fell out of the sky, thus *fallen*."

"Great. What does this have to do with anything?" Pageant wished someone would hand him a concise summary of what they were going through. His head was starting to hurt, a stabbing pain behind his right eye.

Crispy looked from the skeleton to Anne, back to the skeleton, and finally to Pageant. "Boss, as far as I can tell, I think they grafted Anne with DNA from that skeleton on the table. The alien DNA is from one of the Nephilim."

Quick's mouth hung open. She pointed the index finger of her grabber at Anne. "You tellin' me she's got goddamned *angel* DNA coursing through her?"

"Divine powers, right? It would explain so much," said Fang.

Pageant was still confused, but the fog was starting to lift. He needed to reset what they knew. "Everyone, hold up. Let's piece this thing together. MannTech takes over the Katherine System in its conquests because they're the first corp to break the seal and claim it. One of their research vessels finds, what? A human-like civilization on a dying world, but the human-like aliens were giants."

"Accurate so far," said Crispy.

"They pull items from the dying world including printed scrolls and giant skeletons."

"Yup."

"They decode the various fragments and learn that a race of aliens the Bible called the Nephilim crashed on Earth eons ago."

"Yup."

Fang interrupted. "These scrolls are all from Earth. These all lie in museum collections from ages ago. They're all accessible from the central hub." He waved his PPD at them to emphasize his point.

Pageant ran a hand through his thinning hair. He had a flashback to his early twenties when it was so thick that it would stand straight up on its own when he ran his fingers through it. He missed those days. Life was so much simpler, then. "Okay, so they find skeletons and probably other pieces of civilization. Maybe tech? Maybe something else?"

"Who knows?" Crispy threw up his hands. "Could be anything."

"They take DNA from the skeleton. They replicate it. They graft it into the DNA strands of human test subjects. Why?"

Crispy shrugged. "Alien magic? They were trying to bring back the Nephilim."

It was as good an answer as any they had. Pageant still could not fully process what they had found. "This is stupid as hell. You all know this, right?"

Neer pulled herself back to a standing position, leaning on a shot-up workstation. "Nate—think about it. Shea Mannion has alien tech and alien DNA in his possession—nay, in his *control*. This system doesn't exist on maps. It's deep in MannTech space. You pretty much have to make a direct jump in translight to get here. You cannot just stumble across this place. That's why they didn't blow this station up. It's position in orbit around the dying world was too valuable. Even if the rock goes completely black, they can still land raiding parties in exosuits to gather more goods. That rock is a gold mine beyond the dreams of any corporate suit. That planet is every banker's wet dream. What we are looking at here is the potential control of the universe in a single room."

"The skeleton?" said Fang.

"No, it's Anne, you dummy," said Quick.

Everyone's eyes turned to the frail woman in their midst. She looked scared. She was trembling. There was a silence around the room as the full gravity of the situation rested heavily on their minds.

"Shea Mannion is the single-most powerful man in the universe, isn't he?" Anne said aloud what they were all thinking.

"We're all screwed." Happy Yeong's dour, gloom-and-doom voice piped over the comm. He and Sunny had been listening to their chatter over a feed from their PPDs.

"You ain't just spitting seeds, brother." Pageant's stomach lit up with the queasy, tickling sensation he always got just before something unbelievably awful happened. "We gotta get off this thing. Sunny, come get us. Now."

Sunny's voice crackled back across the comm. "Too late, Nate. We got company."

"Aw, hell." Pageant punched the desk he was leaning against. "How bad?"

"Two Cerb gunships and an Apex-class vessel."

Neer went on alert. "Apex-class? That's gotta be Mannion's personal yacht."

"This doesn't bode well for any of us now, does it?" Quick pulled her Mengler and made sure it was loaded, safety off.

Pageant checked his own weapon. "Crispy—five creds says his ship has an absolutely pretentious asshole name, something like *Imperator* or *Magnate*."

"I'd never take that bet, Cap. Rich assholes always have the worst ship names." Crispy followed his crewmates' suit and pulled his own sidearm.

"Really? You're betting?" Neer's face was a mask of disgust. "At a time like this, you're betting? If Mannion decides to launch missiles at this station, we're all dead you know? Credits won't matter."

Pageant gave Neer an appraising look. He looked at the cred-counter in his hand. "So…you're saying I should go all-in?"

Quick rolled her eyes. "Nate, no one's taking that bet. It's an Apex-class ship; of course it has a completely stupid name. I'll bet it's called the SS *Wish I Had a Big Cock.*"

"Sunny, what's the registry coming back as on that Apex yacht?"

After a moment, Sunny responded. "It's the MTI *Archon.*"

"Everyone here owes me five credits." Pageant smashed his hand against his forehead. "Someday, I hope to be a rich enough prick that I can give ships stupid names like that and get away with it."

"I'll never let you get away with it, Cap."

"That's because you're a good friend, Crispy."

"*Archon* is actually kind of a cool name," said Fang.

"You have neck tattoos. You're clearly no kind of judge of tasteful things, Fang. No offense," said Pageant.

"None taken."

"Do you idiots always make stupid jokes when you're about to die?" Reesha Neer clearly did not understand their ways.

The big Maori jogged into the room. Norman was holding his patu on his shoulder, ready for action. "Are we all about to die?"

"Oh, most definitely," said Quick.

Sunny came back over the comm. "He's hailing us."

Pageant was not shocked. "Is it to tell us we're all going to die, because I figured that out without him having to say it."

Sunny kept the channel open so the landing party could hear. Her voice was tinny through the speakers of their PPDs. "This is Yeong Sun-hee of the LTA *Mary Read*. How's tricks, Mannion? Evict any disabled old ladies from their homes lately?"

Mannion's voice came over the comm. He had the barest hint of an Irish lilt, and his voice was slightly higher than Pageant expected after seeing pictures of the corporate overlord. "Ms. Yeong, you have my property. I would like it returned."

"Her. You would like *her* returned. And that's *Captain* Yeong, to you."

"As you say." Mannion was a tycoon. He would not deign to waste time arguing with the lowly captain of an escort attack ship. "I would like *her* returned, please. You have no idea what you have in your possession."

"I'd say we have a really good idea." Mannion could not hear Pageant over the comm, but Sunny echoed him.

"I'd say we have a really good idea. She's got Nephilim DNA. That's pretty impressive, I must say."

There was a prolonged silence before Mannion came back over the comm. "As you can no doubt imagine, she is the product of research worth more than a thousand lifetimes. I have spent a considerable amount of time, money, and initiative in her already, and it is only a drop of what she will return to me, but more importantly: think of what she will return to humanity. She will rewrite history and map the future, Ms. Yeong. PR-ARC346 is more valuable to this universe than you, me, and all the credits we could amass between us over a million years. She needs to be studied. She needs to be protected."

"She's a human being!" Sunny's voice rang out over the comm. Pageant's stomach knotted tightly. He knew that tone. Sunny was going to do something stupid.

"She is a weapon. She is a tool. She is the future. She seceded her humanity long ago." There was a chill to Mannion's voice. It was very matter-of-fact, very plain. He could have been making small talk with someone he was standing next to while waiting in line at a store.

"You forced her to secede her humanity, Mannion. You can't just do that to people."

Pageant's PPD vibrated, an incoming message. He glanced down to see a message from Sunny, coordinates. *Find Opal if this goes badly. I'm counting on you to make sure she has a good life.*

Pageant keyed his comm link. "Sunny, whatever you're doing—don't."

There was no response.

In that moment, stuck in the middle of nowhere, trapped on a barely functioning research vessel orbiting a dying alien world, Nathan Pageant was utterly helpless, and that was not something he enjoyed. In every situation he had ever been in, there had always been something for him to do. He could leave. He could escape to his ship. He could shoot someone. He could crack a joke. He could pilot his ship into another ship, if he wanted. But in that moment, he was helpless and utterly useless. He could do nothing. "Quick, Sunny's about to do something stupid. Any ideas?"

"Blow the research station. We drop to the dying world in coffin pods and hope for the best."

"What would blowing up the station accomplish?"

"It'd be a helluva distraction, Cap."

Pageant frowned. Why did so many ideas his crew managed to come up with involve large-scale destruction?

"Anyone else have any bright ideas?"

"Turn me over to him," said Anne. "I'll go quietly."

Norman was not having it. "Did you not see the bodies? You'll go quietly right back to being a prisoner and a slave to the corp. They'll kill the rest of us on principal. They have to; we know too much."

"If Sunny's smart, she's already sent an SOS into the ether. Maybe some ship will venture into controlled space to see what's up," said Crispy.

"How long will that take?" Pageant checked his chronometer. It had taken MannTech more than half an hour to get to them from wherever in MannTech-controlled space they had been hiding, which was likely nearby. It had taken a top-of-the-line vessel like *Mary Read* more than twenty-four hours to make the translight jump to the Katherine System. They were isolated and alone. No one was coming for them.

Quick was doing calculations on her PPD. "Cap, without at least six people on the bridge of *Mary Read*, I don't think Sunny's chances are very good. No matter how good Happy is—and he's not—he can't pilot, navigate, work scanners and guns, and maintain the rover commands. Even Crispy couldn't do all that. Jubilee-class ships are meant to work with four people, minimum. And more would be better."

"What kind of guns does that Apex have?"

"Not as many as Sunny, but close."

Pageant walked to the single view window on that floor of the research station and looked out at the three approaching ships. The two Cerbs were intimidating, but they were slow. They were big hitters with no finesse. It would only take two or three shots from either of them to incapacitate *Mary Read*. Maybe one, if it hit the right spot. She was still sporting wounds from her tussle with *Despair*, after all.

He craned his neck down to look at the rock beneath them. He could not see *Mary Read* in the darkness below, but he knew she was there. Sunny was probably priming engines and guns. Jubilee-class attack ships had twin snap guns, and a small cadre of missiles. Nothing fancy. It was more than enough to get the job done, though. Especially with their considerable speed and maneuverability. Pageant knew how the fight was going to end before it started, though. He keyed the comm link again. "Sunny, I'm begging you. Don't be stupid."

Silence.

Pageant saw two missiles fire out of the dark shadows of the planet.

Sunny never listened to him before; it only made sense she did not start now.

28

NATHAN PAGEANT COULD only watch as *Mary Read* shot out of the darkness from the shadow of the black rock, trailing after the two missiles. Immediately, the two Cerberus gunships altered course, moving apart to attempt to get out of the missile trajectory. One was successful and the missile intended for it shot wide. The other caught the Cerb's tail and rattled the big ship, but did not hinder it.

Once the Cerbs committed to a new course, Sunny immediately fired two more missiles. As she had closed the gap between them, these missiles were much more damaging. Both hit the Cerbs as intended, smashing into their bellies and causing gaping wounds. They were still not kill shots. Fighting bigger, heavier ships was like a boxing match. It was about sticking and moving, about weaving. It was about using jabs to loosen up a guard before going for a haymaker.

However, having an Apex-class ship in the mix complicated matters.

Archon was not as fast or as maneuverable as *Mary Read*. It was a luxury-class ship meant to shuttle the stupidly wealthy from galaxy to galaxy in the grotesquely high standard of living to which they were accustomed. However, the stupidly wealthy were targets in the galaxy, so Apex vessels had guns and a small complement of heavier weapons. It was like carrying a gun on your hip in a public space. It was a deterrent. People thought twice about messing with you if you were packing heat within easy grasp. Apex-class ships were not assault vessels, but neither were they going to roll over and show their belly if it came to trading shots. They could be dangerous if it was required of them.

While the bigger and heavier Cerbs, *Praetor* and *Kentarch*, lumbered into a defensive position, *Archon* did something Pageant did not expect it to do: it accelerated toward *Mary Read*, opening fire with its own forward-mounted snap gun. A volley of blue-white blasts streaked toward *Mary Read* forcing Sunny to adjust course.

Sunny returned fire with her own snap guns, a twin steam of blue-white light returning to *Archon*, forcing it to roll out of the way.

The rest of the landing party moved to the view window. No one said anything. They could only watch the fight. Crispy had to drag over a chair to stand on to see out of the window, but he did it with only the slightest noise.

On Pageant's right, Reesha Neer grabbed his shoulder for support. She stood wavering on one leg. Her voice was barely a whisper. "It's a suicide mission."

Praetor, the Cerberus gunship tagged by Sunny's first missile, was turning more slowly than *Kentarch*. Sunny hit one of its maneuvering repulsors. *Kentarch* was wheeling hard, however. The big guns aside the ship's prow, twin Akkaron blasters, unloaded a full volley at *Mary Read* the second she was clear of the collateral range of *Praetor*. Sunny had to spin away from that volley, and then cut back hard to make another run at *Archon*.

Pageant saw her strategy immediately. She was trying to keep *Mary Read* between the two Cerbs, and thus negating their ability to fire at her. Either ship firing and missing Sunny's ship would result in a damaging hit on the other. She was making her play directly at *Archon*, which was more vulnerable to direct fire than either heavily armored Cerberus.

The pilot of *Archon* was no idiot. He looped low and away, trying to make Sunny chase him into an area where both gunships would have full range and opportunity to launch fiery hell upon her. Sunny could only pull up and roll back to maintain her position between the two gunships while shooting a harmless retort from her snap guns.

"She can't keep this up forever." Crispy's face was grim. He knew how difficult it was to maintain the engine power, the steering, and the guns, not to mention all the other necessary systems. Some of it could be automated, but adjustments had to be done on the fly. Two people in a ship built for six on the bridge were doing too much. Even if she could continue to dodge the volleys from the ships, it would only be a matter of time before human error happened and exposed her chin for a killing blow.

The two Cerbs began to move toward each other, squeezing the lane closed between them. If they could get Sunny to go too high or too low, she would be vulnerable. Sunny responded by wheeling *Mary Read* close to the already injured *Praetor* and unloading a full volley of guns and missiles. Multiple explosions rocked the bigger ship. It began to list like a wounded whale as the crew fought to make adjustments and repairs.

Crispy shook his head. "She's out of missiles."

"Snap guns can do plenty of damage. She just has to keep hitting the same spots," said Quick. "It's like when a boxer opens up a cut over an eye—just keep hitting that spot until the ref stops the fight. He doesn't have to knock out his opponent."

"Death by a thousand cuts," said Fang.

"More like one cut, but you hit it a thousand times," Quick corrected him.

"You're still using the same knife to make the cut. It's not like you stop using the knife after the initial incision."

"Shut up, neck tattoos." Neer was not in a mood to hear such stupid banter. This sort of thing never happened on MannTech ships. They were rigorous in their adherence to corporate mandates. There were policies and procedures that needed to be followed. There was no place for bickering or banter on a bridge, especially with destruction imminent.

Anne Medea watched the space battle with wide eyes and lips pressed together tightly. "This is all so stupid. Why? Why does it have to be this way?"

"It's the way of the world, unfortunately. Corporations have money. Money makes the rules. That's why the rules punish the just and reward the corrupt. It's been that way since time immemorial, I'm afraid." Pageant reached out and put a hand on her shoulder. She felt so small, so frail beneath his palm, almost bird-like. In what way could she be sharing DNA with that behemoth skeleton on that table? How could such a small form like hers manifest such amazing abilities?

Outside the station, the Cerbs had come together and taken *Mary Read's* attack lane away from Sunny. She was forced to drop below the two ships, and was currently being tracked and attacked by those Akkaron blasters. Each volley, even when it missed, was still rocking the ship with heavy concussive force. *Archon* had taken advantage of Sunny's defensive maneuvers and was now comfortably tailing *Mary Read* from a distance, launching its own snap gun attacks forcing the light attack vessel to twist and squirm through space like a panicked rabbit.

"Sunny's not firing guns anymore," Crispy pointed out. "One hundred percent focus on evasion now. She won't make headway like that for long."

"She's got to jump out of here. Translight will save her," said Pageant.

"But it will screw us. If she leaps, we're stuck here, and there's a couple hundred MannTech acolyte assault troopers who will storm this station, kill us, and take the space witch back, thus solidifying their place as the most dangerous corp in the galaxy and paving the way for Shea Mannion to take over whatever the hell he wants to take over." Reesha Neer knew how this ended if Sunny vanished into the translight.

"Only a couple of hundred?" Quick racked the bolt in her long gun. "Easy-peasy. Let 'em come."

"A couple of hundred for the first wave, at least. If we survive that, they'll send a couple hundred more. We're screwed to the bulkhead here."

Pageant looked down at Anne. "I don't suppose you've got any of that magic left in you?"

Anne's eyes did not leave the ship battle outside. "If I did, I swear to you I'd be using it right now. I don't know how it works. I can't just summon it at will."

"I guess we're truly hosed now," said Pageant.

"There's always the coffin pods," said Quick. Every space station was required to have one-man life pods which could be ejected from the station and sent directly to the nearest planet. If nothing else, the life pods had a wide-broadcast SOS beacon and enough water, food, and air for seventy-two hours of survival. "They'll drop us to the surface of that rock. Maybe we'll figure out a way to live once we're down there."

"Coffin pods could just make retrieval of Anne too easy for MannTech, and make killing all of us even easier," said Neer.

Outside the view window, Mary Read's speed and maneuverability were the only thing keeping her in one piece. The Cerb gunships were getting closer with each volley, though. The gunners were coordinating between the vessels. One was firing to her starboard, the other to her port. Then they would fire fore and aft. Then, they would mix it up, firing fore and port, and then aft and starboard. Sunny could not twist away. She did not know where the blasts were coming from, and it was preventing her from launching any counterattacks.

"She's got to jump." Pageant sent a message to the bridge of *Mary Read* from his PPD. *Jump to translight. We'll be all right.*

There was no reply from Sunny. She had her hands full.

Crispy was watching *Mary Read's* engines for the telltale discharge of ion particles of the translight engines warming up. They gave a puff of fuzzy white light. "There it is!"

The ship turned on a hard pivot, pointed to empty space, and prepared to leap into darkness.

There is a moment of vulnerability in every translight jump when a ship's repulsor engines kill out so the heavier translight engines can fire and assume the responsibility for propulsion. The ship is adrift in that moment, a target.

As if *Praetor* and *Kentarch* had been expecting it, waiting for it, they fired multiple heavy missiles at Mary Read.

Mary Read's ion jets sputtered and flared as they came to life. A bright, white flash of light told the other ships what they were trying to do.

The missiles gained on the smaller attack ship.

"Go, Sunny! Go!" Pageant thumped his fist against the wall impatiently. Beside him, Anne watched horrified, unable to look away from the scene.

Why hadn't *Mary Read* leapt to translight? What was she waiting for? Pageant's skin felt like ants were crawling over every inch of him. "What's taking her so long?"

Pageant turned to his pilot for an answer and saw Crispy standing on the table, watching the battle over all their heads. A single tear was sliding down his cheek. His lips were trembling. Pageant grabbed Crispy by the front of his tac-suit. "Talk to me, Crisp. What do you know?"

"She's not jumping. It's a maneuver. She taught it to me years ago."

"What maneuver? What are you talking about?" Pageant could not keep the panic out of his voice.

Crispy's face told the tale. It was a last-ditch maneuver, a final fuck-you to a ship that was about to kill you. "She's going to fire the translight a moment before the torps hit her. It's going to create a ripple blast just as the translight window opens. It's going to wreck everything nearby."

"How bad?" Quick asked.

"Total. *Mary Read* will be gone, but so will the two Cerbs, maybe the *Archon*, and maybe this station, too."

Anne glanced at Crispy over her shoulder. "Why? Why do that?"

"Because if you're going to die, you have to make it count." Crispy swiped his tear away, but another started in his other eye.

"Sounds familiar," said Pageant.

"Someone should do something. Sunny doesn't deserve this. Not over me." Anne looked around the group making eye contact with each of them. "Someone stop her."

Quick threw up her hands helplessly. "Do what, Anne? You're the space witch. If anyone can help her, it will be you."

Anne turned back to the window horrified. "I don't know how."

Pageant put his hands on Anne's shoulders, a more paternal gesture than a platonic one. "Anne, you're special. You can figure this out."

"Honestly, my powers just manifest when they want to. I don't control them."

Pageant pretended not to hear her. "You shot the gun out of my hand when you thought you were in danger, but you didn't hurt me. You made us intangible when you thought we were going to crash. You made that spear appear when Quick was in danger. It's the danger that triggers it." Pageant turned her to the window and pointed at *Mary Read.* The missiles were almost to it. The fiery white light was starting to strengthen at the engines forming a glossy ion cloud. "She's in danger, Anne. You have to do something."

From behind her, Norman's Kiwi accent whispered to her in a low tone, "You're a guardian angel."

On the *Mary Read,* Sunny fired the translights. A massive burst of white light erupted at the rear of the ship. It made contact with the fronts of the torpedoes.

In Pageant's eyes, time seemed to slow. Anne stepped forward and threw out a hand as if she could recall the torps from space. The gauzy black butterfly mask of light popped out of nothingness and wrapped itself around Anne's face.

The torps exploded in the wash from the translight. The shock wave of the explosion rippled back hard and fast on the *Mary Read*. The translight engines blew a portion of the explosion back at *Praetor*. Between the chop caused between the translight rift and the torpedoes, *Praetor* was slammed broadside. The explosion tore through the front hull panels protecting the bridge and ripped it apart. The ship, suddenly without crew, navigation, or steering, listed hard right and slammed into the side of *Kentarch*, which was still flying too closely to its twin. The sudden collision caused ruptures in several of *Kentarch's* main systems. A series of small explosions rippled down the side of the vessel. *Praetor* was dead. *Kentarch* was crippled badly, maybe permanently.

Archon's pilot fought hard to keep his ship out of the wash from the massive disaster happening before it. The bulk of the explosion missed the smaller, sleeker ship, but no doubt it had jostled anything not nailed down within it.

Mary Read tipped engines-up as the ripples from the shockwave threw it. The poor little Jubilee was beginning the process of being torn in two by the competing forces of the shock wave and the translight rift.

A glowing pink light enveloped the ship. The light stretched back to the station like the tail of a comet. The light rocketed *Mary Read* forward into the translight rift, spinning wildly like a curveball pitch, the ship listing end-over-end on a bad axis. The second the ship cleared the rift, it sealed shut and *Mary Read* vanished from view.

Whatever heading *Mary Read* had been on, that was no longer the case. It had vanished from present reality and was cartwheeling through the translight space, a spiraling dervish with no control, and no heading. As far as translight jumps went, this was a worst-case scenario. *Mary Read* was lost in the nothing space between galaxies and realities.

It was the only way Anne had been able to save it.

29

THERE WAS A pronounced lull in the station after that moment. Anne, physically exhausted from her sudden efforts, collapsed into a pale, sweaty heap. Even a dose of smelling salts and an adrenaline hypo-spray from a first aid kit failed to rouse her. Norman gathered the little woman and held her to his chest. She looked like a toddler in the big Kiwi's arms.

Pageant had not taken his eyes from the screen. He was watching the aftermath of the twin dreadnought hulks floating away incapacitated and in emergency mode. There was an empty feeling in his chest, a hole ripped in his heart. He was initially numb and unable to process what had just happened. It was too big. It was too brutal. His mouth was dry, and he could not speak. When he gathered himself, he could only bring himself to say the only thing he wanted to know. "Where did Sunny go?"

No one answered him.

Pageant spun from the view window pointing angrily toward the spot where *Mary Read* had last been seen. "Where the hell is Sunny?"

No one could tell him. They offered sympathetic looks but said nothing. Pageant grabbed Anne's shoulders and shook her lightly. "Anne? Annie, old pal— wake up. I need you."

"Go easy, right?" Norman turned his body protectively. "She's tired."

"Sunny is missing right now. I need to know where she went."

"Pageant?" Neer interrupted.

"Not now, lady."

"Pageant, look again." Neer was insistent.

"What? What is so important?" Pageant turned back to the view window and saw what Neer was seeing. A cascade of debris, mostly metal torn from the hulls of the Cerbs, was wheeling rapidly through space. It was a projectile mess of large sections of ship panels, twisted metal structural beams, and all the other odds and ends from inside of ships. It was all heading straight for the research station. Some of it would miss, yes. The parts that did not miss would punch holes in the sealed areas of the station.

Pageant punched the glass out of frustration and tried to calm himself. He adjusted his tac-jacket and holstered his pistol. "This is not going to go well for us at all."

"External shields should hold." Neer's eyes drifted to the relatively thin bulkhead of the station. "It's going to do some damage, though."

"Cap, the *Archon* is approaching the station," Crispy called out. "I don't know much about Shea Mannion, but I don't think he's the type who is willing to parley."

Pageant sank to his haunches, leaning back against the wall. "I don't suppose Anne will be able to magic us out of this situation, will she?"

Norman jounced her in his arms for a second. Her head lolled, her face slack. "Don't think so, boss."

"Reesha, you were part of MannTech. What's his next play?" Pageant looked to the woman still standing on her crutches at the view window.

"If I were him, I'd shoot the life support system. If we're cold and deprived of oxygen, there will be a lot less issues with us fighting back. Then, he can come reclaim us just before we die. We'll probably be grateful to be shot and killed after a half-hour at near lethal temps."

"There's a pleasant thought." Pageant had no desire to experience the chill of space. He had heard stories of people who ripped an exosuit and felt the stab of the cold and lived to tell the tale, albeit after suffering through surgeries and skin grafts. It sounded unpleasant.

The MTI *Archon* raced ahead of the approaching rain of debris. It was headed to the open mouth of the vessel's cargo bay.

Pageant nodded at Quick. "If they're going to storm the station, we take a few of them out before they finish the job."

"Sounds like a plan, boss." Quick was always ready for a fight.

The group made their way to the cargo area, taking up defensive positions around the door. Quick watched the approach of *Archon* through the window to the bay and narrated for the rest of the group.

The ship broke the seal of the shields, touched down briefly, and opened a door. A single acolyte, unarmed, climbed out of the ship onto the cargo bay floor, and set something down. The soldier climbed back aboard the ship, and *Archon* reversed, pushing back out into the black and turning away from the station. It looked like it was motoring clear of the vessel and preparing a jump to translight.

"Looks like he put down a transmitter of some kind." With no abundance of caution, Quick opened the interior door to the cargo bay. The ozone-and-fried-meat smell of the engines was still thick in the bay. Quick nudged the device left by the acolyte with her toe. "Hard light. It's a hologram comm."

As if to prove her right, the hologram comm flared to life. Projected from the base was a three-dimensional rendering of Shea Mannion, life-sized and in brilliant, flashy color, if a little hazy and transparent because of the holo-render. Mannion was seated in a chair. He stared into the camera that was recording the projection. He could not see the gang in the cargo bay from where he was, but the transmission device relayed sound.

Unflappable and unfazed, Quick did not flinch. "What's up, dickhead? How're your gunships doing?"

Mannion's lip curled ever so slightly. "Is that the voice of Ms. Huffman I hear?"

"The same."

"Didn't you work for me at one point?"

"I worked for Kendrick Corp against you."

Mannion's eyes lit up. "That's right, that's right. The Battle of Vista Rey, if I recall."

"Is that what you call it? I call it the Vista Rey Massacre."

"Battle. Massacre. I guess it depends on whether or not you're on the losing side."

"I remember MannTech warships firing on civilians."

"Business can be messy, Ms. Huffman. I did what I had to do for my shareholders. Kendrick did what they had to for theirs."

"What do you want, Mannion?" Pageant broke off the banter before Quick escalated it and started firing her gun into space at *Archon*.

"You are trapped in MannTech space. You have my property. I need our project back alive. I'm giving you one last chance to give her to me. If you give her up without a fight, I will let you live. I won't call a ship for you, but you can stay on this station. There is enough food and water for a little while, at least. I won't let you leave it, obviously. I will arrange to have more food and water brought to you when you run low. It won't be much of a life obviously, but it will be a life, and that's my best offer to you."

Pageant glanced at the assembled crew. He knew what their answer would be. A life stuck on a corporate research vessel would be an empty, hollow existence. It was a prison. No communications, no escape. "What happens if we reject your offer, Mannion?"

Mannion made a gesture, a simple raising of his left hand and a move like he was tapping his left finger against something.

Outside the cargo bay, the *Archon* fired two pulses of light from its snap guns. The blasts hit the station and rocked it.

Mannion sat back in his chair and tented his fingers in front of his chest. "You have no more life support, Mr. Pageant. By my estimates, you have about three days' of oxygen on that station. Maybe less after the debris field hits and the station loses some before the shields are able to adjust and compensate. So, let's just say three. After three days, you will have no choice but to seal yourselves into the coffin pods. If you drop to the planet, I will send my acolytes to retrieve you. If you stay on the ship, you'll just be saving me some time. I will get my project back, regardless. Just remember, I did give you a chance to live."

Pageant was impressed with Mannion's play. It was just what Neer said he would do. "Why wait? Come get her now."

Mannion smiled. It was not the smile of a villain, no cartoonish grimace. It was the pleasant smile of an Irish grandfather correcting a child. For some reason, to Pageant, that made the smile all the more unnerving. Mannion leaned toward the projector. His face grew larger, a bit more distorted in the holo-render. "Mr. Pageant, Sunny Yeong's ship crippled my gunships. I have no real complement of troops on *Archon*. I have more ships en route to assist the survivors on *Kentarch*. They will be here in two days, tops. If you really wish for a battle, I'm sure they might be happy to oblige at that time, but you will have only a few hours of oxygen left. By that time, the air will be getting colder and thinner. I have a feeling you will not be up for fighting. *Au revoir.*"

"Wait? That's it? You're just going to leave us here to freeze to death?"

"Coffin pods, Mr. Pageant. You have no choice."

"I could kill the girl right now. Then you'll have nothing."

"But you won't. You know in your heart how valuable she is. You know what she means. Even if she's in my possession, you recognize now how much she means to the universe." Mannion's holo-render went dark. In the distance, *Archon* vanished in a haze as it jumped to translight.

At that moment, the station's red alert klaxons sounded as the local sensors registered the unavoidable impact of the approaching debris field. Pageant opened the cargo bay hatch. "Everyone get inside. If that shield gives for a second, we don't want to be on the wrong side of the gaping maw of a cargo bay."

Crispy piped up. "Cap, we're having a lot more danger than I care to be in, lately. Can I have a raise?

"Sure, Crisp. Take it out of Quick's salary."

Neer shook her head. "More jokes?"

"Who said it's a joke?" said Crispy. "I want more money."

"Jokes beat facing reality," said Quick. "You should try it."

Neer said, "Then, can I have some of Quick's salary, too?"

"You bet." Pageant sealed the hatch to the research station. "Some of Quick's salary for everyone."

"I don't like how you're playing fast and lose with my salary, Cap."

The debris field hit the station at that moment. Through the corridors, the plinks and plunks of metal hitting metal sounded like a bad steel drum rhythm. Then, the heart-stopping sound of a heavy chunk of debris hitting a piece of the station and tearing a hole in it silenced all talk. There was a rip of air as the vacuum of space vented some of the station's oxygen. The rip launched all emergency procedures on the station and sealed every hatch. The crew was locked into a corridor on the living module of the station. It was as safe as any place else they could be at that moment. More plinks. More plunks. Another heavy impact. The tell-tale hiss of air being whisked out of sealed areas.

Reesha Neer did the calculations in her head. "Maybe Mannion shouldn't have bothered leaving. We'll be in those pods in a couple hours at this rate."

30

THE SECOND WORST thing about space without a functioning life support system was the silence. The only thing worse than the silence was the crepitation of the hull as the oncoming cold settled into the vessel. There was a constant popping and crackling as the exposed metal, no longer being properly heated from within the station, began to succumb to the bitterly cold temperatures of the Black. The little noises were only amplified by the silence of space. The thinning air efficiently carried the hollow noises to everyone's ears. It was a symphony reminding them everything Mannion said was right, and their only hope was the coffin pods.

Coffin pods, so named because they were little more than square compartments with homing beacons and a three-day supply of air and water, were the last refuge of a failing research vessel or space station. They were required devices, complete with their own power supply separate from the station's central supply. The rule was a vessel had to have enough coffin pods for at least a third of its crew complement.

Why not enough pods for a full crew complement? Thank the corporations. Coffin pods were expensive. Crews were cheap. The research station had been home to more than thirty researchers and guards. There were ten pods in the life bay attached to the bottom of the station.

Anne was still unconscious when they laid her in the first pod. Pageant sealed it and made sure the oxygen feed started.

Neer took the second pod. "I'm tired of being on my foot, anyhow." She tossed her crutches aside. "Thanks for taking me in. It was fun while it lasted, I guess." She waved at them through the little window and gave a thumbs-up when Pageant asked her if the air was working.

Fang took the third pod. Then Crispy. Then Quick. Norman took the next one. "I hate these things. They weren't built for fellows with my dancer's body." Norman laid in the pod and had to simultaneously suck in his gut and exhale all the air in his lungs to get his girth successfully sealed. It was a tight fit, but it worked. Norman gave Pageant a smile through the window.

Pageant was last, as any good captain should be. The captain should really have gone down with the ship, but there was no ship, and the station wasn't even his to begin with, so all the typical half-baked idioms about sacrificing himself went out the window.

Pageant lowered himself into a pod and stared at the ceiling of the life bay. Ten pods were poised over the drop-floor. Once Pageant got into his pod and sealed it, a timed release would occur. Three minutes after the final pod sealed, the life bay would seal itself against the rest of the station, the floor would drop, and the ten pods would engage little rockets propelling them to the nearby planet.

The pods were thick and hearty, sealed well against the cold of space and tiled for the potentially brutal planetary reentry process. When the pods recognized they were through the atmosphere and fully into free fall, parachutes would slow their descent, and the repulsors that propelled them to the planet would help soften their touchdown.

On the surface of the planet, they would all be given the option to open their pods once they touched down. However, the pods would advise against it given the thin mix of oxygen and nitrogen on the planet below. They might be able to breathe, but every breath would be labored and difficult. Better to stay in the pod and wait for assistance the little computer in the pod would tell them.

Pageant looked around one last time. It might be the last time he saw a space station. It might be the last time he saw anything other than the inside of the little pod. If he was Mannion, he'd come back and blow up all the pods except Anne's and simply remove one more privateer nuisance from the galaxy. It would only help business in the long run for Mannion's company.

If nothing else, it would always stick in Pageant's craw that someone like Mannion got to win. The great karma wheel of the universe was irreparably broken. Rich clowns like Mannion always won. Those corporate heads always got their way. They were the true pirates of space. They could rape, pillage, and burn anything they wanted, and they always got away with it. They hired the best soldiers. They flew the best ships. They forced settlements into grotesque terms for shipping supplies because they knew those settlements had no choice but to accept it. They got richer. The poor got poorer. The wealthy *always* won.

Pageant laid down in the pod, acid burning in the back of his throat, angry at the whole situation. He looked at the coordinates Sunny sent him in her last act of communication. His daughter was at those coordinates. Somewhere, the little girl he'd made with Sunny Yeong was probably playing, or watching some videos on a monitor, or maybe sleeping, patiently waiting for her mother to return to her.

Sunny was who-knows-where. She had been tossed haphazardly into the translight. When she emerged from the tunnel—*if she emerged*—she might be on the other size of the galaxy. Or she might be a million galaxies away. It was quite possible that Sunny Yeong and the *Mary Read* would never emerge from the translight. Maybe the wild jump tore the ship apart. Maybe she was already dead.

Pageant could not help Sunny. He could not help his daughter. At the moment, he could not even help his crew. He glanced to his right. Anne Medea's face could be seen in the little, triangular window of the pod. She looked angelic in the reddish light of the life bay. Her eyes were closed, her lips just slightly parted. Her skin was pale and perfect. Her hair was almost back to its unnatural hi-tech red.

"If you've really got the holy DNA in you, maybe you can whip us up another miracle when you wake up." Pageant pulled the door of the coffin pod closed. The light changed from soft red to a harsh flashing red-and-blue as the drop timer started. Pageant shut his eyes, but the light pressed through his eyelids.

Time to drop: two minutes, fifty-five seconds. The robotic voice of the countdown timer began to announce intervals of time. As if to punctuate why they were getting into the pods, a robotic voice from the station's computer followed with its own announcement: *Air quality low; recommend evacuation of station immediately.*

Pageant listened to the countdown. It updated every fifteen seconds. Then, with ten seconds left, the robot voice counted down the remaining seconds. The floor dropped. Ten coffin pods fell away from the ship, falling to the planet surface hundreds of miles below them.

The silence of space pressed on the pods. There was no sound.

31

THE SHIP APPEARED in an instant. One second, there was nothing, only a hazy ripple in space announcing the arrival of something. The next second, a ship appeared as if by magic, the green tendrils of translight quickly whisking away into nothingness. Where once there was only empty space, a vessel manifested.

The vessel quickly took stock of the situation. The SOS signals from the station and the one still-functioning gunship. The beacons of the drop pods. The expanding debris field in the vicinity. The vessel honed in on the drop pods. They were rapidly descending toward the planet below, an inhospitable rock for human life.

The ship's frontal cargo bay door opened, the rounded belly of the ship rolling open like the maw of a Largemouth bass. The ship swallowed up the ten pods quickly, closing the door and venting life support back into is hold as soon as it had. Ten pods recovered. Heartbeats in seven of the ten.

32

IT HAD DONE it! It had found them! R1 did not know what elation was, as it was still grasping at its burgeoning sentience, but it knew from the signature reports from the PPDs of the people in the drop pods, it had found its crew. Against all odds, it had found them.

R1 turned Shy Opal back to empty space and triggered the translight. It was usually not good for a ship to hop in and out of the translight, but R1 and its team of rovers had been making improvements over the flawed human designs of the ship. The ship was better in terms of its abilities. It was trimmer. It was sleeker. FriendNathan would be happy with the improvements, R1 knew. FriendCrispy would be thrilled.

R1 guided the ship back into translight. It headed away from the scene of destruction. It headed somewhere else. It did not know where. That was unimportant at the moment. At the moment, the only thing important was the fact that it had found its crew.

R1 raced to the cargo bay to free its friends from the pods. It could not yet understand joy, hope, or pride, but it somehow felt all three.

End of Book I

Acknowledgements

I don't remember ever being anything other than a Sci-fi nerd. My earliest memories revolve around *Star Wars*. I had action figures, the bedsheets, the comforter, a Yoda t-shirt. I remember laying on the floor in my room making Luke and Darth Vader fight it out with clashing lightsabers. I always wanted the Han Solo action figure, but the best I got was Han in his Hoth winter wear, and that just wasn't the cool vest-wearing Han I liked. C'est la vie.

After *Star Wars*, there was *Buck Rodgers* (my Halloween costume when I was five), *E.T.*, *Battlestar Galactica*, and *Star Trek*, of course. I read the books, watched the shows, and went to the movies. I was enabled to do most of this because of my mother.

Mom is one of the original Trekkies. Instead of having a social life like a normal college student, she spent Saturday nights in the basement of her dorm at UW-Eau Claire watching the original *Star Trek* while snacking on a bag of Fritos and a jar of peanut butter. She was the one who dragged my old man to movies like *Star Wars*, *Star Trek: The Motion Picture*, and *The Black Hole*, none of which he liked.

My dad likes westerns and cop shows. A child of the '50s, he wanted to be a cowboy. Still does, really. He should have been born in 1860, riding Mustangs across the untamed range of the Wild West with a six-gun on his hip, and he has no patience for modern society or Sci-fi.

My mom introduced me to *Doctor Who*, and I vividly remember watching Tom Baker caper about when PBS was showing the series in America. I remember seeing Baker's Doctor turn into Peter Davison, in his cricket sweater and broccoli stalk. That was cool because I knew Davison from *All Creatures Great and Small* and his legendary run as Tristan Farnon.

(We could even take it up another step and move into my love of crime fiction because Davison also starred in the *Campion* series as Margery Allingham's great detective, Albert Campion.) Mom also introduced me to *Red Dwarf* and *The Tripods*. The latter drove me to dive into John Christopher's wonderful books, and the former permanently warped my sense of humor.

When *Star Trek: The Next Generation* launched in the late '80s, it was on at 12:30 AM on Friday nights on CBS in the Madison area. My mom would set the VCR to tape it, and we would watch them the next day. Whenever my sister and I had to accompany my mom to some event where we would have to sit and be quiet, it was usually preceded by a trip to Waldenbooks in West Towne Mall, and I would inevitably get a ST:TNG book. Sometimes I'd get a fantasy novel, but often it gravitated toward sci-fi. I got the first in Larry Niven's Ringworld series on one of those Waldenbooks trips. Tim Powers's *The Anubis Gates*, too.

Mom was the reason I watched the original *Dune* movie (the terrible one with Sting and Kyle MacLachlan). She was the reason I watched *The Greatest American Hero, Quantum Leap, Alien Nation* (both the movie and the series), *Starman, The Last Starfighter, InnerSpace, Alien*, and all the other great 1980s Sci-fi offerings.

Basically, my mom is the reason I was, and remain still, a massive nerd.

Thanks, Mom.

When Fox launched *Firefly* in 2002, I was hooked from the jump. Sci-fi westerns are always fun, and Joss Whedon managed to make the perfect ragtag bunch of hoodlums space opera western. I'm still mourning its mishandling by the Fox brass. I contend if they had handled the show properly, put it on in the Sunday night timeslot *The X-Files* had recently abandoned instead of trying to make it a Friday show, and marketed it half as much as they marketed their reality trash shows, it would have run for seven seasons, maybe more. Instead, we got thirteen episodes and a movie. I know *Firefly* lives on in some novels and graphic novels now, but it's not the same.

This book came out of me wanting to do my own version of that show. I combined some elements of *Firefly* with some of the elements of a Sci-fi trope that I enjoy greatly: emerging robotic sentience and sentient vessel books like those done by Anne McCaffery, Adrian Tchaikovsky, and Gareth L. Powell. This book also came out of me wanting to write a space opera because I love the genre.

I can only hope I did all those books, shows, and movies that laid the groundwork for my love of science fiction some justice in my own attempt.

I started writing this thing in 2016, believe it or not. It languished on my hard drive for years, occasionally resurfacing for me to add another chapter or two, wondering if it would ever be finished, or if it would ever be good enough to publish. Recently, I brought it out, polished it up, and realized I really liked it.

When you write a book, the only way to do it is to write something you like, and then hope that everyone else will like it, too.

Well, I like this one.

It was fun to write. I like the characters a lot. I can only hope enough people like this so I can continue writing more of it.

As always, thanks to you, the reader. I can't do this without you. As a nobody in a crowded market, it's always an honor when someone deigns to pick up your book and read it. It is always appreciated. The emails I get from people around the world are humbling. Thank you all.

Thanks to the family unit for letting me do this nonsense even though it doesn't pay and delivers zero glory.

Thanks to the other writers, librarians, booksellers, and everyone else who has suggested something I've written to friends or been kind to my work in the past. Maybe the stars rain blessings upon your houses.

We'll see you at the next book.

Sun Prairie, Wis.
October 2024

Other Books by Sean Patrick Little

The Survivor Journals
After Everyone Died
Long Empty Roads
All We Have
We Still Remain

The Abe & Duff Mystery Series
The Single Twin
Fourth and Wrong
Where Art Thou
Bought the Farm

The Shelby Ree Mystery Series
Welcome to Meskousing

www.ingramcontent.com/pod-product-compliance
Lightning Source LLC
Chambersburg PA
CBHW022350020726
47500CB00002B/210